THE ENTICERS

THE ENTICERS
Natasha Peters

NEW ENGLISH LIBRARY

First published in the USA in 1981
by Fawcett Popular Library, a unit of
CBS Publications.

First NEL Paperback Edition January 1983

NEL Books are published by
New English Library,
Mill Road, Dunton Green,
Sevenoaks, Kent.
Editorial office: 47 Bedford Square,
London WC1B 3DP

Printed and bound in Great Britain by
Collins Glasgow

0 450 05542 6

British Library C.I.P

Peters, Natasha

The Enticers.
I. Title
823'914[F]   PR6066.E/

ISBN 0-450-05542-6

THE ENTICERS

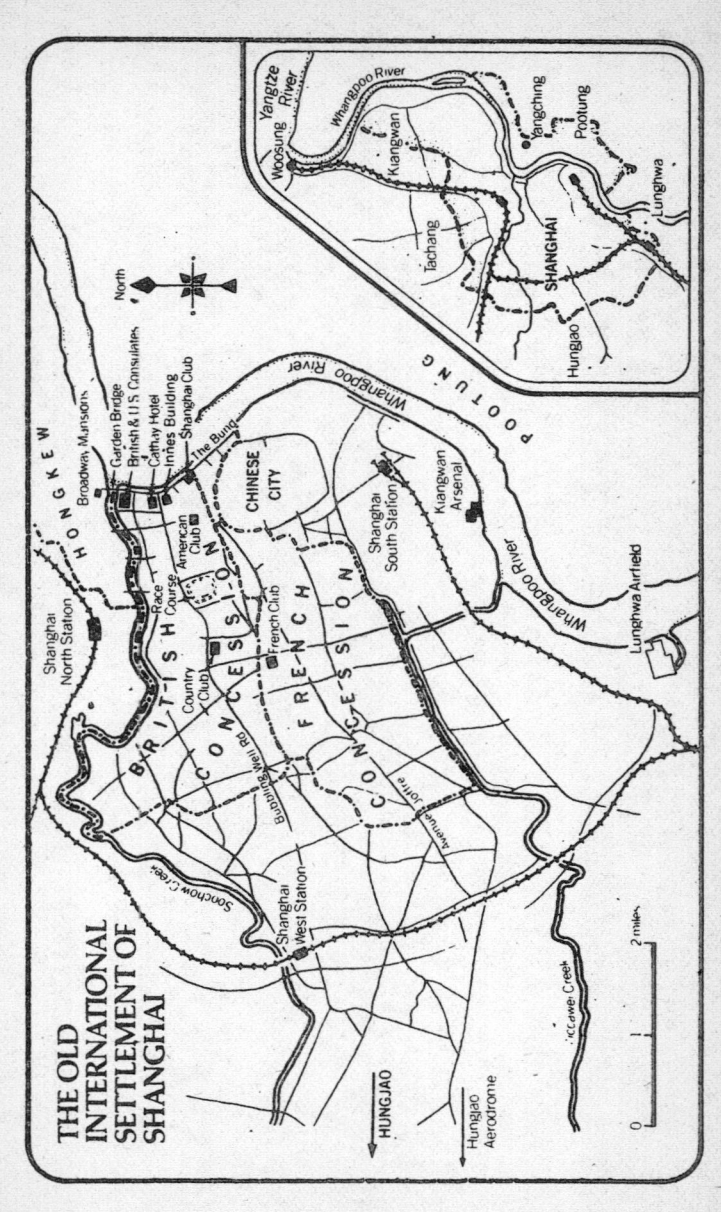

THE OLD INTERNATIONAL SETTLEMENT OF SHANGHAI

North

Yangtze River
Whangpoo River
Woosung
Kiangwan
Taichang
Yangching
Pootung
SHANGHAI
Lunghwa
Hungjao

POOTUNG

Whangpoo River

HONGKEW
Shanghai North Station
Broadway Mansions
Garden Bridge
British & US Consulates
Cathay Hotel
Innes Building
Shanghai Club
The Bund

Race Course
American Club
CHINESE CITY
Shanghai South Station
Kiangwan Arsenal
Lunghwa Airfield

BRITISH CONCESSION
Country Club
French Club
Bubbling Well Road
FRENCH CONCESSION
Avenue Joffre

Soochow Creek
Shanghai West Station

HUNGJAO
Hungjao Aerodrome
Kiawei Creek

2 miles
0   1   2

Chapter One

The factory whistles of Pootung and Chapei and Hongkew shrilled like distant demons, and the bells of the Catholic church over on the Avenue Foch tolled the Angelus. The clock in the study downstairs began to chime with an overblown dignity and syrupy slowness that always reminded Anne of her father launching into a sermon.

'Damned noise.'

Anne jumped up and slammed shut the windows over her desk. Even so, she could still hear the muted voice of the clock, nagging about time passing, time wasted, time lost –

She fell back into her chair and scowled at the small stack of tests she had just brought home. She lit a cigarette, and resisted the urge to apply the flame to the papers. They would be god-awful, of course. Fresh testaments to her inadequacies as a teacher. She couldn't blame herself totally: the nuns at the École des Filles always kept the brightest students for themselves, and left the half-wits to her, the infidel.

'Small-minded virgins,' she muttered. And the girls. 'Hopeless morons.' And herself, wasting her life pounding facts into their little heads. 'Fool.'

The thickening haze of cigarette smoke made her cough, and she waved the sheaf of tests briskly to disperse it. The exertion brought a flush to her cheeks and dislodged her glasses so that they slid down her nose on a small tide of perspiration. Her clothing clung to her skin. The air was hot, sticky, and sodden, typical for June in Shanghai, and a preview of the misery that summer would bring. The whites would flee to cool mountain retreats, but the Chinese refugees who lived in the streets would die of heat, starvation, and rampant disease.

The whistles and bells ceased their assault, and Anne opened her windows again. High-pitched laughter floated up from the kitchen, along with the jingle of crockery and the click of mah-jongg tiles. In the room on the other side

1

of her wall, a radio squawked a mindless dance tune that was ten years out of date. She could smell pork and cabbage, steaming laundry, the fragrance of roses.

The music stopped abruptly and there was a tap at her door. Kit sauntered in without waiting for a reply. She was wearing a navy blue blazer and white pleated skirt, but her costume didn't look conservative, or conventional. Instead of tying the streamers from her red silk blouse into a bow at the neck, Kit had tossed them over one shoulder, so that they fluttered behind her like scarlet banners. A white hat like a rhinoceros horn emerged from the dark froth of her curls, just above her right eye. Her purse and pumps were red. An oversized red handkerchief billowed from her breast pocket, mocking the display of patriotic colors. The effect was at once bizarre and enchanting, and only Kit could have pulled it off.

'Can you imagine,' Kit said, 'all set for an afternoon of fun, and not a cigarette to my name.'

'Poor child.' Anne didn't look up. 'Well, what's on the agenda today? Golf at the country club? Tea at the consulate? Or the usual mix of cocktails and venom in someone's drawing room?'

Feigning acute exhaustion, Kit flopped down on Anne's narrow bed and fanned herself with her gloves. 'My dear, have you forgotten? The seventeenth of June is Bunker Hill Day! The Royalists meet the Rebels on the polo field. The loathsome Limeys will win, as usual, and gloat like crazy, and we Yanks will break our faces trying to smile through our tears. If you ask me, there are no good losers, only good liars.' She poked around among the books and papers on Anne's nightstand. 'Honestly, I don't know how you can find anything in this cesspit – ah, here we are! Quite stale, of course, but I'll take the pack. I'm that desperate.'

'You're quite welcome, I'm sure.' Slouched down comfortably in her chair, her legs stretched straight out in front of her, Anne watched a thin strand of smoke spiraling upward, snaking out the window. Over the years she had burned up a lot of cigarettes – and a lot of minutes – in this posture.

'I have an idea,' Kit said brightly. 'Why don't you come

with us today? Get out of this miserable cell for a while. It'll do you good.'

Anne made a noise somewhere between a laugh and a snort. 'You must be joking.'

'Why not? It'll be fun. Hurry and throw on something decent. I'll send the elders on ahead, and we can go over in my car.'

'No. I have work to do. I also loathe the company of your asinine friends, and I wouldn't go if you paid me. Polo! What a disgusting waste of time.'

'Oh, yes, and your time is *so* precious,' Kit drawled. 'Well, that's the thanks I get for being good-hearted. I don't know why I bother. My God, Mouse, if I had to live inside your skin for just one day, I'd go crazy!'

Years ago, their mother had scolded Kit for making a nasty remark about Anne, eight years her senior and a hopelessly unattractive teenager: 'Don't be catty, dear.' Kit had retorted, 'Then tell Anne not to be such a mouse.' No one else ever used the nickname.

'It's just unbelievable,' Kit went on. 'You teach school. You come home. You sulk in your room. It depresses people just to be around you. Why don't you do something with your life?'

'What did you have in mind?' Anne ground out her cigarette. 'Marriage?' Faint sneer.

'Why not? What's wrong with marriage? But no decent man will look at you twice if you don't fix yourself up.' She eyed Anne's baggy grey slacks and white shirt. 'Revolting!' she shuddered. 'Who designs your clothes, Custom Coolie Apparel Limited? And your hair! For God's sake, cut it off, pin it up, or crimp it, but do something. It looks like old rags.'

Anne pulled herself up in her chair. 'Any more ideas before you go?' she said coldly.

'Lots.' Kit cheerfully ignored Anne's icy glare. 'Get rid of your glasses. They make you look a hundred years old. If you can't see where you're going, then get some nice man to lead you around by the hand. You could, you know. Under that sackcloth, your figure's pretty decent.'

Anne gave a bark of scornful laughter. 'Thanks so much!'

'I mean it,' Kit said with the easy warmth of one who can afford to be generous. 'You're thin and your legs are good. You're a little heavy on top, but men like that sort of thing. You know, dearie, a good brassiere would change your life.'

Their mother called up the stairs that the car was ready.

'You'd better hurry up if you don't want to miss the kickoff,' Anne said.

Kit stood up and shook out her skirt. 'They don't have kickoffs in polo, silly. Besides, we're having tiffin first at the clubhouse. With cocktails and dancing. Lovely!' On her way out of the room she paused at the door. When she spoke again, her voice was cool and hard. 'I don't know who you think you're punishing by behaving like this. It might have worked once, even gotten you a little sympathy, but it's old hat now. Frankly, my dear, you've become a crashing bore. Why don't you update your act? Be civilized for a change. The results might surprise you.'

Anne's eyes flashed angrily. 'Shut up, will you? The way I live is nobody's business but my own, and I'm sick of people preaching to me about it! Just leave me alone. Go on, get out!'

Kit, pleased with the reaction to her dart, smiled and strolled out. Anne lit a cigarette and smoked furiously for some minutes, then composed herself and gave her attention to her work. She looked down at the topmost test paper. The spelling was ludicrous, the punctuation haphazard, pure guesswork. She could just decipher the smeared signature at the bottom of the page: Josepha Chang. She might have known. Josepha. The face of a fairy princess and the brains of a chicken. They'd been over this stuff a thousand times – it wasn't that hard – hours of extra work, special tutoring, and – nothing. Nothing!

She snatched up the tests and shredded them, quickly and viciously. She would tell the girls to do them over, that they were all terrible, unacceptable. An occasional show of wrath always shamed them into trying harder.

She stood in the middle of the room and looked around. The blue curtains were limp and sunburned, and like the worn Chinese rug and the festoons of drawn-up mosquito netting over the bed, they smelled slightly of mildew. Sour cigarette butts overflowed ashtrays, and piles of books teetered precariously on every surface. A scuffed violin case and heaps of music gathered dust under the dresser. There were no prints or photographs on the faded papered walls, no cherished mementos of childhood, no evidence that she had spent the greater part of her twenty-eight years there. It might have been a room in a boardinghouse, or a transient hotel. Most of the time she didn't notice how bleak and miserable it was, but today it sickened her. Damn Kit.

Wandering out into the hall, she rested her forearms on the sill of the open casement window that overlooked the driveway. The limousine that she called Christ's Cadillac murmured drowsily, like a great black beast rousing itself from sleep. The Chinese chauffeur made soothing swipes at its front fender with a white cloth, and when Reverend Leonard Fox emerged from the house, the man leaped to open the car doors. Anne's father looked at his pocket watch, tapped his foot, then turned and demanded in an amused, exasperated bellow, 'Where are those women of mine?'

Anne shrank away from the window.

'Marian! Kit!'

Laughing, Mrs. Fox and Kit emerged from under the portico. Mrs. Fox's face was shaded by the brim of her straw hat, but her figure was trim and youthful. Anyone seeing her and Kit from that angle and distance would take them for sisters.

The car slid slowly down the drive, and Anne let out her breath in a long sigh. Except for the servants, who were as unobtrusive as the furnishings, she was alone in the house. She could look forward to an afternoon of delicious solitude, a rare and unexpected treat.

A breeze, hot and unrefreshing, stirred the fronds of the palm trees at the center of the circular driveway. A blanket of clouds hung low over the city, trapping the rising steam from the Yangtze delta and the heat of four million sweating bodies. Anne took off her glasses and stuffed them into the pocket of her slacks. She rubbed her eyes, then raked her hands through her hair and scooped

5

the whole mass into a pile on top of her head. The breath of wind felt cool on her damp neck and shoulders.

Arms still upraised, she stepped away from the window and caught a glimpse of her reflection in the glass. She blinked at the watery image for a moment, not recognizing herself. One of the nuisances about wearing glasses, she thought, is that you forget what you look like without them.

The face beneath the upswept hair was an imperfect oval, broader at the forehead than at the chin. Without the thick lenses, her eyes looked larger and darker, and her nose smaller. She drew herself up and smiled slowly. The shadow woman behind the glass looked like a stranger from another time, a Belle Époque beauty: long-necked, full-bosomed, narrow-waisted, serenely proud and confident. Mysterious. Desirable.

Well, why not? One man had found her beautiful, years ago. One man had loved her, wanted her. Beauty was her birthright, just as it was Kit's. Maybe Kit was right. A little attention to her hair, some new clothes —

Oh, yes, she could transform herself. Refurbish her unattractive exterior, shuck the old contentious attitudes that were as much a part of her costume as her unremarkable clothing. But why bother? So that she could attract a pack of drooling idiots, like the men who trailed after Kit? So that she could be like every other woman in Shanghai, devoting endless hours to preening and anointing and preparing herself for the contest that had no winners, the frenzied pursuit of happiness? Why make the effort? To please her father? To look like a full-fledged member of the Fox family, instead of an outsider, a lodger in the house.

She dropped her arms, and her hair fell limply around her shoulders. She put on her glasses again. The image in the windowpane looked drearily familiar and unromantic. Presenting the real Anne Fox: pseudo-Marxist, sullen nonconformist, lonely spinster. Cheers and applause? Not even hisses and catcalls. Only bored yawns.

Shoving her hands deep into her pockets, she turned her back to the window. The afternoon stretched in front of her like a long gray shadow, and her solitude seemed more like a penance than a promise.

Lying on a satin nest inside a carved sandalwood box, the hand looked like a piece of white jade, cold and bloodless except for the vivid streaking of blue-green veins. It was a worker's hand, coarsened and hardened by time and hard use, the nails rough and cracked, the grime so deeply embedded in the seams that no amount of washing in life could have cleansed it completely. The severed edges of skin at the base were dried, and they folded over the shrunken flesh, exposing the knobby carpals of the wrist and twin prongs of radius and ulna.

James Innes wrinkled his nose with distaste, although because of age or curing or the concealing fragrance of the sandalwood, the object had no repellent odor.

'Attractive, is it not?' Sun Yu-sing said with the controlled enthusiasm of the connoisseur. 'A most convincing piece of evidence, certainly to one of Tu's limited mental capabilities and superstitious bent. Although I have always despised the superstitious strain in my countrymen's makeup, I will admit that it has its uses.'

'Jesus,' Innes muttered.

'Perhaps I should supplement the gift with an artful photograph of the old man cradling his blood-soaked stump,' Sun said. 'I wish we had thought of making a phonograph record. They tell me he howled piteously.'

'You weren't there?'

'Certainly not.' Sun dabbed at his lips with a scented handkerchief. 'I detest violence.'

Innes smiled wryly. 'I know. Well, where's the old guy now?'

'I have removed him to Hong Kong and instructed our people there to kill him if they do not hear from one of us every ten days.'

'So damned complicated,' Innes growled. 'I don't like it.'

He turned away. The wall behind his desk was made entirely of glass. At his feet lay the Bund, the hub and financial heart of Shanghai. The most powerful taipans in the Far East ran their businesses from there. Jardine-Matheson, Butterfield and Swire, the Bank of China, the

North-China Daily News – they were his neighbors now. The street rippled with the movement of pedestrians and vehicles and the centaur-like combination of the two, the ricksha. The silvery Whangpoo River, dotted with the white man's destroyers and gunboats and the yellow man's frail junks and tiny sampans, mirrored the motion on land. Two of Innes' small freighters steamed toward the factories and warehouses at Pootung on the opposite bank, and an Innes & Company tugboat nosed an ore-filled barge to a steel mill upstream.

Layers of ferroconcrete and glass muffled the din of the city, but Innes could hear the ricochet of hammers and the whine of drills as workmen put the finishing touches on the newest addition to Shanghai's already impressive skyline. Shining letters of stainless steel had already gone up over the main entrance twelve stories below: INNES BUILDING.

'Perhaps you prefer the elegant simplicity of being blown up the next time you enter your car?' said Sun. 'Our friend Tu is profoundly irritated by your refusal to take his demands seriously. That first bomb was just a warning. The next will have a permanent effect. There is no way you can protect yourself once he has decided to destroy you. You cannot trust anyone. You could be betrayed by a servant, a woman, a coolie on one of your ships.'

'Or a compradore?' The old Portuguese word was a holdover from the early days of China's trade with the West. It described the Chinese merchant who acted as go-between in business transactions, without whom trade in the East would have been impossible.

Sun was not offended. 'Even a compradore, if he so desired. Why have you never learned to trust me?'

Innes came back to the desk and took a cigarette out of a silver box. His lighter flashed. 'When I've stopped being useful to you, you'll try to get rid of me, Sun. I'm warning you right now, it won't be easy.'

'That day will never come,' Sun assured him. 'I am your friend.'

'You never had a friend,' Innes said. 'Friends cost too much and the return on your investment is poor.' He scowled at the disembodied hand, its fingers curving gently around nothingness. 'What if the old man dies? Of natural causes, or an accident? Your plan won't be worth much then.'

'We will still have the corpse,' Sun reminded him. 'Tu Yueh-sen would be a very poor son indeed if he endangered his father's immortality by failing to ensure the proper disposal of his whole clay. If Tu continues to behave aggressively, we will execute the old man ourselves. And send Tu the head.' He closed the box gently.

The heads of decapitated criminals were displayed on pikes, as a warning to potential evildoers. Family members were permitted to reclaim the heads after a certain amount of time had passed. Innes had often seen them transporting their unhappy burdens in baskets slung from bamboo poles. Unless the deceased's relatives buried a whole corpse, the dead man's spirit could wander forever, searching for its lost head and causing trouble to the living.

He said, 'You guys make Al Capone look like an amateur.'

'Oh, surely your American gangsters resort to kidnapping from time to time. Here in China the taking of hostages is an old and much-revered custom. Mutilating them in stages is equally respectable. Tu could retaliate, certainly, but he won't dare. It is filial obligation to take every precaution to save his father's life. The plan is foolproof. Even if the agents of the Green Dragon Society were to locate the old man, our men would kill him before they could save him.'

'I still don't like it,' Innes said stubbornly. 'I can take care of myself.' He didn't have to touch the reassuring leaden bulk of the gun under his left arm, warmed like a living appendage by the heat of his body.

Sun said, 'We have outwitted Tu. He will accept that, and respect you for it. Surely you have better things to do with your time than dodge bombs?' Sun glanced at his wristwatch: ten minutes past noon. 'The polo match later today, for example. Your team will win.'

Innes' frown became a grin. 'Are you willing to bet

money on that?'

'I already have. Ten thousand dollars. I got excellent odds, which means that your secret is still safe.'

Innes laughed aloud. 'You're a slick son of a bitch, Sun!'

Sun dipped his head. 'I endeavour always to serve my friend.'

Dr Gilbert Lawrence felt a surge of excitement as the *Chichibu Maru* entered the Whangpoo River. The journey up the broad throat of the Yangtze had disappointed him: China remained tantalizingly distant, and he could hardly distinguish the parched islands of the delta from the mud-colored water and the overcast sky. But now, between narrower banks, those shadowy outlines gained color and substance. Gilbert could make out the scrubby lines of trees and the dark drainage ditches that marked off brilliant green rice paddies. Villages textured with thatch and brick rose out of the flatlands. Moving figures appeared, peasants in broad-brimmed straw hats, and the bulky gray masses of water buffalo.

The freighter prepared to dock at Woosung, twelve miles downriver from Shanghai. The Whangpoo was shallow, made navigable only by constant dredging, and farther up could not accommodate oceangoing vessels. This part of the river was busy and crowded. Small sampans wove in and out between gigantic freighters and gleaming passenger ships. Blunt-nosed tugs hauled strings of barges. High-sterned junks with sails like veined bat wings seemed hardly to touch the surface of the water. A little gray gunboat passed so close to the side of the *Chichibu Maru* that Gilbert could make out the expressions on the faces of the crewmen, and he fancied he could hear the snap of their Union Jack as it whipped in the wind.

'The only law in China: armed strength,' wheezed the man who stood beside Gilbert at the rail. He was middle-aged, rumpled, and unshaven, with breath soured by alcohol and a queasy stomach, and a wistful look in his eyes that didn't match the cynical tone of his voice. He introduced himself as Albert McClure, the new Reuters man in Shanghai.

'Old one got the DT's,' he explained. 'Hard to keep a good man – or a man good – in Shanghai. They all become satyrs, soaks, sodomists, or dope fiends. Forgive that last item. I haven't found an *s* word that scans properly.' His accent was British; his vowels had a Cockney twist. 'Your first trip to Shanghai?'

Gilbert admitted that it was, and asked if Mr. McClure had been there before. McClure had, many times. He'd covered the riots that followed the May Fourth Rebellion in 1925, and the strikes that paralyzed the city in '27. He regretted missing the big news last year, 1932, when the Japanese bombed the city. They excused the attack by claiming that the Japanese nationals living there needed to be protected from rampaging Chinese students, who had been aroused by the Nationalist Government's anti-Japanese propaganda campaign.

'I was in Singapore, drinking stengahs and trying to write something worthwhile, God help me. I shouldn't have bothered.'

'I read about it,' Gilbert said. 'Dreadful. Was much of the city destroyed?'

'None of the parts that count for anything. Our small yellow friends confined their show of militaristic might to the poorer Chinese sections, like Chapei. They didn't touch any of the banks or businesses on the Bund – they have a lot of money tied up in the International Settlement. But I'll get another chance at the story. If not here, then someplace else. Another Manchuria, another Korea. They haven't finished flexing their muscles yet.'

They glided slowly past a freighter with INNES LINES stenciled in red letters on the smokestacks. The sides of a huge warehouse on the shore boasted letters thirty feet high: INNES. A bug-eyed red dragon with outstretched claws and curving tail formed the final *s* on INNES.

'Jim Innes and I used to get drunk together,' McClure smiled reminiscently. 'He started small, running opium up the Yangtze in a makeshift gunboat. Had a couple of surplus tommy guns mounted fore and aft to discourage pirates. And look at him now: one of the richest white men in China.'

11

'Are there still pirates on the rivers?' Gilbert asked. 'I thought Chiang Kai-shek had wiped them out.'

'Son, piracy is just a fancy word for thievery done on water. Unless you eliminate poverty, you're going to have thieving. Chiang may be a hell of a leader – and I'm not saying he is – but he's not that good. Between the Japs and the Commies he had his ass in a vice, and by the time this country is done with war, there are going to be a lot more beggars on Nanking Road.'

The docks at Woosung hummed with activity. Swarms of coolies moved cargo up and down ramps, pushing, hauling, lifting, straining, and chanting as they worked: 'Ai-i-ya!' The stink of their sweat mingled with sulphurous smoke and fragrant oranges, bilge flushings and musty cotton in bales, acrid fuel oil and earthy peanuts. Clusters of sampans closed in around the *Chichibu Maru*'s stern. The boat people waited for the kitchen refuse to come gushing out so that they could net the scraps, lay them on the roofs of their boats to dry, and feed them to their children.

'You'll never see a seagull in Shanghai,' McClure remarked as he and Gilbert boarded the small tender boat that would carry them the rest of the way to the city. 'Pickings are too poor.'

'It goes on for miles, doesn't it?' Gilbert marveled as the riverbanks grew dark with factories, warehouses, and wharves. 'I must say, it's not quite what I expected.'

McClure grunted. 'No gentle hills spiked with pagodas and moon gates, you mean? Oh, farther out the countryside looks more like the pretty pictures in the guidebooks, but not Shanghai. Money and power: that's why Shanghai exists. You don't come here unless you're after one or both.' He gave Gilbert an appraising look. 'Which is it for you?'

Gilbert confessed somewhat proudly that he was a medical missionary. McClure nodded. 'Thought so. You have just the right look of complacent innocence. Well, a man of God couldn't find a better training ground than Shanghai. There's more sin here than in all the rest of China put together. Shanghai is like a great restaurant of vice, with the longest menu in the world. Anything you want – small children, animals, six Japanese girls at one time – anything! And everywhere you go, the sweet stink of opium. If hell had clouds, they'd be opium smoke.' He shook his head reverently at the wonder of it. 'It's magnificently evil.'

'Then it must offer equally magnificent opportunities to do good,' Gilbert said somewhat sanctimoniously.

'Yes, if that's your vice,' McClure winked. 'But it's easier to avoid mud in a pigyard than it is to resist temptation in Shanghai. I'd watch my step if I were you, parson.' He nudged Gilbert's shoulder and grinned.

Gilbert recoiled a little. He was becoming tired of Albert McClure. 'If you don't mind a little advice yourself, Mr McClure, stay away from liquor. It's poison to a man in your condition.'

McClure shook his head. 'Son, I don't even take the advice I pay for, but thanks just the same. People can get addicted to poisons, didn't you know?'

'In my profession we call it something else,' Gilbert said gravely. 'It begins with an s.'

McClure's eyes brightened and he mouthed the three syllables silently. 'Yes, that's good. Quite good! I hope you don't mind if I use it: satyrs, soaks, sodomists, or suicides! Many thanks!'

The tender boat arrived at the Customs House on the Bund, and Gilbert prepared to set foot on Chinese soil for the first time. He breathed a silent prayer of thanks. He had safely reached journey's end, and soon he could begin the work that God had sent him here to do.

'I cannot endure this,' fumed Reverend Leonard Fox. 'The crass impudence of the man!'

'Oh, Leonard,' sighed his wife, fanning herself, 'everyone else is staying and putting a good face on it. Don't make a fuss, please. If you don't want to watch, run down to the clubhouse and have a cup of tea or something.'

'I would dearly love to leave,' said Kit, 'but I don't see how I can if I have to present that stupid trophy afterward. This is awful. What if he wins? Oh, look!'

At that moment, Innes and the captain of the British team wheeled their ponies around, kicked them into a gallop, and hurtled on a collision course toward the bamboo root ball in the middle of the field.

The first shock of the 1933 playing of the Bunker Hill Polo Tourney came when James Innes, who had never been known to look at a horse, much less attend the tourney, led the Americans onto the field. The crowd gasped. Ordinarily the only mounts available to polo enthusiasts in China were shaggy Mongolian ponies hardly broken to the saddle, but every member of Innes' team rode a sleek polo pony, that swift combination of thoroughbred and quarter horse.

More astonishing still, the Rebels, as Kit called them, had learned how to play. The British team hadn't lost a game in twenty years, and they usually won by an embarrassingly wide margin. But this year they were faced by confidently aggressive opponents, who were mounted on superior animals and led by a fanatic who took incredible risks. So far they hadn't scored at all.

'Unsportsmanlike!' growled Leonard Fox halfway through the first chukka. 'Innes is trying to buy victory as he buys everything else. Well, he can't buy respectability.'

The two ponies closed in on the ball. The players lifted their mallets and prepared to swing, but unless one pulled his horse aside, they would surely collide. The crowd drew a collective horrified breath. One of them must back down, jerk his pony aside at the last second −! But neither swerved. The two men might have been medieval jousters bent on unseating and slaughtering each other.

The ponies met chest to chest with a sickening thud. The force of the impact drove them upward, rearing. Hooves slashed the air and they went down in a tangle. Innes pulled his feet out of his stirrups and fell clear, but the other player was pinned under his own pony, who flailed his legs desperately but could not rise. Men gathered around the fallen. Innes jumped to his feet unhurt and examined his mount, who had been extricated from the mess and stood shaking his head dazedly. The British player lay inert on the stretcher that bore him away. His Mongolian pony, one leg dangling uselessly, was led off the field. Everyone knew the brave shaggy creature would have to be put down.

The chukka was not over yet. Innes walked his lathered pony to the string and picked out a fresh animal. He mounted quickly, and as he galloped onto the field, he swirled his mallet in a full circle over his head to show that he was undaunted by the spill and ready for more. A smattering of grudging applause greeted his return.

The members of the Fox family, patriotic Americans, rooted silently for the British team.

'Trash.'

Anne pitched the book into a corner. 'What drivel,' she muttered disgustedly, uncoiling her long legs from the chair.

During that idle afternoon, she had picked up one of the frothy romances that provided the bulk of her mother's literary diet. Curious about the outcome, she kept reading until she reached the inevitable embrace on the last page.

'Ridiculous happy endings. Pap.'

She crouched over the radio in the corner of her father's study. After the usual interval of whooping and whistling she found real music. Heifetz playing a Mozart violin concerto. Every time she turned on the radio these days she got Heifetz, even though it had been two months since he stopped there on tour. But that's the way it was in a place like Shanghai, where civilized pleasures were rarer than rubies and those who craved them savored them like a gourmet in the jungle.

She listened closely. The piece wasn't difficult. She used to know it well. For the first time in years she wanted to get out her violin, just to see if she could finger along. She flexed her fingers in midair, and she knew immediately that it would be impossible. She snapped off the radio and sat steeped in misery so thick that she could hardly breathe.

The doorbell chimed. She was dimly aware of Wang's slippered shuffle as he hurried to answer it. In a minute he stood in front of her.

'Young fellah come. I tell him you see.'

She scowled up at him. His pitted face was as round as a soup plate, fringed by thick black hair, inset with eyes so

15

small they really did look like raisins. Kit made cruel fun of him and called him Dough Face, but Anne knew that his simple, homely exterior concealed a formidable foe.

'Tell him Kit's gone out,' she said crossly.

'No want Missee Kit. Want you.'

'But I don't want to see anyone. For heaven's sake, Wang, tell him to go away.'

Wang shook his head and informed her that he had put the visitor on the screened porch. He would serve tea in a few minutes. Anne knew she was lost. He could be incredibly stubborn. 'Nice-lookin' fellah,' Wang said encouragingly as she hauled herself out of her chair and pushed her hair out of her face. 'You like.'

'Like hell,' Anne said.

'Jesus Christ!' said James Innes, wiping champagne out of his eyes.

'Oh, Mr Innes, I'm so sorry!' gasped Kit. 'I can't imagine how that happened. How dreadfully clumsy of me!'

To celebrate the American victory, Innes poured champagne into the loving cup he had accepted on behalf of his teammates. Just as he raised the great goblet to his lips, Kit tripped on an invisible flaw in the clubhouse carpet and lurched into him. While he sputtered angrily, Kit whipped out her enormous red handkerchief and dabbed at his dripping face. The other men in the room sniggered, Britons and Americans alike. Innes had made fools of them too many times for them not to find this turnabout amusing. Their gleeful snorts all but drowned out the sympathetic murmurs of the ladies present.

Although the women of Shanghai's white society, like their husbands, made a show of shunning James Innes in public, many of them would have welcomed some time with him in private. There was a quality of excitement about Innes, a surging and irrepressible vitality that the longer-established taipans lacked. Physically he was an attractive mongrel, stronger and tougher than the thoroughbreds, and dangerously unpredictable, like a tame jungle animal who could revert to his wild ways at any time. He moved with a taut, well-controlled grace, as

16

though holding his destructive energies in check. Even when he rested, tension knotted his forearms and bowed his broad shoulders. Loose curls like billows of black smoke softened the broad line of his forehead and the menacing arcs of his brows. His blunt nose, blue-black cheeks, and massive hands bore the scars of a hundred violent encounters, and the glint in his blue eyes showed his readiness to engage in a hundred more. His wide mouth was usually bent into a grin that his competitors saw as rapacious and impudent, but which their wives found beguilingly boyish. The taipans' daughters were awed and secretly excited by his strength, but they wondered about his capacity for gentleness. The taipans' wives knew that Innes would not disappoint; he would know when to be gentle, and when not to be.

But as Kit applied her handkerchief to the craggy contours of Innes' face, she thought she had never seen an uglier man. She had heard the whispers, in the ladies' lounges and drawing rooms of Shanghai, and wondered at the stupidity of some women. What could they possibly see in someone like Innes? He was coarse, rough-speaking, alien, a monied thug trying to buy his way into a world that he couldn't understand and couldn't appreciate. She thought of his hands on the loving cup, calloused worker's hands with a rich man's manicure. That was Innes in a nutshell: a ditchdigger scrubbed clean and decked out in top hat and tails.

Innes couldn't very well push her away. He had to stand there like a fool and endure her mocking ministrations. Her brown eyes were bright with mischief, and she kept up a patter of false concern and apology. He wanted to spank her, the cruel spiteful little bitch. He glared down at her lovely face, framed with a tumble of dark curls and set off by a silly hat that looked like a white shark's fin jutting out of a turbulent sea. Her red lips were pursed, cooing, and a dimple danced around the left corner of her mouth. He decided that he'd rather make love to her. It would serve her right if he took her, right there on the clubhouse floor. They'd lynch him, but it would be worth it.

She read his thoughts in his eyes and felt a sudden spasm of fear. For her, his potency represented neither a promise nor a challenge, but a threat. She stepped away from him.

'I do hope you'll forgive me,' she said coolly.

'I hope you'll forgive me for disturbing you, Miss Fox,' said Gilbert.

'Kit's not here,' Anne said brusquely. 'Why don't you telephone later? You might catch her in.'

'I'm afraid I haven't made myself clear. My name is Gilbert Lawrence. My father is a Presbyterian minister in Philadelphia and an old friend of your father, and I promised to call on Reverend Fox as soon as I could. I happened to be in the neighborhood –'

'Oh. I see.' Anne chewed her lip. Wang was right, the fellah was damned good-lookin'. He might have stepped out of the glossy pages of one of those silly magazines her mother and Kit devoured. Slender, patrician, even fair-haired. Eyelids a little heavy, lips a little full, but why quibble? He had a jaw like a movie star and a nose that royalty would envy.

Suddenly she hated herself for looking like a frump and she hated him for finding her looking like one.

'I suppose you might as well sit down.' She stepped onto the porch, part of the veranda that had been screened off and furnished with rattan and wicker, colorful cushions, plants in pots. Overhead a large-bladed fan whirled lazily, producing a faint but welcome breeze in the stifling stillness of late afternoon.

Gilbert lowered himself into a wicker easy chair that creaked under his weight. Anne flopped onto a settee opposite him and swept her hair away from her face with an impatient swipe of her hand.

'Father's not here right now. They're all over at the Polo Grounds.'

'Oh, really? I passed the Race Course on my walk. I thought there was something going on.'

Anne stared. 'My God, you walked? In this heat?' She was more impressed by the immaculate condition of his white suit. Just like God, she thought irritably, to give the good-looking ones the power to repel dirt.

'I enjoy walking,' Gilbert said. 'I was rather proud of

18

myself for being able to resist the blandishments of the ricksha men.'

'You should have hired one.' Anne shifted so that she could extract her pack of cigarettes from her pocket. She lit one and puffed furiously for a minute before it occurred to her to offer one to her guest, who declined with a gentle shake of his head. 'He would have pulled you all around town for a few cents.'

'Actually, I didn't want to,' Gilbert confessed with an amused grimace. 'I rode in one this morning, from the dock to my hotel. I found it rather embarrassing, being pulled around like an Oriental potentate by another human being.'

He would always remember that first ricksha ride. The ricksha coolie wore only tattered blue shorts and a straw hat shaped like an inverted bowl. His bare feet slapped on the filthy pavement and he kept up a steady patter of warning cries. From where he sat in cushioned comfort, Gilbert could see the sweat pouring down the uneven groove of the man's spine, and he had felt conspicuous and ashamed.

'Why, the poor man wasn't even wearing shoes,' he said in a tone of mild outrage.

'He doesn't need them,' Anne said. 'His feet are as thick as elephant hide. Look, pulling people is his job. He doesn't do it for fun. He doesn't even own his own ricksha. Often after he's been gouged by the owners at the end of the day, he doesn't have enough money left to buy a bowl of rice.'

'Oh.' Gilbert looked abashed. 'I didn't think of it that way. You're right, of course.' Then, trying to redeem himself a little in her eyes. 'Well, the next time I go out I'll have to stock up on small change. I gave all I had to a beggarman, and then a pack of them practically chased me into the Wing On Department Store!' He laughed at the memory of that adventure, although he had been terrified at the time.

'That was stupid,' Anne snorted. 'Word will go around the Beggars' Guild that you're an easy mark and they'll never leave you alone.'

'But he hardly gave me room to walk,' Gilbert

protested. 'He was missing an arm – I'd swear the stump was gangrenous! I really should have taken him to the hospital.'

'He would have run away if you'd tried it,' Anne said. 'He wasn't gangrenous: he'd probably just smeared some rotten meat and blood on himself. A lot of them pretend to be worse off than they are. The bad cases don't have the strength to beg – hunger and disease carry them off very quickly here. If the professionals see you're an unlikely prospect, they'll shove off pretty quickly.'

'I guess I have a lot to learn about life in China.' Gilbert hesitated to say anything more about his first impressions of Shanghai. This odd woman seemed determined to make him feel like a perfect greenhorn, a fool.

'Shanghai is not China,' Anne informed him. 'Don't ever confuse the two. Shanghai and the other treaty ports are monstrosities created by the white men who came here to steal. I know, they call it business, trade, commerce. But it's stealing. It's exploitation. The peasants are lured to the cities by the promise of jobs, but even the ones who do find work aren't paid enough to feed their families.' She stopped her tirade and shrugged. 'Never mind. In a few days you'll be as hard as I am. You can't go breaking your heart over every wretched thing you see here. You'd go mad.'

She stared at the glowing tip of her cigarette.

'This is a fine house,' Gilbert offered, desperately trying to guide the conversation into safer waters. He wondered how soon he could decently make his escape. How long do polo matches last, anyway?

'It's hideous,' Anne sniffed. 'I call it California Bastard: Spanish Mission with a little Moorish Castle thrown in. It was the home of a stocking manufacturer from Queens, New York. It's a little grand for a minister's house, don't you think?'

'Well, I suppose –'

'The original manse was on the other side of the church. It burned down the year before we got here, and the stocking mogul thought he could earn divine credit by donating his house to the Presbyterians, who could have sold it and used the money to rebuild a simple manse. But that didn't seem to occur to them. Typical.'

She kicked off her sandals and drew up her knees. She smoked without paying attention to her ash, which sprinkled the carpet, the cushions, her clothes. Silence yawned. Just as Gilbert was about to make his excuses and depart, she said, 'Well, what brings you to Shanghai, Mr Lawrence? Do you toil for God or Mammon?'

'I'm a physician, Miss Fox. I'm being sponsored by the Philadelphia chapter of the Medical Missionary Society of America. I've studied at the seminary, although I was never ordained. I'll heal bodies and perhaps save a few souls along the way.'

Anne was unimpressed. 'Oh, Lord, another do-gooder.'

Gilbert bridled. 'You object to do-gooders, Miss Fox?' he demanded.

'Oh, yes, indeed. I'm one myself, you see. Inveterate. My own motives are absolutely pure and selfish: I want to be loved.'

Gilbert didn't know how to respond to such a bald admission. 'We all do, I suppose.'

'Not you.' She gave him a penetrating look. 'You've never had to worry about that in your life.' She strummed the rattan on the arm of the settee. 'A lot of people come here, thinking they can change things. It doesn't happen that way, ever. China changes you, instead of the other way around.'

Gilbert said warily, 'That sounds like a fair warning. You've seen a lot of us come and go, I imagine?'

'Oh, yes. Almost every missionary who comes to China passes through Shanghai, and the Presbyterians usually stop here to see Father. We're up to our ears in universities and hospitals and do-gooding institutions, and our collective pride in helping the downtrodden is thrilling to witness.' She leaned forward and stubbed out her cigarette, and immediately lit another. 'The Chinese aren't like us, you know. They have suffered so much that they've learned how to suffer gracefully. You'll never hear one complaining, as we would. There's a word they use in Shanghai: *maskee*. You'll hear it a lot, from people who are sick or hungry, who have lost their families or been

21

cheated in a business deal. It means, "Maybe things will be better tomorrow. Maybe not." God doesn't provide for the Chinese. No amber waves of grain. No food. No fuel. Only rocks and hardship and too many children. *Maskee*.'

'But surely missionaries can relieve some of that suffering,' Gilbert argued.

'How?' Anne demanded. 'By preaching the resurrection and the life? You missionaries are too stupid to realize that you've failed before you've even begun. How can you teach Christian morals to a Chinese who's had to sell his daughter to a brothel because he has no other choice? That's a reality we can't even comprehend, much less change. But there are missionaries who go back to the States or wherever and blame China because it failed to measure up somehow.'

'According to your way of thinking, I shouldn't even be here.' Gilbert felt annoyed and exasperated. He had expected a warm welcome from his father's friend, and instead he found himself arguing with a woman who treated him like a door-to-door salesman. 'Is that what you mean?'

Anne frowned. 'No, not really. The whites came to China to make money. They opened the door, carved up the Empire into this concession and that concession, instituted the ultimate arrogance of extraterritoriality, which says that no matter what crime a white man has committed, he has a right to be judged under the laws of his own nation. Not Chinese law, mind you. White man's law. The missionaries rode in on the merchants' coattails. They brought the Word, and salvation – none of which mean anything to the Chinese. But they also brought the modern world, schools and hospitals, science and technology. To the Chinese, though, you're one and the same, merchant and missionary. You look alike, you smell alike. You both came to exploit, although you people take your dividends in converts instead of cash. They'll let you go on doing it, because the whites have gunboats and they don't. They'll learn what they can from both of you, pick your brains while they pretend to believe what you say. But when the time comes, they'll throw the lot of you right out – doctors, priests, Standard Oil, the works. Me included.

Because we're the foreigners here.'

Gilbert was profoundly shocked. He had never before heard anyone speak about missionary efforts except with respect and wholehearted approval.

'Surely your attitudes are rather cynical, Miss Fox!'

Anne said, 'You think so? In Pidgin English the word for missionary is "joss-pidgin-man." "Joss" means luck, fate, God. "Pidgin" is any kind of business or enterprise. "A man whose business is God." And religion is big business here, believe me. There are ministers, including my father, who live as well as the taipans, the wealthy entrepreneurs. Not for them the lean and humble Christian example. They send letters home to their boards saying that conversions are up fifteen percent over last year and please keep the donations coming in. Investors, returns, upward curves, profit and loss statements. Business.' She unfurled her legs and stretched them out in front of her, and glared at her toes.

This impassioned speech made Gilbert's head swim. 'I, ah, I take it you're not religious,' he said lamely.

'I'll believe in God when He believes in me,' Anne declared. 'It's only fair.' She gave him a defiant look, then suddenly her face broke into a smile of surprising beauty. 'What an awful bore I am! I wouldn't blame you if you ran screaming from the house.'

Gilbert, who had been contemplating just such a move, lied gallantly. 'I'm not bored at all. I find what you say rather interesting. Different, certainly. Refreshing.'

She laughed aloud. 'You'll do all right in China. You can lie with a straight face!'

Wang came in then, bearing a tray loaded with a tea service and plates of cakes and sandwiches. He grinned at Gilbert and semaphored his eyebrows at Anne, who ignored him. She was still miffed at him for getting his own way.

When Wang departed, Anne sat up straight and poured some tea into cups. 'I really ought to apologize, Mr – Dr Lawrence. I'm not always so bad-mannered. I've been a bear all day, for no good reason. My father tells me it's rude to say what you think to people who believe the opposite. I don't agree, but if you think I was rude, I'm sorry.'

Gilbert swallowed tea and wondered how to respond to such an impenitent apology.

'Well, what do you think of Shanghai so far? Are you disappointed because it looks like Philadelphia, except that the streets are filled with Chinese?'

Gilbert laughed. 'I wasn't really expecting a colonial outpost all set about with fever trees, but I confess I'm rather overwhelmed by the sheer size and urbanness of it. Have you lived here long?'

'My father was a missionary up-country until I was eight. Then my mother became ill, and rather than go back to the States he asked for a posting in Shanghai. They gave him the Bubbling Well Road Presbyterian Church and all that that entails: rich congregation, a seat on the Municipal Council, membership of the Shanghai Club. He blossomed. Preaching to peasants isn't my father's style, although he does one service on Sundays in Chinese for the Christian compradores and their families. I've lived here ever since, except for an interval in Paris when I studied music. My little sister was born here. She's a real Shanghai girl. We both had perfectly normal childhoods. Music lessons. Dancing lessons. Girl Scouts. Recitals. Problems with prepositional phrases and acne and grubby little boys in bow ties who walk all over your feet. We Shanghai girls don't bind our feet or dine on hummingbirds' tongues or cultivate any bizarre bad habits, just the garden-variety ones that all girls have.'

Gilbert munched a sandwich. 'In spite of your denials, I refuse to believe that living here isn't as fascinating and exotic as I want to think it is. Do you work, Miss Fox?'

Anne shrugged. 'I've done some interpreting and translating. Right now I'm teaching at a school for Chinese and Eurasian girls that's run by an order of French nuns. I'm not especially good at it, not one of your born teachers. But the girls are decent, and they seem to tolerate me all right.' She made a face. 'Doesn't it stick out all over? Spinster schoolmarm on her afternoon off?'

It did, but Gilbert refrained from saying so. 'You didn't go to the polo match this afternoon. Don't you like sports?'

'No.' Anne swung her legs around and draped them over the arm of the settee. 'I detest anything that smacks of the white man banding together against the foreign element. Like a sheep in a snowstorm. The whites in this town are about as interesting as sheep, too. They're so desperate for amusement that it would be funny if it weren't so sad. You wouldn't believe the mindless dinner parties. There's no worthwhile conversation, only gossip and an airing of prejudices. The British run society here; we Americans ape their teas and their tiffins and take on British coloration. You'll see what it's like. A fete or a ball every time you turn around. Today is Bunker Hill Day. The first of July brings Dominion Day. Then the glorious Fourth! And a month from now Bastille Day. The French really put on a show. First a parade, then the most elegant picnic, with mousses fluted and tinted like cockades and rivers of champagne. And of course a lot of talk about the superiority of French culture.'

'Yes, I noticed the division on the map, the British at the north end of the city and French Concession to the south.'

'That's the French.' Anne made a sour face. 'Hooray for me and damn everybody else. It's a crazy treadmill here. You keep running and running and doing the same things and seeing the same people all the time. You learn too much about their lives and reveal too much about your own. The women are the worst. Always probing.'

'Perhaps they're bored,' Gilbert said reasonably. 'Their men are occupied with business, I suppose.'

'Listen,' Anne said, standing up abruptly, 'how would you like to see the garden? It's my special province. I like to grub in the dirt. At least plants don't argue back.'

Gilbert followed her out through the screen door. She wasn't unattractive, he thought, although she didn't bother to take any pains with her appearance. She obviously had a keen mind, and she certainly knew a lot about China and the Chinese. But how did a missionary's daughter get such misguided ideas?

Like most dwellings in China, the stocking mogul's estate was surrounded by a high wall. One end of the lawn behind the house was studded with croquet hoops. At the other end a couple of palm trees supported a fringed canvas hammock. Anne pointed out a camphor tree, flame trees, oleander, palmetto, paulownia. A man in a coolie hat straightened up from one of the borders and waved to them, then bent over again.

'Our new gardener,' Anne said. 'We always had a Japanese gardener because Father had some idea that the Japanese had a greater reverence for life than the Chinese. Then last year the Japanese bombed Chapei and their reverence for life became suspect. Father sacked poor old Cato, who didn't know what it was all about because he was too deaf to hear the bombs. It was awful. We both wept. Lu tries very hard, but we're having difficulty communicating. I came out last week and found him pulling up the sweet Williams I had raised from seeds a cousin in the States sent me. I asked him what for, and he said it was because they had no meaning.' She laughed suddenly, infectiously.

Gilbert grinned appreciatively. 'As a joss-pidgin-man I should appropriate that metaphor for a sermon: we should all be so ruthless in uprooting the meaningless from our lives.'

'If you did that in Shanghai, you'd have no life,' Anne remarked. They stopped at a rose bed. 'Another failure,' she said, poking at a bud that drooped on a wilted stem. 'I've slaved over these brutes for years and they're still not growing right. Too hot. Too damp. Of course they're not helped by being dug up and moved twice a year. I ought to keep my hands off for a while. But see that mildew? They just don't belong here.'

'Another metaphor?' Gilbert asked.

'Perhaps.' Anne picked off the bud and threw it away. 'But I can't see myself living anywhere else. I've been here twenty years. Twenty! After Shanghai, even Paris was dull.'

'Do you still pursue your music?'

'No,' she said. 'No, I don't play anymore.'

Gilbert had a sudden inspiration. 'You know, I'd love to see Shanghai through the eyes of a native. I know it's presumptuous of me to ask on such short acquaintance, but our fathers are friends, and if you could spare the time to show me around, I'd be most grateful.'

She gave him a suspicious look. 'You're just being kind, aren't you? Please don't bother.'

'I am not being kind, Miss Fox,' he said firmly. 'I'm being rather selfish, actually. I think you'd make a fine guide.'

'There really is so much to see,' she said hesitantly. 'Shanghai's a fascinating place. I'll show you the old part of the city first. The walls are gone now, but it's the same as it's been for a hundred years, like going back in time. And the Five Star Pavilion – the original tea house on all that Blue Willow ware. It's shabby and overrun by tourists, but it's genuinely lovely. There's a temple to the town gods – all Chinese cities used to have one.' She was becoming animated. 'And there are some people I'd like you to meet, one in particular –'

'I must get in touch with my sponsor here first thing tomorrow,' Gilbert said, 'but my afternoon will probably be free.'

'That's all right,' Anne said. 'I still teach in the morning. Too hot in the afternoon, but not too hot to sightsee. I won't drive you too hard. Why don't we meet for lunch?'

She looked genuinely pleased and excited. Gilbert felt happy that he'd made the gesture. Her father was an important man in Shanghai, after all. It wouldn't hurt to be nice to Anne Fox.

This is the best part of a friendship, Anne thought as they strolled through the garden. The very beginning. It's an adventure, like exploring unknown territory without a map. You paddle up uncharted arteries. There are false starts and cul-de-sacs. You get lost, you find your way again. You take a journey to the heart. You search for the source, the treasure that is the real person. With a lot of people you don't even bother to start out because you know it's not worth it. But Gilbert Lawrence is worth it, I can tell.

A horn blatted, tires squealed, car doors slammed. Anne's eyes lost their light. 'They're back,' she said. 'We'd better go in.'

Reverend Leonard Fox welcomed Gilbert warmly. He

asked about Gilbert's father, whom he had known at Yale Divinity School, and spoke of him fondly.

Gilbert could see a strong resemblance between Anne and her father. They had the same light brown hair and gray-green eyes and the same large bones, except Reverend Fox's were padded with hard bulk and covered with a beautifully cut white linen suit. He wore no clerical bib and collar, but a handsome blue silk bow tie on a cream-colored silk shirt.

Leonard Fox introduced his wife, Marian, who was as petite and fragile and dark as her husband was tall and robust and fair. She said, 'I remember a picture your parents sent years ago, when you were still in short pants. You were a lovely little boy, and you've grown into such a handsome young man!' She smiled enchantingly.

Gilbert flushed with pleasure, obviously not immune to compliments from charming ladies.

'A handsome young man?' came a voice like a chime. 'Where?' Kit joined them on the porch.

Gilbert had been in Shanghai only a few hours, during which time he had observed that the city was full of small, dark, beautiful women. But he knew he'd never see one like Kit Fox. Nor was he prepared to find her so attractive. Something Anne had said had led him to expect a gawky brat in pigtails, a younger version of herself.

Reverend Fox performed the introductions and they shook hands. Gilbert was acutely aware as he held Kit's cool hand that his own palms were sweaty. When he sat down he wiped them surreptitiously on his trousers.

Kit flowed into the settee opposite Gilbert's chair. She crossed her slender legs and smiled warmly.

After the precarious nature of conversation with Anne, social intercourse with the rest of the Fox family was refreshingly safe and sure, free of pitfalls, free of passionate outbursts and prickly silences. Gilbert's offhanded remarks elicited not diatribes but breezy, offhanded answers. They greeted his announcement that he was a medical missionary not with ponderous scepticism but with enthusiasm and respect. This was the response he was used to, the one he expected. He began to relax.

'Henry must be very proud of you,' Leonard Fox beamed. 'We're proud of you, too. While you're in Shanghai, Gilbert, we want you to think of this manse as your home.'

'Work like yours is so important to the Chinese,' his wife said.

'Oh, I think Dr Lawrence just has a lust for adventure,' Kit teased. 'I hope we can satisfy it. Why else would a handsome young man want to bury himself in China?'

Gilbert smiled. 'I suppose I've always felt the lure of the mysterious East. A lot of Americans have. But when I was in the second year of seminary, I heard a talk by a Methodist minister who had just returned from Manchuria. He spoke about the dreadful conditions of the countryside, the poor hygiene, the urgent need of Chinese for Western medicine. I've never been a good talker – I wouldn't have made a very good preacher – but I knew that here was one way I could serve. I changed my course to medicine, and here I am.'

The senior Foxes smiled approvingly. Kit's eyes glowed. Gilbert found himself blushing as she looked at him, and he was grateful when Anne came in carrying a pitcher of lemonade and a tray of glasses. Odd, he hadn't even noticed her slip away.

'Hullo, Mouse,' Kit greeted her gaily. 'Give me a fag, will you?'

Anne tossed down her crumpled pack of cigarettes and stretched out on the chaise in the farthest corner of the room, where she was partially obscured by a rubber plant. Gilbert lit Kit's cigarette. Most women, he had noticed, looked a little silly when they smoked. Louise, his fiancée, for example. Anne was particularly awkward. But Kit did it so naturally that she might have been illustrating the fine art of inhaling and exhaling.

'How was the polo match, Miss Fox?' Gilbert asked Kit. 'Was our side humiliated?'

'Humiliated, but not the same way as before,' Reverend Fox grumbled.

'Dr Lawrence, I forbid you to address me as Miss Fox,' Kit said severely. 'There are two Misses Fox, but only one Kit. Please, I insist.'

'She has always insisted on Kit, from the time she was two years old,' her mother said fondly. 'Leonard started to call her Kitten because she was such an adorable child, but she absolutely hated it! Kit it had to be. She was stubborn, even at that age. But it suits her so well, don't you think? Much better than Katherine.'

Her name did suit Kit perfectly: hard-edged, breezy, as sharp as a knife, as clean as a scalpel cut.

Anne said from her corner, 'I have always thought that the reason we didn't hear more from Anne Brontë was because of her name. What I could have done if I'd been an Emily or a Charlotte.'

Gilbert liked the way Kit wore her hair, in fluffy curls instead of pasted-down waves, like Louise. Gilbert thought that style tortured and unnatural-looking, like the way Louise shaved off her eyebrows and penciled them back in. Kit's brows were lush and dark, with a serpentine shape. Her eyes were brown with gold lights, and they seemed to know all his secrets, and he found he didn't mind. He realized that he was staring, and he cleared his throat and looked away.

Kit said, 'The polo was marvelous. Even you would have enjoyed it, Anne.'

'I doubt it.'

'Did we score?' Gilbert asked.

'Score? My dear, we won. It was the most stunning upset.'

'We didn't win, we cheated,' her father declared with heat. 'It's a scandal.'

'How do you cheat at polo?' Anne wondered drowsily. 'Dope the horses?'

'Ponies, dear,' Kit corrected her. 'We might as well have. It was that monster, Jim Innes. He outfitted the whole American team with real, live, genuine polo ponies from England. It must have cost the earth. But he has it, of course. It was the most unbelievable show. The British on those over-sized canines, and Innes and the rest of the Americans on the sleekest creatures you ever saw, all with pedigrees as long as their arms, or rather legs, which is more than one can say for Mr Innes, you may be sure.'

'Our British cousins were not pleased,' Reverend Fox

remarked sourly.

'They were livid!' Kit laughed deliciously. 'They did manage to score a couple of times, when Innes couldn't quite manage to get to the ball. The rest of the time they didn't have a chance. Those English ponies didn't even need riders to tell them what to do.'

'I thought it was rather exciting,' Marian Fox said, sipping her lemonade through a straw. 'Poor Brad Harvey was knocked unconscious, though. Dreadful.'

'He'll be lucky if he lives,' Leonard Fox said darkly.

'It really was a rout,' Kit said. 'We were all cringing in our seats. I don't know how I can show my face in the British Country Club again. It was so embarrassing!'

Gilbert was confused. 'But surely, to have a victory after all these years –'

'I think it sounds jolly,' Anne said. 'If anybody but Innes had come up with the scheme, you'd have cheered your silly heads off.'

'It was typical of the man,' said her father with deep disgust. 'He has no scruples, even where sport is concerned. He had no business practicing his cutthroat tactics on the playing field, in a friendly game that is supposed to exemplify the spirit of amicability between nations in Shanghai.'

'That sounds like a quote from your benediction at the annual Chamber of Commerce banquet,' Anne said. 'Just one big, happy, greedy family.'

Reverend Fox swelled with annoyance. He was about to retort but Kit interrupted with a laugh. 'Daddy's just trying to say that what Innes did isn't pukka,' she told Gilbert. 'It was rather – well, nasty.'

'The other members of the team were plainly uncomfortable at the reception afterward,' Reverend Fox said, shooting a black look in Anne's direction. 'As well they should have been. I can't imagine what possessed them to join forces with that madman. Have they no self-respect?'

'Maybe they were just tired of losing,' Anne suggested.

'After the match I presented him with the trophy,' Kit told Gilbert. 'I was the token pretty girl in the reviewing stand this year, the one that ends up in the press pictures – see tomorrow's *News*. Innes practically grabbed the cup out of my hands.'

'Oh, Kit, he didn't,' her mother protested.

'He did, darling,' Kit insisted. 'You really were too far away to see. He had the most arrogant leer – as if he'd really earned that cup single-handedly! Then he waved it over his head, in the direction of the consuls and the bigwigs, just rubbing their noses in it. The taipans were seething. They couldn't even muster polite applause.'

'Well, I applauded vigorously,' Marian said. 'I thought he deserved it.'

'He deserved a good kick in the pants,' Reverend Fox said.

Gilbert marveled. 'He sounds like a terrible person.'

'Oh, he is,' Kit said earnestly. 'Everyone in Shanghai despises him. He's always involved in something unsavory and despicable.'

'He's smarter than the competition,' said Anne. 'They're just jealous.'

'That's not so,' said Leonard Fox. 'I have nothing against a self-made man who has gotten to the top by means of hard work and intelligence and sacrifice. But Innes has none of these things. He's like a jungle animal, corrupt to his soul, utterly ruthless and un-Christian, without manners or morals. His money came from opium. It still does, I'm certain. It's well known that he's hand in glove with Tu Yueh-sen, the head of the Green Dragon Society. A bunch of terrorists. Innes is no better than a gangster.'

Gilbert said, 'I saw his name along the docks, on warehouses, even on the Bund.'

'Oh, yes, he's quite prominent in Shanghai, is our Mr Innes,' said Leonard Fox grimly. 'Uses legitimate businesses as fronts. Now he's gotten to the stage where he'd like a little respectability. After all, his money's just as good as the rest, isn't it?' He snorted derisively.

'It's all filthy,' Anne opined.

'He has the longest Rolls-Royce in the world,' Kit said. 'It's painted money green and trimmed with gold, naturally. I hear he wants to join the Shanghai Club.' She explained to Gilbert. 'A Shanghai institution. You probably saw the physical institution on the Bund: white

32

marble, looks a little like the Parthenon. So very exclusive, my dear. Only the most important men in Shanghai are invited to join.'

'You mean the biggest robbers,' said Anne.

'Hah. They'd blackball not only Innes, but any man who proposed his membership,' Leonard Fox said. 'He can buy his way into most things, but not that. Kit fixed his wagon, today, though. Saved our face a little.'

He told the story proudly, while Kit steadfastly maintained that the stumble had been purely accidental.

'About as accidental as those ponies of his.'

Mrs Fox got unsteadily to her feet. 'I'm feeling rather tired all of a sudden,' she said. Gilbert noticed that her face had gone white. He stood up. 'I must lie down. Perhaps if I rest now I can come down for dinner later. You will stay, won't you, Gilbert?'

'I'll come up with you, Mother,' Anne said.

'No, no, dear,' her mother waved her away. 'I wouldn't dream of taking you away from your guest.'

She went out, tripping slightly on the sill. Gilbert moved toward her but a slight pressure on his arm held him back.

'She'll be all right,' Kit said.

'Is there anything I can do?' Gilbert asked.

'Marian, ahem, suffers from the heat,' said Reverend Fox with an embarrassed cough.

'Like hell she does,' Anne said.

'I really shouldn't intrude on you further,' Gilbert said. 'I've already made a nuisance of myself, appearing unannounced.'

Kit and her father tried to persuade him to stay. Anne wandered back to the chaise and held herself aloof from the argument, as if it made no difference to her whether Gilbert Lawrence dined with them or not.

'It's just us and a few old friends,' Reverend Fox said. 'Billy and Laura Morrison and the Westons.'

'That's not Dr William Morrison, by any chance? The head of the Medical Missionary Society here? He's my sponsor here.'

'The one and only,' Kit said. 'Uncle Billy's a lamb, and you'll love Laura. You see, you must stay. It was meant.'

'It won't hurt you to meet him socially, Gilbert,' Leonard Fox said wisely. 'Has he handed you an assignment yet?'

'There was some mention of my joining the staff of the university hospital in Chengtu, Szechwan,' Gilbert said, 'but nothing really definite. I don't know where I'll end up – not that it matters. They didn't expect me this soon, and I left rather suddenly. I wired, but I don't know if he received the message.'

'Szechwan's a tricky spot right now,' Reverend Fox said, shaking his head doubtfully.

'Perhaps you can persuade him to keep you on at a hospital right here,' Kit suggested.

'Kit can't believe there's life in China outside of Shanghai,' her father laughed.

'I can't believe there's life in Shanghai,' Anne said.

'Poor Anne,' clucked Kit. 'Those dreary Communist cell meetings got you down? Step out with my crowd some night. We'll show you how to live it up in Shanghai.'

'God forbid, Anne shuddered.

'Actually, I was rather looking forward to working in the provinces,' Gilbert told Reverend Fox. 'I know Shanghai is already full of excellent physicians, but out there –'

'All the same, it won't hurt you to get things between you and Bill Morrison on a friendly footing right away,' said Leonard, giving Gilbert a fatherly pat on the shoulder.

'Father means if you want to get ahead in the mission game, you've got to get in good with the chief joss-pidgin-man,' Anne said.

Her father glowered at her, and there was an awkward silence that even Kit's bright laughter couldn't fill.

Dr Morrison and his wife might have been brother and sister. They were both pink and white and stout. Kit likened them to a couple of Toby mugs. They were distraught that Gilbert's cable hadn't reached them.

'We could have met your ship', they said. 'What a shame.'

'I managed quite well,' Gilbert assured them. 'My

departure was a little frantic. A space on the *Chichibu Maru* opened up at the last minute and it seemed wiser to take it than to waste the summer waiting. I'd already finished my residency in Philadelphia, you see. I was sure I could be useful in Chengtu.'

'I'm afraid Chengtu is off limits right now,' Dr Morrison said sadly. 'I'd like to get my people out of there, but travel's difficult, impossible really'

'Why is that?'

'The natives are blowing up joss-pidgin-men,' Anne said. 'I hear they're even taking heads.' Laura Morrison squealed girlishly.

'It's this eternal warring between the Communists and Chiang Kai-shek's armies,' Dr Morrison explained. 'Unfortunately the upper Yangtze's been cut off, and there's no other way to reach Chungking. It's just too dangerous at the moment, my boy. I know you're disappointed, and being young you'd be willing to risk it. But I don't want to risk losing you! Doctors are far too precious in China.'

'But where is your wife, Dr Lawrence?' Laura Morrison asked, looking around as though Mrs Lawrence had somehow become misplaced. 'In your last letter you said you were plannng to be married in the spring.'

There was an interested silence. Gilbert avoided meeting Kit's eyes. He said, 'Louise didn't want to live so far from home. She really didn't understand why I wanted to work in China, and I didn't feel it was fair of me to insist. We are no longer formally engaged.'

'Very sensible,' Dr Morrison said approvingly. 'Lots of women never get used to the life. Too hard, too different from what they know. Still, a woman can be a great comfort to a man out here, especially when he finds himself the only white man in a village full of Chinese.'

'I don't know what else the village would be full of,' Anne remarked.

'I don't know what I would have done without my Laura.' Dr Morrison beamed at his wife, who blushed becomingly.

The Westons arrived then. Arthur Weston was a wealthy British exporter. He had a large number of exotic birds in an aviary in his mansion, which was farther up on

Bubbling Well Road. He was also an enthusiastic private collector of Chinese art objects. Myrna Weston was pale, shy, clearly overshadowed by her expansive husband. Anne despised them both, but they contributed generously to the church, and to Reverend Fox's salary, and were frequent guests at the manse.

Dinner would have been more relaxed and pleasant without Anne's occasional dormouse outbursts. Marian Fox sent down apologies and regrets that she didn't feel well enough to join them. The food was delicious, a combination of American and Chinese cuisines that included stir-fried dishes and steamed dumplings as well as broiled pork chops and mashed potatoes. Wang and a female servant waited on the table. Gilbert noticed that Anne ate only Chinese food, and that she used chopsticks.

The Westons had attended the polo match, and so had the Morrisons. They shared Leonard and Kit Fox's low opinion of James Innes. Gilbert was to discover that denigrating Innes was part of the conversational fabric at Shanghai social gatherings.

'The man is a menace,' Arthur Weston declared. 'Now he's even entering the curio market. Every time I locate something truly precious and valuable and try to buy it, I discover that he's been there before me. He's buying up everything – Ming, Sung, jade and porcelain, prints and paintings. He even snapped up a fourteenth-century Peking temple carpet, a gorgeous thing. Paid thousands for it. His funds are limitless,' he added bitterly.

'Does he send his things out of the country?' Anne asked innocently.

'Why, I don't think so.'

'Then maybe it's a good thing he's buying them, instead of an exporter,' she said. 'At least those works of art stay here, where they belong.'

Weston flushed. He sold carloads of Chinese antiques to dealers from around the world. Reverend Fox looked annoyed and embarrassed. He seemed about to rebuke his older daughter for her rudeness when Kit asked Mr Weston how his book on Chinese mythology was progressing.

'Oh, very well, my dear. How kind of you to be

interested. It's just a little book,' he told Gilbert modestly. 'Nothing terribly learned, just a collection of stories I've heard over the years. You would be amazed at the richness of Chinese legends, the vast number of spirits and demons that have no counterpart in Western mythology.'

'That's why converting the Chinese is so difficult,' Laura Morrison said, spooning dumplings onto her plate. 'They have to discard thousands of gods and goddesses. You think you've persuaded one of them to accept Christ as his savior, and the next time you turn around, he's setting out glasses of water around his house so that he can trap demons in them. It can be incredibly frustrating.'

Anne gave what sounded like a derisive snort and slid lower in her seat.

'Yes, be warned, Dr Lawrence,' said Arthur Weston. 'You're going to encounter a lot of superstitious resistance to your work. You might even encounter some demons yourself.' He twinkled at Kit, who favored him with a smile. 'They say in China that if you meet a young lady who is particularly lively and attractive, you should peek under the hem of her dress. If you see the red tip of a fox's brush, beware! You've been victimized by a fox-fairy.'

Everyone laughed, and Gilbert said, 'I'll try to be alert. Are they very dangerous?'

'Mischievous more than malicious. They often take on the appearance of a woman you know, perhaps the woman you love. The confusion is generally amusing. Impecunious scholars seem to be especially marked for their attentions.'

'You're in no danger, then, Mr Weston,' said Anne. 'I mean, you're hardly impecunious.' Weston's mouth tightened with anger and Leonard Fox began to swell.

Gilbert said quickly, before Reverend Fox could erupt, 'I don't think I'm in any danger, either. I may be impecunious, but I'm no scholar.' The awkward moment passed.

'I've been thinking, Gilbert,' said Dr Morrison, 'the staff at the Aldershot Clinic is short an internist. Their man had a bad go-round with malaria and he's still recovering. If you wouldn't mind filling in there until the situation in Chengtu clears up, we'd be most grateful.'

'I'd be delighted to be of service, sir,' said Gilbert.

'The clinic is simply wonderful, Gilbert,' Laura Morrison gushed. 'Brand-new and fully equipped.'

'And we lucky whites get the full benefit of all that lovely equipment,' said Anne, stabbing her chopsticks into a bowl of pork slivers and Chinese cabbage. 'Well, why not? We deserve the best. We made this country what it is today.'

'Anne means to say that the clinic is for paying patients only,' Reverend Fox explained hastily. 'After all, it was very costly to furnish.'

'And we do treat Chinese,' said Laura, tearing open a roll and applying a generous layer of butter. 'Why, just last week the wife of Shanghai's Buddhist abbot came in for minor surgery.'

'That was very liberal,' Anne said. 'But what would you have done if he'd sent in one of his concubines?'

'Anne.' Her father's tone carried a stern warning. Sulking, she put down her chopsticks and lit a cigarette. No one else had finished eating. Her father gave her a furious look, which she ignored.

'I'm in your hands, Dr Morrison,' said Gilbert, concealing his disappointment. If he had wanted to treat rich whites, he could have stayed in Philadelphia.

'I'll only ask for a few hours a week,' Dr Morrison said. 'Leave you plenty of time to get used to us and begin language study. Yes, this will work out very well. You'll get a jump on Chengtu if you start now. There's a summer course for beginners starting up at Shanghai University next week, in fact. Anne here can give you a hand. She's quite a little linguist. Chatters away just like a native.' He gave Anne a broad smile. His eyes nearly disappeared in folds of fat.

'I know it sounds like chatter,' Anne said, 'but I even know some vocabulary.'

'I'm impressed,' said Gilbert. 'I have absolutely no talent for languages myself. I know I'm going to need all the help I can get.' His smile was friendly, and she flushed slightly.

'Oh, yes, Anne's our resident Sinophile,' said Kit smoothly. 'Anytime we have to read a menu or need help with the servants, we run to her.'

Gilbert's head swiveled around to Kit again, as smoothly as if she controlled it with a string. Sinophile, thought Anne with grudging admiration. Where did she get that?

'It's settled, then,' said Dr Morrison with a decisive nod. 'Come to my office first thing in the morning, Gilbert. We'll work out a schedule.'

'I absolutely forbid it, Uncle Billy,' cried Kit. 'You haven't given Gilbert a chance to catch his breath. Come on, three days' grace at least. He hasn't even seen the city yet.'

'You know I can't refuse you anything, Kitty,' said Dr Morrison fondly. Gilbert felt Kit stiffen at the name, and he winked at her.

She said, 'Have you found anyone to show you around Shanghai yet, Gilbert?'

Gilbert gave Anne an anxious look. She stared steadfastly at the cigarette ash piling up on the dinner plate. 'Well, actually, your sister was kind enough –'

Kit laughed. 'Oh, so you've already been booked on a tour of the slums and the charity institutions! Are you really so eager to see the seamy side of things? Anne, dear, I beg you, don't blight Gil's first impressions of Shanghai by dragging him through the muck. He'll see enough of that when Uncle Billy puts him to work.'

Anne shrugged. 'We hadn't made any definite plans.'

'It's settled, then. I'll pick you up bright and early, say around eleven. Cocktails and an early lunch at the Cathay – we'll run into a dozen marvelous people there – and they have the most divine French chef!'

Anne said, 'You're lucky, Dr Lawrence. Now you'll see the real Shanghai. Don't neglect the Casanova and the Delmonte, Kit. We don't want Dr Lawrence to think Shanghai's all soup kitchens and brothels. I'm sure he'll go mad for the new Filipino dance band at the Golden Gate.' She stood up and tossed down her napkin. 'Will you all excuse me? I have to go out for a while.'

The gentlemen rose unenthusiastically as she left the room. Dr Morrison said to Reverend Fox, 'Is she still running around with those Marxists, Leonard?'

'If she is, it's the fault of that priest, Jacquinot,' said

Leonard Fox angrily. 'He's bewitched her.'

'I hope I haven't offended her,' said Gilbert anxiously.

'Offended Anne?' said Kit. 'Of course you have, dearie. You can't help it. I'm in the doghouse around here from Sunday morning to Saturday night, and I'm used to it. She thinks me utterly frivolous and shallow, you see. Maybe she's right.'

Her dimple danced coyly at the corner of her mouth. 'It might not be seemly for a medical missionary to be seen with someone like me.'

Mrs Morrison said, 'What nonsense, Kitty. Dr Lawrence will fit right into your crowd. All the brightest young people. Everyone who matters.'

'I'm looking forward to it,' said Gilbert with utmost truth, as Kit Fox enfolded him in her smile.

The Morrisons gave Gilbert a lift back to his hotel in their enormous Packard limousine. Their uniformed chauffeur drove sedately, hardly faster than Gilbert had walked. The back seat, equipped with jump seats, could accommodate six persons, and seemed to Gilbert to be more spacious than his hotel room.

'Poor Leonard,' sighed Laura Morrison. 'I don't know how he manages, with Marian being so ill most of the time. And Anne -- ! What's the matter with the girl anyhow? And what's all this about a priest, Billy? She's - she's not going to convert, is she?' She sounded genuinely alarmed.

They gossiped unself-consciously in front of Gilbert, like parents in front of a child they have trained to be discreet. He paid little attention, and watched the buildings on Bubbling Well Road slide past as he thought about luminous brown eyes and rose-petal-pink skin.

'It's Jacquinot, the Jesuit,' Dr Morrison said. 'A very forceful personality, and a fine mind. Not a bad friend for her to have. I don't think she's in any real danger from him. She's still pretty skeptical. I do think she might have confided in me, but perhaps we're too close to the family. No, I'm not too worried about Anne. She's alert to her responsibilities.'

'I do wish she'd get married,' said Laura. 'That would

settle her, and take her off Leonard's hands, too.'

'It didn't settle Kitty, or take her away from home very long,' her husband grunted. 'She really ran circles around that poor fellow. Wonder when she'll try again?'

Suddenly Shanghai looked ugly to Gilbert. He felt utterly bone-weary and exhausted. It had been a long day.

Back in his hotel room he undressed quickly and crawled under the mosquito netting that covered the bed. He wasn't used to it, and didn't think to tuck the bottom edge under the mattress, and several mosquitoes found their way in and whined around his head. He pulled the sheets up and fell asleep without writing in his journal and without saying his prayers.

Chapter Two

'Why so quiet today, Gil?'

Kit's little red Bentley bounced over the narrow rutted track. She took a corner too quickly and the rear wheels slid a little in the soft roadbed. Suddenly they were almost on top of a boy herding a huge water buffalo. Kit leaned hard on her horn and aimed the car at the narrow space between the two obstacles. The beast kicked up its heels and bolted, and the boy reeled backward into a ditch. They sped past.

'What's the matter?' Kit asked over the roar of the engine. 'Aren't you enjoying my Shanghai?' The close call and its horrific possibilities left her unperturbed.

'Of course I am,' he shouted, grateful that the throbbing of the motor concealed the tremble in his voice.

'Liar,' she said cheerfully.

He had had nearly a week of Kit's Shanghai: long, leisurely lunches at expensive restaurants where there wasn't a chopstick in sight, a little tennis or golf in the afternoon, cocktail parties, late dinners, and finally dancing in a series of nightclubs, sometimes as many as five in one evening. He never crawled into bed before four in the morning, and although he never drank anything alcoholic, he always awoke with a raging headache.

She wouldn't let him pay for anything, and he never saw any cash changing hands. Everyone simply signed their names to chits, and paid their bills at the end of the month.

'It's a marvelous system,' Kit told him. 'You never have to carry any money, except a few coins for a taxi or a ricksha. We're almost a cashless society.'

He met the members of her set, horse-faced young Britons and sleek Americans with names like Binky and Dusty and Boo. The young women giggled a lot, and wanted to know all about the current fashions in the States, the newest films, the popular dance bands. No one mentioned the current economic depression, which was having its effect in Shanghai as everywhere else. Many branch offices had closed because of problems in their home countries. Markets for all goods were slack and prices fell. Factories in Pootung, across the Whangpoo from the city, were closing their doors. More people starved. But Kit and her friends played on, attending cricket matches and horse races and amateur theatricals, rowing on the Soochow Creek, riding their Mongolian ponies out in the countryside, arranging houseboating parties and lawn parties and costume parties, planning jaunts to the mountains when the heat in Shanghai became unbearable.

Gilbert noticed with amazement that as beautiful as Kit was, none of the girls in her crowd seemed to be jealous of her. She treated everyone, male and female alike, with the same offhanded friendliness, and she had a charming way of belittling her own superior qualities. Anne did that, too, but then Anne's self-deprecation was sincere and believable, while Kit's was as false and endearing as her smile.

He was grateful for her attentions, but eager for them to end. His attraction to her irritated him because he felt that it was something he couldn't control, and he was afraid that if he saw much more of her, he couldn't cure it. It was especially strong when they danced. She slid into his arms, assuming a position of remarkable intimacy, and moved her body lightly against his. He loved the smell of perfume on her hair. His hand rested stiffly on the cool flesh of her naked back, just above the deep scoop of her shimmering gown. He wanted the dance never to end. Only later, when he was alone in his room, did he realize that he was falling under a sort of spell. He could tell that the other men had already succumbed, even the married ones. They were all in love with her, and Gilbert didn't want to be just another scalp hanging from her belt. He knew that she didn't care a scrap for any of the men who obviously adored her.

He detested the nightclubs and dance halls with their noise and their liquor and their smoke. Most of the clubs were located on the Avenue Edward VII, which divided the International Settlement from the French Concession.

The street was known around the world as Blood Alley.
The clubs were famous for their hostesses, mostly lithe
Oriental and Eurasian girls who wore tight-fitting dresses
slashed to the thigh and high-heeled pumps. They all had
scarlet lips and painted eyes and rouged cheeks. They sat
at tables, alone or in small groups, and waited for
invitations to dance or drink. Kit seemed especially
fascinated by them, and she delighted in comparing their
relative merits. She laughed at their crooked seams and
garish makeup and hideous frocks.

Gilbert was no different from other doctors who liked
to think they were immune to shock because they had
witnessed every phase of the human experience and had
seen the human organism at its most vulnerable and
pathetic. But he was truly shocked by these women, who
paraded themselves boldly and offered their bodies for
hire without a glimmer of shame or regret.

He noted with surprise that several of the hostesses
were fair-haired and blue-eyed.

'White Russians,' Binky Hartshorn explained. 'Came
here by the carload after the Revolution in '17. Of course,
they're all counts and countesses and princesses.' Laughter from the rest. 'Not good for much, really. Sold off all
their jewelry and had to live somehow. Couldn't work.
Couldn't even speak decent English. So the men became
beggars and the women whores.'

'It was awfully bad for us whites,' someone else said.
'First time the Chinese had ever seen a white man
begging. We really lost face.'

Gilbert was not surprised to meet his old shipmate,
Albert McClure, in the Casanova one night. He introduced him to Kit and her friends.

'Fox?' McClure's nose twitched when he heard Kit's
name. 'Your father's a preacher-wallah, isn't he?'

'Oh, God, you mean you can tell by looking that I'm a
preacher's daughter?' Kit laughed. 'I'm going to have to
do something about my appearance.'

'You don't have to do a thing about it except put it next
to mine and let me whirl it around the dance floor a little,'
Albert McClure leered appreciatively.

Later Gilbert said, 'You didn't need to be polite to him

for my sake. I don't care much for him.'

'I thought he was sweet.' Kit said. 'And he's a lovely dancer.'

Gilbert wondered about her mysterious ex-husband, whom no one mentioned. He began to wonder if he had dreamed Dr Morrison's reference to him. He could have satisfied his curiosity simply by asking her, but he didn't want to. She might have thought that it mattered to him, that he cared, and he would have felt like a fool.

She was unlike any other woman he had ever known. She was as lithe as a cat, as graceful as a swallow in flight – but no, animal metaphors were too easy, too facile. To compare her to anything earthly and familiar was to do her an injustice. To think of both her and Louise as women was to insult one of them; either Kit was more or Louise was less. Both were feminine, to be sure, but Kit was female, the essence of femaleness. Louise was sisterly, dependable, predictable. There was nothing hidden behind her eyes, nothing implied in her movements. A shrug of the shoulders was just that, not a tantalizing glimpse into that other something, that Femaleness. He couldn't picture Kit engaged in any of the homely, domestic activities that he associated in his mind with woman's role. Kit sewing? Suckling a baby? Making coffee in the morning, and frying an egg? No. Oh, no.

Louise was just an ordinary woman, like Anne, although she wasn't given to argument or passionate outbursts. She was sane, calm, sensible – like Philadelphia. But Kit was as strange and exotic as Shanghai itself. On the surface things seemed deceptively normal, familiar, and comprehensible. You could almost persuade yourself that Shanghai wasn't really that different from home. But then you'd round a corner and find yourself in a place that didn't look anything like home, a place that was mysterious, ancient and arcane.

He remembered walking down a market street near his hotel. There was the usual narrow path between a jumble of stalls and pushcarts that were piled high with displays of vegetables and fish and ginger root and red-painted ducks pressed as flat as platters. A cat snorted on top of a heap of greens. Chinese merchants and customers chattered excitedly and looked right through him, and he knew they had taken in every detail of his appearance. Then he saw a knot of people clustered around a doorway off to one side. Being taller than the rest, he could see right over their heads. A man squatted in the doorway. Beside him stood a bucket of live, writhing snakes. He withdrew one and dropped it onto a piece of newspaper spread out at his feet. With lightning swiftness he hacked it into pieces with a cleaver. As the pieces of snake wriggled and roiled, the man jabbered and gesticulated. Gilbert knew he was divining hidden meanings, perhaps even telling the future. One of the members of the rapt crowd saw Gilbert then and murmured a warning. The seer wrapped up the bits of snake and melted away into the interior of the building and the crowd dispersed. It was ugly, fascinating, and a little frightening, a glimpse of a world he would never understand.

He shivered even as the hot delta wind seared his face, and he wondered how he could ever have thought of such a horrid incident in connection with the beautiful woman who sat beside him.

Kit turned the car off the main road onto a precariously narrow path between two rice paddies. They crossed a bridge over a stinking drainage canal. A dead dog lay in the low water at the bottom. His body was bloated by the sun and his legs stuck straight up into the air. Kit paid no attention; she had been born in China, and she didn't even see the horrors that made newcomers cringe. They came to a dusty halt near a stream and a bamboo grove. A ruin lurked behind a screen of willow trees. A temple, Kit said.

She jumped out of the car and said brightly, 'You're bored stiff, aren't you, Gil? Can't wait to get your hands on a nice case of beriberi or leprosy. Well, your torment is almost over. It was very sweet of you to cooperate with me this long.'

She bustled, unfurling a blanket in a shady spot under a willow, ordering Gilbert to take the hamper out of the trunk. She flopped down on the blanket and folded her tan naked arms under her head

'It's horribly quiet here,' she said 'I don't know how long I can put up with this.'

46

'You're addicted to noise,' Gilbert said, lowering himself onto the far edge of the blanket. 'I don't know how anyone in Shanghai can hear himself think.'

'I don't bother to think,' she said sleepily. 'Why should I?'

She looked incredibly lovely. Her dress was white, with a fitted sleeveless bodice and full skirt. Her breasts were small but round and full. Her legs were brown and smooth. No woman had a right to look like that, Gilbert thought. He found himself longing for Louise's shaved eyebrows and crimped hair.

'You're very intelligent, Kit,' he said severely. 'You ought to do something useful.'

' "Useful" is a dirty word. Almost as obscene as "work," or "duty." Ugh, dreary! Please don't preach, Gil. You sound like Anne, and that's a bore.'

'You're cruel to her.'

'Stuff,' Kit snorted. 'Half the time she doesn't even hear what I say. Of course we squabble. We're sisters, remember? And I'm the baby. I have to stand up for myself.'

'All the same, she doesn't have many friends and —'

'Dear me, criticizing already!' Kit rolled onto her side and looked at him. 'Five days and you're trying to tell me what to do. That was a brief friendship. Well, I could do some criticizing too, dearie. You've been a great disappointment to me. I've done my darnedest to show you a good time and you've behaved like a perfect bear, glowering and moping. You've endured me and my friends and suffered patiently and not said a word because you've been brought up properly, but all the time you've been hating it, haven't you? We don't have to do any more of this if you don't want to.'

'My class in Chinese starts tomorrow,' Gilbert said, picking at a pill of fuzz on the blanket. 'I'll be rather busy, I'm afraid.'

'La, our Gil's going back to school,' Kit chortled. 'I hope you brought your letter sweater with you. What did you go out for? Football? Basketball?'

'Lacrosse, actually,' he admitted. 'And track. I'm a runner.'

'I'll say you are. Louise must have been a pretty swift little girl herself to catch you.'

'I'd rather not discuss Louise, if you don't mind,' he said stiffly.

'Why not?' Kit asked. 'Feeling guilty for the way you treated her, running out on her minutes before the wedding? And to China, no less! I feel sorry for her. Your message couldn't have been more clear. Or maybe you really do miss her, Gil.' She sat up and wrapped her arms around her updrawn knees. 'I know what's the matter with you, you're homesick!' She gave him her false, bright smile. 'It might help if you talked about her, you know. What's she like, Gil? Terribly intelligent – unlike me? Fascinating? Intense? Poetic? I know, she's a scientist! You met her over the dissecting table.'

She could see the blood rising to his face but she kept on, goading and teasing. He wanted to strike her. Instead he stood up without saying a word and stalked away through the willow grove, to the ruin.

Only two walls remained standing, and most of the stucco had fallen away from those, exposing ancient pitted brick. Only faded patches of red paint indicated that the place had been something other than a simple dwelling. The tile roof had caved in and the temple was open to the sky, but the willows shaded it and a new roof of wisteria vines had grown over one corner so that it felt quite cool inside. The floor was a jumble of shattered tiles, crumbled brick, clumps of grass, heaps of earth. Over the years pigs rooted there, children played there, lovers met. Anything wooden – arches, altars, pillars, doorframes – had long ago been removed and used for fuel.

Gilbert wished he could be alone there for a while, to meditate and to pray. God was close, ready to listen to the outpourings of his troubled heart.

Kit appeared in the doorway. 'I'm sorry, Gil. I can be an awful bitch sometimes.'

'You've been married,' he said accusingly.

'That's right, I have. But I'm not now.'

'You're divorced.'

'Right again. I can't think of a better way to end a marriage. Except murder, but people object to that.'

48

'You might have told me.'

'You might have asked,' she said reasonably. 'It's no secret.'

'You're using your maiden name again.'

'Why not? I was a Fox for nineteen years and a Matthews for six months. I didn't want to drag that name around with me for the rest of my life, like a ball and chain. The marriage was a mistake. It's gone, erased.'

'So it's that simple, is it?' he asked bitterly. 'As though it never happened. Does he feel that way, too?'

'Dickie? Lord, I don't know. After the wedding we went to England to meet the family. Six months later I was back here, divorce papers in hand, ready to pick up where I left off. Except now I had money of my own, thanks to a very generous settlement. Dickie stayed home. He's probably afraid to show his face in Shanghai again.'

'Why? Why shouldn't he come back here?'

Kit shrugged. 'Men don't like to look like fools. People might say that he wasn't man enough for me. In fact, they do say it.'

'Is it true, what they say?'

'Isn't that getting a little personal, Gil? It just didn't work out, that's all. We weren't suited to each other. Come on, don't give me that "Get thee behind me, Scarlet Woman" treatment. It went out with the bustle. We can still be friends.'

'But not more,' Gilbert said firmly.

'Why, Gilbert, do you want to be more than friends?' she asked softly. She stood very close to him. He turned his head away because he couldn't bear the knowing look in her eyes. She put her fingertips on his cheek and moved his face around again. He could feel the warm wind of her breath. 'There's nothing to stop us.'

He wasn't aware of anything else but her. Her heat, her perfume, the sweet softness of her skin. She threaded her arms around his neck and kissed him.

'No.' He pushed her away and stepped out into the dappled sunlight of the bamboo grove.

Her laughter was as cool and light as the ripple of the nearby stream. 'Oh, Gilbert, honestly.' She followed him and watched amused as he closed the hamper, folded the blanket, carried the things to the car. 'What's the matter, sweet? Haven't you ever been kissed before?'

'Of course I have.'

'Then what is it? You can't say you don't find me attractive.'

'Then I won't say it.'

'I don't believe you. You're angry with me because of one innocent kiss! Oh, God, you're turning out to be one of those Gospel-quoting, tiresomely good men.'

'I can't help what I am,' he said. 'Will you get in, please? I'll drive if you like.'

'Sure.' She tossed him the keys. 'Help yourself. But I'm not quite ready to leave yet.'

'Then you can stay here.'

Kit sat down and pushed her slender hand through her curls. 'Oh, you won't abandon me, Gil. You're too much of a gentleman. Come over and talk a bit. I won't bite, I promise. Come on.' She patted the grass, as if she were trying to coax a recalcitrant puppy. Gilbert hesitated, then obeyed reluctantly. He stood in front of her, a good three feet away. She smiled. 'You don't need to treat me like the town bad girl, you know. The fact that I'm a divorcée and therefore not a virgin doesn't automatically class me with the hostesses in the clubs or the whores in Blood Alley.'

'I know that,' he mumbled. He didn't like the way she tossed around words like 'whore' and 'virgin.'

'You're annoyed because you're in love with me. You've just found out that I'm unmarriageable by your own high missionary's standards, so you think we ought never to see each other again. Well, am I right?'

'I am not in love with anyone,' Gilbert said stiffly. He sat down and rested his elbows on his knees. His sleeves were rolled up. His forearms were tanned and smooth. The sunlight brought out glints of red-gold in his hair. 'I just wish you had told me, that's all.'

'You're saying it doesn't make any difference, but obviously it does.' Kit's eyes narrowed suspiciously. 'I'll bet that old bitch Laura Morrison warned you off, didn't she?'

'No, no one said anything.'

'I heard what Fat Billy said that night: a wife is a good thing to have out here in the bush. You're ambitious, aren't you, Gil? You want to play up to him, get a good slot. If he wants you to have a wife, then you'll get a wife. But who? Why not the best? Kit Fox! Divorced? Whoops, better not!' She swung her shoulders. 'What rubbish. As if you needed to please him or anybody else. You're in China now. If you want to doctor the damned peasants, then go ahead and doctor them, in any part of the country you choose. You don't have to answer to Uncle Billy, or ask his permission.' A sneer crept into her tone. 'I'm afraid you're still a little bit of a child, Gilbert. Wanting someone to lead you around by the hand and wipe your nose.'

'That's not true.'

'Then stop being such a little prude. If you want to kiss me, then kiss me. If you want to make love, then we'll make love. There's nothing so terrible about a couple of healthy young people doing what comes naturally. Uncle Billy's not looking over your shoulder.'

'I am not trying to ingratiate myself with Dr Morrison,' Gilbert insisted. 'Nobility and goodness are not just words to me, Kit. I can't help others and try to guide them along the right path of Christianity if I can't follow it myself. I don't mean to offend you, or hurt your feelings, but I feel it would be a mistake for us to see each other again, like this, alone.'

He knew he sounded like an idiot. He didn't have to look at her; he could sense that she was trying not to laugh out loud.

'I'm sure that the lovely Louise would agree with you,' Kit said mockingly.

'Please leave her out of this.'

'Why? You didn't leave poor Dickie out of it. Odd, how I always find myself prefixing his name with "poor." If you didn't want to be tempted, you should have persuaded her to come along. Didn't anyone warn you about Shanghai? Beautiful women at bargain rates? Or did you really think you were above it all because you're a man of God? Uncle Billy's no fool. He knows that men get lonely. He knows if you have a wife waiting in your hut, you won't go looking

51

for a doe-eyed maiden to help relieve your sexual tensions. That sort of behavior gives missionaries a bad name.'

'I wish you wouldn't talk like that.'

She laughed. 'Poor Gil! He's terrified that I'll seduce him, and just as terrified that I won't, that he'll have to do it himself. And now that I've put the evil idea into his mind, he won't be able to concentrate on work or school or anything else.' She stood up and shook out her skirt. 'Come on, laddie boy. I can see I'll never get any lunch if we don't get back to town. Sorry I embarrassed you.' As she passed behind him, she ruffled his hair playfully.

Furious, he grabbed her wrist and pulled her down into his lap. He kissed her hard, but she didn't respond. He could feel her lips curving into a sneer.

She got to her feet and said coldly, 'You're right, of course. If you feel uncomfortable with me, we certainly shouldn't see each other again.'

'Kit—'

'You still have the keys. Let's see if you're a better driver than you are a lover.'

Gilbert started work at the Aldershot Clinic the same week he began his study of Chinese at Shanghai University. The clinic was well staffed and underpatronized, and his duties there were routine and familiar. But he found the Chinese language strange and complex and impossible to grasp. He began to think he would never learn enough to be useful.

'Don't worry about it,' said Dr Morrison reassuringly when Gilbert confided his fears a week later. 'Took me a dozen years before I could make myself understood in just one dialect. You have some free time. What you need is a private tutor. I gave Anne Fox a call when I heard you were coming in today She ought to be here any minute.'

'Wouldn't a native Chinese be better?' Gilbert said. He wanted to avoid further contact with the Fox family.

'Anne's done a lot of good work for me,' Dr Morrison said. 'She's a born teacher.'

'That's not what she says,' Gilbert recalled glumly.

'She s one of those people who can't judge her own

worth. She'll be right along, I'm sure.' Dr Morrison heaved himself out of his chair and escorted Gilbert to the door. 'Let me know how you two get along,' he said heartily, dismissing Gilbert with a thump between the shoulder blades. 'And don't worry about a thing. You're under no pressure at all. The chief of staff at the Aldershot told me this morning that he's very impressed with your work. You've made a good start, my boy.'

Gilbert thanked him for his help and went out to the waiting room of the offices of the Medical Missionary Society in the Jardine Building on the Bund. Kit was right. He was a baby. What was he doing in China? Healing the Chinese? Teaching them? He'd be lucky if he didn't spend the rest of his life probing solid English flesh and listening to the woes of bored British and American housewives at the Aldershot.

The door from the corridor opened with a bang and Anne Fox burst in. She looked terrible, hair hanging loose and limp, clothes awry, shoes scuffed. When she saw Gilbert, she stopped in her tracks.

'Oh. You. I didn't know – Dr Morrison just said he had a tutoring job for me. I didn't realize –'

Gilbert rose to greet her. 'He did mention it that first day,' he reminded her.

'Yes, I know. Look, I hope you don't think – this wasn't my idea,' she said quickly. 'I never mentioned it to him – reminded him – I mean, if you'd rather not work with me, we certainly don't have to, and I'll make the excuse and tell him I'm too busy or something.'

'It sounds like you don't want to help me,' Gilbert said.

'Oh, no, it's not that. I just didn't want to place you in an awkward position of being saddled with someone you'd rather not –'

'It is you who have been placed in the awkward position, Miss Fox,' he said a little sheepishly. 'I want to apologize for ducking out of our date.'

Anne set down the load of books she was carrying. 'That wasn't your fault. Kit's pretty hard to resist. I've never known anyone who could refuse her anything.'

'I can understand that,' Gilbert said with feeling.

She looked around anxiously. 'Can we get out of here?'

she whispered. 'I mean, I don't have to see Uncle Billy, do I? I can call him later.'

'You don't like him, do you?' Gilbert said.

She made a face. 'No. He's my archetypal joss-pidgin-man. I've seen pictures of him and Laura when they first came out to China thirty years ago. They were thin!' she said in an outraged voice. It was an unlikely condemnation, and Gilbert smiled. 'It's true,' Anne said stubbornly. 'You've seen what they look like now. Thirty years of ministering to the undernourished Chinese, and they've gotten fat. That's obscene. In my unprofessional opinion, it's a sin.'

Gilbert picked up her books. Anne protested that she was capable of carrying them herself and tried to take them from him. The pile spilled. As they stooped to retrieve the books, their heads knocked together and Anne lost her balance and sprawled backward on her rump. She laughed and rubbed her head ruefully.

'Serves me right. I'm not used to gallantry.'

Gilbert helped her to her feet and gathered up the books. They were all in French and had lurid covers and titles like *La Blonde Morte*. He tucked the stack firmly under his arm.

'Shall we go? You read French, I see.' He held the door for her and followed her to the elevator.

'I do, but these aren't for me. They're for a friend of mine.'

'The French priest?'

'Oh, you've heard about him.' They stepped into the elevator. 'Yes, he's going on a holiday – his first in twelve years – and he loves this sort of thing when he wants to relax. Catholic missionaries aren't like Protestants, who head for the mountains as soon as the temperature here goes over eighty. My parents are leaving in two weeks. There's nothing like pampering yourself in God's service. I'd really like you to meet Father Jacquinot. He's a fine person, a real scholar.'

'Is he a Communist?' Gilbert asked.

'Officially he's forbidden to take any part in political activity, but I suspect his sympathies are socialistic rather than capitalistic, like mine. Then so were Christ's.' They walked through the lobby and stepped out onto the Bund.

'Have you had lunch?' Gilbert asked.

'If you want to sound like a native, you'll adopt the Anglo-Indian affectation and call it tiffin,' Anne said.

'Very well. Will you have tiffin with me, Miss Fox?'

'I suppose so.'

She took him to a Chinese restaurant off Nanking Road, behind the Wing On Department Store. When they were seated she spoke to him in Chinese.

'What's that? I'm afraid I don't understand.'

She repeated the question and answer. He mimicked the sounds. She corrected his pronunciation. They repeated the procedure until she was satisfied. She ordered for them, and while they were waiting she taught him the words for table, chair, chopsticks, salt, tea.

'I have a textbook,' Gilbert said desperately. 'If you could just help me with my exercises –'

He was stopped cold by a look that said if he wanted her help, he should obey her instructions.

Their food arrived. Anne instructed him in the use of chopsticks and as they ate taught him the names of the dishes in front of them. A couple of waiters came out to watch, and drew up chairs to join in. Anne seemed very relaxed with them, and joked with them. Gilbert felt irritated and self-conscious. He was sure they were laughing at his clumsy attempts to pronounce the queer-sounding syllables.

When they were out in the street again, he said, 'That was agony. I hope the next time you'll at least let me enjoy my lunch in peace.'

Anne replied, maddeningly, in Chinese. She dug some change out of her pocket, climbed aboard the rear section of a halted streetcar, and motioned him to hurry up. They fell into conversation with a woman and a small boy, who had an ear infection. Anne told the woman that Gilbert was a doctor, and he found himself examining the child in the middle of the crowded third-class section. Their fellow passengers carried flapping ducks, bags of crabs, baskets of fish.

Gilbert prescribed aspirin and drops of warmed oil, Anne translated, and then it was time to get off. They passed under an old archway, and found themselves in another world. There were no modern buildings here, only brick and tile dwellings that had stood for so long that any distinguishing architectural features had long since weathered away. The streets were too narrow to accommodate cars, and Anne and Gilbert dodged bicycles and rickshas, handcarts and wheelbarrows. They were shunted aside by coolies carrying baskets slung on bamboo shoulder poles and by women bearing huge loads in slings on their backs. Many families newly arrived from the country lived right on the street, taking their meals and relieving themselves in full view of the public, sleeping in doorways, dying.

'Do you like statistics?' Anne asked as they stepped around an emaciated corpse. 'Last year the Public Benevolent Society provided free burial for thirty-six thousand corpses, in the International Settlement alone. Thirty-three thousand of those were infants. I feel guilty whenever I put a bite of food into my mouth. William and Laura Morrison have gotten fat on the flesh of babies.'

She took him to a street lined with shops that sold pets of every variety: monkeys, cats, snakes, birds. She presented him with a tiny bamboo cage containing a single cricket.

'Crickets are good luck. Welcome to Shanghai.'

Crossing a zigzag bridge over a scummy green lake, they came to the Five Star Pavilion, familiar to thousands of possessors of Blue Willow pattern china. They sat on a bench near the ancient tea house and Anne drilled Gilbert on the parts of the body and elementary afflictions such as headache, broken bones, sore throat, stomachache. Gilbert sweated, scowled, strained to remember.

Finally she said, 'That's enough for today.'

'Shouldn't I be taking notes?' he asked.

'Wouldn't do you any good. There isn't any good system for phoneticization into English yet because there's no way to deal with the four tones properly. Just concentrate on what the word feels like when you say it. The only way to learn is by listening and speaking. I ought to find you a Chinese family to live with. No English or pidgin allowed.'

'I'd go mad.'

'But you'd learn.'

'I envy you your skill with languages,' he said.

'Speaking Chinese in China isn't a particularly rare skill, although speaking good Chinese in Shanghai is. The local dialect is awful. It's skills like yours that are needed here. How do you like the Aldershot?'

He said diplomatically, 'Dr Morrison was right. It's a fine hospital, fantastically equipped.'

'You must be a pretty decent doctor. The Aldershot is Uncle Billy's pet and he hogs all the best medical talent in the city. How many Chinese have you treated so far?' she demanded.

'None,' he said. 'It's just as well. I'll never learn to speak to them anyway.'

'Of course you'll learn. You didn't do badly at all.'

'And I didn't do brilliantly, either. I know, I have no talent for languages. I wouldn't have made it in the ministry – the Greek and Hebrew would have been beyond me. As it was, I barely passed the Latin I needed for medical school. I suppose you've studied Chinese a long time?'

'On and off over the years. I learned most of it by talking to people. I never could see any sense in living here and pretending it was New York City, like so many of the whites do. Take a stroll on the Bund one morning. You'll see elegantly dressed women parading up and down with their chows and their poodles, exactly as if they were showing off on the Champs Élysée or Fifth Avenue. But we're in China! There are four hundred million people out there who have an ancient culture, a grand history, a fascinating language. Why can't we learn their ways instead of forcing them to learn ours? Why do we just have to see how much money we can squeeze out of them?' She stopped herself. 'There I go again. I wish you'd say something when I get up on my soapbox. I do it at the drop of a hat – the same hat I talk through.'

Gilbert said, 'No, I like to listen to your ideas. You're not a bit like Kit, you know.' His heart gave a queer little jerk when he said her name aloud.

Anne said, 'Do I know? Oh, yes. Kit is special and

magical and delightful. Everyone adores her. Nobody knows what to make of me. I'm odd, different. Always have been. Rotten in school. A crybaby. So shy I'd walk clear around the block to avoid encountering someone I knew slightly. The only thing I could do better than Kit was play the violin, although I have no doubt that if she had wanted to learn she would have been brilliant. She didn't study it because she thought she looked funny when she held it under her chin. She could always do anything she set her mind to. She's bright and sharp. Breezed through school. No trouble with anything, not even maths. Mother wanted her to go to Vassar – alma mater, you know. Father was more ambitious; he leaned toward Oxford. But Kit had ideas of her own, as usual. She was ready for life.'

'And so she got married,' Gilbert said softly.

'Poor Richard.' Anne said. 'He didn't know what hit him. He's probably still wondering. She set her cap for him and he jumped in with both feet. I'm probably mixing my metaphors horribly.'

'What went wrong?'

'Lord, I don't know. I hardly knew the man. But he wasn't terribly bright. I guess she just got screamingly bored. It was funny. She turned up here six months after they had left on their honeymoon. No warning, not even a wire. Father shouted and Mother took to her bed and I moped and tried to figure out what it all meant. That's the way we deal with crises in our house. First she announced she wasn't going to keep Richard's name. Then she rang up all her old friends and got up a party right away. In any other city – no, with any other woman – they'd have plastered her with some kind of stigma because she was divorced. But not Kit. It was as though it never happened. Welcome home. Open arms. "Can you come and dine I've got the most divine young man I want you to meet."'

They crossed the zigzag bridge over the brackish water that surrounded the island. Anne said, 'It's built this way because demons are very stupid, and they can only move in straight lines. If you cross this bridge you'll lose the ones that are following you.'

Gilbert resisted sneaking a look over his shoulder. He

knew that his particular demon wasn't stupid. Evading her wouldn't be so simple as walking a crooked line.

'I saw a man killed once on Nanking Road,' Anne went on. 'We were crossing the street at the same time, almost side by side, and then all of a sudden he darted out in front of a lorry. He cut it a bit too fine and it hit him and threw him twenty feet.'

'Good heavens!' Gilbert was horrified.

'They do it all the time. It's another way of losing your demons. But you have to move quickly, of course. Boats do it, too. Little sampans try to cross in front of the bows of steamers. Sometimes they get shorn in half and everybody drowns.'

'But that's terrible,' Gilbert said. 'Such appalling superstition.'

'Why is it so terrible? We in the West invented God and the devil for the same reasons, to frighten people into being good, and to try to give some meaning to the filthy things that happen, wars and famine and so forth. The Chinese aren't so different from us. They want to make some sense out of life, too. You Christians treat adversity as a blessing because it's supposed to toughen your spirits and make you worthy of the hereafter. The Chinese treat it as a curse and they blame demons. But it's the same coin.'

She picked up the stack of mystery novels. 'I just want you to know that I don't blame you for what happened. I'm used to it. It doesn't bother me anymore.'

She started to walk away. Gilbert called after her, 'But we haven't made arrangements to meet again. We haven't discussed payment.'

'I don't want your money,' she called back. 'Call the house and leave a message. I'm generally free in the afternoon. If you want to ride back to your hotel, take the Number 5 car.' The crowd swallowed her up.

Gilbert dined with the Morrisons that night. Reverend and Mrs Fox were there, and some other people, but neither Anne nor Kit. He watched his hosts consume a vast quantity of food and his own appetite suffered.

Marian Fox was particularly lively and talkative that evening. Gilbert noticed that her color was good, but her pupils were dilated. She ate and drank very little. After dinner she cornered him and talked animatedly about her daughters, especially Kit. Gilbert listened eagerly and prompted her with questions when she seemed about to take another tack. When she reached into her purse for photographs, Leonard Fox said waspishly, 'For heaven's sake, Marian, Gilbert doesn't want to look at those.' Gilbert said eagerly, 'Oh, but I do!' and feasted his eyes on Kit in petticoats, Kit in a school play, Kit on horseback. Anne appeared in one picture, almost inadvertently. She squinted into the sun, and her forehead was drawn into a worried pucker. She was a gangly, homely sixteen. Next to her stood Kit, an adorable eight-year-old, in ribbons and curls.

Gilbert met Anne at a tea house near the Aldershot a couple of days later. After she took him through his paces and they relaxed a little, he said, 'I know it's none of my business, but your mother is taking some kind of drug, isn't she?'

She looked stricken, then said, 'I suppose we could hardly hope to hide it from someone like you. Yes, she takes laudanum. I guess the pain of living is too much for her. Well,' she shrugged, 'opium addiction is a common enough affliction in China. It's no disgrace.'

'I'm sorry to hear it.' Gilbert said sympathetically. 'But there are cures.'

'None that she would be willing to take. She has no reason to stop. She has a ready source of supply here in Shanghai. My parents haven't been back to the States on furlough in years. She refuses to go. She's afraid she won't be able to get her drug. It's so easy here. You can get a tincture of opium at any chemist's with a prescription, and at any corner store without one. She's in no real danger from it. She never increases her dosage. She's been taking the same amount for years. But neither can she stop. It would be too painful, and if there's anything Mother can't stand, it's pain. She says that's what got her started in the first place, my being born. I was a disgracefully large baby, nearly ten pounds. And she was so tiny. She's been a semi-invalid ever since.'

'But it's not your fault.' Gilbert said.

'I know that, in my head. But I grew up feeling that I was to blame for her sickness, don't you see? And then she got pregnant with Kit. That was a horrid miscalculation. She put my father through hell for it. Kit was very sick for a couple of years after she was born. She almost died. You see, she's a miracle child in every way. They couldn't help spoiling her.'

'You're jealous of her.' Gilbert suggested.

Anne looked startled. 'Is that how I sound? Jealous? I don't mean to. I love Kit very much. I just have a very good idea of my own liabilities and failings and her stunning lack of them.'

'I'm sorry. I shouldn't have said that.'

Anne gazed at the smoke swirling upward from her cigarette. 'I wonder what it's like, to smoke opium. You see them everywhere in China, thin people with yellow skin and yellow eyes that can't focus clearly on anything. Dried up and fragile, like autumn leaves. I wonder if the dreams are really beautiful, if they're worth what they put themselves through.'

'I can't believe that they are.' Gilbert said.

'The Chinese have us to thank for opium, did you know that? A hundred years ago the British and Americans wanted to trade with China. They wanted tea and silk and porcelain. But the Chinese wouldn't take any of our goods in trade – they didn't want anything that we had. They traded for silver only. They were sufficient unto themselves, and they believed they had everything they needed within their own borders.'

'The Central Kingdom,' Gilbert remembered.

'That's right. Every place else was peripheral, inessential. They treated the white men very badly, like second-class citizens. Ironic, that, when you look around Shanghai now. We certainly have paid them back in kind.'

'Then what happened? About the opium, I mean.'

'Well, the silver continued to flow out of the Western treasuries. The balance of trade became lopsided. And then the whites discovered that they had a vast potential market for opium. Indian opium, which the British Government owned under the auspices of the East India Company. They traded freely, until the Chinese saw what

61

it was doing to their people, turning their soldiers into passive babies, impoverishing the farmers, devastating whole families. They declared it illegal to trade, and imposed a ban. But we continued to smuggle it in, paying out squeeze to corrupt officials. Things haven't changed much. Bribery and corruption are part of life here.'

Gilbert remembered watching Albert McClure bribing his way past the customs officer, and he nodded. 'I guess we joss-pidgin-men have a big job ahead of us,' he said with a rueful smile.

'In the old days the joss-pidgin-men were part of the system. Who do you think interpreted for the traders? Tracts went over one side of their ships, and crates of opium over the other. One of the Chinese generals confiscated tons of the stuff and burned it, and in retaliation the British declared a war. That was the First Opium War, not quite a hundred years ago. Nanking Road is named for the treaty that ended it, and humiliated the Empire. The greatest trading houses in China were founded on opium. Oh, they've diversified since, and they don't talk about the past. Now they own breweries and mills and factories and banks. But the money that built the foundations of those financial empires came from opium. We have a lot to answer for.'

'What's the answer?' asked Gilbert. 'Communism?'

'I don't know anymore. I used to think it was. But when you put ideals into action, they get horribly distorted. It's so much easier to put deeds into words, after the fact. The Chinese Communists have done some ugly and violent things. I won't believe that violence is the answer. But perhaps it is, the only answer. Something is dreadfully wrong when thousands of people die of starvation and exposure every day in Shanghai alone, and Standard Oil sends home seventy million dollars to be divvied up among its well-fed stockholders.'

On his way back to his hotel, Gilbert passed a grain shop. Huge sacks bulging with wheat, corn, and rice sat like burlap Buddhas on the sidewalk. The grain merchant's plump wife presided over the business from her seat under a canvas awning. A set of scales sat on the table at her elbow. She fanned herself idly and sipped tea from a delicate china cup. On the curb in front of the shop squatted a filthy beggar boy. He was so scrawny that Gilbert couldn't determine his age. Gilbert's first impulse was to dig out some change from his pockets. Then he went over to the woman.

'Ten pounds of rice. please.' he said. pointing to the open sack and holding up both hands with all his fingers spread out. 'Ten.'

The woman weighed out the rice. poured it into a brown paper sack. and secured the parcel with a string. Gilbert handed over his money. and while she was still watching. he carried the rice over to the curb and thrust it at the boy.

'For you. Take. Yours.'

The woman started to scold shrilly. The child looked frightened and seemed about to run away. Smiling. Gilbert pressed the rice on him. and he grabbed it and scampered away. He could give it to his family. or sell it for cash. Gilbert didn't care.

The grainseller's harangue was still ringing in his ears as he walked away. Gilbert felt better. more sure of his mission now. less intimidated by the vastness of the need in China. He had corrected a social imbalance, restored equity in a small corner of Shanghai. It was a little thing. hardly more than a gesture, but it showed him how to proceed. He would help when he could. not letting the evil he didn't see daunt him. He thanked God for showing him the way. for giving him the opportunity to serve. and to learn.

He arrived at his hotel at about four o'clock. He had been considering a move to rooms closer to the Aldershot. but he'd been too busy to look for a place. He still had a couple of hours before he was expected at the hospital for evening rounds. Time to catch up on his letter-writing, and to attend to his neglected journal.

In the lobby he encountered an elderly missionary couple whom he had met before and he walked up the stairs with them. They told him that they were returning home to the States the next day, and he wished them luck.

'You know, Dr Lawrence,' said the old minister, 'I

don't feel so bad about leaving now. I feel that the future of our work in China is in good hands when I see someone like you: young and strong and stalwart, clear-eyed and optimistic. Mildred and I talked about it some last night. You're a fine young man. You will pick up and carry on where we left off.'

Gilbert thanked them and they parted. He climbed the next flight of stairs alone. It was wonderful, how when you're feeling confused and disturbed, God sends messengers of hope, he thought. He was still nursing warm feelings when he got out his key and opened the louvered door to his room, and saw Kit Fox lounging on his bed under festoons of drawn-up mosquito netting.

'Hullo, Gil. I've been waiting for you.'

She was wearing a silk print dress with short sleeves and a flowing skirt. She had kicked off her sandals and stretched her stockinged legs out in front of her. A broad-brimmed hat of yellow straw hung on the bedpost. She smoked a cigarette in a white ivory holder.

He gaped at her from the doorway. 'What are you doing here?'

She laughed. 'I really didn't expect you to fall on my neck with glad cries, but really, Gil, couldn't you at least pretend to be happy to see me? Come on in, stay awhile.'

He didn't move for half a minute. Then he heard voices of people approaching and he came to his senses. He stepped into the room and closed the door quickly.

'You startled me, that's all,' he swallowed.

'You've been neglecting me, Gilbert,' Kit said with mock severity, 'while you've been courting my sister.'

'No, I haven't. I mean, I haven't been courting – that is, we've been studying. Chinese,' he finished lamely. His mouth felt dry. He took off his jacket and sat on the chair farthest from the bed. 'You shouldn't be here, Kit. It might look – awkward.'

'Oh, I suppose it might, if awkwardness were in the eye of the beholder.' She plumped up the pillow behind her back and curled her legs under her. 'Why don't you offer me something to drink, Gil? I'm very thirsty.'

'I don't have anything. Only water. Would you like a glass of water?'

She said, 'That would be lovely.'

He ran the water in the bathroom sink until it felt less tepid. He wondered if she had read his journal, or the letter he had started to Louise. Frantically he tried to recall what he had written: the usual amusing stories, interesting deviations from the Philadelphia norm, a few rather condescending observations about the Chinese in general and their hygiene in particular. He cringed. He filled his tooth glass and carried it out to her. As she took it his hand wobbled and he sloshed a little on her lap.

'Oh, I'm sorry, I didn't mean –' He started to dab at the wet spot with his handkerchief, and noticed how the water made the silk transparent so that he could see the pink flesh of her thigh. He snatched his hand away.

'I hope your bedside manner isn't always so clumsy,' she teased. He started to return to the safety of the remote chair, but her mocking laughter pulled him back. 'You don't have to run away from me, Gilbert. I promise I won't make my tongue-lashing any harsher than necessary. Now, why haven't you called me?'

'I've been very busy, starting at the hospital and my classes –'

'Too busy to pick up the phone for a minute to thank me for showing you such a good time,' she clucked. 'It would have been the polite thing to do, even if you didn't mean it. I tell you what, I'll let you make it up to me. Come and play tennis with us tomorrow. You look like you could use a little exercise.'

'Sorry, I can't. Have to work and –'

'I bet you're meeting Anne for a lesson. You don't want to miss that. I think it's sweet. I'd just love to see the two of you together, little heads bent over your grammars. *Yi, er, san, si, wu, liu, chi, ba, jiu, shi!*' she counted rapidly. 'See, I'm not a total ignoramus.'

'No, of course you're not,' he said nervously. 'But Anne's a wonderful teacher. You'd be surprised. She's quite demanding, but patient. And she's willing to go over and over a thing until I get it right.'

'Oh, I can do that.' Kit's smile was naughty. Gilbert flushed. 'I'm sure our little Anne is very capable. But so am I, Gil. I would never demand of a student more than he was able to give. If he were a shirker, though, I would be terrible in my anger.' She leaned toward him a little. The bed rolled under them slightly like a small boat on a calm lake. 'Have you thought about me at all, Gilbert? I've thought about you.'

'Of course I've thought about you,' Gilbert said without looking at her. 'I meant to call, I really did. Look, you'd better go, Kit. I have some things I need to do. Some writing, and studying. I don't know how you got in here in the first place.'

'Squeeze,' she said. 'You can get anything in Shanghai, if you're willing to pay the price. Even admittance to a monk's cell.'

'I'm sorry you wasted your money.' He strode purposefully to the door and grasped the knob. 'You'd better go.'

'I don't consider it wasted,' she said without moving. 'What would you have liked me to do, wait in the lobby? What a lovely chat we could have had down there, sitting up straight in those horrid chairs. "Hello, nice of you to drop by." "Nice to see you again." Oh, honestly, Gilbert.'

She had opened the window, but the room was still stiflingly hot. Automobile fumes and food odors and noise drifted up from the street.

He watched relieved as she swung her legs over the side of the bed and poked at her sandals with pointed toes.

'Are you really going to throw me out, Gil?' she asked wistfully, looking at him through her eyelashes. 'Why do you hate me so much? I wish you'd be a little kinder to me. I don't mean any harm.'

She approached him slowly and rested the palms of her hands on his chest. He was so taut that she could feel him trembling. He closed his eyes. She rose up a little on tiptoe and kissed the corner of his mouth lightly. She kissed him again and again, soft little kisses that she might have given a child, all the while pressing closer, winding her arms tighter around his neck, sucking the will out of him.

She said, 'There, that wasn't such a dreadful initiation, was it? Even the lovely Louise couldn't have been kinder.'

'Shut up,' he said thickly, into his pillow.

She stroked his naked shoulder. 'Did you know there are cultures where the young girls are initiated by the older men and the boys by older women? I think that's a fine idea. By the time you reach the marriage bed, you're no longer inept and scared. You ought to thank me. The future Mrs Lawrence ought to thank me. Dear Louise.'

He twitched. Poor Louise. Calf eyes and penciled apostrophes, corrugated waves. Thank God they hadn't married. Thank God they had decided to wait. She hovered, remote and saintly, in the periphery of his brain, while the demon whispered over his shoulder.

'You were very good, Gilbert. You surprised me. You're a quick learner.'

He hadn't learned anything. He had simply obeyed her commands, spoken and unspoken. He, too, had been surprised by his willingness and utter concentration. He forgot everything else: God, medicine, Louise. Kit had driven them all right out of his mind. He had been in the grip of temporary madness. He wasn't responsible. She had been a whirlwind of naked flesh and flashing teeth and knowing fingers and yawning cavities like wounds begging to be staunched. He had simply acted as one acts in a medical emergency, instinctively, like a machine.

'Gilbert,' she murmured, sliding her hand over his iliac crest. 'Dearest.'

'I wish you'd go.' He tried to shrug her off.

'No *tristesse*,' she breathed. 'Wastes too much time. Come on, more love. Please? We've already sinned once. Twice won't make it a bigger sin, only a better one.' She caressed his swelling skillfully and darted her tongue in and out of his ear. He couldn't help himself. He rolled over and covered her, and she sighed deeply.

Someone knocked on the door. He jerked his head up. Kit's fingernails dug into his back.

'Oh, Dr Lawrence!' quavered an elderly voice. 'Are you there, dear? Yoo-hoo!'

In a panic he started to pull away from Kit, but she wrapped her legs around him and held him firmly. She moved under him, arching and heaving. He felt himself reeling between the madness of pleasure and the terror of being discovered.

'Oh, dear. Do you think he's in the bathroom?' More tapping.

'I don't hear any water running. Maybe he's gone out again, Mildred.'

'But he just came in,' Mildred protested.

'So did we, and we're on our way out again. Use your head, woman.'

'Oh, Homer, I did so want to ask if he had any message for us to take back home. He mentioned a fiancée –'

The bed squeaked deafeningly. Gilbert thought his heart would stop. He couldn't remember locking the door. Someone rattled the knob.

'Such a fine young man. He reminds me of our Horace.'

'What on earth are you talking about? Horace is at least four inches shorter, and he has dark hair and wears glasses. How can he remind you of Horace?'

Kit couldn't help herself. She laughed out loud.

'Shut up,' Gilbert hissed in her ear. 'Shut up, shut up, shut up!'

He didn't realize that he was digging his thumbs into her upper arms. She cried out in pain. The bedsprings sang.

The voices outside the door fell silent.

'I think there's someone in there, Homer,' said Mildred in a stage whisper.

'Come along. It's none of our business.'

'But he's such a sweet young man. Oh, I can't believe it. This must be the wrong room.' They went away, still arguing in whispers.

Gilbert pulled away from Kit. 'Get out,' he rasped. 'Get your clothes on and get out of here, and don't ever come back.'

'Oh, Gilbert,' she said muzzily, 'don't be such a –'

'For the love of God, will you leave me alone!' he cried. He turned his back to her and pulled on his trousers. 'Don't touch me. Just get out of here.' He stumbled to the window and leaned out, gasping for air.

He was afraid to turn around. He couldn't be certain that he was alone. He thought he remembered hearing a softly mocking 'Goodbye, Gil,' and the sound of the door opening and closing. But what if he was mistaken? What if he looked around and saw her lounging on the bed with one silk-sheathed leg tucked under her, her hip hitched high, a cigarette burning between her fingers like a stick of incense in front of a lewd idol?

He hated Shanghai: the faceless, shapeless people, the heat, the stink. Most of all the noise, jarring and incessant, amplified by heat and humidity, funneled into his room by the thicket of signs that covered the sidewalk like acoustical baffles. If he had had the means at hand at that moment, he would have laid the entire city to waste without a qualm. Leveled it. Destroyed it and everyone in it.

A Chinese girl stood on the balcony directly across from his window. She leaned her elbows on the railing and watched the passing scene, and she twitched her hips in time to the music from her radio, which she had turned up full volume so that she could hear it above the din in the street. Accompanied by cigar-box banjo and wood block percussion, a female vocalist wailed a Chinese love song. She sounded like a cat being threaded through a mangle.

The girl looked over at him. Their eyes met and she gave him a friendly grin. He whirled away from the window, his heart pounding.

The bed was tumbled but empty. He skirted it warily, afraid to touch it. A laugh or a moan might come flying out of the folds like a moth. He could smell the contaminating stink of Kit's perfume from three feet away. His pillow lay on the floor. A lipstick-smeared handkerchief littered the nightstand. The looped-up mosquito netting looked like a shroud.

He lowered himself into a chair. He felt a growing heaviness deep inside, in a place no surgeon's probe could reach. Tears stung his eyes and he covered his face with his hands.

Sin did this. Made you feel so utterly alone. Cut off from mankind, and God, and yourself.

Chapter Three

Anne ran through the streets of the French Concession. Sobbing with exhaustion, her heart bursting, she stumbled up the steps of the Jesuits' residence on the Avenue Dubail and threw herself at the bell. The houseboy answered the door: Père Jacquinot was not at home. Perhaps he had gone to his office at Aurora University. Despairingly, Anne retraced her steps.

In her hand she clutched the early edition of the *North China Daily News*. Her father always read it at breakfast, and he had tossed it into her lap that morning with a curt 'You'll be interested in this.' An article on page one described the discovery of six well-decayed bodies under the floor of a house on the Rue Albert. The reporter speculated that Chen Ping-ho, one of the chieftains of the Chinese Communist Party, had ordered the execution of the entire family of a man who had betrayed a Communist hiding place to agents of the Kuomintang. Each victim had been trussed up, arms and legs tied behind his back, and buried alive. The report called Chen the Butcher of Shanghai, and cited the incident as typical of the viciousness of the Communist mentality.

Father Paul Jacquinot was in his sixties, and by 1933 he had spent more years in China than he had in his native France. He was small in stature but fairly robust, bald and bearded. He liked to tell children that the force of gravity had pulled all the hairs on his head downward and out through his chin. He maintained that except for the days when his right arm pained him, he was never ill. He had been without that arm since the day it was crushed in a bad fall from a pony in the mountains of Szechwan. Legend had it that he had amputated the gangrenous limb himself, but in fact he had commandeered the help of a frightened peasant and his wife. Ignoring his protests, his superiors reassigned him to lighter duty in Shanghai after the mishap. He taught philosophy and Greek at Aurora University, and also at the Roman Catholic seminary. He was chaplain to the order of French nuns that ran L'École des Filles, the school where Anne taught. His passion for butterflies had grown into a scholarly treatise on Far Eastern Lepidoptera. He was a fanatic chess player and an enthusiastic musician, lending his raspy baritone to British-organized oratorio performances, amateur opera, and to any group that would have him.

Anne sought him out when she returned to Shanghai in 1925 after misadventures in Paris and Switzerland. She felt as raw as a burn victim then, ill at ease with old friends, incapable of enjoying the things that used to give her pleasure: music, poetry, little magazines. Father Jacquinot was an old friend and mentor of the man she had loved in Paris, and although they rarely talked about Chen anymore, she found comfort in the company of someone who knew her history. He persuaded the nuns at L'École des Filles to offer her a job, overriding their objections to a non-Catholic by reminding them that as an unbeliever she was a potential convert.

Anne and the priest met often, two or three times a month, to play chess or simply to talk. So unfailingly kind and gentle was he that Anne was unprepared for the attack that greeted her announcement that she wanted to become a Catholic.

'Are you willing to accept the Pope as the Vicar of Christ on Earth?'

'The Pope? Well, I don't know. I hadn't really thought —'

'Do you believe that in the sacrifice of the Mass, the bread and wine actually become the body and blood of Christ?'

'I'm sure I could come to believe it as firmly as some of your rice Christians,' she retorted.

'Chen turned his back on the Church. Perhaps you share his sympathies.'

'If I did, I wouldn't be here now.'

'Then why are you here?'

'I told you, because I want to be a Catholic.'

'Why? What do you think the Church can give you? Tell me, if I were to leave Shanghai tomorrow, how would it affect your decision?'

And on it went, until she discovered her own motives, so obvious to him all along.

She threw open the door of his small office. 'Did you see this, Father?' brandishing the newspaper. 'Do you think it can be true? I can't believe it! I won't! It's just too horrible. How could he do such a thing? It's not true!'

Father Jacquinot smiled warmly. 'It is very good to see you, too, Mademoiselle Anne. Yes, I had a very fine holiday, thank you. I even found a couple of new specimens, very beautiful. One of my students is mounting them now. Alas, this clumsy hand of mine would only destroy them.'

She collapsed into a chair. 'I'm sorry for bursting in like this. I couldn't help it. Then you haven't heard? About the house on Rue Albert?'

'I have been back in Shanghai for only one day, long enough to realize how badly holidays spoil one. Now, let me see this newspaper of yours.' He put on his glasses and read quickly, moving his lips a little. He grunted at the gratuitously sensational descriptions of the dead, and when he finished he shook his head. 'Ah, such a terrible thing. Those poor people.'

'You think it's true!' Anne gasped. 'But he wouldn't do such a thing, Father. Not Chen!'

He gave a Gallic lift of his shoulders. 'These were certainly executions, and as such were ordered not by any subordinate or lower-echelon member of the Party but by a highly placed official. Chen is the head of the Communists' intelligence organization. He would act quickly to stem further betrayals – as quickly as a Jesuit acting to halt the spread of heresy. Remember, he was trained by Jesuits, by me. I am very sorry, Anne. You want me to deny absolutely that our friend could have taken any part in this atrocity, but I cannot. Neither can I confirm it. I can only say that it is not impossible. I know him.'

'You don't have to be so damned rational all the time,' she cried. 'I know him, too, and I know that he's not capable of such evil. He was always so gentle.'

'Yes, because you yourself inspire gentleness, like a butterfly. I don't need to tell you that a man is different in the bedroom than on the battlefield – fortunately. Chen is fighting a war.'

'But not this way,' she said passionately. 'Two old people, a pregnant woman, three children, one only five years old. They're calling him the Butcher of Shanghai! You should have seen my father gloat. Oh, God, this is awful. If only I could see him.'

'For what purpose?' the priest demanded. 'To persuade him not to do such nasty things? Ridiculous. He would laugh in your face, as he laughed in mine.'

'Then you have seen him! When? Why didn't you tell me?'

'The interview was painful for both of us, and quite fruitless. It took place about six months ago.'

'Did he ask about me?' she said. Her heart gave a fearful jolt.

'No, *chérie*, he did not,' Father Jacquinot said gently. In this case a lie was certainly justifiable. 'He is married now. Perhaps you heard.'

She lowered her head. 'No. I didn't know.'

'I had such hopes for him,' Father Jacquinot sighed. 'He is brilliant, clear-thinking, yet compassionate. But we have no right to place our hopes in another. The things he wants for his country are very different from what I want for China. He thinks he is saving her, and I say he is destroying her. But I am old and shortsighted. And, as he so cuttingly reminded me, I am not Chinese. Truth is an elusive thing, Anne. You cannot hold it in your hand and look at it and measure it and say it has this or that shape. No, Anne, we must let him go, you and I. He has made his choice, and we are not part of his plans.'

'If things had been different,' Anne said in a husky voice, 'if I hadn't let my father persuade me to leave Paris – if Chen hadn't been away – we would have been married now – and none of this —!' She covered her face with her hands and wept softly.

'It is useless to weep,' the old priest said gruffly. 'We don't know what God has planned for us, much less for the ones we love. Listen, I want to tell you a story. Dry your eyes at once.' He produced an enormous handkerchief from the pocket of his cassock. 'Pay attention. Once in that part of France known as Brittany, where the poor people eat stones when they have no bread, lived a widow and her six children. She worked hard to support her family, traveling three miles every day to the house of a nobleman where she was second laundress. The children all worked, too, but because the oldest was only twelve years of age at the time of this story, they were unable to contribute very much. The widow was thrifty, and she was able to put enough money aside to buy a sow, which she planned to raise in her little yard. The sow would produce one litter a year. She would keep one piglet, perhaps two, to provide meat for the family. The others she would sell. Now, it was springtime and the weather was rainy and chilly. One of her children, the youngest who was only two years old, became very ill. His fever was high, and his lungs were so clogged that he could hardly breathe. She did everything she could for him, but he got no better. Out of desperation she consulted a physician, who told her that the child must have expensive medicine in order to live. The poor woman was in a quandary: should she spend her money on this medicine for the child, or should she go ahead and buy the sow? The child was frail, always sickly. Even if she bought the medicine, there was a good chance that he would die, if not now then at another time. She had five other children, all healthier than this ailing babe. The sow would pay for itself after a short time, and feed them all on the profits from her piglets. Well, Mademoiselle Anne, what do you think the woman did?'

Anne mopped her eyes and shrugged. 'She bought the medicine, of course.'

'She did not!' Father Jacquinot crowed. 'She put the life of her child in the Lord's hands. It costs nothing to trust in God. And she bought the pig. Some would say that she was cruel to deny her child a chance of life. Others would say that the physician might well have been mistaken. And in fact he was: the child lived. It was a miracle, everyone said so. But two months later, the sow sickened and died. And how that woman grieved for that pig!'

Anne found herself choking with laughter through her tears. 'That's the silliest story I've ever heard,' she sputtered. 'I don't believe it, not a word.'

Father Jacquinot pulled himself up impressively. 'You

cannot disbelieve,' he said, 'because that same child that did not die stands here before you now.' He thumped his chest. 'Do you see what I am saying? We are all babes, ignorant of the consequences of our actions. We do the best we can, and leave the rest to God. You have lived in China all your life, but you have learned nothing about resignation and acceptance. I understand better, because peasants are the same all over the world: they are happy to see the sun come up in the morning, and they expect nothing more than to see it go down again. You are no better than a cripple, Anne, paralyzed by sorrow and self-pity and hatred. Your losses weigh on you like so many stones: Chen, your baby, your father's love, your music. The Chinese are wiser than you are. They don't inter themselves before they die. Chen did love you, but when he lost you he did not permit himself to become immobilized by grief. Grief is the lot of almost every Chinese, a familiar demon. Forget Chen. Forget this.' He swept his hand scornfully over the *North China Daily News*. 'Stop agonizing over things you cannot change.'

He waited patiently until the storm of weeping subsided, then patted her shoulder.

'Now tell me, what have you been doing in my absence? You were tutoring a young American doctor, as I recall. Is he making good progress?'

Anne hiccoughed and said from the depths of his handkerchief, 'No, he's having an awful time. It's like trying to teach someone who's tone deaf how to sing.'

'But you are patient and persistent and he will learn, I have no doubt. He is handsome, a real gentleman, eh?' Anne nodded grudgingly and Father Jacquinot laughed. 'Ah, that is good. I would like to meet your student. You must bring him to visit me sometime.'

'I would,' Anne said, taking some deep breaths, 'except I suspect he has the usual Presbyterian's prejudice against priests.'

She tripped over the words, mangled them on a second attempt, and abandoned the effort.

Gilbert and Anne met the next day in a restaurant near the Aldershot. Gilbert seemed distracted and preoccupied. He couldn't concentrate at all. The words he had learned melted into each other into a stream of nonsense syllables. He looked unwell, too: pale around the mouth, drawn, his eyes dark and smudged with shadows.

After a few minutes Anne said, 'We don't have to go on. You're feeling unwell, aren't you? What's the matter, something you ate?'

'I don't think so. I don't know, really. Just tired, I suppose.'

'You're trying to do too much,' she said sympathetically. 'Your work and the class and these meetings with me. Listen, why don't we not meet for a week or two, until you feel —'

'No,' he said sharply. 'I'd fall so far behind the class that I'd never catch up, and unless I learn the language, Dr Morrison won't let me leave Shanghai, and I have to, I have to get out of here. No. I'll be all right.'

'Of course you will,' she said. 'And you will learn, honestly you will. One day very soon everything will begin to fall together, to make sense, and you'll find yourself chattering away just like one of Uncle Billy's natives. I've worked with students who were much more backward than you, and you should hear them now.'

He felt calmer. He knew that when he was with her, Kit couldn't touch him.

He measured some sugar into his tea and whirled his spoon slowly. 'I wrote a letter to Louise last night, my fiancée.' Anne nodded. 'When I decided that I wanted to come to China we talked it over. Seems like we talked about it for months. She had no desire to leave her home and her family, and she was wise enough and honest enough to say so. I think she was right. I think she would have hated it here. She's very sensitive to suffering, and to ugliness. We agreed that it would be foolish to remain engaged. If either of us met someone else, we shouldn't feel bound.'

'That was sensible,' Anne said. 'She must be a wonderful person.'

'Why do you say that?' Gilbert demanded.

Anne said without any trace of mockery, 'Why, because you wouldn't have wanted to marry her if she wasn't.'

'Oh. Yes. She is a very fine person. Anyway, I wrote to her last night. I told her that I wanted her to consider herself free of any promises. I was afraid she might still be hoping that I'd come to my senses and come home.' He pushed his hands through his hair.

'But Gilbert, I'm sure she'll understand if you write to her again, right away, and tell her that you were upset and lonely and even ill and that you didn't mean what you said in your letter. You could even ask her to join you here. She would, I'm sure of it.'

'No, you don't understand. I don't want her to come. I don't want to see her again.'

Anne sighed. His distress made her feel so inadequate and helpless. Having weathered so many emotional storms herself, she felt that she ought to know exactly what to say and do for someone else. But it wasn't that easy. Nothing in life was easy.

'Why don't we walk a little?' she suggested.

They shouldered their way through the crowds on Nanking Road and strolled along the far side of the Bund to the park that overlooked the juncture of Soochow Creek and the Whangpoo River.

'This used to be where they had the sign "No Dogs or Chinese Allowed,"' Anne said as she paid a few cents at the entrance gate. 'That was a long time ago – I don't remember ever seeing it. I imagine it was taken down as a result of the Boxer Rebellion, which gave the whites something to think about: what if the four hundred million suddenly turned hostile? All the gunboats in the world couldn't protect them.'

They leaned on the sea wall and watched a tugboat hauling a long string of barges up the Soochow Creek. Coolies snored on top of loads of pasty-looking bricks. Laundry spread out on the bricks dried in the sun. On the foredeck of one barge a woman cooked her family's lunch over a small spirit flame. The ragtag procession passed under the Garden Bridge and out of sight.

'Some of these people live their whole lives on boats,' Anne said. 'There's a village of sampans anchored in the Soochow, above the bridge. I'll take you there sometime. You can walk from one boat to the next, for over a mile, without ever touching the water. Mothers tie their small children to the boats so they won't fall in. A lot of people who lost their houses in the bombings last year went there. They sleep and eat on the boats, and give birth, and die. Not such a bad life. You can cut loose anytime and go where you please.'

The park was well used. They strolled past crisply uniformed British nannies and Chinese amahs minding their rampaging charges. Studious young Chinese pored over textbooks. A couple of old men practiced the balletic movements of *tai chi* under the canopy of a banyan tree, while nearby a foursome rattled mah-jongg tiles. As Gilbert and Anne neared the gate on the Bund, they met Reverend Fox and a woman, a well-corseted blonde of middle age who twirled a parasol on her shoulder.

Anne stopped cold, then turned her back on the approaching pair and watched the mah-jongg game with sudden intense interest. The couple passed, nodding pleasantly to Gilbert. Anne, her face white, moved toward the exit.

'Who was that with your father?' Gilbert asked when they reached the Bund.

'No one. My old violin teacher, Olga Kerensky.'

'Why didn't you speak to them?' Gilbert wondered.

'Because I can't. I won't.'

Gilbert asked no more questions.

'Well, that was quite a snub,' said Olga Fyodorovna Kerensky to Leonard Fox. 'I feel bad. We used to be such good friends.'

'I'm sorry, Olga. I'll speak to her about it if you like.'

'No, don't do that. It would only anger her. And it really doesn't matter. Although someday, I think, someone ought to explain things to her.'

'You're suggesting that I should?' Leonard shook his graying head. 'No, I'd never be able to do it. You know what she's like. We never could talk.'

'One of the tragedies of being a parent,' Olga sighed, 'is that you must always be so much older, and the gulf must always be so wide. The young man she was with — very handsome. Is there a romance in the works, perhaps?'

'Romance? With Anne?' Reverend Fox snorted. 'She's giving him lessons in Chinese, that's all.'

'A pity. She needs someone to love. I suppose he's married?'

Fox told her about Gilbert, and added, 'I can't imagine any man finding Anne attractive enough to marry.'

'One did, long ago.'

'Yes, and can you imagine what would have happened if I hadn't intervened? The Butcher of Shanghai as a son-in-law. My God.'

'They might have been quite happy together,' Olga said with the warmth of a woman who believes in the saving power of love. 'He might have turned out different, with a wife and a child to think about. Love has a softening effect. Are you really happy with the way she is now, surly and slovenly and utterly miserable?'

'I did what I thought best at the time,' Leonard Fox said coldly. 'I have no regrets. We've both seen marriages that crossed racial lines – tragedy. There are reasons for excluding Chinese from clubs and events. The children of such marriages belong neither to one race nor the other. They are born outcasts and they remain outcasts. She knew all that when she plunged into that miserable affair. She should have had more sense.'

Olga shook her head slowly. 'So should we all, at one time or another in our lives.'

'I've never been sorry about us,' Reverend Fox said staunchly.

'Nor have I,' she murmured. 'Nor have I.'

Gilbert strode briskly toward the Aldershot. He was so deeply immersed in thought that when an automobile horn blatted at his elbow he jumped a foot. He whirled around and saw Kit sitting behind the wheel of the little red Bentley she had bought with the money from her divorce settlement. She smiled and waved. He wanted to walk ahead resolutely, to ignore her, but he knew that she would follow, lean on her horn, and create a public spectacle. He went over to the curb.

'What do you want?' he demanded.

In the weeks that had passed since that nightmarish

encounter at his hotel, she had achieved the dimensions of an obscene Jezebel, all pulsating orifices and stinking paint. He was rather startled to see that she was modestly dressed for golf. Her face was shining and free from paint, and her hair looked windblown and glorious.

'I just wanted to see if you were still feeling low about our last meeting. I can see you are. Poor Gil. Hop in. Let's go for a drive and talk things over.'

'I don't want to go anywhere with you,' he said through his teeth. 'I don't want to see you again. Stop following me!'

'Following you! Silly, I happened to be riding along and I saw you and pulled over to say hello. Dear me, I didn't know we weren't friends anymore.'

He leaned stiff-armed on the door of the car and said in a low, harsh voice, 'I'm sorry I ever set eyes on you. Sorry I came to China. For God's sake, leave me alone, can't you? Haven't you done enough harm?'

'Oh, Gilbert,' said Kit disgustedly, 'stop acting as though I raped you. What's the matter with you, don't they have sex in Philadelphia? The best thing about virginity is losing it. It's not as though you were helpless and couldn't defend yourself, you know. My dear, you didn't even try. You were hardly the unsuspecting little chicken dozing on its roost when the big bad fox came along looking for a meal. You wanted me from the minute you laid eyes on me, and I wanted you. You did your share.' She traced a pattern on the back of his hand with a polished fingernail. 'I bet you'd like some right now,' she said in a silky murmur that made the hairs on the back of his neck stand on end.

He leaped back, away from the car. 'You're disgusting, horrible. Can't you see what you're like? You're no better than those women in Blood Alley. If anything, you're worse, because they do what they do in order to live, and you do it out of boredom.'

'How dare you parade that holier-than-thou stuff in front of me,' she snapped. 'As if you were more sinned against than sinning! You damned pious hypocrite.'

'You're an animal,' Gilbert hissed. 'Sneaky, sly, cunning. You don't care what you do, who you hurt, as long as it gives you a little excitement. I don't know how you've fooled everybody for so long. They all think you're just marvelous, even Anne. What a joke. What a lie. You're hideous, ugly as – as sin. You're a slut posing as a saint.' He spat out the words with cutting deliberateness. Kit winced. 'You're wanton and vicious and the very sight of you sickens me. If you were a rotten limb, I could amputate you. If you were a tumor, I could cut you out. But you're insidious. You're poison. You'll poison this whole city if someone doesn't stop you. You don't have the right to breathe the same air as the lowest, filthiest beggar in the street.'

He backed away and walked a few staggering steps before breaking into a stumbling run. Kit sat absolutely still. She felt drenched in bile, as though someone had just vomited all over her. Scorned. Humiliated. Tears trickled down her cheeks and she made no move to brush them away. After a little while she started her engine and pulled out into traffic with a roar, nearly running down an old Chinese man and cutting off a ricksha coolie, who cursed her passionately.

The nurse who accompanied Gilbert on his rounds that afternoon remarked on his preoccupation, and he apologized and blamed the heat – the usual convenient excuse for malaise in Shanghai in summer. All the while he felt knives of terror stabbing him, stinging the backs of his legs, gouging at his middle. He recognized the symptoms of panic: dry mouth, accelerated pulse, shallow breathing. Finally his visits to his patients were over and he retreated to the safety of the doctors' lounge.

He felt worse than he had that afternoon in his hotel room, after his body so eagerly betrayed the spiritual values he held so dear. Then he lost faith in himself and despised himself for his weakness. Now he worried about his professional competence and wondered about his sanity. He knew that prayer wouldn't help him. He had prayed until his knees were raw, and his prayers always sounded like so many whining excuses: I couldn't help myself, I lost control, just that once. I'm sorry, Lord. Sorry, sorry, sorry. But what was the point of lying to himself anymore? He knew now that it could happen again. Even as he stood there on the curb and reviled her with a coarseness and vehemence that sickened him, he knew that he still wanted her.

He paced the floor and tried to think clearly. He couldn't go home, back to Louise, back to his parents, back to all the people who had praised his spirit of openheartedness and selfsacrifice. He couldn't admit defeat. Chengtu was still cut off by fighting. He didn't want to arouse Dr Morrison's suspicions by requesting a posting to another mission outpost, or to another city like Canton or Nanking. And he couldn't possibly hide from her in Shanghai. She was everywhere. She had a host of friends, her spies. She would find him. What could he do?

He tried to remember the last time he felt safe, at peace. With Anne, walking in the park, watching the boats gliding upstream. Yes, Anne. Calm, warm, reassuring. She cared about him, he could tell, and she believed in what he wanted to do, for all her absurd talk about joss-pidgin-men. She was Kit's sister, and surely sisterhood was a bond that not even Kit would violate.

Anne was proficient in Chinese, which was more than he would ever be, even if he studied for a lifetime. Competent, compassionate, dedicated to helping suffering humanity. The perfect missionary's wife. Dr Morrison would agree. Hadn't he thrown them together with just such hopes in mind? He would have to treat them as a unit, a team, doctor and linguist. He would send them away from Shanghai immediately, far away, as the moon, to a place where Kit couldn't touch them.

As his wife's sister Kit would be untouchable. The jackal that gnawed at his vitals whenever he thought about her would subside. He could start anew, with a renewed mission and a renewed sense of purpose. St. Paul said that it was better to marry than to burn. Yes, yes it was, much better.

Albert McClure noticed the little red Bentley blocking the sidewalk in front of his favorite pub on lower Nanking Road. He went inside and seated himself at the bar, called for a double gin with a splash of tonic, and looked around with the habitual curiosity of the professional observer. He was surprised to see Kit Fox sitting a few stools away from him. She was dressed in a tweedy skirt and white blouse and brogues, and she looked girlish and out of place. She glanced over, bleary-eyed, and pushed the tumble of curls out of her eyes.

'I know you,' she said. 'Don't tell me. Mishter McClure, the Reutersh man.'

'Very good, Miss Fox.' Albert slid his drink along the bar and sat beside her. 'I didn't recognize you at first, away from your usual setting.'

'I came in here because it looked like a fine place to get good and sh—stinking after what I've been through,' she said thickly. 'Have you ever been raped?' she demanded, peering at him intently. 'No, of coursh you haven't. Silly question. Well, I have. Just a few minutes ago.'

'Good heavens!'

'Not the way you think. But violated. Against my wishes. I bet you didn't know that someone could rape you with words.'

'It hadn't occurred to me,' Albert admitted, 'but now that you mention it, I can see that it's possible.'

Kit called to the barman to bring her another double scotch. 'I didn't do anything wrong, not a thing. Meant no harm. But he acted like God Almighty, passing down judgment. Said terrible things to me. Sickening. I couldn't defend myself. Just sat there like an idiot and let him spew his filth all over me. I should have run the son of a bitch down with my car. Shouldn't be sitting here getting blotto. No man is worth making yourself sick over, and I'm going to be one sick little girl a few hours from now. I hate his guts. Make no mistake about that. I hate him and I wish he— I wish I—' She began to cry noisily.

'Come on, old girl,' Albert said kindly, 'I'd better get you home. That your car outside?'

'No, no,' she moaned, 'can't go home. Can't let anybody see me. You won't tell. Swear you won't tell.'

'Word of honor. Where shall I take you, then? You have friends near here?' She waggled her head. 'Then you'd better come up to my room. Practically upstairs, it is. You can sleep it off in peace and quiet. I'm supposed to be working anyway.'

'Why are men so stinking?' she wondered as he half-carried her out into the cruel sunlight. 'Makes no sense. A little fun, no harm done, and the next thing you know, I'm the whore of Babylon. Poison. Vermin. I hate him!'

'Sure you do, old girl. Come along, easy does it.'

'Will you, Anne? Will you marry me?'

She was certain that he had come down with a raging tropical fever and she touched his forehead, which was slightly glazed with perspiration.

He managed to smile. 'No, I'm not raving, Anne. I mean it. In the past few weeks I have come to admire your learning, and your patience, and your kindness. I know we share the same desire to help the Chinese. We could work well together.'

'It's a joke,' she said. 'That's what it is. I don't think it's very funny, Gilbert.' She started to rise from the park bench but he caught her arm.

'Anne, please!' There was a note of desperation in his voice.

She gazed at him searchingly. 'You do mean it,' she said in an astonished whisper.

'Yes, I do.'

'Oh, Gilbert.' She sat back and stared, dumbfounded. 'I don't know what to say.'

'I know it's too soon for avowals of love,' he said, moistening his lips and speaking rapidly. 'But that will come in time, I'm sure. We do have mutual respect, and admiration for each other's finer qualities, and tolerance for each other's weaknesses. And most important, we share a common goal.'

She said slowly, 'You're good and fine and brilliant, Gilbert, and I'm very honored. But you don't want to marry me. You really don't. You've been lonely and homesick —'

'That's not true,' he protested.

'I'm full of flaws you don't even know about. I'm moody, and lazy, and — I'm just not good enough for you, Gilbert.'

'You're not in a position to judge your own worth,' he said, trying to infuse his tone with a little warmth. 'You don't think you're a good teacher, for example, but everyone else thinks you're just fine. I don't find you flawed. Far from it. You're one of the most interesting people I've ever met. But of course, if you don't want to marry me, then you shouldn't. I won't press you. I won't even mention it again.'

She shook her head wonderingly. He seemed so calm, so sure of himself, discussing their marriage as coolly as he might discuss one of his cases at the hospital. She herself felt that she might vibrate apart at the seams at any moment. Suddenly she had a future. Suddenly she had a life.

'I would be honored. I ought to thank you. I just never expected —' she stammered.

'Then you accept?' She nodded shyly, then eagerly. Gilbert let out his breath. 'Good. It's settled then.' He found her hand and gave it a little squeeze. He supposed he ought to kiss her, but he couldn't bring himself to do it. So he just pressed her hand and gave her what he hoped was a fond smile. 'Well, I don't suppose we can go on with our lesson. Unless you feel up to it —'

'I don't know how I feel,' she said with a nervous laugh. 'Just like that? It's settled?'

'Yes, it's settled. We can tell your parents tonight, if you like. Perhaps we can be married before they leave for the mountains.'

'Gilbert.' Anne gnawed her lower lip. 'I must tell you something.' She knotted her hands in her lap and turned away from him slightly. 'I was in love once before, when I was studying in Paris. Father didn't think him suitable, and he put a stop to things. I didn't want you to think — that is, I wanted you to know — I thought I should tell you —' she floundered unhappily.

She was trying to tell him that she wasn't a virgin. Well, what difference did it make? At this point he couldn't afford to be choosy.

'I understand, Anne,' he said. 'You were young, and far from home. It's not so unusual. It would have been more unusual if you hadn't found anyone to love you.

You're a fine person.'

Anne gave him a grateful look. She had done her duty; she had told the truth. Or at least part of the truth. She wasn't really trying to hide anything, but what was the point of dragging all that old stuff up again? She would be a good wife, the best wife he could have.

* * *

After dinner that night Gilbert and Reverend Fox found an opportunity to be alone together in the minister's study.

'Gilbert,' Leonard Fox cleared his throat portentously, 'I just want to say, ah, um, well, I hope you're not doing this out of some kind of pity for Anne. I don't know what she told you about what you saw the other day. Madame Kerensky is an old friend, nothing more.'

'Anne said nothing to me about that, sir,' Gilbert said. 'I don't consider it any of my business.'

'It's not that I want to discourage you from marrying Anne,' Leonard Fox said quickly. 'I merely wanted to be sure that, ah . . .' He hesitated.

'— that I knew what I was doing,' Gilbert finished for him with a smile. 'I do, sir. Anne and I are very sympathetic. I think she will be very helpful to me in my work, and I promise I'll do my best to make her happy.'

'I can't say that I'm not pleased about this, Gilbert. I know your father will be pleased, too. I'll write to him at once. Anne can be difficult, I know. You have seen that the relationship between us is a little strained. Did she tell you about that unfortunate affair in Paris?' he asked cautiously.

'She did, yes.'

'Good.' Reverend Fox relaxed a little. 'I'm the villain of that piece, you know. We haven't been able to talk civilly since then, and it happened seven – no, eight years ago. A long time to carry a grudge, to nurse a hurt. But women are talented that way. I've never known a man who could nurse a grudge like a woman can.'

'I'm sure things between you will improve,' Gilbert said encouragingly.

'I hope so. Gilbert, if you like, you and Anne may live

here at the manse until you're able to leave for Szechwan. There's plenty of room. I don't know if you and she have discussed plans yet.'

Live in the same house with Kit? Gilbert swallowed a yelp. 'We haven't, but I think we would both prefer to start out on our own. The warring in Szechwan could drag on for months, Dr Morrison says, and I believe we'd be more comfortable in a small apartment for the duration. I'm earning a salary at the clinic and —'

'You must permit us to help out, Gilbert. A wedding present.'

'Thank you, Reverend Fox. That's very kind of you.'

'You might call me Father now,' said Leonard Fox, pumping his prospective son-in-law's hand. 'Welcome to our family.'

Anne was too excited to sleep. She walked in the garden until her feet were dew-soaked, then she went back to her room and paced and smoked. At a little after three o'clock, she heard Kit come in. She waited a few minutes, then crossed the hall and tapped softly on her sister's door.

Kit had already thrown off her wrap and gown and dancing slippers. She sat in her slip in front of her dressing table mirror and brushed her hair vigorously. Her maid, Ling, padded silently around the room and made order out of Kit's chaos.

'Hullo, Mouse,' Kit said, surprised at seeing Anne up so late. 'You're not becoming a night owl like me, I hope. Have you got a fag?'

'Of course.' Anne gave her a cigarette, lit it and one for herself, and perched on the side of the bed.

Kit had decorated her room herself, and it was lovely. A thick celadon-green Chinese rug covered the floor. A delicate white and green toile hung from the windows and covered the bed and chairs. All the furniture was white. A vase full of crimson roses provided the necessary warm complement to the cool greens.

Anne said, 'I couldn't sleep. I'm all up in the air tonight. I feel like I'll never sleep again.'

'What's up?' Kit asked, applying cream to her face and

tissuing it off again. 'Another row with Daddy?'

'No, nothing like that. I'm so excited – I hope you'll be pleased, too. Oh, I'm sure you will. Gilbert – Dr Lawrence and I are going to be married. He's so fine, so dedicated, Kit. You have no idea. We're going to work in Chengtu as a team. He's got it all planned.'

'I'll bet he has,' Kit said softly.

Anne plunged on. 'I've even been thinking about taking a course in nursing. Don't you think that sounds like a good idea? I couldn't wait to tell you, Kit. I'd like you to be in my wedding. It won't be big – nothing like yours. Mother and Father agree. Just family, and the Morrisons. And it will be soon, just as soon as possible. Gilbert doesn't want to wait because if the Yangtze opens up we'll have to leave for Szechwan on short notice. Will you be my bridesmaid, Kit?' Her eyes shone with excitement and hope.

'Of course I will.' Kit's smile was thin. 'I'd be delighted.' She sat on the bed and put her bare arm around Anne's shoulders. 'I'm very happy for you, darling. Thrilled. I've been longing for you to get out of this house, out of Shanghai. I think it's wonderful.'

Anne put her arms around Kit's tiny waist and kissed her cheek.

'I knew you'd be happy for me. We don't have an awful lot in common. I'm so much older and we're not interested in the same things, but we're sisters, just the same. I haven't always been patient with you, and I'm sorry. I won't keep you up any longer, but I wanted you to know.'

She went back to her room. Kit remained seated on the bed. That sly bastard, hiding behind Anne's dowdy skirts. She knew why he was doing it, the coward. It was a deliberate slap in the face. Little Kit wasn't good enough for him because she was divorced. Dreadful. But Anne! Oh, God, it was laughable.

She wanted to scream, to throw something, to shatter glass, to smash windows, to hurt someone. She moved back to her dressing table and sat again in front of her mirror. The face that stared back at her was still beautiful, if a little pinched and wild-eyed. She had pretended for so

long that she didn't care about anything that the sudden-
ness of finding herself plunged into a maelstrom of
feelings came as a shock, like being tipped into icy water.
First that business outside the Aldershot, then waking up
hours later in Albert McClure's dingy hotel room. The
memory of that humiliation still pained. And now this.

She picked up the brooch she had worn that night, a
delicate stalk of wheat in gold and diamonds that Richard
Matthews had given her before their wedding. The pin on
the back was long, nearly three inches, and as sharp as a
needle. She touched the tip to the palm of her left hand.
The prick of pain gave her a point of concentration that
eased the jumble of her other feelings. She pressed,
harder and harder, and stared at the face in the mirror,
distorted now by an ugly grimace.

Ling turned around and saw her mistress with her face
twisted and white and the pin thrust clean through her
hand. A trickle of blood ran down her slip, from her knee
to the floor, and stained the green carpet. Ling screamed.

Chapter Four

In the days that preceded the wedding, Gilbert kept up his routine of work and study while in the grip of the fear that Kit would somehow spoil his plans. Everyone smiled understandingly at his displays of nervousness and apprehension, and attributed them to the natural terror of a man about to take that decisive step into matrimony.

Anne alternated between fits of paralytic helplessness and hysterical frenzy. For once even her father indulged her moods and accepted them as the natural order of things. If marriage is a big step for a man, for a woman it is the culmination of the thousand dreams of childhood adolescence, and young womanhood, and it carries with it the promise of total fulfillment in motherhood.

Only Kit, if she had been able to analyze the situation rationally, could have guessed that both bride and groom invested their forthcoming nuptials with some rather extraordinary expectations. This marriage was no simple union of loving hearts, but the instrument of reparation, redemption, and salvation.

The only blight on Anne's happiness came as the result of a visit to Father Jacquinot, soon after Gilbert's proposal. At first the priest was delighted with the news.

'My dear child, it is wonderful! I wish you both so much happiness. You must bring your young man to call upon me, I insist. I will not invite myself to your wedding – I know your father would not be pleased. But I am curious about him. I am a great romantic, even though I am an old man.' He kissed her on both cheeks and stepped back to admire her flushed face and radiant smile. 'Ah, you bloom with joy. You love him, don't you?'

'Yes, I think so. Not the way I loved Chen, but that was long ago, and I was so young and naive. Gilbert is good and kind and I know we will be happy together. A lot of people start out marriage with a lot less, and they still learn to love each other. I know we will.'

'You have told him about Chen?' Father Jacquinot

motioned for her to sit down and he eased himself into the chair behind his desk. The interview took on the look of a professional consultation.

She didn't meet his sharp gaze. 'Yes. I said that I was in love before, with a man I met in Paris.'

'That's all? But surely you told him the rest, about —'

'No, not yet. I tried, but I couldn't. Listen, Father, he's rather straitlaced and he might not understand. But I'll tell him someday, I promise.'

The priest frowned. 'No, Anne, you must tell him now. Everything. If he really loves you and wants you for his wife, he will understand. The past won't make any difference. But if he should find out from anyone else – it would be very bad for you both.'

'But he won't find out,' Anne said. 'No one knows the whole story except my family and you. Not even Uncle Billy knows everything that happened. It's over, finished, and it happened so long ago. You've been telling me that I should forget the past and look ahead, and that's just what I want to do. A secret isn't the same as a lie. It's simple diplomacy.'

Father Jacquinot said, 'It is a lie if your intention is to deceive. Anne, diplomacy is for strangers, people who need to observe certain forms for the sake of outward appearances. But in this case, silence is the same as deceit. Tell him. Your past is not so shameful. He is a Christian man, is he not? Then he will understand, and help you with your sorrow. Don't you see that if you don't speak now, this secret will stand between you like a stone wall? It will not diminish in importance over the years. And it will harm your close relationship with your husband.'

'I don't believe that,' she said stubbornly. 'It all happened years ago. It's ancient history. You've kept telling me to put it behind me, and now I am.'

He snorted. 'It should be ancient history, but it is not. For you, your hurt is still as fresh as it was the first day you came to see me. Just a few weeks ago, in this very room, you wept for a man who had stopped loving you eight years ago. You cannot bury the past, yet you think that somehow after you are married it will stop tormenting you and conveniently disappear. You are deceiving yourself, hurting yourself more than anyone else by this folly.' He scowled and tugged at his beard, an ominous sign.

'The past will disappear,' Anne insisted. 'It must. Don't you see, Father, he's holding out a lifeline to me. If I don't take it, I'll go under. I know I will.'

'Nonsense. You are not drowning, not dying. The only person who has been holding you back from happiness is you yourself, Anne. No one else. You came here because you wanted me to confirm the rightness of your actions, to tell you it's all right to go into marriage without telling your young man about your past. But I cannot do that. The problems that you choose to ignore do not go away. They reoccur again and again, like infections in a wound that never heals properly.'

Anne's lower lip trembled. 'I can't believe you don't want me to be happy. I thought you were my friend.'

Father Jacquinot threw up his hand in despair. 'I am your friend, Anne, and I want nothing less for you than you want for yourself. But no one else can make you happy. Not me, not Dr Lawrence, not your papa, not Chen. You.'

They sensed the chill of estrangement, and they both knew that their friendship would never be the same. Seething with anger at what she considered betrayal, Anne walked away from the university campus. She had persuaded herself that she was doing the right thing, and mentally she accused Father Jacquinot of employing a double standard: it was perfectly all right for Chen to forget her, to marry again, to lead his life as he wanted, but not Anne. Oh, no, she had to grovel and apologize for the rest of her life. Well, she wouldn't do it. She wouldn't let this chance for happiness slip away. At the same time, she felt curiously adrift, as though she had slipped one of the moorings that anchored her to her old life.

Father Jacquinot understood that this break was necessary. He was part of her past, her last link with Chen. He had consoled her in her bereavement, and supported her during the years she spent in a self-constructed limbo of self-pity and anger. But new loves demand new loyalties. All the same, he feared for her, and kept her in his prayers.

Reverend Fox, performed the simple wedding ceremony at the manse. Anne looked dowdy and self-conscious in a pale blue suit that gave her sallow complexion a greenish tinge. In dazzling contrast, Kit shimmered in a floor-length frock of the gauziest silk imprinted with full-blown peonies. She didn't speak to Gilbert at all, but he could feel her watching them closely, sneering as he and Anne exchanged vows, laughing at them silently.

Afterward Wang served refreshments in the dining room. Mrs Fox asked Gilbert to refill her punch cup, and when he turned away from the punch bowl he came face to face with Kit. His heart gave a terrified flutter.

Kit was coldly contemptuous. 'I ought to congratulate you, I suppose. That was fast work. I know you'll be very happy.' Her scorn dashed like acid in his face.

'I did what I had to do,' he said tonelessly. 'I didn't want to hurt you.'

'Oh, don't worry about me. It doesn't matter to me if you make a fool of yourself. I don't give a damn what you do.'

Laura Morrison came toward them, her eyes fixed on the platter of cookies near the punch bowl. Kit put on a smile and said something bright, and Gilbert was spared further recriminations.

The newlyweds spent a week in Hangchow, a city of lakes and temples, one of the most beautiful places in China. Gilbert steeled himself in anticipation of a wedding night that was just one more part of the price he had to pay for security.

He found it all too easy to fault his new wife. He hated himself for blaming her because she wasn't like Kit, but he could not avoid comparing them. Anne was clumsy. Kit was graceful. Anne was hard and angular where Kit was soft and supple. Anne's breasts were large, attractive enough, he supposed, but gross and matronly compared to Kit's. She had none of Kit's knowing tricks in bed, and she was hampered by shyness and a paralyzing desire to please. She was surprisingly physical – Gilbert would have expected such a politically oriented person to have scant interest in sex. She loved to touch him, to fondle his hand when they sat close together, to kiss him, to snuggle close to him at night, her head pillowed on his shoulder.

'I'm sorry,' he told her, 'but I can't sleep with someone touching me.'

She apologized, unable to conceal her hurt at being rebuffed, and retreated to her own side of the bed.

Her fidgeting nearly drove him mad, and the smoke from her cigarettes threatened to asphyxiate him. Finally he asked her somewhat sharply if she would try to refrain from smoking in his presence.

She blushed furiously and said, 'Yes, of course I will, Gilbert. I'm sorry. I didn't realize it bothered you.'

But then her fidgeting increased so markedly he was almost tempted to ask her to resume her smoking.

They were both relieved when their brief honeymoon ended and they could return to Shanghai. They rented a furnished apartment near Soochow Creek. Gilbert hated the place. The furnishings were shabby and the walls and ceilings hadn't been painted in years and were patterned with stains and flyspecks. There always seemed to be children playing on the front steps, white children and Indian children and Eurasian children, and they were noisy and boisterous and careless with their toys. When the wind was right – and it seemed to be right most of the time – the stench from the honey boats that hauled the excrement of Shanghai's millions to the farms around the city was so noxious as to be unbearable. The fact that Anne loved her new home and never noticed its shortcomings only aggravated his loathing.

They hired a cook and a number-one boy named Wu, who kept the apartment less than immaculate and who stole from the housekeeping money. The Lawrences had their first quarrel about Wu.

'The man is a thief.'

Anne was unimpressed. 'Not really. He's squeezing us a little, but that's perfectly normal.'

'I cannot tolerate thieving in my house, Anne. He must go.'

'But you don't understand the system, Gilbert. We pay him so little, far less than for a comparable servant in the States. We can't pay him more because we'd lose face and look like fools. Then he would despise and take even greater advantage of us. This way he scrapes a little off the top, and filches a bit, and it's our job not to notice. Please don't say anything to him. It would only embarrass him and he'd quit and we'd get another just like him, or worse.'

He couldn't very well contradict her. She was an old China hand and he was still ignorant about ways of doing things in Shanghai. He muttered something about the futility of trying to teach morals to an intrinsically corrupt people. Anne leaped to the defense of the Chinese by saying that they were basically honest, but that years of exploitation by the whites had corrupted them. Gilbert wasn't in any mood to listen to her socialistic nattering, and he told her so. Her hurt made him feel guilty, and angry, and he slammed out of the house.

He worked hard, and prayed for an opportunity to leave Shanghai. The Communists and the soldiers of Chiang's armies were still battling furiously in Szechwan. Shells fell on Chengtu. Missionaries fled to safer zones for the duration of the fighting, and some were able to reach Shanghai by circuitous routes that skirted embattled areas. Gilbert met some of these people and he marveled. He would have braved gas-poisoned trenches and showers of shells if it meant escape from Shanghai.

Anne gave up her teaching job and began a course in nursing at the Shanghai General Hospital. She and Gilbert saw less of each other. They spent one evening a week with her parents, although both disliked the visits. Gilbert dreaded encountering Kit, although when he did glimpse her at the manse, on her way to a party or a dance, his heart contracted and the jackal inside him growled and stirred hungrily. Anne found it difficult to accept the fact that her marriage had rehabilitated her in her parents' eyes, made her an acceptable human being again. Her father treated her like a daughter instead of an affliction. He was bluff and hearty, even teasing. Her mother was so delighted in their apparent reconciliation that Anne didn't have the heart to drag out her old repertoire of contentious attitudes, just to remind her father that she still hadn't forgiven him. She was a loving wife now, and the role of loving daughter didn't seem such a difficult one to play anymore. Certainly the role of acid-tongued spinster no longer applied.

'I say, Kit, didn't your sister marry that doctor fellah you were showing around last summer?' Binky Hartshorn munched the olive from his martini.

'No, Binky, *he* married *her*. There's a difference.' Kit said with a touch of venom.

Binky looked puzzled. 'Then they married each other, didn't they? Ha, ha!'

'You're too smart for me, Bink. You ought to find yourself a pretty little physicist.'

Binky laughed again and signaled to the waiter for another round. 'You know, I saw her the other day.'

'Who, the physicist?'

'No, your sister. Funny how I can't remember her name. Didn't even recognize her at first, all done up and her hair combed. She's rather pretty, don't you think?'

'Well, why not?' Kit shrugged. 'We're sisters, after all.'

'How many years older are you?' Binky asked with a stunning lack of tact. 'Two?'

Kit raised her eyebrows a full inch and said with menacing sweetness, 'No, Bink darling, not two. Twelve. I am twelve years older than Anne. I don't look too bad for an old hag of forty, do I?'

* * *

Kit called Anne and they met for lunch at the Cathay a few days later. Bink was right. Anne did look almost pretty. She stood straighter and held her head higher. Her hair was neatly braided and pinned in a wreath across the top of her head. She wore a very stylish pink challis dress trimmed with black that flattered her figure.

'So the proletariat is wearing dresses from Maurice these days.'

'Mother bought it for me after we got home from Hangchow,' Anne said. 'I didn't want her to – it was scandalously expensive – but it gave her pleasure.'

'You're looking remarkably well these days, Mouse.

You're not pregnant already, are you?' Kit lit their cigarettes.

Anne flushed a little. 'Oh, no, not yet. We've only been married two months.'

'Not too soon to get started. Does Gil want kids?'

'Yes, of course he does. That is, he's never said he didn't want them. He'll be a wonderful father, don't you think?'

'Yes, super,' Kit agreed. Then with feigned offhandedness, 'How is he? I never see him these days.'

'He's so busy at the hospital and with his language studies. You're never around when we visit Father and Mother, Kit.'

Kit blew a smoke ring. 'I'm the happy busy bee, dearie, buzzing around outside the hive while the rest of you are holed up inside making honey. I have three new beaux, as usual, and more things to do than I have minutes in the day.'

'I think you're looking a little tired, Kit,' Anne said worriedly.

'And old?' Kit asked with a harsh laugh. 'Do I look old, too?'

'Old, at twenty! Certainly not!' Anne was amazed.

'I suppose you're going to tell me that I ought to find something useful to do with my life.'

'No, I won't preach to you,' Anne said. 'I know you're not really interested, even though there's so much a person could do here —'

'That's right, I'm not interested. I'm the original *maskee* girl, remember? A real flapper, a relic from the good old days of yesteryear. I don't care what I do, who I hurt. I'm a fox, sneaky and sly and quick and brown, a varmint loose in a coop full of sleeping chickens and lazy dogs. You know what happens to foxes, don't you? They get hounded by the pack until they find someplace to hide, or until they're cornered and get ripped to shreds.'

'Kit, what on earth are you talking about?'

Kit's hands trembled. She folded them around the stem of her cocktail glass to still them. 'I don't know. Too much high living, I guess. Sorry. Tell me – tell me more about Gil.'

Anne talked about some of Gilbert's successes at the Aldershot, about what a fine doctor he was and how much Dr Morrison and his colleagues valued him.

Kit listened, hating him, loving him, knowing that Anne would get prettier and prettier and she, Kit, uglier and uglier and Gilbert would look at her in a few years and wonder what he had ever seen in her. What did it matter? He was only a man, not particularly extraordinary, with only good looks to recommend him, a bit of a bore in bed. Ah, it was only the old forbidden fruit syndrome. Kit the Fox lusting after Gilbert the Grape, hanging too far out of reach but so beautiful and tempting that every time she told herself she knew it was a lie. He and Anne would have kids, beautiful babies, and Gilbert would dote on them even though he didn't love Anne, and those horrid little babies would stand between them like a fleshy pink wall and he'd get further and further away from her.

'— and when he's cross with me I know it's because he's so dreadfully tired. I'm a terrible wife. He deserves much better. That's why I feel so lucky.'

Kit stood up abruptly. 'Listen, Mouse, I've got to run. Sign the chit for me, will you? I've just remembered something – something rather important.' She had to get out. Her head was bursting and a scream was pulsating in her throat and if she had to listen to any more she'd go crazy.

Anne stared after her sister's retreating back.

'She seemed so tense,' she told Gilbert at dinner that evening. 'I've never seen her like that. I'm rather worried. Odd. It was always the other way around. Nobody ever worried about Kit. She always knew what she wanted. She was never afraid of anyone or anything. So sure of herself. I might have been the younger sister and she the older. She ruled the rest of us from the time she was born. What do you think, Gilbert? Maybe you should have a talk with her. She admires you.'

'I don't think that would help.' he said, choking down a morsel of pork. He hated the way the Chinese cooked, chopping their meats into wormlike bits, tossing them together with stringy vegetables so that it all looked like that snake. He put down his fork. He refused to use chopsticks at home. 'She's right, too much high living, too much alcohol and tobacco can take a toll. A good rest is all she needs. When you see her next, advise her to take a trip. A long vacation, away from Shanghai. A change of scene would do her good.'

Kit walked through the stainless steel and glass doors of the new Innes Building, Number 47, The Bund, and took the elevator to the top floor, to the offices of Innes & Company. She spoke to a receptionist, who passed her on to Charlie Fong, Innes' private secretary, a smooth-faced Chinese who spoke Oxford-accented English. Fong told her that Mr Innes was speaking on the telephone, and promised to announce her as soon as the line was free.

'Please don't bother. I'm sure he won't mind if I wait in the office.'

The young man, presuming she was one of his employer's more intimate friends, nodded pleasantly and held the door to the inner office. Innes was sitting behind an enormous teakwood desk. His back was turned to the room and his feet were propped up on the sill of the vast window that overlooked Shanghai harbor.

Kit lowered herself onto a white leather couch near the door. The office screamed new wealth unrestrained by taste. It was furnished in white and chrome, and felt about as welcoming as the inside of a refrigerator. The wall opposite the window was mirrored and covered with shelves displaying antique Chinese treasures. A couch and two chairs rested on that object of Arthur Weston's envy, a blue and white fourteenth-century Peking temple carpet.

Innes laughed into the phone. 'Is that what the old son of a bitch says? . . . No, I don't believe him either. If he doesn't sell to me, somebody else is just going to come in and grab it and he won't get a copper cash for it. . . . Damn right, lean on him a little. That land isn't worth a thing to anyone else. . . . I don't give a damn who's buried there, he can dig 'em up and move 'em. . . . So he's hiring a diviner to give him a reading on the *feng shui*,' the propitious balance of wind and water. 'Get to the guy first and pay him off. Simple.'

Kit crossed her legs and fished in her bag for cigarettes. Her hands shook a little. Innes heard the rasp of a striking match and looked over his shoulder. She smiled the mysterious half-smile that showed off her dimple.

He heaved his feet off the sill and whirled around, staring. 'Call you back,' he said, and hung up.

'Good morning, Mr Innes,' Kit said politely.

'Ah. Good morning. Mrs Matthews, isn't it?'

'Not anymore. I'm using Fox again. But just plain Kit will do very nicely.'

'Sure. I didn't hear you come in.' He stood up and rolled down his shirt sleeves, then pulled on his suit jacket. He was thick-set, swarthy, and muscular. His jaws were blue-black; he was one of those men who always needed a shave. 'Charlie didn't announce you.'

'No, I presumed on old acquaintance and came right in. I hope you don't mind.'

He sat down again. 'Not at all.' God, she was a beauty, a real thoroughbred. Trim and elegant. Expensive. Her gray suit was silk, with a tight-fitting jacket and narrow skirt and ruffled blouse of pink crepe de chine. A pink beret rode the dark waves of her hair. He cleared his throat. 'Well, what can I do for you today, Miss —ah, Kit? Hunting up money for charity?' He opened his top drawer and pulled out his checkbook. 'I'd be happy to help out.'

'I'm glad to hear that,' she said, amused. 'However, I'm not here on behalf of anyone except myself. I don't know whether you'll consider it charity or not. It's strictly a personal matter.'

'Oh?' He leaned back in his chair and waited. Dealing with the Chinese had taught him to be patient, not to rush things. She approached the desk and perched on the corner, crossed her legs high, and held a cigarette expectantly. He leaned forward and snapped his gold lighter.

'How would you like to marry me, Mr Innes?' Kit asked as she bent into the flame.

He stared, scowled, then his face broke into a broad smile. 'What's the joke?'

'No joke. I just asked if you'd like to marry me. If you

would, then we will. Nothing more complicated than that.'

'I'm afraid I don't understand. Last time we met, I had the impression that you didn't like me very much,' he said.

'And I had the impression that you liked me a lot,' she said. 'I'm sorry if I was mistaken. I suppose you're shocked. We ladies are so bold these days, usurping all the usual male prerogatives.'

His smile widened. 'Oh, I don't mind giving up a few of those now and then. But I think I'd like a fuller explanation, if you don't mind.'

'Why not?' She lifted her shoulders and smiled at him through her cigarette smoke. 'You're a businessman. You don't like to jump into things without looking. Certainly not something so final and important as the marriage bed. Well, how can I best sell my idea to you?' She wrinkled her brow prettily and pretended to ponder. 'It seems to me, in my ignorance, that the best business arrangements are those that benefit both parties. Now, what you have to offer is obvious.' She looked around appreciatively. 'But what do you need? I thought it over, and decided that a man in your position ought to be more visible socially. I attend all the best parties, and you're simply not there.'

'I'm simply not invited,' he said.

'What you need is an entrée into our peculiar little society, Mr Innes. It would be easier if you had a wife, a hostess. Someone who was well connected. A woman like that could open doors. You'll never get in any other way.'

'Maybe I don't want in that badly,' he said. 'They don't have anything I want.'

'No? Oh, well, I guess I've wasted my time, and yours. I've done my best. I have nothing to offer but my important friends and my reputation. I have no special skills, except social ones. Dowries are a bit passé – not that my father could ever come up with enough money to run your cars for one day. And he wouldn't try. He hates your guts.'

'So I've heard. I'm afraid this doesn't make much sense. Why me?'

'Why not? You're the richest man in Shanghai, aren't you? You are the company you work for. You don't send your money home, you spend it here, and you spend it grandly. They're still talking about that polo match.' She tapped her cigarette ash into an object that looked like a chrome lifeboat. 'You can't blame a girl for looking out for herself. If there's one thing I know how to do, it's spend money. There's no poverty so demeaning and horrible as the genteel kind. I've always hated it. And I've always loved expensive toys. Fast little cars. Gold watches. Pretty trinkets. Several men in this town can provide all these things, piecemeal. Only one man can provide them all. I'm not really eager to spread my favors around. Awfully tiring, and the prospect of growing old without financial security is a worry to me, I confess. I'm ready for marriage. I am not being immodest when I say that I can have my pick of candidates. I know you haven't demonstrated any interest in being one of them, but perhaps that's only because you haven't had the opportunity. It comes down to this: you support me, and I enhance your respectability. Doesn't it sound like a fine idea?'

'No, it sounds like a joke. I'm not buying jokes today, Miss Fox. Now if you'll excuse me, I'm a busy man.' He reached for the phone.

She leaned across the top of his desk and covered his hand with hers. 'No joke, Mr Innes,' she said, looking him in the eye. 'I am quite serious.'

He scanned her slim figure appraisingly. 'Are you pregnant?'

She looked startled, then sat back and laughed. 'No, you dear man, I am not! I may be bold, but I am not a fool. Well, what do you say?'

'I need time to think it over.'

'No, you don't. You wouldn't give anyone else time to think over one of your offers. You're either interested or you're not. I think you are. I think you've made your decision.'

'You've been married before,' he said. His blue eyes were cold, and shrewd.

'Yes. Do you mind?'

'No. Why should I? I just don't want to be number two in a series. If this is some scheme to collect a fatter alimony than Matthews is paying you —'

'I assure you, divorce is not uppermost in my mind. Marriage is. I don't blame you for not wanting to be lumped with Dickie Matthews, though. You know what they say, that he wasn't man enough for me.' She gave him a challenging look. 'Do you think you are, man enough?'

He said, 'I wish I knew what you were up to.'

She said, 'I'm just trying to work out an arrangement between us. I'll be a good little wife, supportive, encouraging. I'll do my best to get you into the right circles, make them accept you. I think I can even be helpful to your business. I can be very persuasive. I hear things, murmurs of the tom-toms that you don't get up here. For instance, did you know that Jack Carlyle was thinking of selling his business? Nice little import-export affair.'

Innes said, 'I don't believe it. He's doing very well. Why should he sell?'

'Because Dorothy is pregnant. She lost their first baby and she blames China. Dirt, disease, horrid filth. You know. He adores her, and he doesn't want her to go back to England without him. Isn't that sweet? No one else knows yet. She just found out herself a couple of days ago and I was the first – besides Jack – to hear the good news, from her very own lips.' She smiled. 'We're best pals.'

He sat back in his chair and blew out his breath. It was crazy, but here it was, in his lap. He didn't delude himself. He knew she wasn't in love with him, didn't even find him attractive. But he'd never had any trouble with women like that. In bed they were all the same: they start out hating you and then they can't get enough of you.

She looked at her watch. 'I have a luncheon appointment in a few minutes. Sorry I can't invite you along. Yet.'

She slid off the desk and ran her hands over her hips to smooth her skirt. Innes said, 'You have debts. Gambling. I can make you a loan —'

She gave a trill of laughter. 'You still aren't convinced that my motives are pure! No, I am not pregnant, and I don't need money fast. I just want to get married. What do you say?'

103

He shrugged. 'Why not? When?'

'The day after tomorrow. That will give you a little time to shop for a ring. I'm partial to yellow diamonds, pear-shaped. I'll pop up at five, and we can go over to the registrar's. I'll take care of the details.'

He followed her to the door. 'I wish I knew what this was all about.'

She faced him. 'What difference would it make? Are you going to back out?'

'No.'

'Well, neither am I. I knew you wouldn't be afraid to take a chance.' She fingered the lapel of his suit. He obviously didn't know a thing about clothes. She'd have to take him in hand if she didn't want to be a complete laughingstock. 'After all, that's how you got where you are. See you Thursday, Jim.' She rose on her toes and gave him a light kiss.

He grabbed her shoulders and kissed her long and hard. She caught his wrists and pulled away.

'Don't be so impatient, darling,' she said breathlessly. Her smile was strained. 'There will be plenty of time for that after the wedding.'

'I know that,' he said with a grin. 'I just wanted to look at your eyes, to see if you were drinking or doping.'

In the corridor outside the doors to Innes & Company Kit wiped her mouth viciously with her handkerchief. God, he was loathsome.

That Thursday evening the Lawrences and the Foxes dined at the manse. After dinner they played bridge in Reverend Fox's study. Anne always partnered her mother, who was giddy and erratic in her play. Neither Gilbert nor her father, both excellent players, had any patience with Marian's peculiar methods of bidding. The radio played Vivaldi's *Four Seasons*. Anne's fingers twitched; she had mastered the solo passages as a student, long ago. She thought how well the 'Autumn' segment suited the October evening: it was rainy and blowy outside, and she could imagine frost-tinted leaves swirling in the wind. Actually it was seventy degrees, and the wind shredded the banana leaves and tossed the blooms on the roses.

Marian Fox studied her cards and opened the bidding.
'Two spades.'

Anne sighed inwardly. That meant her mother had the
ace. She might not have any other decent cards, but she
was perfectly capable of going to game on the strength of
that one card.

'Three clubs,' Gilbert said halfheartedly.

'Three hearts,' Anne said loudly so that her mother
would be sure to comprehend the change in suits.

'Oh, dear,' sighed Marian, frowning at her cards.

'Pass,' Reverend Fox sighed.

His wife wrinkled her nose. Gilbert smiled at her. She
had been very animated that evening, so much like Kit.
She must have been a beauty when she was young, just
like — He shook himself and tried to concentrate on the
game.

'Five hearts!' Marian trilled. Gilbert passed.

Anne groaned aloud and passed. Both men smiled
superiorly, and Leonard passed and threw out a lead.
Marian put down her cards. She had all of six hearts with
the queen high. Anne whooped and the men scowled.

Tires hissed in the driveway. Doors slammed.

'That must be Kit,' said Marian, leaving her chair to
peer out the rain-splashed bay window. 'She's home early.
But I don't recognize that car.'

Gilbert trumped his partner's ace. 'Really, Gilbert,'
Leonard muttered crossly.

Anne beat his trump and raked in the trick. 'Thank you,
dear,' she said to Gilbert.

Gilbert heard the unmistakable chime of Kit's laughter.
Shivers of nervousness raced through his body. He hadn't
seen her in weeks.

'Hullo, everybody. Congratulations are in order. We've
just been married.'

Their heads swiveled, mouths dropped open, and eyes
stared. Marian Fox sagged limply into the chair under the
window, her eyes not wavering from her daughter. The
other three cardplayers froze in their attitudes and gaped
at Kit, who stood with her arm looped casually through
that of James Innes. Innes loomed large in the close, cozy

room. A belted topcoat hung from his shoulders like a cape and dripped water on the carpet.

Reverend Fox was the first to recover. 'Really, Kit, I hardly think —'

Kit extended her left hand to display an enormous diamond and a slender gold band. She hitched a new silver fox stole higher on her shoulder. 'No joke, folks. Absolutely true. Everybody, this is Jim Innes, my new husband. Husband, meet the family. Daddy, better known as Reverend Leonard Fox of the Bubbling Well Presbyterian Church. Mummy, who's a darling. My big sister, Anne, affectionately known as Mouse. And the pale young man with the slack jaw is Gilbert Lawrence, M.D., husband of aforesaid Mouse.'

Gilbert snapped his mouth shut.

Innes nodded. 'Evening.'

Leonard Fox stood up quickly. 'Kit, this isn't funny. I wish you'd take your friend back to whatever seedy nightclub you found him in and —'

'They don't believe me!' Kit cried in mock distress. 'They want to see proof. Quick, Jim, give me the papers, there's a dear. See?' She flapped the license at them. 'We tied the knot, as they say, at six o'clock this evening, in the office of the registrar. Then we had a jolly dinner at the Petersburg and sat at Sasha's very own table. He and Jim are best buddies, isn't that nice? Then we danced a little, but we didn't want to stay out too late because I simply didn't want to keep this a secret much longer and we rushed home so that I could introduce him to all of you.'

'Oh, Kit,' said Marian faintly, 'did you really do it?'

'Yes, darling, I really did it. Well, what do you say? Shall we have some champagne to celebrate?'

'I think you've had too much champagne already,' said her father angrily. 'Sir, I hold you responsible for this. My daughter is not yet twenty-one. She's clearly out of her mind. I will have this marriage annulled at once. This is a cruel farce, a shabby trick. I won't allow it, do you hear me? Get out of this house at once!'

'Oh, Daddy,' sighed Kit, 'if you throw Jim out, you'll just have to throw me out, too, and you don't want to do that.'

She went over to her father and took his arm. He was dangerously pale, trembling with rage. Anne had seen him like that before. Old memories and dreads flooded over her. Gilbert walked to the window and turned his back on the rest of them. Kit watched him closely.

'You had no right,' Leonard Fox said to Innes over his daughter's head. 'I won't have it. My little girl —! No! You know how I feel about you. If this is some kind of fiendish revenge on me for hating you – by God, I never loathed you so much as I do now. Leave this house at once!'

Innes said softly, 'I'll wait in the car, Kit.' He went out.

'It's a joke, isn't it, dear? One of those mad things you're always doing?' Her mother wavered between laughter and tears.

'It's a mad thing, I guess, but it's no joke. Come on, Daddy, cheer up. He's frightfully rich. I could hardly have done better.'

Gilbert pressed his hand over his eyes.

Reverend Fox pushed Kit away from him. 'Rich? You married that man because he's rich? I'd rather have you naked in a gutter somewhere, married to a coolie, than married to that – that monster. He's filth!'

'Jesus,' Anne murmured. 'Do you have a cigarette, Kit?'

Kit handed over her purse. 'Help yourself, Mouse. Light me one, will you?'

Anne struck a match repeatedly. It failed to light. Kit said, 'Let me. I'm sorry you're being so beastly about this, Daddy.' Her voice shook, but the hand that held the flame to their cigarettes was steady. 'After all, I was a good girl the first time around and it just didn't work. Married just the right guy, big jolly wedding, tons of flowers. And it was a flop. Well, it's my turn to choose now.'

'You chose Richard Matthews,' said her father sharply. 'No one else did.'

'But you approved, didn't you? Everyone approved, and wished me well, and sent lots of ugly gifts, and sent me off to be happy for the rest of my life. I was young and foolish and I still believed in romance and it was quite a shock when the whole thing blew up in my face. Men are beasts, all of them, without exception,' she said pointedly, aiming her darts at Gilbert's back. 'If I decide to marry one who doesn't make any bones about his beastliness, then what of it? At least he doesn't try to hide behind a mask of hypocrisy. Well, it's up to you. If you don't want me to come around anymore, I won't. I'll pick up a few things while I'm here, and send for the rest of my stuff in the morning, and you'll never see me again. We're on our way to honeymoon at the Cathay, in Mr Innes' penthouse.' She lifted her chin and pulled up her furs.

A moan escaped Gilbert's lips.

Reverend Fox shuddered and sat down heavily. He buried his face in his hands. 'Kitten, my Kitten, my little girl, my baby.' He began to sob.

'Oh, Daddy!' Kit knelt by his side and put her arms around him. 'Don't, please.' Marian Fox gazed at them helplessly, hardly comprehending what was happening to her family. Gilbert didn't move a muscle, but he could feel himself dying slowly, of terminal anguish.

'I can't take this,' Anne breathed. Going out into the hall, she closed the door firmly on the rest of them. It would be all right, she knew. Her father wouldn't give Kit up, no matter what she'd done, no matter whom she married. His little girl. His baby.

Tears stung her eyes and she brushed them away angrily. How was it, when you thought that wounds had healed and the frail places were covered by scar tissue, that hurts could suddenly open up and pain pour over you like liquid fire? Eight years ago her father had said of Chen, gentle and scholarly Chen, 'No better than a coolie.' One thing had led to another, and when it was all over Anne had felt as though her legs had been cut off. She still felt shooting pains in her amputated limbs.

She jerked open the front door and stepped out under the portico to suck in some clean moist air. Innes' Rolls was parked at the bottom of the steps. She went down and tapped on the window. The chauffeur hopped out and opened the rear door. She poked her head inside.

'Mr Innes, I'd like to speak to you for a moment if I may.'

'Sure, come on in,' Innes said, sliding over to make

room for her.

She entered the car. The seats were leather, glove-soft, rich to the touch. The cozy little cabin behind the glassed-off driver's compartment was warm and dry and it smelled of tobacco and scotch whiskey and wet wool. Innes' bulk seemed to fill the small space.

Anne felt a little frightened at bearding the enemy in his own steel-clad den. She knew him by reputation, of course, and she despised him for what he was. But she didn't know yet who he was. She needed to measure his strength and assess the depths of his viciousness. She needed to discover his weaknesses, if any. Suddenly the enemy had a face.

The face was in shadow, of course. The only light inside the car came from a small lamp on the ceiling.

She took a breath. 'I want to apologize for my father's behavior. No matter what his feelings about you are, he had no right to treat you like that. Parents seem to think that they own shares in their children's lives, even after they're grown, like stockholders, and this gives them the right to approve and disapprove, a license to meddle. Kit can fall in love with anyone she chooses. It was wrong of him to behave the way he did.'

'Looks like we caught you by surprise,' Innes said. His voice was deep, smooth. 'Cigarette?' She accepted one from a glittering gold case. He snapped his lighter. She noticed his hands, calloused and immense, but with a rich man's clean skin and buffed nails. 'So she didn't tell anybody about this, not even you?'

'Oh, especially not me.' Anne smoked nervously. 'I'm a bit older – one foot in the next generation. She would never confide in me. And certainly not about something like this.' She faced him squarely. 'I may as well be frank, Mr Innes. My feelings about this matter are rather confused. I don't approve of the way my father behaved toward you, but at the same time I understand why he acted that way, and I can sympathize. I mean, if my daughter came home with someone like you, it wouldn't matter that I was a missionary and a spokesman for God, I'd probably do just what he did and throw you out.'

'So you don't think Kit should have married me,'

Innes said.

Anne lifted her chin. 'You're the last man in Shanghai I'd want my daughter to marry, or my sister.'

'Why's that?'

'Because from what I've heard, you're your own favorite charity. You squeeze every nickel you can out of the coolies who work for you and you never give anything back to any institution or organization that would help them. You made your money destroying people by selling them opium. Some people even say that you're involved with the Green Dragon Society.'

Anne stubbed out her cigarette. She had devoured it quickly, hardly pausing between puffs. Innes rolled down the window to clear the air of smoke haze.

'Now that part's not quite accurate,' he said calmly. 'If I am involved with them, it's only because I'm on Tu's shit list. He's like everybody else, mad because I won't contribute to his favorite charity. There are a lot more beggars in Shanghai than anybody thinks, but most of them don't look the part. They're either wearing dog collars, or diamond necklaces, or sidearms. In this town everybody's got his hand out, grabbing for money he doesn't have to earn.'

'Oh,' Anne said coldly, 'so you consider that you earn your money?'

'You bet I do. I built Innes & Company out of nothing, and I'm proud of it. I started out with one small boat, and now I have a fleet of freighters. I own one tenth of the prime land in and around Shanghai, and I'm going to own more. The other taipans can afford to be generous – somebody else did the work for them, made their money, took the risks. In just a few years, I've achieved what it took them a hundred to accomplish. I'm as big as any man in this town, and I did it all myself. I didn't inherit my money from my father. My father didn't have two nickels to rub together. Nobody's ever given me a damned thing, and I don't want anything from anybody. You know why your father hates me? He came to the office one day, with his hand out, and I told him to get lost. I've been in China long enough to know that if you give a beggar a hundred cash, ninety percent of it is going to find its way into somebody else's pocket. I'm not working just so some pasty-faced missionary can live in a fancy house and wear silk neckties. I don't have time to attend charity bazaars. I'm a busy man. I don't sit on my butt and delegate authority to flunkies. I work hard, eighteen hours a day, sometimes more. Do I earn my money? You're damned right I do, lady.'

'And of course you're too busy to take a look at what you and the rest of them have done to this country, the hunger, the poverty.' Anne's voice trembled with anger.

'You can't blame us for that. The Chinese were a lot worse off before we came.'

'I could argue that point.'

'I bet you could. People like you and your old man give me a pain, Mrs Lawrence. Your solution to problems is to whine, blame somebody else, deplore the nasty business-man for every evil on this earth, and then ask him for the money to make it all better.'

'I have never been guilty of my father's kind of hypocrisy,' Anne said. 'I wouldn't take a dime of your filthy money if it meant saving every orphan in China. In my opinion the only real solution to China's ills is to throw you and the rest of the exploiters into the China Sea. Right now you're all little gods, living like bloated potentates on next to nothing: servants by the score, easy women, easy money. But it won't last. It can't. It's as fragile and as hideous as those opium dreams you peddle.'

'You'd better wake up and take a look at the real world, Mrs Lawrence,' Innes advised. 'Nobody's getting richer than the Chinese. They're not about to kill the goose.'

'A handful of corrupt compradores doesn't make a nation, Mr Innes,' she said tartly. 'You'd better read a little history: Russia in 1917, France in 1789. The aristocrats didn't turn themselves out. The people —'

'I hate to disappoint you, but the Chinese aren't going to rally around the Commies any more than they have around Chiang,' Innes said. 'You armchair revolutionar-ies are all the same. Overeducated, overprivileged, full of half-baked liberal ideas that you get out of books. You're eager to give away somebody else's money because you've never had to work a day in your life. Why don't you try

111

earning a little money of your own for a change?'

'Because earning money in China means killing people. Every dollar you earn here takes rice out of a starving child's mouth.' Even as she spoke, she knew she was wasting her breath. Men like Innes were blind to the human costs of their actions.

'Forgive my French, Mrs Lawrence, but that's a lot of sentimental bullshit. I employ a lot of people. I feed a lot of children, more than all the missions in this town put together. How many families are you supporting?'

'What? That's hardly a relevant question.'

'Oh? Just what do you think would happen to this town if we capitalists pulled out?' Innes demanded. 'You'd have panic, starvation like you've never seen before. The flow of goods and services would stop. The dance hall dollies would battle the whores for customers, and they'd put out for a lousy bowl of rice. The ricksha coolies, the waiters, the little merchants, the house servants, the pimps – they'd all starve. You know why this town is always full to the brim: because the Nationalist Government is corrupt and ineffectual and it hasn't done a damn thing for the people except tax them until they bleed. The peasants pour into Shanghai because there's a slim chance that they might find work. Just a small job that pays a few cash a day can keep a family from starving. The Chinese didn't build Shanghai; we did. Sure, people starve to death here. They freeze in the winter and they die of the heat in summer and they get ground up in the machines. I've seen the bodies in the alleys and doorways, same as you. It's too bad, but that's the way it is. But you'd see a lot more bodies if Innes & Company left Shanghai. A lot more.'

He sat back, arms folded, well fed and complacent, so sure of himself and his world, the epitome of everything she despised.

'Well, Kit obviously married the right man this time,' Anne said with a bitter laugh. She gripped the door handle. 'I won't bother to remind either of you that money isn't everything. It wouldn't do any good.'

'That's the smartest thing you've said yet,' Innes said.

The door opened and Kit climbed in. 'God, I'm glad that's over. It was hell. Give me a drink, will you, Jim?'

Innes produced a small silver flask and handed it to her. She uncorked it and took a swig.

'I'd better get back,' Anne said. 'Mother must be in a tizzy.'

'Oh, dear Dr Gil is tending to her,' Kit said, shuddering as the liquor seared her stomach. 'She'll be all right. At least I got Daddy calmed down a little. I haven't seen him that upset since — well, you know, Mouse. But it won't last.'

'No, it won't last. He worships you.' Anne hugged her. 'Goodbye, Kit. I hope you'll be happy.'

'We'll all get together soon,' Kit promised. 'Night, Mouse.'

Anne climbed out of the car. Sanjay, the Sikh chauffeur, closed the rear door and took his place behind the wheel. The Rolls glided away down the drive.

'Well, how do you like your in-laws?' Kit asked Innes.

'Let's just say I reciprocate their feelings for me,' he said dryly. 'Your sister called me a thief and a bum. She implied that I was perfect for you.'

'That's the Mouse for you,' Kit laughed. 'Painfully honest. She's never approved of me. Thinks I'm light-headed and frivolous.'

'Just the way I like my women,' Innes said. He grasped his bride's hand and squeezed it warmly. 'I guess I married the right sister.'

In front of the manse, Anne lifted her face to the sky. The misting rain felt good, clean and cool. She didn't want to go back indoors. Raindrops rattled the palm and banana fronds and whispered on the grass. The sounds of the city were muted. Foghorns echoed hollowly from the Whangpoo. A distant train whistle shrilled. An airplane motor droned overhead. She sighed and closed her eyes. The world is a very sane and sensible place when you're the only one in it.

'I just can't believe she married that man,' Anne said for the fortieth time. 'Arrogant and conceited, utterly without conscience or compassion. And the way they did it – I wouldn't expect consideration from him, but Kit knows better. She didn't have to be so secretive about it. It's

113

almost as if she set out deliberately to hurt us.'

Gilbert managed to turn a despairing moan into an elaborate yawn.

They undressed. As usual Gilbert turned his back to her. She suspected that he did it not so much from modesty or shyness, but because he didn't like the sight of her nakedness. She slipped on her nightgown, lit a stick of incense to discourage mosquitoes, and crawled under the netting.

'She must be in love with him,' she said, plumping her pillow energetically. 'It's the only reasonable explanation. She wouldn't have married him if she didn't love him.'

'For God's sake, will you stop talking about it,' Gilbert burst out impatiently. 'I'm sick to death of hearing about them. It's over, done. There isn't a thing we can do about it now.' His voice caught in his throat and he struggled to regain his composure. He saw Anne's astonished expression and mumbled, 'I'm sorry. I didn't mean to shout at you like that.'

'It's all right,' she said softly. 'I forgot how much you'd been affected by all this.' He jumped a little. 'My parents aren't easy to handle when they're upset, and I wasn't any good at all tonight. But you were so calm. I know they were grateful for your help, as I am.'

Gilbert turned off the light and climbed into the bed beside her. She still felt cold from standing out in the rain and moved close to him. He didn't put his arms around her, but lay stiffly, gazing open-eyed at the ceiling like a corpse. After a few minutes he turned over on his side, away from her.

Father Jacquinot was right. She didn't understand how something so insubstantial as a secret could have come between them, but it had. Something was wrong. Their marriage was out of joint, spastic and uncoordinated like a palsied person who would never be normal. She blamed herself. She was the deceiver, the betrayer. She tried hard to compensate for her deception, to be a good wife, but her failures were consistent and humiliating. It seemed that every time she apologized to Gilbert for her shortcomings and promised to do better, she would turn around and do something that irritated him profoundly:

she sprinkled the sink with hair combings or forgot to buy toothpaste or left soiled underwear heaped on the floor. She was slovenly in her habits, an indifferent housekeeper, much too lenient with Wu and the cook. She liked to read in bed with the lights on when Gilbert wanted to sleep, and she lay in bed until the last possible moment in the morning. When they went out together, she always made them late. Gilbert hated that most of all, but she couldn't seem to cure herself. In fact her habit of lateness was getting worse.

She wondered how other couples coped with their differences. How would Kit and Innes cope with theirs? Perhaps they were better matched, in their self-absorption and love of material comforts, than she and Gilbert. They would be happy. Anne felt a pang of envy.

She could tell by Gilbert's shallow breathing that he was wakeful, too. Was he also wondering about their marriage, and regretting it? She wished he would touch her, and knew he wouldn't. That had been her greatest disappointment and her greatest shame: he didn't find her attractive, and he didn't desire her. His perfunctory weekend performances left her feeling dissatisfied and hungry for more, but she had no right to demand more because she was such a rotten wife.

Lying next to her husband, she should have felt secure, serene, content. But instead loneliness skittered furtively around the cluttered chamber of her heart like a rat, a filthy threatening thing, difficult to trap, exposing itself only at night, when everything was quiet.

'Well, it's been quite a day.' Kit kicked off her shoes and tossed her new fur over a chair. Innes settled himself in an armchair in the corner of the bedroom and watched her undress. She did it with leisure, unself-consciously. He might have been a piece of furniture, or her husband of many years. She took off her suit jacket and unbuttoned her blouse. 'I'm exhausted.'

'I've had a pretty good day. I bought out Jack Carlyle this morning,' Innes announced with a touch of pride.

'Did you?' She unzipped her skirt and worked it down over her hips, unfastened her stockings, pulled off her slip. 'You're a fast worker. There must have been others interested. I suppose you didn't give them a chance.'

'Why should I?' He lit a cigarette and narrowed his eyes against the smoke.

'I don't suppose you're going to give me a chance either.' She unhooked her brassiere, peeled off panties and garter belt. She assumed a bold stance, her hands on her hips. 'Well, how do you like your purchase? Do I measure up to your high standards?'

He swallowed. She was perfectly formed, slim and high-breasted, tawny, lovely. 'You surpass them,' he said. 'You're beautiful.'

She shrugged and sat on the edge of the bed to remove her stockings. She lit a cigarette and tossed her head to disperse the smoke. 'You wouldn't have married me otherwise. I don't have anything else you want, not really.'

'You don't need anything else.' He stubbed out his cigarette and stood up. When he removed his jacket she saw that he was wearing a shoulder holster and a small gun under his left arm.

'Jesus. I didn't realize this was a shotgun wedding.'

'I always carry it. Have to.'

'Why?' Kit asked. He's enormous, she thought disgustedly as she watched him undress. There won't be anything left of me in the morning. Look at him, sweating like a horse. He probably thinks he's the biggest stallion in Shanghai.

'A lot of people aren't satisfied with hating me from a distance, like your father and sister,' he said. He walked around the room, turning off all the lights except the sconce near the bed. Kit lay back, waiting and watching him. In the shadows her sneer looked like an inviting smile.

He lowered himself beside her and touched her face with his calloused hand. She trembled and braced herself. It's worth it, she told herself. Even if he tears me in two, it's worth it. Just to see their faces. Especially Gilbert's. White, so white and sick. He looked like he wanted to vomit. Good for him. Good for me. He's thinking about me right now, doing this with Innes, and it's making him sick. I hate him. I hate all of them.

Innes pulled her close. She could smell the whiskey on his breath, and the cigarette smoke. She felt as if she was being squeezed in a vise, or buried under an avalanche of flesh and hair. He was massive, heavy, ready.

'Please.' She pushed against him. 'Let me go.'

Her eyes were wide. He had seen their light in so many faces: fear. She was terrified of him.

'There's nothing to be afraid of,' he said in what he thought was a soothing murmur. His voice rumbled in her ear like a bulldozer.

Inside her head she was screaming, 'No, no, no,' when he came down on her and thrust her legs apart and sank his fingers into her breasts and pressed his wide hideous mouth over hers.

What have I done? Dear God, what have I done?

Her body throbbed, her head ached. She felt as if she had bathed in filth. Next to her Innes snored contentedly.

Gone to hell in a Rolls-Royce.

Chapter Five

Innes made it a point always to be there when the *Eastern Star* set sail from the docks of Whangpoo, twelve miles down-river from Shanghai. The ship, named for the game little craft that started him on the road to fortune, was his good-luck charm, and one of twenty freighters owned by Innes & Company. These plied the China seas and the Pacific, ranging as far as Singapore and Hong Kong, Manila, Honolulu, and Nagasaki. The old *Eastern Star* had carried opium up the Yangtze to China's heartland.

Now Innes and his compradore, Sun Yu-sing, stood together on the bridge of the ship. Gleaming red letters on the twin smokestacks that towered over them spelled out INNES, as did the sides and roof of the enormous godown or warehouse whose stenciled letters were forty feet high and ended with the writhing red dragon that was the company symbol. The godown, like a busy anthill, disgorged and absorbed a stream of sweating coolies who loaded the holds of the *Eastern Star* with silk goods, bales of raw cotton, bolts of cotton cloth, tung oil, Ningpo varnish, pig bristles, and rice. The ship would sail within the hour for Port Arthur and Vladivostok, and would return in a couple of weeks with a cargo of furs, hemp, leather, and machine parts.

Sun, who despised the chill of the morning air, wore a fur-lined coat with the collar pulled up around his ears. Innes wore a rough tweed jacket and slacks. His shirt was open at the throat. The smoldering stump of a cigar lodged in the corner of his mouth.

Sun said, 'The opium is of the finest quality, I have their assurances. Benares, of course. All absolutely guaranteed.'

'No,' Innes said. 'I thought I made it clear that I want nothing more to do with opium. We don't need it and it hurts the firm's reputation.'

'Of course, I understand, my dear Innes. But I thought we might make an exception in this case. We could clear three million with no difficulty.'

'I doubt it. You'd have to pay a lot of squeeze to get that load past Customs,' Innes pointed out.

'I have taken that into consideration. But we must act quickly, my friend. The Japanese are flooding the country with opium they bring in through Manchuria. The price will go down sharply, and very soon. This may be our last opportunity to take a profit on opium.'

'Then it's an opportunity I prefer to pass up. I said no, and I meant no, Sun.'

Sun shrugged. 'As you wish.' He concealed his annoyance and began to make plans to bring in the opium without his employer's knowledge. 'I have found something I think will interest you. A jade bowl from the seventeenth century, set in a gold filigreed basket. A charming piece. The owner is strapped for cash and I think we can get it for a good price – seven thousand Mex.'

Innes had at first thought it strange to hear silver referred to in that way. But he learned that any silver dollar was called a Mex, after the coins minted of pure Mexican silver that were the only money the Chinese would accept in the early days of trade with the West. Silver was safe from the instability that undercut the Chinese dollar, and some businessmen still preferred hard currency even to the American dollar.

Innes said, 'Sounds good. Send it over this afternoon and I'll take a look at it.'

Sun nodded. 'You will be enchanted, I promise you. There is no better investment than art.'

'Yes, there is. Land.'

'Perhaps, but there is something comforting about knowing that if your land is overrun, you can at least carry some of your wealth away with you. We are in a good position in Shanghai. This Japanese aggression has inspired many Manchurians to sell their precious objects to protect them from the barbarian. Market forces prevail, prices fall. We can only benefit.'

Sun excused himself and went to talk to the foreman of the coolie stevedores. On paper the coolies were paid thirty copper cash a day; they took home fifteen. The man got five and Sun the remaining ten.

Innes remained on the bridge, enjoying the sight and sounds of his creation: Innes & Company. The outward signs of wealth were important to him. He defined himself by the structures he built. If anyone asked him, Who are you? he would reply, I am Innes & Company: shipping, manufacturing, mining, real estate.

Although he never acknowledged the debt publicly, he owed his success in large part to Sun Yu-sing. Sun was a provincial official who had been schooled in New York and Oxford and whose assignment to a cultureless backwater rankled. Eager to practice his English, and perhaps to enrich himself with a little opium-dealing among the locals, Sun offered to interpret for Innes when his trade brought him to the grubby little town of Pu-Yi just west of the Yangtze Gorges. In other circumstances Sun Yu-sing would have slept with a pig rather than consort with an ill-bred foreigner, as Innes obviously was. But he was desperate to escape slow death from boredom and poverty in Pu-Yi. At their first meeting he looked beyond Innes' rough exterior and saw a man who was brave to the point of lunacy and inordinately ambitious. Sun shared the ambition, but he was a coward who feared pain and danger and dreaded discomfort even more than death.

Sun invited the stranger to his home, dined with him, talked companionably about trade and art and the political situation in newly republican China. He treated Innes like an honored guest, an equal. Innes absorbed Sun's knowledge as a thirsty plant absorbs water. This is jadeite, this is nephrite, another variety of jade. This is Ming, this is a cheap Sung copy.

Sun's friendly overtures continued through the night. When Innes retired he found in his bed a servant girl scrubbed and perfumed and dressed up like a concubine.

From the outset Sun's attitude was at once patronizing and obsequious, exactly like that of an impoverished prince deigning to instruct a wealthy barbarian. Innes disliked and distrusted the man, but endured the insincere purring, the subtle jabs at his ignorance because he needed someone like Sun. He couldn't continue his

one-man operation forever; the dangers were considerable, and the prospects limited. He wanted to expand, but
he couldn't buy ships, hire agents, or broaden his trade
without the assistance of a compradore, go-between,
someone who knew China and spoke Chinese. Individual-
ly he and Sun could accomplish little. Brilliant but timid,
Sun would continue to waste his sweetness on the desert
air, and the intrepid Innes would go on courting adventure
and death on the Yangtze. But together, they could own
half of China.

Sun wanted no official partnership, only, he said, the
opportunity to serve his friend. When Innes sailed for
Shanghai for the last time in the rusty *Eastern Star*, Sun
went with him. The boat carried a cargo of objets d'art,
cases of Western and Chinese books, and Sun's family: his
mother and grandfather, his wife, his small daughter
Ai-ling, and three concubines, including Innes', who
regarded the change in her status with amazement and
despair.

Sun Yu-sing shared in Innes' success without exposing
himself to the glare of publicity and its attendant dangers.
Innes had a knack for generating capital and applying it to
unlikely but astoundingly profitable ventures. In the
mid-'20s he used all his new capital to buy acres of mud
flats which the burgeoning city of Shanghai swallowed up
a few years later, when it experienced the greatest spurt of
growth and prosperity in its history. Sun's hand guided
and smoothed every transaction and removed every
obstacle to success, even the noisome demands of Tu
Yueh-sen, the kingpin of the Green Dragon Society, who
extracted exorbitant sums of protection money from every
taipan in Shanghai, except Innes.

Eventually Innes gave up his dealings in opium. Under
Chiang Kai-shek the government began to close in on
poppy growers and traders and to prosecute opium
smokers. The interference of an officious bureaucracy
could easily have been discouraged by some discreetly
placed bribes, but Innes decided that the profits from
opium no longer outweighed the risks of handling it.
There was also the social stigma attached to open trading
in opium. This hurt Innes & Company's relations with the

Christians in the business community, particularly the all-important British bankers, who had conveniently forgotten the origins of their own wealth. Innes had never concerned himself with the moral implications or the human consequences of his trade, merely with the profit picture. Opium had served its purpose. It had enriched him, raised him above the faceless herd, given him power. He had tried the Foreign Smoke once, out of curiosity. Its effect on him had been negligible, less than a bottle of bad scotch. He had had no dreams, no visions, only troubled sleep and nausea upon awakening. He couldn't understand what the fuss was about.

He had it all, the whole corrupt and unlovely city of Shanghai at his feet, great wealth, grudging respect even from the people who hated him. His company was growing fast. He owned miles of valuable real estate, a fleet of ships, an oil refinery, and shares in some of the richest companies in the East. His marriage to Kit Fox was the icing on the cake, or so everyone told him. She was the most beautiful and coveted woman in Shanghai, a prize worthy of a merchant prince. She added credibility to his stature as leading citizen. The fact that she had divorced Richard Matthews, heir to one of the great fortunes in the Far East, only added luster to Innes' kingly image.

He shivered a little in the damp air and experienced a fleeting longing for the freedoms and the simple physical pleasures and dangers of his old opium-running days. The dangers that swirled around him now were too vague and nebulous to fight. He thought about Kit, and he felt an old horror creeping over him, the horror of nothingness, of being nobody, insignificant and unimportant, impotent.

What men could not do with guns or bombs or clever plots, Kit could achieve with a laugh: she could remind him that he was a charlatan, a mountebank, a poseur. Nothing.

Sanjay, his Sikh chauffeur-bodyguard, drove him back to his offices on the Bund where he remained long after the phones had stopped ringing and his staff had gone. Finally, reluctantly, he went home to his marble palace on the Avenue Joffre.

He had bought the house to please Kit, and he felt

gratified when she professed to admire it. Later he overheard her telling one of her friends that she really hadn't expected to spend her married life in a mausoleum. He gave her permission to redecorate, and squads of workmen descended on the place. They stripped away all the shining ormolu that he liked because he associated it with the homes of the very rich, painted out the watery imitations of Fragonard and Boucher on the ceilings, ripped out the mahogany paneling and the leaded glass windows and painted all the dark woodwork her favorite shade of celadon green. The exterior of the house was still ornate and impressive, with fat columns supporting a high portico. There wasn't much she could do to change that. But inside, the house looked clean and modern and, to his eye, plain and impoverished. He hated it.

He handed his briefcase and topcoat over to a sullen houseboy. 'Missee home?'

The boy jerked his head toward the drawing room. A burst of laughter confirmed his gesture. Innes went in. Kit and her friends sprawled on green velvet sofas, their fingers entwined around the slender stems of cocktail glasses. When they saw him, their laughter faded abruptly.

'Ah, the empire builder returns,' Kit drawled. She wore green silk lounging pajamas. Her legs were tucked under her and she didn't rise to greet him. 'Have a drink, Jim. I think I've finally taught that idiot Ting how to make a decent martini.'

'I'll get it for you, old boy,' said her friend Binky helpfully. He shambled over to the bar in the corner.

Innes stood awkwardly in the middle of the room. He glowered at Kit, who ignored him. Binky handed him a tiny glass filled with colorless liquid. An olive in the bottom turned a sightless eye up to him. Innes scowled at it. A girl called Bootsie gave a shrill whoop of laughter, then stifled it quickly by covering her mouth with an audible slap. Her face reddened, and a chorus of muffled sniggers joined her little peeps of irrepressible laughter. Innes didn't move, but Kit discerned a tiny tic on the left side of his face, the first warning of a coming explosion.

'I'm going to throw you all out now,' she said brightly.

Ordinarily she wouldn't have minded a scene, but she needed his cooperation tonight and had to keep him sweet. 'We're attending a very important dinner party and we can't be late. Run along like good children.' She offered her cheek to be kissed and shepherded her party toward the entrance hall. When she came back into the drawing room Innes was still standing where she left him. As she watched, he closed his fist around the martini glass. Gin dribbled through his fingers. He opened his hand and tiny shards of glass fell to the carpet with a tinkle. His leathery palm was unscathed.

'Run up and change, will you, Jim?' Kit said, ignoring the display. He wanted to let her know that he could crush her like that anytime he wanted to. But she wouldn't acknowledge that she knew it, and she wouldn't show fear. 'Anne and Gil are expecting us at eight-thirty.'

'I don't feel like going out,' he said.

'And I don't feel like going alone.' Smiling, she strolled over to him. 'Don't be a stick, darling. You don't want to give the Mouse the satisfaction of being able to say that you think you're too good to visit a missionary's humble home. Besides, I want you to come. Please?' she cooed, touching his chin with her fingertip. 'As a favor. I'll be good tonight, I promise.'

'Liar.'

She had humiliated him too many times, repelling his advances, pleading headache or stomachache, or yielding to him so passionlessly and unenthusiastically that he lost all desire for her. Yet whenever she offered herself, because she wanted something from him, he took her, even though he knew he was a fool for giving in to her blackmail.

Bullying, cajolery, pleading, threats – he had tried them all, without success. She despised him, and she always had. Why then had she married him? He asked himself the question ten times a day. Yes, she liked spending his money, but there were other rich men in Shanghai who would gladly have paid her bills. Why?

She did keep one promise: she forced Shanghai society to accept him. At first his reception was frigid, but when the taipans became aware that the enemy had a face, they also perceived that he lacked horns and a tail. He was more well-spoken and intelligent than they had expected him to be. And of course he was a proven money-maker. Obviously a man worth cultivating. He breached the portals of the Shanghai Club as a guest of several of the members, and he drank at the famous bar, reputedly the longest in the world. Die-hard foes like Arthur Weston and Leonard Fox kept the membership rolls closed to him, of course, but he had no doubt that even their resistance to him would vanish someday, with Kit's help.

The ladies were more easily won. At first they tolerated him for Kit's sake. But they soon found themselves succumbing to his easy charm and rough-hewn good looks. A few of Kit's friends even pronounced him to be madly attractive.

'I'm not lying,' Kit pouted a little. 'I mean it. When we get home tonight —'

'Now,' he said. 'Payment in advance, or no deal.'

Her eyes snapped with anger but her smile never wavered. 'But there's no time, darling,' she protested.

'We'll make time.' He pushed her down on the couch and pulled down her pajama bottoms. She shuddered and closed her eyes. The assault was mercifully short, and afterward they went up to their separate bedrooms to change. She deliberately didn't bathe herself, and when they arrived at the Lawrence apartment an hour later, the musky odor of his sex still clung to her. Gilbert smelled it as he helped her off with her fur.

Gilbert knew very well that it was physically impossible to die of shame. Certainly strong emotion could precipitate a stroke or a coronary, but the state of being ashamed or embarrassed never killed anyone. Yet the flush never left his cheeks. Kit remarked on it, and he was forced to complain about the heat and open a window, admitting a blast of damp, chill air. Once he excused himself from the table and fled to the bathroom, where he took a sleeping pill in the hopes that it would calm him. He wished he could hide there all night.

When he came back to the table, Kit was complimenting Anne on the food.

'Your cook is an absolute dream, Mouse. If you don't guard him carefully, I'll steal him away from you.'

Anne smiled. 'I'll tell him you liked it.'

The food had been terrible. Gilbert hated Kit for praising it, especially after she had left half the items on her plate untouched. At least the china matched. Borrowed from a neighbor. But the silver was the usual collection of odds and ends picked up at secondhand stores. The linens were threadbare, worn out with use and laundering, as thin as cambric. His glass was cracked. He kept his hand wrapped around the break so that Kit wouldn't notice.

They adjourned to the living room to sip coffee from an ill-assorted set of chipped cups. Gilbert saw again, with painful clarity, the stained ocher walls, the sagging chairs, the badly fitted slipcovers, the hideous carpet. Anne's arrangement of roses on the end table looked worn out by its efforts to bring beauty to the place.

Anne poured coffee, spilling a little onto her lap. Gilbert bit back the admonishment he would have given her had they been alone. No, she couldn't be careful, because she simply didn't care how she looked. Her pink and black dress had been beautiful when it was new, but now the thin wool was stretched and pilled, and the shadows of too many hastily eaten lunches at school lurked in the folds of the skirt. She was hopeless. He couldn't bear to look at her, but he knew that if he looked at Kit he would see mockery in her eyes, perhaps even pity.

'Gilbert, would you give this to Kit, please?'

Their fingers touched as he handed Kit the coffee cup. He looked away and saw Innes gazing into the blue smoke from his cigarette. He hadn't said much all evening. Probably plotting his next million-dollar coup, Gilbert thought angrily. And Kit, what was she plotting? A new romance, a new car, a cruise? She had all Innes' filthy money at her disposal. He wondered if she earned it, and tortured himself briefly by imagining them together, making love. A lump like a sob rose in his throat, and he coughed noisily.

'That air is too much for you,' Anne said. 'I'll close the

window.'

'Oh, this is so cozy,' Kit said, wriggling deeper into the sofa cushions.

'It's only temporary,' Gilbert said. 'We didn't know how long we would be here. As it is, we're away most of the day.'

'If you hadn't made yourself invaluable to Uncle Billy and his pet hospital, you'd be out of here by now,' Kit told him. 'Can't you persuade Gil to lose one of his patients, Anne?'

'He's too good a doctor,' Anne said proudly. 'He couldn't do that even if he wanted to.'

'How's the Chinese coming, Gilbert? Are you fluent in six dialects yet?'

Gilbert flushed, and Anne said, 'He's studying privately with Dr Sung at Aurora now. I'm afraid I wasn't a very good tutor.'

'You were fine,' Gilbert said sharply. 'It's just that —'

'I understand,' Kit said warmly. 'It's hard for married people to teach each other anything.' She flashed a look at Innes, who either ignored her or didn't hear. 'You're simply too close, and you tend to take correction personally. Anne, this coffee is delicious.'

'Would you like another cup?'

Gilbert winced. The coffee had been vile, like everything else.

'Oh, no, thank you. Are you still nursing?'

Anne shot an anxious look at Gilbert. 'No. I found I couldn't do it. I did miserably on my six-weeks exams. Luckily I got my teaching job back. My replacement didn't work out. The nuns welcomed me with open arms.'

'Awful hard work, nursing,' Kit said sympathetically.

'It wasn't that. It was the people. Sick and in pain, and I felt so helpless.'

'The whole point of training for nursing or any medical career is to become helpful,' Gilbert said. 'You could have stuck it out. Silly sentimentalism.'

'I couldn't bear it,' Anne said softly. 'I wanted to help them all, to take their suffering away, and when they died —' She chewed her lip and studied her hands. Gilbert's cup rattled on his saucer. The odor of stale, unsettled

127

argument hung in the air.

'I'm with you, Mouse,' Kit shivered. 'I couldn't take it, even for a day.'

The talk was desultory, boring. Gilbert wondered why the Inneses didn't just get up and leave. Kit told an amusing story about lunching with both the German and Japanese ambassadors, and Anne told a dull one about a prank played on her by the girls in her senior English class. The evening wore on. Gilbert didn't even try to stifle a yawn. Perhaps his in-laws would take the hint and go home.

'You didn't grow these roses, did you?' Kit asked. Anne admitted she had. 'Still trying, aren't you! I think it's marvelous of you. Listen, why don't you take Jim out to show him your rose garden. I'm sure he'd love to see it.'

'What?' Innes looked up, startled.

'Go on, darling. I want to ask Gilbert something medical, personal. You know, female complaints.' She smiled sweetly. She was always nice to him in public. One of the games she played.

'Would you like to see them? The roses?' Anne asked, awkwardly extending the invitation in a more formal manner.

Innes hauled himself out of his chair and followed Anne out through the kitchen to the tiny yard at the back of the house. Gilbert watched them go with trepidation.

'What was that all about?' he asked, facing her squarely for the first time. Her gown was teal blue with tiny capped sleeves, gathered into a bunch at the side and fixed with a green silk flower. He had to look away. He couldn't bear her beauty. 'You're not ill, are you?' His tone was gruff.

She laughed. 'My, you're full of concern. No, not ill. My periods have been frighteningly irregular, though. Why do you think that is?'

His cheeks darkened. 'Why don't you ask your own doctor? I'm really not in a position to make a diagnosis.'

'He's out of town.'

Gilbert shrugged. 'You can't expect your body to keep perfect time if your own schedule is erratic. Maybe you're pregnant.'

'I doubt it. I had an abortion last week in Nanking.'

'Nanking,' he said stupidly.

'Why not? It makes a nice break. But maybe you would have done it yourself? Would you, Gil? As a favor to an old friend?' She sucked on her cigarette thoughtfully. 'I was really annoyed with myself. I generally take precautions, but Innes is so unpredictable. Some day his impulsiveness is going to get him into trouble. Still, he knows what he wants and goes after it, I'll say that much for him. He's like me in that respect.'

'Does he know?' Gilbert was appalled. Nice women didn't discuss abortions, much less have them.

'Why? Do you think it's your duty to tell him? Go ahead, I don't care. If he wanted kids he should have married someone else. I am definitely not the mothering kind. Anne is, though. I'm surprised you two haven't started a family yet.'

Gilbert murmured something noncommittal about being busy and there being plenty of time. He couldn't take his eyes off her now. A missionary's daughter, he thought incredulously. But wild and savage, as untouched by her exposure to Christianity as a cannibal. He was horrified, and fascinated.

'I can't believe she's still brooding about that baby of hers after eight years,' Kit remarked. 'It was a terrible trauma for her, I know. Poor sensitive soul. But honestly, lots of women have babies they can't keep. She certainly got a lot of mileage out of hers. Is she still being boring about it after all this time? You shouldn't let her get away with it, Gilbert. Be firm.'

'What are you talking about?'

'Oh, that business in Switzerland,' Kit said. 'You know. I suppose she's still brooding over it. The way she carried on – complete with nervous breakdown. It's probably just as well she gave up nursing. Just too sensitive and unstable, poor thing.'

'I don't know what you're talking about,' Gilbert said wonderingly.

'Oh, Gilbert, you don't have to hide anything from me. I'm her sister, remember? But you don't mean —' Kit sat up straighter. Her eyes were wide. 'Surely she told you!'

'Of course she did.' Gilbert spoke quickly, without

129

conviction.

Kit went on, taking no notice of his discomfiture. 'She still resents Daddy for interfering. But what could he do? My dear, a Chinese! If there's anything Shanghai doesn't need, it's another mixed-breed bastard. And look what Chen has become – a Communist. The Butcher of Shanghai.' She took her compact out of her purse and touched some powder to her nose.

'Chinese,' Gilbert said. 'Communist.'

'I never saw him, of course,' Kit said, getting out her lipstick. 'I was still a kid when she went to Paris on a music scholarship from the Shanghai Jaycees. Her violin teacher, Olga Kerensky, got a letter from her telling all, and Olga ran straight to Daddy to let him know that Anne was planning to marry a Chinese. He hopped the next train across Siberia – boiling mad, as you can imagine. Wrenched the poor girl out of the yellow man's arms and put her in a nursing home in Switzerland and made her give the baby up. She was simply devastated, of course. But you know Anne: she can be more devastated than anyone. She had a complete breakdown after the baby was born. They had to put her away for a year in a Swiss sanitarium. She made a big show of never touching her violin again. She wanted to punish us for not taking Chen and the babe unto our Christian bosoms. She could still play if she wanted to, but perhaps we should be grateful. She made a god-awful racket. You ought to be glad she gave up music before you came along.'

'Oh, I don't know,' Gilbert said, grasping at the feeble straw of fact while he floundered in a sea of bewilderment. 'I'm rather fond of music.'

'But you won't let her get away with such infantile behavior, Gilbert.' She applied lipstick and snapped her compact shut. 'I know you. You'll take control. She needs a strong man.' She smiled warmly, but her eyes were bright with mischief. Gilbert squirmed. His cheeks burned. 'You're a little flushed, Gilbert,' Kit said in a voice like velvet. 'It must be getting warm in here again.'

He wanted to die. He knew he was a fool, and now she had exposed him as a dupe as well.

'Not that you're interested, but the roses are over there.' Anne gestured vaguely and sat down on a discarded packing case under the kitchen window. 'Do you have a cigarette, Mr Innes?'

'Sure.' His lighter flared, briefly illuminating the scruffy little yard behind the apartment. 'Nice flowers,' he said, casting a look over his shoulder.

She made a face. 'Don't bother. It was good of you to play along with Kit's obscure little game.'

'I've learned that playing along is easier than arguing,' he said, lighting his own cigarette.

'How long do you suppose she wants us out of the way while she picks Gilbert's brains?'

'Why, am I boring you?'

She grunted. 'The other way around, I should think. We're not exactly in your league, socially.'

'I don't have a league,' Innes said. 'I leave that stuff to Kit. She gets a kick out of it. You don't seem to like it much. You didn't stick around our housewarming party very long.'

Anne remembered that party. Kit's admirers and sycophants rubbed up against overfed leaders of the business community. A dance band played appropriate music, loud and passionless. Servants carried trays of drinks and hors d'oeuvres circulated while fifty starving Chinese – not professional beggars – clamored at the iron gates on the Avenue Joffre. The sight of so much waste and sumptuousness sickened her, and she and Gilbert left soon after arriving.

She said, 'I'm sorry. I suppose we hurt her feelings by running out like that, but we weren't really enjoying ourselves.'

'Don't worry about Kit. She didn't even notice that you weren't there anymore. Not that she would have cared. Too decadent for you, huh?' he grinned.

'Yes, Mr Innes,' she said. 'A bit too decadent. I was surprised that she invited us at all. She knows how I feel.'

'Oh, that was my idea. Since you're the only members of the family she's on speaking terms with, I thought you ought to be there.'

'I'm afraid I can't appreciate your consideration,' she

said. 'I think you just invited me because you knew I'd hate it. It was your idea of a joke, like inviting a cripple to a ball. Very funny.' She felt a flush of anger.

'Good for you to see how the other half lives,' Innes said unrepentantly. 'Hard work pays off.'

'So does stealing, until you get caught.'

'There you go, calling me a thief and a bum again,' he said, shaking his head. 'I don't think I like it.'

'You will forgive me, but I don't care if you like it or not. It's the truth.' She stood up. 'Do you think it's time to go in yet?'

'What's the rush? Afraid I'll talk you out of your half-baked radical ideas?' He lounged against the wall of the house and crossed his arms. 'The best way to keep from losing an argument is not to start one.'

Anne pulled herself up. 'No, Mr Innes, I am not afraid of losing an argument to you. I'm just tired of fighting you and all the other Inneses in Shanghai. It doesn't do any good. I couldn't persuade you to start paying your coolies more. You'd tell me that rich men don't stay rich by giving it away, and that the poor devils would only spend their extra money on opium dreams, which would make them unfit for work at all. It's sickening and wrong but it's been this way for a hundred years. I can't hope to change it, so I'd better just keep my mouth shut.'

'You'll never do it,' he laughed. 'Preaching's in your blood. Cheer up. Not everybody's as stubborn and selfish as I am. You'll make a convert or two before you die.'

'Thank you for those encouraging words, but I am not in the business of converting people. All I can do is speak out when I see something wrong. I'm not a missionary.'

'You do a pretty good imitation of one. They all hate my guts, and so do you.'

Anne frowned. 'Hate you? No. Oddly enough I don't hate you. I hate and despise your money and the way you make it, but for some reason I can't condemn you. I leave condemnation to people like my father, who's like all the other missionaries I've ever known: single-minded and absolutely convinced of the rightness of what he's doing. How can I hate you? I don't know anything about you. I don't know who you are or where you come from or what makes you act as you do. I don't know how I'd act if I were in your place. What would I be like if I had all the money and power in the world?' She shook her head. 'I can't even imagine it. To have anything I want, and the power to build up and to tear down and to rule men's lives – It's probably nothing like I think, is it?'

'It's slippery,' Innes said. 'When you're at the top of the heap, there are always a lot of characters grabbing for your ankles, trying to pull you down.'

'How do you get rid of them?' Anne asked.

'Kick their teeth in,' he said cheerfully. 'How else?'

'You like it, don't you?' She looked at him curiously. 'You like the fighting, the surviving. It's all part of the fun, getting there, staying on top. You really were an opium runner, weren't you?'

'One of the best, which means one of the craziest. I had a power launch, the *Eastern Star*. She was a good little boat, even though half the time I had to hold the engine together with string and chewing gum. I took her up and down the Yangtze a thousand times. I got to know that river pretty well. A river is like a female, the biggest dangers are the ones you don't see: the sandbars, the rocks, the trees that will tear the bottom right out of you. The rapids. Have you seen the Yangtze in flood time?' Anne nodded. 'We rode right over the banks, over farms and villages, Corpses would bump up against the hull. Men. Animals. Kids.'

'All that, just to sell poison,' Anne said.

'Someone else would have done it if I hadn't.'

'I suppose you needed to tell yourself that, to justify what you were doing.' Anne flipped her cigarette away.

'I didn't need any justification,' Innes said. 'I did it because I had to, because opium is still the quickest way to make a fortune in China. It's all there, for the taking, for any man who has the guts to do it. And when you have that fortune, there's nobody who can take it away from you, unless you're fool enough to let them have it, and I've already told you, I don't give to charity. The people want opium. The missionaries can't change that. The government won't – they'd lose millions in squeeze.'

He dropped his cigarette and smeared it out with his

133

toe. He opened his flat gold cigarette case and offered it to Anne, who took one. They smoked in silence for a while.

Innes chuckled. 'I was just remembering how I bargained with the buyers. I did it all myself, without any go-between, without speaking a word of Chinese. I kept a twelve-bore shotgun cradled in my lap, and I shook my head. If I shook my head long enough, they'd meet my price. I sold opium to bandit chieftains and officers in the Nationalist Army and to mandarins. Strictly cash. I turned down everything else, even things worth ten times the opium their owners wanted to buy. I was pretty ignorant in those days.'

Anne said, 'I was remembering one of the up-country missions where I grew up. A man came begging one day. He'd been a farmer, and he lost everything he had because of opium. He sold his possessions, his children, and finally his land, just like the men in our 'Evils of Opium' tracts. He was as withered and brown as a stick. My mother gave him some food, but he didn't eat it, even though he was starving to death. He died that night, outside our door. The next day the local warlord rode in to pay a call. He was as pink and bloated as the farmer had been thin and wasted. My father was rude to him. It was the first time I'd seen him be rude to anyone. The man got angry, made a few threats probably, and went away. Afterward I asked Father why he had been mean to a guest, and he said it was because the warlord ordered the farmers to plow under their wheat and plant poppies. The poppy fields were so beautiful in the springtime. So fragrant. The flowers looked like any other flowers, nodding innocently in the breeze. Then the lancers would come and cut the seed heads and workers would collect the milky gum that oozed out. You could see it drying in the sun on the rooftops, becoming opium. Becoming death.'

Innes said, 'Not everybody who smokes gets addicted. Not every addict dies. I did some rum-running in the early days of Prohibition, and I didn't worry about making alcoholics out of my customers. The man in the marketplace gives the public what it wants. How wisely they handle the merchandise is their business.'

'That's ridiculous. You wouldn't put guns in the hands of children. Opium is just as lethal. You just don't want to look at the consequences of what you're doing.'

'I'm not doing anything now. I haven't handled opium in years.'

'That doesn't exonerate you for what you did in the past. And you're not even sorry!'

'Sorry is for little kids who don't want to get their asses whipped anymore. I'm not sorry for anything I've done. Why should I be? There are plenty of missionaries around, spreading the sorry as thick as the shit on the honey boats. They're like you. They want me to be sorry for drinking liquor, sorry for smoking tobacco, sorry for screwing pretty women.' He grinned broadly. 'You're all wasting your time. I'm sure as hell not sorry for that, and neither are the women.'

Anne snorted disgustedly. 'Now you're just trying to shock me. Believe me, I could care less about your vices.'

At the bright sound of Kit's laughter their heads turned. 'I suppose we can go in now,' Anne said. 'Even Kit can't possibly find medicine that amusing.'

He followed her through the back door. Inside the kitchen she stopped and faced him. 'Mr Innes, I'm going to be brazen enough to ask for a favor. It's not for myself,' she explained quickly.

'Oh, in that case I'll consider it,' he said. 'As long as there's nothing immoral or illegal about it.'

She gave him an exasperated look, but went on. 'One of the girls I used to teach, Josepha Chang, is having a hard time finding a decent job. I'll tell you right off that she's not brilliant and her English isn't as good as it should be, but she can do some typing and maybe answer the telephone. I wouldn't ask, except she's rather special, and I don't want her to end up like so many of them do, in the dance halls or bars. If you know of anything —'

'Sure. Send her over tomorrow. I'll tell my man in personnel to find her something.'

'Thank you.' She looked embarrassed.

Innes said, 'You're going to have to revise your opinion of me, Mrs Lawrence. I may be a thief, but I'm not a bum.'

'That remains to be seen,' Anne said.

As soon as Kit and Innes left the house, Gilbert's fury exploded.

'Why didn't you tell me you'd had a baby? And by a Chinese! My God, what a fool you've made of me.'

The strength left Anne's legs and she sat down quickly. 'Did Kit tell you that? I can't believe it. Why? Why would she do it?'

'Are you saying it's not true?'

'Of course it's true. I would have told you —'

'When, in another twenty years? My God.' He couldn't stand to look at her cow eyes and awkwardly splayed limbs. He turned his back to her and shoved his hands into his pockets.

'I don't know why it's so important,' she said softly. 'It all happened so long ago.' But she knew it was important. Father Jacquinot was right. It would destroy them.

'You deceived me. You lied to me. Your whole family deceived me. If Kit hadn't told me, I might never have known. Don't I have a right to know what kind of person you are? You were too ashamed —'

'That's not true. I'm not ashamed. I loved him and I was proud to have his child and they had no right to take it away from me. No right.' Two crimson patches appeared on her cheeks.

'A mixed-breed bastard,' Gilbert hissed.

'Don't you dare call her that!' Anne cried.

'A Chinese! How could you! A heathen barbarian.'

'He wasn't. He was more civilized than you are. How dare you preach to me!' Her anger rose within her, pushing her out of her chair, drawing her fists into knots, drawing her into herself. 'He was fine and good and I will not apologize for what happened, to you or anyone else.'

'He was filth! Chinese filth!'

She stared. 'You hate them. All of them. You do!'

'Yes, I hate them,' he spat out. 'They're horrible, animals. And you – you're no better than they are. Your father should have let you marry him. You would have been perfectly happy, living in a hole like this, eating worms with sticks, drinking the swill they call tea. You don't know how to act, how to dress, how to be human. You're deceitful and sly. You — you tricked me!' She marveled at how in his great anger he managed to keep his voice at a conversational level. But of course, he didn't want the neighbors to overhear. 'And the sanitarium. You didn't tell me about that, either. You didn't think it was important that you were a mental patient. Did you think I wouldn't care about that?'

'It was all wrong. I didn't belong there. They had no right to shut me up like that. They said I was being unreasonable, irrational. What did they expect when they took my child from me?' She put her hands on her head, feeling again the infuriating helplessness, the horror of being shut away from the world.

'They had every right!' He whirled on her angrily. 'I only regret that they let you out. You don't belong in the real world, with the rest of us. You have the morals of a cat, the soul of a — a —' He groped for a word.

'Not the soul of a Christian,' she said tightly, 'full of hate and spite. You're like all the rest. A hypocrite. You're like my father. You only care about showing the world what a good man you are. The show, that's what's really important to you, isn't it? But you don't care about anyone, because your soul is too mean and small.'

They glared at each other. 'I won't forget this,' Gilbert said.

'You mean you won't forgive. I'm not surprised,' Anne said. 'You don't have it in you to love or forgive. You never loved me, did you? Why did you marry me?'

'I wish to heaven I knew.'

She got a light coat out of the closet in the foyer and left the house. Gilbert's eyes fastened on her vase of roses. He picked it up and hurled it through the open window, into the night.

Kit sat at her dressing table and filed her nails. Innes came into the room without knocking. She knew his step and didn't look up.

'What do you want?'

'You know what I want.'

'You've already had it once today. Isn't that enough?

I'm not in the mood tonight.'

'You never are.' He stood behind her. Their eyes met in her mirror. 'Why did you marry me?' he asked.

'I wish to hell I knew. Why, do you want a divorce?'

'No. I was just curious. You didn't even know me.'

'I knew your reputation. That was enough.'

He put his enormous hand around her neck. His fingers almost completely encircled it. She didn't move.

'You'd like to crush me like you crushed that glass, wouldn't you?' she said with a smile. 'Go ahead. I won't scream.'

'You really wouldn't care, would you?'

'Not for long.'

He dragged her to the bed. Eyes closed, she lay motionless under him. She had learned that resistance only excited him, and made her a participant in a sexual contest in which he had to be the victor. But if she refused to play along there was no contest, only a one-sided display of virility in front of a bored audience.

Her body might have been filled with ice water. His member shrank inside her.

'Might as well try and screw a goddamned statue,' he said disgustedly. A shadow of a smile appeared on her lips but she didn't open her eyes. Rage supplanted passion, and he shook her. 'Why, damn you?' he rasped. 'Why!'

Her eyes opened. They were clear, dry of tears, burning with anger. 'Because I hate you. I hate the sight of you. Now get out of here and leave me the hell alone.'

The air-conditioned lobby of the Innes Building felt like a cooling bath after the thick humidity outside. Innes tossed the stump of his cigar into an ashtray and headed toward the bank of elevators. He stopped short. Kit was waiting there, too. She wore a dark red dress with a shawl of the same fabric. Fingers of black silk fringe beckoned him. He came up behind her and grabbed her arm, his fingers digging into the soft flesh above her elbow.

'If you're looking for me —'

She turned, startled. He dropped his hand and his mouth fell open. The eyes that looked into his were wide and brown, but smooth-lidded, epicanthic. Chinese eyes.

'I'm sorry,' he said. 'I thought you were someone else.'

She smiled diffidently and dipped her head. The elevator doors slid open in front of them and they stepped inside. He nodded to the liveried elevator operator. The girl murmured, 'Twelve floor, please.' His office was on the twelfth floor.

She kept her eyes lowered and didn't notice that he was staring at her in amazement. The resemblance between her and Kit was really remarkable. They were the same size, the same build, with slender hands, small feet, crisp dark hair. The Chinese girl wore hers cut close to her head, with long bangs that barely covered the arched brows over her dark eyes. The shape of her face was like Kit's, oval, with a little point at the chin.

He stood aside to let her get off first, and followed. He said, 'I think I hurt you back there. I'm sorry.' She smiled and shook her head. 'I did. What's your name?'

'My name is Josepha Chang, tuan,' she said in a small breathy voice that he had to strain to hear. She was self-conscious about her English, and spoke it slowly, with studied deliberateness.

'I'm Innes,' he said. Chang? Oh, yes, the girl Anne Lawrence had sent over. The mission girl.

'Yes, tuan, I know,' she whispered, not daring to raise her eyes. She used the old form of respectful address, tuan, which meant 'white man.'

'What kind of job did they find for you?'

'I am filing, please. In the department of manifestos.' Cargo manifests, shipping department, his mind clicked.

'How do you like it?'

'I like very much, please. Nice job. Missee Anne say you very nice man, give me job. Thank you, tuan. Thank you.'

'It's all right,' he said gruffly. 'See that you do your work well, and you'll always have a job.'

She looked up, her large eyes bright with tears of shyness and fear and joy. 'Yes, tuan, I will work very hard. Thank you, tuan. Thank you.' She backed away a step or two, bowed, and then broke into a run. He looked after her and smiled. She was a pretty little thing, as fragile and delicate as porcelain. He should have known

139

she wasn't Kit. Whenever he held Kit he could feel the steel under her flesh. But this girl felt as though he could break her with one twist of his wrist.

Innes saw Josepha again a week later, in the corridor outside his offices as he was on his way to lunch. She wore the same red dress and fringed shawl, and her bobbed hair was capped by a pert red beret. She carried a tiny black purse. He asked how she was getting along, and she answered shyly, and smiled at him. She seemed less terrified of him.

The doorman performed with a flourish and they stepped out onto the Bund. They strolled toward Nanking Road, Sanjay following discreetly.

Innes said, 'Miss Chang, I still feel bad about hurting you that day. It would please me if you would let me make it up to you somehow. May I buy you lunch?'

She said quickly, 'Oh, no, no, tuan, is not necessary. You did not hurt me, not at all. I cannot —'

'Of course you can,' he said firmly, tucking her tiny hand under his arm. She gasped and tried to pull away, but he held her firmly. 'One lunch isn't going to upset the balance of employer-employee relationships, is it? You have to eat, and so do I. We might as well keep each other company.'

He took her to the St. Petersburg, the Russian restaurant owned by his friend Sasha Chernov, an émigré pauper who enhanced his image by posing as a nephew of the assassinated Czar. Josepha's eyes widened when she saw the lush interior, even gaudier and more opulent than the private offices at Innes & Company. She drank champagne and liked the taste. She nibbled a bit of caviar on a piece of bread and made a face, but would have eaten it anyway – lest she offend her host – if Innes hadn't laughed and taken it away from her. Waiters brought in shashlik on flaming swords. Josepha laughed delightedly and clapped her hands. Innes smiled indulgently, and he and Sasha exchanged glances and approving nods.

He said, 'Mrs Lawrence thinks very highly of you, Miss Chang.'

She looked puzzled, then her brow cleared. 'Ah, yes, Missee Anne. She very nice lady, very good friend. She give me this dress. Red is color for good fortune.' The dress was more stylish than anything Anne ever bought for herself.

'It was good fortune that brought you to work for my company,' Innes said. Josepha murmured a demurral and looked down at her hands. 'I have a lot to thank Mrs Lawrence for. I mean, Missee Anne.'

'I also have much to thank her for,' Josepha said softly. 'She buy me from brothel keeper. I run away from him, and she hide me, and when he find me, she pay him twenty dollah. I will pay back, when I earn enough. This will take two months, maybe more.'

Innes resisted the temptation to reach into his wallet and pull out a twenty. He asked, 'And what will you do with the rest of your money? Do you have a boyfriend?'

'Oh, no, tuan.' She looked up. Her expression was serious. 'I will send to my father, in north. My family is very poor, and he will be happy for much money.'

'Much money makes us all happy. But if he was such a nice guy, how did you end up in a brothel?'

'He sell me,' she said without rancor. 'Family have no money, no food.' A man from Shanghai had come and liked her, she said, brought her to Shanghai to be a singsong girl. But the brothel keeper liked her too, and bought her.

Josepha was one of the lucky ones. Singsong girls entertained in private clubs and restaurants. Many died of beatings, and disease. Most were sold to brothels. Only a few achieved the pinnacle of the singsong girls' ambition and became the concubines of rich Chinese.

'I tell you what, Josepha,' Innes said, throwing down his napkin. 'It's such a beautiful day. Too beautiful to stay indoors in a stuffy office. Let's take the rest of the afternoon off. We can go for a ride in my car, or we can take the sight-seeing boat down the Whangpoo. Would you like that?'

She protested, and he quickly allayed her anxieties by reminding her that he was the owner of Innes & Company. He had a right to make reasonable demands of his employees, and he could certainly explain her absence to her superiors. They took the sight-seeing steamer down to Woosung, where the Whangpoo poured into the mighty Yangtze. They sat in a private cabin and sipped tea while they watched the traffic on the river, and Innes regaled her with tales of his own days as a river man. He pointed out two freighters tied up at the docks and he told her about the first *Eastern Star*. She was impressed, as much by his kindness as by his wealth, which seemed boundless and magnificent.

They had cocktails at the Trocadero, and dinner at a fine French restaurant on the Avenue Dubail, only a few blocks from the Innes mansion. She began to feel tired, but tried not to let it show. Innes suggested that they go dancing, and since he was her host – and she only a lowly female – she agreed enthusiastically. They whirled to a Filipino dance band at Ciro's, and to an American Negro jazz band at Marty's near the Quai de Français. Finally he whisked her over to the Flaming Orchid, and as he put his arms around her slender waist and prepared to lead her out in a fox-trot, she uttered a cry of pain and sagged in his arms. He half-carried her back to their table.

'What is it? What's wrong, Josepha?'

'Is nothing,' she reassured him, pain distorting the fixed smile on her lips. 'Only a bad place on foot. Will be better soon. Sorry, so sorry.'

He bent over and looked at the crippled foot. Ignoring her protests he removed her shoe. Her foot was bloody. He took off the other shoe. That foot was bloody as well.

'Jesus,' he breathed. 'Why didn't you tell me?'

'Is nothing, nothing,' she cried. 'Only little hurt. Please, please, we dance again, yes?'

'No. We're going home.' In the car he asked her if her feet hurt her often. She said yes, every day, so that by evening she could hardly stand. His mouth tightened dangerously. She felt frightened and wept into her handkerchief. The car pulled up at the Cathay Hotel, and he lifted her in his arms and carried her to the private elevator that went up to his penthouse.

He set her gently on the couch in the sitting room and knelt down in front of her. He took off her shoes and tossed them aside, and lifted up her skirt to unhitch her garters. She squealed and tried to push his hands away, but he told her curtly to be still, and she obeyed. He was her employer, her master. She had been brought up to be thankful to men just for letting her live.

He peeled off her stockings with great care, easing them tenderly over her bloody toes. He went to the bathroom and returned with a warm, wet cloth, and he wiped away the caked blood. She sat quite still, covering her face with her hands to hide her shame.

Her toes were folded under the soles of her feet, which had been bound when she was eight years old, and unbound when Anne rescued her at age thirteen, too late to reverse the considerable damage to the bone structure. Because Josepha wanted to appear normal, she stuffed her feet into Western-style pumps that pinched and constricted them.

'I will be better tomorrow,' she said from behind the screen of her hands. 'You will see. I will be at office first thing—'

'No,' he said. 'No more work, no more standing, no more office. You're staying here.' He plied the cloth around her tiny toes. She was so fragile, so delicate, so vulnerable.

'Stay here?' she repeated incredulously. 'No, no, I cannot! I go now, please.'

She tried to rise. 'Sit still,' he commanded. She trembled. He cradled her feet in his two hands, which were large enough to engulf them. Then he bent his head and kissed them softly. She gasped and braced herself, but he didn't hurt her. His hands and his mouth were as soft as a child's, or a lover's. He let out his breath in a weary sigh and rested his head on her lap.

'Stay, Josepha,' he said. 'Stay with me.'

She stroked his dark head lovingly.

'I will stay, tuan. I will stay.'

'Maurice, you make all my wife's clothes, don't you?'

'Yes, Monsieur Innes,' Maurice cooed into the phone, 'and a very great honor it is, too. Such a pleasure to dress that lovely figure.'

'I want everything in her wardrobe duplicated. Everything. Coats, dresses, underwear. Everything except shoes.'

Maurice grew agitated. 'I understand, monsieur. But what has happened? Has the wardrobe been damaged somehow? Oh, great heaven, what a disaster! I must call Madame immediately.'

'No, you must not call her. She's not to know anything about this.' Innes paused. 'The clothes aren't for her.'

'But monsieur, I cannot—'

'Who pays your bills, Maurice?'

Maurice struggled to regain his composure. 'I only wanted to say, monsieur, that it might be wiser to obtain exact measurements before proceeding with the task. Illusion is one thing, but exactness is everything.'

'Telephone for you, Dr. Lawrence.'

'Thank you, nurse. Hello, Dr. Lawrence speaking.'

'Hullo, Gil. Can you spare a few minutes to minister to an old friend?'

He gripped the receiver and huddled closer to the wall phone. 'What do you want? Why did you call me here?'

'I called you because I need a doctor. You are a doctor, aren't you?' She was her usual flippant self, but her voice sounded strained and her bravado forced. He thought he heard her choke off a sob. 'Gil, I need you.'

'What is it? What's happened? Kit, are you all right?'

'Yes, yes, of course I am. Oh, God, I don't know. Just come, Gil. Please. Hurry.'

'I'll be there as soon as I can. Don't worry. Everything will be fine.' He hung up. He was sweating. He tried to imagine what could have happened to her. Another abortion? Pills? What if it was a trick? What if it wasn't?

He took a taxi to the house on the Avenue Joffre. A houseboy admitted him and led him upstairs to Kit's room. Kit was lying on top of the coverlet on the bed. She was wearing a flowing robe of pale blue silk. One arm was thrown across the upper half of her face.

He put on a show of cool professionalism. 'All right, here I am. What seems to be the problem?'

She sat up weakly. Her eyes were swollen with crying.

'He's so awful to me, Gil. You have no idea. He's a brute, an animal. I — I hate him!'

She flopped down and rolled over on her side. He felt a

rush of fear and love, and he approached the bed. 'He hurt you,' he said. 'Where? Tell me what happened, Kit.'

'I'm so ashamed, Gil. I suppose I deserved it. I was a bitch to him. But I couldn't help it. He's so horrid. Oh, God.' She sobbed brokenly. Gilbert sat down on the side of the bed and put his hand gingerly on her shoulder. Her cries tore at his heart.

'It's all right, Kit. Don't cry. Where does it hurt? Please, I want to help.'

She sat up shakily and wiped her eyes on her sleeve. Then she opened the bottom part of her robe gently. Her white thighs were smeared with ugly purple bruises.

'He beat me, Gil,' she whispered hoarsely. 'And then he raped me.'

He touched the worst of the bruises and she flinched. It was genuine, not a trick of light, not theatrical makeup. He quivered angrily. 'I could kill him for this. How long – how long has he been treating you like this?'

'From the very beginning, Gil.'

'Oh, God. Why did you marry him, Kit? Why?'

She put her hands on his shoulders and looked into his eyes. 'Don't you know?' Her robe, loosened at the waist, dropped down over her shoulders to reveal fingerprint-sized contusions on her breasts. She lay back slowly, drawing him down with her, guiding his head. He made a moaning sound, halfway between a sigh and a sob, and closed his mouth over an erect nipple.

'Don't you know?'

Chapter Six

'Hallo, Jimmie! What you bring me?'

'What makes you think I've brought you anything, monkey?'

Josepha flung her arms around Innes' neck. He whirled her around and kissed her warmly. She shrieked, and they collapsed laughing on the sofa.

'You've put on weight, monkey,' he said sternly. 'No more chocolates for you.'

'I no put on weight!' she cried. 'You bring me mo' chocolate, eh?' She patted the pockets of his coat. Her hand came to rest on a promising bulge. He slapped his hand over hers.

'Listen carefully,' he said. 'I have not put on weight. Not "I no put on weight." *I have not put on weight.*'

'You no put on weight, I no put on weight,' she said with a saucy toss of her curls. 'Lemme see what you bring me.'

'Let me see what you have brought me,' he said with jaw-breaking preciseness. Josepha laughed at him. 'That's it.' He threw up his hands. 'We're not going out tonight. We're not going anywhere, ever again. I'm not taking you out until you learn to speak proper English. You embarrass me in front of my friends.'

'Pooh,' she retorted, 'you no proper gentleman! Friends no care how I talk, only how I look. Lemme see what you bring.'

He sighed despairingly and removed his hand from hers. She rooted in his pocket and withdrew a flask of Worth perfume, its neck wrapped around with gold string. It was Kit's favorite scent.

'Ah, lookee!' she burbled happily. 'You say I am pretty as flower, now I smell like one, too!'

'Splash a little of this stuff behind your ears and we'll go out,' he said. 'No place fancy – you're not worthy of the St. Petersburg. But I'm hungry. We'll grab a bowl of noodles someplace, where no one knows me.'

'I wear prettiest dress,' she said, wriggling excitedly and touching her hands to her newly crimped hair.

'No, you can't wear anything else but perfume,' he said, pulling her closer. 'I, your master, forbid it.'

'You very naughty man. You want me arrested for badness on the street.' She kissed the tip of his nose.

'You can't get arrested for badness in this town,' he said. 'But they might arrest you for ugliness.'

She gave a mock-angry yelp and pelted him with a pillow. He grabbed her wrists and grinned while she pretended to struggle. She fell exhausted onto her back and he threw himself on top of her.

'Come on, monkey, tchin-tchin.' He tried to kiss her. She turned her face away.

'No, I no kiss big ugly man like you!'

'I'll take the perfume back.'

'No, no kiss. You shamed of me. You no love me.'

'I'll take you to that French restaurant you like so much,' he said, forgetting his threats.

'Well, maybe little kiss,' she pouted. 'Just one.' She pursed her rouged lips and sighed contentedly when he slid his hands under the lacy froth of her negligee and kissed her deeply. 'You like me, Jimmie? You happy here with me?'

'I happy here, monkey. Damn, you've got me doing it, too.'

'I got you doin' lotsa things,' she giggled and parted her legs. 'I bad influence.'

'I *am* a bad influence,' he began to correct her automatically. She unfastened his belt and unzipped his trousers. She fondled him gently, and the speech lesson ended.

'You like me when I am old, Jimmie?' she asked later, twirling a curl of his hair around her finger.

'Old? You'll never get old, monkey. Come on, get dolled up. I'm hungry.'

'We go dancing after? I want to dance in pretty silver dress.'

'Sure, if you're up to it.' He watched her scamper into the bedroom. Specialists had looked at her feet and advised surgery to correct the bone deformation, but she

147

wouldn't hear of it. She was terrified of doctors and sickness and hospitals, and besides, her feet were so much better since she didn't have to walk or stand all day, and she could even dance for a little while in the evening if she rested beforehand. He had had special shoes made that would cushion and support her twisted feet.

She emerged from the bedroom half an hour later. She wore a silver lamé dress and dragged a silver fox jacket behind her as she tripped along on three-inch heels. She stopped in front of the mirror to adjust her straps, and to powder her nose from the little gold compact he had given her. Innes sucked in his breath. Sometimes the resemblance was incredible, really incredible. He could almost believe —

She turned and smiled radiantly. 'I ready now. We go soon, Jimmie? I very hungry.'

He sighed. 'I *am* ready now, and I *am* very hungry. Can we go soon?'

'Yes, we go right now.' She handed him the fur to drape around her shoulders – a little ceremony he had taught her and which she enjoyed – and she wriggled with pleasure and caressed the soft pelt with her cheek. She was like a kitten, small and warm and cuddly. She loved warm places and soft things and good food, and she purred when she was happy, which was most of the time.

Innes was particularly critical of her table manners at dinner that night. She pouted and spilled her water. Waiters hovered. Innes fumed and scolded. Josepha deliberately dropped all her silverware onto the floor under their table. Waiters hurried to replace it. Innes snarled at her and she wept a little. He kissed and petted her in the car as they rode to the Park Hotel for an after-dinner drink.

They went on to the Flaming Orchid to dance. He bought her a rose from a flower seller and helped her pin it over her left ear. She admired the effect in the mirrored wall behind their banquette.

'Is nice,' she said, patting the flower gently. She moistened a finger and adjusted a curl over her right eye. 'Curly hair very pretty.'

'Ugly girls always look better with their hair curled,' he

remarked, offering her a cigarette. She stuck out her tongue at him and pushed the cigarette case away. Smoking made her sick, she said, and she did look rather awkward and ridiculous holding the smoldering stick between thumb and forefinger, as far away from her face as possible. He gave up insisting that she try to like it. He had also given up trying to make her like alcohol. She would drink champagne in minute quantities, but she preferred ginger ale.

'You should have been a bar girl,' he told her. 'All those girls drink ginger ale.'

'But for bar girl you pay for champagne and get ginger ale,' she told him. 'For me you pay for ginger ale and you get ginger ale.'

They waltzed together. She told Innes she had learned to dance from the other girls at L'École des Filles.

'Did the nuns know about that?'

'Oh, yes. Soeur Marie-Claire, she teach us tango. Very nice dance.'

'Where did a nun learn to tango?' Innes wondered.

'From Soeur Marie-Étienne,' Josepha told him. 'She learn from her brother in Paris. He was no good, she say. We pray for him.'

'You prayed that he'd come to Shanghai?' Innes teased.

'Oh, you very bad man,' she clucked disapprovingly.

'Maybe you'd like to join the convent?' he suggested. 'If I'm so bad and you'd rather be good —'

'No,' she said primly, 'I will stay with you and be Christian influence. Is more important.'

They danced two more dances and he noticed that she was dragging slightly and trying not to show it. As they walked back to their table, he said, 'I've had about enough, I think. We'd better be getting back. I have to get an early start tomorrow.'

'What for?' she demanded. 'I not tired. Why you no go work later tomorrow?'

'No can do. I have a lot of new bills to pay since I took pity on you and started giving you food and shelter,' he said, slinging her fur over his arm. 'Don't give me an argument or I'll send you back to the files.'

He spoke sternly but she knew he was joking, and she

laughed at his show of masterfulness. They skirted the dance floor and threaded their way through the tables near the doors. One of Innes' business acquaintances called to him and Josepha went ahead alone. Just then the doors flew open and Kit swept in, followed by her entourage of horse-faced young men. She was wearing a silver lamé dress and half-wearing, half-dragging a silver fox jacket. Kit and Josepha came face to face, mirror images of each other. Their gowns were identical, like their jackets. Their hairstyles were similar although Kit's hair had more natural curl and looked fuller than Josepha's. Incredibly, Kit wore a red rose over her left ear.

She stared at the Chinese girl, and at Innes, coming toward them. Her eyebrows slid up into her hairline, and her jacket slipped off her shoulder. One of her young men hurried to restore it. Innes wrapped Josepha's fox around her, resting his hands protectively on her shoulders.

'Well,' Kit drawled, giving Josepha a searing appraisal. 'Somebody in this town has good taste. I'm glad to see. But who, exactly?'

Josepha looked up at Innes, her face filled with confusion and hurt. 'Jimmie, I no understand, what is —'

'Shut up. Would you mind letting us pass?' he said to Kit.

'Dear me, not at all,' she said with exaggerated politeness. 'All rise, all rise! The empire builder is coming through. Make way, make way for the empire builder!' she called loudly, bowing low and sweeping her arm in front of her as Innes hustled Josepha out in front of him.

'Make way for the empire builder and his whore!' Kit's laughter was loud, brittle, tinged with fury.

Josepha wept all the way home. 'I no understand. You have other woman and you no tell me? You buy for her same as for me? She is concubine, too?'

'She is wife,' he growled. 'For God's sake, stop that damned noise. Where's your handkerchief?'

'I no got hand —'

He shoved his linen square under her face. 'Here, mop up the flood. I'm tired of it.'

She sniffed, and wept surreptitiously. 'You throw me

out?' she whimpered. 'I go tonight?'

'Oh, is that what's bothering you? No, I'm not throwing you out and you don't have to go tonight or ever, is that clear? Just make believe this never happened. Nothing has changed.'

Inside the door of the penthouse, she dropped her fur on the floor and kicked off her shoes. 'I no understand,' she said, shaking her head. 'I think you love me. Me!'

'I do love you, God damn it!' he shouted, exasperated. 'Can't you get anything through that thick little skull? I want you, not her. I don't love her, she doesn't love me. We're married but it doesn't mean a thing. It's not important. You're important. Forget what happened tonight. I have.'

She nestled against his shirtfront and gazed up at him with tear-filled eyes. 'You say you love me! You never say you love me before.'

He plucked the rose out of her hair and crushed it. 'Of course I love you. I wouldn't put up with you for a minute if I didn't love you. You're much too stupid and ugly.'

She sighed at the familiar loving insults and pillowed her cheek on his chest, safe and happy in the strong enclosure of his arms. Then a thought came to her. 'How she get same dress, same coat?' she asked shrewdly.

'Accident. Pure coincidence. You savvy, coincidence?'

'Sure. You buy two of everything. That is coincidence.' She pulled away slightly and touched her marcelled hair. 'This is same, too, no? Is also coincidence?'

'Yes, God damn it!' he roared, exasperated. 'What's the matter with you, Josepha? Aren't you happy here? Don't you like the things I buy you? I suppose you were happier standing on your goddamned bleeding feet all day in the filing room? That's the thanks a man gets.' He pushed her away from him. 'Work, Jimmie, slave, Jimmie, buy this, buy that, and then they object because they see another woman wearing the same darned dress. What in hell difference does it make?' he demanded, shouting. She cringed, sinking down on the couch and drawing up her knees protectively. He loomed over her, his rage full-blown and magnificent.

'If I want to dress fifty women in Shanghai in the same

goddamned dress, I will, do you hear me? I don't have to explain to you or to anyone. And I don't have to apologize, either. Where do you think you'd be without me? Those damned nuns didn't teach you a goddamned thing. Five years in that school and you still talk like a damned coolie. You females are all the same. Greedy bitches, all of you. Out for yourselves, for what you can squeeze out of a man. You don't care about me, only about what I can buy for you. Christ, I can't get through my own door without a ticket – a trinket for the resident greedy bitch. You're right, if I had any sense, I'd throw you out tonight, back in the gutter where you came from!'

He stamped over to the window and wrenched at the curtain pull. The drapes opened jerkily, revealing the lights of Shanghai. Impudent, brighter than the stars they obscured, they danced on the surface of the Whangpoo, skimmed across the water, soared across the sky. Boat lights, searchlights, headlights, neon lights in crimson and green and gold and blue, carnival lights for a carnival town.

Josepha smiled. He had chosen her as his concubine because he didn't love his wife. He loved her, Josepha, not that ghost woman with the laugh of a demon. She slithered out of her dress and underthings, then she stood behind him and put her arms around his waist.

'I sorry, Jimmie,' she said. 'I no mean hurt. You very good to me. No one is ever good to me before. Please, no be angry anymore.'

He stood stiff and unbending. He was furious with himself. It was inevitable that Kit find out about Josepha, of course. But that they should meet face to face like that – so that she could see that he had produced a cheap carbon copy of her —

'No more angry,' Josepha pleaded, sidling around to his front and twining her slender arms around his neck. 'Why be sad? I love you, you love me. Is all we need, no? Come on, Jimmie, tchin-tchin. One little kiss no hurt. Please, before I go away from here.'

He complied, images of Kit swirling in his mind. He lifted Josepha in his arms and carried her to bed, and the last vestiges of his anger were spent in furious lovemaking that left them both panting and shiny with sweat.

'Jimmie,' Josepha said in a thick, sleepy voice, 'we have many babies someday?'

'Babies?' He roused himself enough to produce a scornful snort. 'Christ, no. I don't want any brats around.'

'Not today, but someday,' she said, tracing her fingertip through the thicket of hair on his chest. Chinese men were smooth, almost hairless. White men were as woolly as bears. 'We have son, maybe. You like, have son.'

'No, I don't want any half-breed bastards hanging around.'

'But is alla same,' she argued. 'Chinese men have concubine, give sons, give names. Same son, white man call bastard. Why is that?'

'Because when you have a kid and you're not married to the woman, the kid's a bastard, savvy? And I don't want any. So shut up and go to sleep, will you?'

He rolled over and let out all his breath in a long sigh. Josepha lay perfectly still, mulling over what he had said. He had a wife. All very well. And she, Josepha, was his concubine, even though she didn't live in his house. She remembered the hatred in the face of the ghost woman and she shivered. It was just as well she didn't have to live under that woman's roof. He had no sons by the ghost woman. She knew that because she had asked him once. His wife was probably barren – not surprisingly. Yet he didn't want Josepha's sons because they would be bastards. If she gave him these bastards, he would cast her out, back into the street to make her own living. She saw herself trying to dance on bleeding feet in a dance hall, sipping ginger ale from champagne glasses, growing older, becoming ill. She slid lower in bed and looked at the gray blankness of the ceiling. It looked like her future.

Gilbert slipped into the lobby of the small hotel and cast a furtive look around him. Two spidery palms flanked the desk. The chairs in the center of the room were upholstered in cracked brown leather, well worn and pocked with cigarette burns. Brimming ashtrays gave off an acrid, unpleasant odor. The runner from the door was threadbare, stained, colorless. Even though the afternoon was cool, a ceiling fan swirled lazily overhead, drawing the contaminated air down from the rooms upstairs and wafting it into his face. He smelled stale perfume, sweat, moldy talc, opium, sex.

He felt nauseated. He couldn't stay. He turned quickly to make his escape and bumped up against Kit, just coming in the door. She laughed and steadied him with her hands on his elbows.

'Hullo, Gil. Not thinking of running out on me, were you? What's the matter, don't you like my choice of love nest?'

'No, I hate it,' he hissed, wishing she wouldn't talk so loudly. 'You weren't here. I thought you weren't coming.'

'How do you know I wasn't here?' she asked. 'Did you ask for me at the desk?'

'Under what name?'

'My own name, of course.' She walked to the desk and swatted the bell. A clerk who had been dozing under a newspaper shook it off and yawned. 'We want a room,' Kit said.

'How long you wantee?' the man asked, rubbing his face as if he were washing it. 'One night? One hour?'

Kit gave Gilbert an appraising look. 'You'd better make it an hour. I don't think my friend could go the whole night.' She signed the register, 'Reverend and Mrs Fox.'

'Your parents —!' Gilbert gasped.

'Why not? Aren't they allowed to have a little fun?' she asked, taking his hand and leading him up to room 3-B. She shed her clothes without ceremony, Gilbert, turning his back to her so that he couldn't see her mocking smile, did the same. 'Have you heard the latest?' She sat on the edge of the bed and stripped off her stockings. 'Innes has a Chinese whore. I saw her last night. But that's not the best part: he's dolled her up to look just like me! Hairdo, furs, the works. Maurice tells me he's duplicated my whole wardrobe for that cheap little doxy. I don't know whether to be flattered or insulted. What do you think, Gil?'

'Think? Well, I don't know what to think.'

'I mean, should I sack Maurice and find someone else to dress me, or should I play along with the joke, pretend I don't care? And I don't, really, although it gives me a funny feeling, knowing there's a slanty-eyed version of me walking around Shanghai. I tell you, it was like confronting your *Doppelgänger*, and finding out that you really had brown skin and Chinese eyes. What a nuisance. I've got to give him credit, though. If he did it to get my goat, he certainly succeeded. I didn't think he had the wits to come up with something like this.' She lay back and closed her eyes. 'Light me a cigarette, will you, Gil? They're in my bag.'

She knew he hated smoking, hated her to do it. She also knew he couldn't refuse her anything. She heard him fumbling in her bag, heard the match strike, and stretched out her hand for the cigarette. He wedged it between her fingers.

'You should be home for dinner right about now. What did you tell the Mouse?'

'I said I had a patient with some post-operative difficulties. She doesn't care. We haven't had much to say to each other since that night you told me about her. She sleeps on the couch in the living room.'

She knew he wasn't ready for love yet. First he would have to unburden himself, unload a hefty parcel of guilt and self-loathing. After his confession he would feel cleansed, and he would be ready to sin again. She didn't know why his breast-beating and garment-rending didn't bore her to distraction. She didn't love him. She didn't even pity him. Perhaps she just enjoyed watching him torment himself.

He rambled on while she finished her cigarette, his mood swinging from deep despair to passionate longing, with occasional outbursts of anger.

'I think I must be going mad. It's not as though you cared about me. You don't. You despise me. And I despise you, Kit. I hate you for doing this to me.'

'Fiddlesticks,' she scoffed. 'You're doing it to yourself. Why can't you just relax and enjoy it?'

'Because it's wrong. It's the worst wrong there is. Betrayal.' He uttered the word in a whisper thick with horror.

'Innes betrayed me, Anne betrayed you,' Kit said breezily. 'Turnabout's fair play and all that. Two wrongs may not make a right, but four wrongs ought to make something exciting.'

She was tired of talk. She stubbed out her cigarette and turned to him. He sat hunched on the other side of the bed, his hands hanging heavily between his knees. He had a nice back, lean and muscular, if a little pale. Kit hitched herself closer and combed her fingernails lightly down his spine. He shivered; little prickles of gooseflesh raised the hairs on his arms.

'What's the matter, Gil? Has it gone stale already? I thought you wanted me.'

'I do,' he said, shaking his head as though he still couldn't believe it. 'God help me, I do.'

'Come here, darling.' She reached for his hand. 'Lie down next to Kit and tell her all about it.'

Her fingers felt like little grappling hooks. He closed his eyes and tried to imagine Jesus in the room with them. His eyes sorrowful, sad. Kit stroked the inside of his arm and he shivered. Absurd. Here he was, naked and ready, still debating with himself about the rightness or wrongness of his actions. It was obvious to both of them that he had neither the will nor the strength to leave her.

He closed his eyes and let himself fall back. His head was pillowed on her abdomen. He imagined he was a baby, nesting safely inside the bony cage of her pelvis. He could hear the rhythmic pumping of her heart as he floated weightlessly inside a sac of amniotic fluid. He felt numb, free of pain, free of care. Innocent.

She stroked his forehead and murmured soothingly, as a mother should, lulling him, reassuring him. At times like this he could almost persuade himself that she cared about him. She shifted a little and his cheek came to rest on the hard mound of her pubic bone, covered with hair that felt as soft as moss. Her perfume mingled with the woodsy scent of her womanliness, like the bowered entry of a forest, fragrant with the promise of cool darkness, rich earth, soft beds of leaves.

Suddenly her loving hands clamped vise-like on the sides of his head. She tugged and twisted, guiding him as if he were a blind man, burying his face in her mossy blackness. He could taste her musky sweetness. She moved again, shutting out all light and sound, smothering him, burying him alive. At the same time he felt her mouth close around his vulnerable organ, welcoming, warm, and soft, yet ringed with sharp nails that could wrench and tear, like a medieval torture instrument. He thought that the two of them must resemble some grotesque two-headed monster, intent on devouring itself.

The bed looked like a small patch of battle-scarred terrain. Before they left the room he started to draw the covers up to conceal the telltale wrinkles and stains, the shards of shattered innocence, the ruins of illusion. The motion was the same as when a patient died and he pulled the sheet up over the corpse.

'Don't bother,' Kit said. 'They know what we've been up to. This was a nice place. At least we started out with reasonably clean linen. Maybe we should come back.'

He would rather die than show his face in this hotel again, yet he knew that if she wanted to meet him here, he would come. 'You always get what you want, don't you,' he said bitterly as he trailed her down the stairs.

'Almost always. I wanted you.' She tossed the key onto the front desk. The man under the newspaper didn't stir.

'Did Innes really rape you and beat you?'

She laughed. 'If the truth be told, darling, I had a run-in with a particularly nasty-tempered pony.'

'I thought it might be something like that. I didn't want to believe — You must think me a perfect fool.'

She laughed. 'Far from perfect, darling. But getting there! 'Bye. I'll call you.'

Anne picked up the phone.

'Mrs Lawrence, this is Jim Innes. Listen, something's wrong. Can you get over here right away?'

Her legs felt watery, weak with fear. 'Oh, my God, something's happened to Kit.'

'No, Kit's all right. Listen, please come. I'm at the Cathay, the penthouse. I'll send the car.'

'No, don't bother. A ricksha will be just as fast. I'll be there as soon as I can.'

After she hung up she gave herself a minute to collect her wits. Not Kit. What then? Was he drunk? He didn't sound it; a little tense, perhaps, but not incapacitated or incoherent. She looked at her watch. Nine o'clock. Gilbert had already telephoned that he had an emergency at the Aldershot and probably wouldn't be home for hours. She threw on her old baggy raincoat and knotted a scarf under her chin.

A fine rain was falling, chill and penetrating. The Chinese were saying that the winter would be a bad one, with snow and sleet in January and February. People would die by the thousands because they had no shelter, no warm clothes. Her ricksha coolie was barefoot, but at least he wore a jacket over his short pants. Ragged and far too big for him, it looked like German army surplus from the world war. His feet slapped the wet pavement and he kept up a raucous shouting at pedestrians and other vehicles. Headlights gleamed confusingly on the shiny surface of the street. The rubber tires slipped a little at an intersection and they narrowly avoided a collision with a lorry. Anne closed her eyes and prayed.

The people in the lobby of the Cathay were dry, overfed, bejeweled, beautifully groomed. They looked at her strangely as she asked directions to the penthouse. She was rain-soaked and mud-splashed, hair askew, clothes awry.

'Mrs Lawrence.' Innes appeared at her elbow. He was wearing the vest and trousers of a gray flannel suit. His necktie was loosened and his shirt sleeves were rolled up. 'This way. You should have let me send my car.'

She followed him to the elevator. 'Kit's all right? You're sure?'

The doors closed and opened again a few moments later. She hadn't been aware of any sensation of being lifted, but he gestured for her to precede him out.

'Not Kit,' he said. 'Josepha Chang.'

She stared at him, unable to assimilate the fact. 'Josepha, here? Why?'

'She's in the bedroom.' He led the way. 'I was away for a few days. I had to fly to Manila. When I came back I found her like this. She won't let me call a doctor. She keeps asking for you.'

'I know,' Anne said dazedly. 'She hates being sick.'

The bedroom was spacious, decorated in Kit's favorite color of celadon green. The bed looked like a giant cradle. The headboard was tufted and high, encrusted with gilt. Hangings of sheer silk and lace looped down from a coronet-like affair on the ceiling and golden cupids bore the panels away in four directions to the corner posts of the bed.

At first Anne thought the bed was empty, then she saw a dark head lying like a fallen black bird among the snowy silk and lace pillow shams. He lied, she thought. It is Kit. She sat on the edge of the bed and leaned over the sleeping girl to brush the curls away from her face. Not Kit. Josepha.

'Josepha, it's Missee Anne,' she said softly. The flesh under her hand was blistering hot, beaded with sweat. She looked questioningly at Innes, standing helplessly a few feet away. 'She's very ill. How long has she been like this?'

'I don't know. I've only been home for half an hour, forty-five minutes at the most. She won't let me do anything for her. She won't even let me touch her.'

Home. He calls this place home.

Anne spoke more sharply. 'Josepha, wake up, it's me, Anne. Can you hear me? Josepha!'

Eyelids fluttered. 'Missee Anne, you come.'

'Of course I came. Now, what's the matter? How long have you been sick?'

The girl whimpered a bit. She was frightened. 'You be angry,' she said.

'Oh, that's not true,' Anne said, smoothing the damp hair away from her face. 'I have never been angry with you, not even when you've been very naughty. Come, tell me.'

The girl tossed and muttered something incoherent. Anne looked around. The dressing table was cluttered with brushes, mirrors, jars of cream, flagons of scent, crumpled cleansing tissues. Feathered mules lay on the thick carpet near the bed. A robe bordered with marabou feathers draped the foot of the chintz-covered chaise lounge in the corner. Josepha herself was wearing a nightdress of dainty silk trimmed with exquisitely fine lace. Anne began to understand.

She spoke to the girl in Chinese, addressing her by her Chinese name, Chang Mei-ling. Josepha began to cry softly. Anne patted her hand and murmured encouragingly. She drew the coverlet back and recoiled a little at the stink of infection. The sheets were slick with yellow pus and blood.

'Where's the bathroom?' she asked Innes. He pointed.

She opened the bathroom door. A bloody bundle lay on the floor in the corner, between the toilet and the green marble tub. Innes looked over her shoulder.

She closed the door firmly and turned to face him. She shoved her fists into her coat so that she wouldn't strike out at him. Her eyes smoldered.

'Couldn't you even send her to a decent clinic to have it done?' she hissed. 'Is this all she's worth to you?'

Innes' puzzled frown deepened. 'I don't know what you're talking about.'

'She's had an abortion, one of those cheap back-street jobs. It's turned septic, poison. She'll probably die.'

Innes looked thunderstruck. 'But that's impossible. She wasn't pregnant. I would have known. She couldn't – I was only gone a few days.'

'We've got to get her to a hospital right away. Is your car available? We'll take her to the Aldershot. It's the closest, and the best.'

He nodded and went out to the sitting room to phone down to Sanjay, his chauffeur. Anne looked for something warm for Josepha to wear. She opened the closet doors and stood amazed. She recognized Kit's silver fox jacket, her Persian lamb coat, her teal blue gown, her favorite Chinese robe. She couldn't fathom what it meant, but there was no time to puzzle over it. She grabbed the Persian lamb coat, which was floor-length, and carried it to the bed. She had some difficulty getting the coat around Josepha, who had slipped into unconsciousness. Innes appeared at her side and helped her dress the limp form. She saw his tenderness and hardened her heart.

He lifted Josepha in his arms. 'I'll take her down,' he said. The dark curly head lolled against his shoulder.

Anne led the way. The Rolls was waiting at the curb.

Innes cradled Josepha on his lap during the short drive to the Aldershot. Her breathing was shallow, panting. Her eyes were half-open, unseeing.

'I didn't know,' he said softly. 'Christ, why didn't she tell me?'

'Maybe she thought you wouldn't be interested,' Anne said.

Innes didn't hear her. 'We talked about babies. She brought it up – no reason. She must have known then. I told her I didn't want any half-breed bastards.'

Anne winced. 'Nobody does,' she said. She huddled in the corner of the car and stared bleakly out the windows.

The nurse at the reception desk recognized Anne. 'Why, Mrs Lawrence, what a surprise. I'll tell Dr Lawrence —' She saw Innes with Josepha and stopped, confused.

'She's had an abortion,' Anne said. 'It's septic. She's very bad. You've got to do something quickly.'

The woman's mouth drooped disapprovingly. 'I'm afraid I can't authorize admittance without the permission of an attending physician. There are rules —'

'I know what kind of rules you people have here. You don't treat Chinese. But by God, you're going to treat this one.' She said to Innes, 'This way.'

They hurried along the corridor, the nurse yapping at their heels. Anne threw open the door of an empty examining room and groped for the light switch. She wrenched back the curtains that surrounded the table in the middle of the room and Innes laid Josepha down gently. Angry female voices trilled in the corridor outside.

Anne opened the coat and began to clean away the slime on the girl's thighs. Innes muttered, 'Oh, God,' and turned away.

'Not pretty, is it?' she said. 'Why don't you get out of here? You've done enough harm already.'

'No. I want to stay.'

Gilbert Lawrence entered the small room. He looked stern and immaculate in a starched white linen coat.

'What's all this? Anne, what are you doing here? You know better than to come bursting in here. There are other hospitals that handle cases like this.'

'She's my friend,' Anne said without looking up. 'I'm not going to throw her to the uncaring butchers at the General, if that's what you mean. Are you going to help her or aren't you? Or do you have to have special permission from God Almighty and the Board of Trustees to treat a Chinese?'

Their eyes met. Gilbert flushed angrily. He looked at Innes with loathing, then went over to Josepha and lifted her wrist.

'Her pulse is very weak. Nurse —' He rapped out instructions and the nurse scurried to obey. 'You two wait outside. I'll call you if there's any change.'

Anne said, 'I want to stay. I can help. She knows me. If she wakes, she'll be afraid. She hates doctors.'

The nurse drew the curtains around the table. Innes went out. He could hear them bustling, talking in low voices. Metal instruments clanked on trays. The nurse came out and returned wheeling an IV stand hung with jars of plasma and blood. He lit a cigarette. It burned down and singed his fingers before he realized that he hadn't smoked it at all.

Anne emerged from the examining room and walked past him without speaking. She picked up the telephone at the front desk. The nurses on duty looked at them both curiously. Grist for the hospital gossip mills, Anne thought. She spoke rapid French and hung up.

'What is it? What's happening?' Innes asked her.

'They can't do anything more for her.' She slumped wearily against the wall. 'I called Father Jacquinot. Josepha is Catholic.'

'What chance —' He was almost afraid to ask.

'No chance,' she said. 'Girls like that never have a chance. She's a born concubine. She's sweet and simple and about the only thing anybody could teach her was how to make a man happy. It's part of the culture. You can't change them. You try to persuade them that they don't need to kowtow to men all their lives, that with a little education and help— Oh, Christ, what's the use?' She passed her hand over her eyes, then drew herself up and said with crisp callousness, 'Gilbert thinks she had it done two days ago. He's given her sulfanilamide, but it's

162

probably too late to stem the infection. She's not very robust, as you know. They can't' – she swallowed – 'they can't get her fever down.' She turned her face aside to hide her anguish.

'I'm sorry,' Innes said lamely.

'Yes, sorry.' She pushed herself away from the wall and faced him angrily. Her face was blotchy and tear-streaked 'You're sorry for yourself, you mean. Now you'll just have to find yourself a new mistress, won't you? What a bore. But perhaps I can supply one for you. What would you like this time, another Chinese? Or maybe you're ready for a change. How about a nice half-breed bastard, very pretty, very cheap?'

Tears coursed down her cheeks. Innes absorbed her anger expressionlessly.

She dragged her sleeve under her nose. 'You make me sick, all of you. Taipan is just another word for plunderer. This isn't your country. You don't care about the people. You come here and rape and take. You chew up the land and spit it out. You chew up the workers and spit them out. Dead coolie? So what. Plenty more where he came from. Dead mistress? It's the same thing. You plant the seeds of half-breed bastards in their bellies and you never give them a thought afterward. The kids end up in Shanghai garbage cans, or in the marble toilets of the Cathay.'

'Don't,' he said softly.

'Why shouldn't I?' she demanded viciously. 'If you don't want to listen you can just go away, back to the booze and the laughter and the music at the Troc or at Ciro's. What are you doing here anyway, trying to salve your conscience a little?'

'I love her,' he said simply.

Anne covered her face with her hands.

'I don't expect you to believe that,' Innes said. 'I know what you think of me – what your husband thinks of me. I'm sorry you had to get involved, either of you.' He grunted. 'She asked if I'd still want her when she got old. I said she'd never get old.'

Father Jacquinot came down the corridor. He carried the viaticum and did not speak. The nurse met him and led him into Josepha's room. As he passed Anne and Innes he smiled encouragingly and nodded. Gilbert and the nurse came out, leaving the priest alone with Josepha.

'I've given her something to rouse her a little,' Gilbert told Anne. 'You can have some time with her when he's finished.'

Anne could hear Father Jacquinot speaking softly in Chinese. There was a long pause; he spoke again, more loudly and Josepha murmured in Chinese. Anne moved away. She didn't want to listen.

Gilbert came over to her. 'I've done all I could. No one could have done more.'

'I know that. Thank you.'

'I do not appreciate the awkward position you put me in. In the future —'

'It won't happen again,' she said stiffly. 'You don't need to worry.'

'I have another critical patient,' he lied. 'I won't be home until late.'

She shrugged.

He hesitated, as though he wanted to say more, then he walked away. He was supposed to call Kit if he could meet her. He needed to see her.

Father Jacquinot appeared in the doorway. 'Anne, Monsieur, come in, please. We have not much time.'

Anne shook her head vehemently. 'I won't watch her die. I don't want to remember her this way.'

Innes said, 'Please. She'll want to see you.' He put his hand under her elbow and led her inside. They took up positions on either side of the bed. Anne held Josepha's hand. Father Jacquinot prayed silently in the corner.

Josepha's face was white and waxen. Anne spoke her name. Her eyes fluttered open. She said in Chinese, 'I will die without children. No one will honor me after I am gone.'

'We will. We love you, Mei-ling. We will carry you in our hearts forever, and in that way do you honor.'

Josepha sighed. She turned her head and looked at Innes. 'I sorry, Jimmie,' she said weakly. 'No, is not right. *I am sorry.*'

'That's pretty good, monkey,' he said, touching her

cheek. 'You gave me quite a scare. *Maskee*. I'll save the beating until you're better.'

She smiled. 'You think I ugly now?'

'You've never looked prettier,' he said. His voice sounded husky. 'Hurry up and get well, and we'll go dancing.'

'Dancing,' she murmured happily, 'I go dancing in pretty silver dress.' The light went out of her eyes.

Anne fled from the room. Father Jacquinot joined her in the corridor a few minutes later.

Anne said, 'I'll never understand this country. They don't care about their own, and they don't want anyone else to help them. Helping them – it's like trying to empty the sea with a teacup. For every one you save, a million die. Even the ones you think you've saved. How do you do it? How can you stay here year after year, failing?'

The priest shrugged. 'Is my work any different from a farmer's? He plants, cultivates, and hopes that the good God will provide enough sun and rain to make a harvest. But the harvest is never a certainty, only a hope. We work because we must. We must try to make a living out of the earth. We are not put here to succeed or fail, simply to try.' He said, 'You are angry because she disappointed you.'

'That's not true.'

'You saved her life, and you felt you had a right to arrange it. You wanted so much for her, I know. But not what she wanted for herself, Anne. You were destined to fail.'

'I wouldn't have failed if it hadn't been for that man,' Anne said. 'He just couldn't keep his hands off her. That's all they know, men like him: taking.'

'He hardly kept her prisoner in a dark cell,' Father Jacquinot pointed out. 'She made her own choice.'

'He seduced her with money and comfort. How could any girl with a background like hers resist those things?'

'Of course, you would have preferred her to live austerely and plainly, like yourself, and devote herself to noble causes,' he mocked gently. 'Oh, Anne, her mind wasn't large enough to encompass any cause but her own well-being. You offered friendship, but he offered much more – not just fur coats and glistening baubles. She would never have been able to fulfill your hopes for her, and she was wise enough not to try. A man's demands are simpler. She could satisfy them, meet his needs. She felt wanted, necessary.'

'I can't believe you're defending him,' Anne said, outraged. 'As though you were members of the same club – and so you are. Defense of your own sex crosses class lines and blood lines and even the lines of that silly cassock you're wearing. It's disgusting.'

'I defend no one,' the priest sighed. 'I do not try to judge, merely to understand. Understanding is the key to forgiveness. Understanding of yourself as well as others.'

'How very modern of you,' Anne sneered. 'Have you forgotten that he's married to my sister? He committed adultery. He betrayed his vows. Am I supposed to overlook that little item?'

'Yes, because what happens in any marriage but your own is none of your concern.'

Father Jacquinot gazed at her intently, as though he could read in her eyes the story of her own foundering marriage, which he himself had predicted.

Anne wiped her nose impatiently and jammed her handkerchief back in her pocket. 'I tried to call Josepha at work, just to see how she was getting along. They told me she was no longer there, at Innes & Company. Then I got a note. She said she'd found a better job. She enclosed twenty dollars. It was as if she wanted to square things, to pay her debt so that she wouldn't feel beholden. What am I supposed to do with that twenty dollars?' she demanded. 'Ransom another kid from a brothel, and have my heart broken all over again?'

She saw Innes emerging from the examining room. He looked dazed, benumbed. She turned her back to him.

Father Jacquinot said, 'You will always be brokenhearted if you try to mold someone into an image not of their own making, Anne. You must love your friends and your children for themselves, not for what you wish them to be. That is dishonest, and foolish.'

'At least I didn't murder her,' Anne said loudly, for Innes' benefit.

'We will not talk of murder,' the priest said sharply, 'but of the will of God. You still have not learned to accept life on its own terms, Anne. You are always fighting, arguing, blaming, trying to change the unchangeable. You make difficulties where none exist; you walk a crooked line even on the straightest road. "If only!" you cry. "If only I had done this and this and this —"' Ridiculous!' He shook his head.

Anne flushed deeply, and her eyes glistened with tears.

'I will not scold you anymore, Anne,' Father Jacquinot sighed. 'We have covered this ground too many times. I am very sorry about poor Josepha. It is always sad when something beautiful goes out of our lives.'

'Yes,' Innes said softly, 'she was beautiful.'

'You will permit us to make the last arrangements, Monsieur? The sisters at the school would like her to be buried in their cemetery. They were very fond of her. We all were.'

'I want the best for her,' Innes said. 'The best. I'll pay for everything.'

'It is not necessary —'

'God damn it, I said I wanted the best, and I'll have it, if I have to bury her myself!' he shouted, his face reddening. Anne looked at him, startled.

'Of course, I understand,' Father Jacquinot said soothingly. 'We will respect your wishes. Everything will be of the finest, I assure you, Monsieur. Do not worry about that. Well, I will wish you good evening. I am sorry we could not have met under happier circumstances.' He moved closer to Anne and took her hand. 'You are angry with me. I shouldn't have spoken so roughly to you.'

'I suppose I deserved it,' she shrugged.

'We have not had a chance to talk for many months. You will come and see me soon.' Anne nodded. The priest bade her good night, and added in French, 'Look after him. He has had a bad shock. Remember, do not judge. Try to understand.'

He went out. Anne and Innes drifted toward the doors. Although they maintained a wide physical space between them, Anne felt linked to him by their shared loss. That link was stronger than his marriage to her sister. They stood outside the clinic. The Rolls waited at the bottom of the steps. Innes lit a cigarette. His hands trembled.

She felt a spasm of pity for him. She reminded herself that he was responsible for Josepha's death. But wasn't she just as responsible? She had arranged for Josepha's employment at Innes & Company. She had planned a career for her protégée and pushed her into a world where she didn't belong, which she couldn't wait to escape.

Droplets of rain glimmered on Innes' bare head. He looked forlorn and lonely, naked without his characteristic cloak of bluff and bravado.

Anne wanted to ask him, 'Where will you go?' But where could he go? Back to the blood-bed at the Cathay penthouse? Back to the mansion on the Avenue Joffre, and Kit, the wife he had betrayed?

She cleared her throat. 'I hate to impose on you, but would you mind dropping me at my house? It's rather late.'

He nodded curtly. They didn't speak during the ride to the apartment on Soochow Creek. The rain started again. The windshield wipers squeaked a little. Sanjay sounded the horn from time to time. Through the rain-smeared windows Anne could see people leaping out of the path of the car, oddly smudged and elongated people who seemed melted by the rain.

The car rolled to a stop. Anne said, 'Will you come in?' She could see that he was about to refuse. 'Please, just for a few minutes. Gilbert's not home – he'll be very late – and I don't want to be alone yet.' This was a lie. She wanted nothing more than to be alone, but she didn't want to think of him riding solitary around the city, or drinking in a nightclub while saxophones bleated in the background. 'I'll make coffee. I even have a bottle of scotch somewhere.' Kit had given it to them, to assure that she would have something to drink when she visited.

Sanjay held the car door for them. Innes followed her into the apartment. It looked as bleak and shabby as ever, but he didn't notice. Anne took off her coat and scarf and threw them over the back of a chair. Innes' shirt looked limp. The cuffs of his trousers were muddy.

He said, 'There's blood on your coat.'

Anne glanced at it. 'Oh. It doesn't matter. Such an old thing. It can be cleaned.'

'I'll pay for the cleaning.'

'Don't be silly,' she said brusquely. 'Please sit down. I'll put the coffee on.' She went into the tiny kitchen and got out the aluminium pot. It flew out of her hands – knocked out of her grasp by one of the mischievous household demons that haunted her – and landed on the floor with a nerve-jangling clatter. She cringed, and was about to call out, 'Sorry,' until she remembered that Gilbert wasn't home to scold her for being clumsy and for making unnecessary noise.

She brought out Kit's bottle of scotch and a glass and set them on the table near the couch where he was sitting. He sloshed some scotch into a glass and thrust it at her. 'Have some.'

'No, thank you. I don't like the taste.'

'Drink it down fast,' he said, pressing the glass on her. 'You won't taste it.'

She hesitated then obeyed because she didn't want to anger him. Shuddering, she handed the glass back. 'It's horrible. I don't know how people can drink anything that vile.' But the liquor warmed and numbed her. She felt calmer.

He poured a generous measure for himself. 'You get used to it.' He emptied the glass in two swallows, and poured another. 'You can get used to anything. War. Blood. The Argonne. You get used to it because you have to. You know there's nothing better and there's no use hoping. It's not like being poor. You know there's something better and it's just out of reach.'

'You were in the war?'

'I enlisted,' he shrugged. 'Didn't have anything better to do and I decided what the hell, might as well learn to kill. That part has come in handy.'

'And I suppose you also learned how to survive,' Anne said, perching on the edge of a chair.

Innes laughed. 'I already knew that. I'd lived on the streets since I was twelve. By the time I went into the army, there wasn't much I didn't know. I should have learned my lesson about women. The rich ones, the

169

so-called ladies, would step on your face to get into their cars. The poor ones who had kids of their own were nicer. The whores were the best. I lived with one for two weeks, until her pimp found out about it and beat the shit out of me. That's when I enlisted. I wanted to come back and kill him.' He clenched his fists, strangling the memory of that first enemy. 'I never did, but I haven't lost a fight since then.'

'Where did you grow up?' Anne could see that he needed to talk.

'New York. Lower East Side. I was born in Ireland. My folks brought me over when I was three. My old man was a dockworker until he hurt his back and couldn't lift. He drank. My mother was a schoolteacher. She was too good for him. I suppose she married him because he knocked her up. I was born five months after the wedding.'

'Maybe she loved him,' Anne said.

'Not him.' Innes shook his head and poured himself another glassful of scotch. The level in the bottle dropped to the halfway mark. 'Not that son of a bitch. I never knew him to say a kind word to anyone, and he treated her like dirt. She tried to pay the rent and buy food right after she was paid, before she got the money home, because the old man would beat her up and take it, and drink it up. He beat me regularly. I hated his guts. I couldn't wait to get out. I ran away once. My mother cried and said, "Ah, Jamie, don't do this to me. If I lose you, I've lost everything, I've no reason to live. Stay, for my sake."'

'What happened?'

'She died. Tuberculosis, they said, but I think she just got tired of fighting him. Women have a way of disappointing a man,' he said with a grim laugh. 'I've never known it to fail. You think you're all right, everything's fine, and they pull the rug from under your feet, you land on your head and the world's upside down. There's nobody can ruin things so fast and so neat as a woman.' Anne heard the echoes of old bitterness in his voice. 'I went to the funeral. The old man was drunk, blubbering like a woman. His pals had to hold him up, to keep him from falling into the grave. I never went back to that house. I lived on the street. Worked odd jobs, stole

170

some. But it was never enough. A few cents here, a dollar there. Chicken feed. Nothing. A little bit of money is worse than no money at all, because it's not enough. Never enough.'

He turned his head and stared glumly at a framed photograph of Anne and Gilbert on their wedding day. Anne had a sudden vision of him as a child, a frustrated, lonely little boy furious at his mother for dying, for abandoning him.

He looked up and saw the questioning look on her face. 'Well, say it, whatever you're thinking.'

She said, 'I was just wondering, how much is enough? All you have now, is that enough? Does it make you happy?'

'I'm not looking for happiness,' he said. 'I'm not a priest, or a missionary's daughter. I don't believe I'll feel happy if I give it away. I've worked too hard making it.'

'I know that.'

'You don't know anything. People like you and your sister look down on a man because he's had to work, because he didn't have his money handed to him when he was born. You know what Kit calls me? The empire builder. She makes it sound like an insult. That woman could make Jesus Christ Himself feel like an idiot for getting hung up on the cross.'

Anne said, 'I grew up hearing her laugh at me, but I don't pay any attention. I know she sounds cruel, but I don't think she means any harm.'

'She's a bitch,' Innes said. 'She knows exactly what she's doing every minute of the day. She's got everything all planned out, and she's just sitting back and laughing at the rest of us because we're in the dark, ignorant.'

'I think you give her too much credit,' Anne protested. 'She's not deliberately malicious.'

'So she's got you buffaloed, too. You just wait and see.'

Innes lit a cigarette and stared morosely at the plume of gray smoke. Anne picked at a fingernail. Suddenly there was a menacing hissing noise in the kitchen. The coffee was boiling over. She jumped to her feet and ran to save it.

'This is going to be awful,' she said, appearing a few

minutes later with a tray loaded with pot and cups. 'It infuriates Gilbert that I can't do anything so simple as make coffee. I'm afraid there's no milk.' She sat on the end of the sofa. 'I can never remember to remind Wu —'

'That's all right. I don't take it.' He watched her pour. 'I made trouble between you and your husband,' he said.

Anne's hand shook and she spilled some coffee into her saucer. 'What? Oh, no, you didn't do that.'

'He was mad as hell.'

She smiled weakly. 'He's always irritated with me about something. I'm afraid I'm not a very good wife. I'm not very good at anything, except getting angry.'

'I deserved it. I should have taken better care of her. She was your friend. She liked you, respected you. She told me what you did for her. I'm sorry.'

Innes took a swallow of coffee and tried not to grimace. Anne tasted hers and gagged.

'God, that's awful. Don't drink any more,' she said.

'If I knock it back fast, I won't taste it,' he said with a feeble grin. He set down his cup and helped himself to another shot of scotch.

'I said some very harsh things to you tonight,' she said. 'Father Jacquinot was right. I shouldn't have judged you and sentenced you to hang. After all, Josepha made her own decisions. About living with you. About the abortion. You're not to blame.'

Innes gave Anne a cigarette, lit it, lit one for himself. 'There was another Chinese girl, a long time ago. I met her at Sun's place in Pu-Yi, the first time I was there. He wanted to buy some opium, although he never said so straight out. He never says anything straight out. He gave me the girl. He called her a concubine, but I think she was just a servant. She had big feet, not bound.'

Anne nodded. Peasants didn't bind their daughters' feet. A woman with bound feet would be of no use to a farmer.

'That girl hated me. I could see it in her eyes. Hate – and fear. Every time I touched her. She never cried, though. And she never – refused me.'

'No,' said Anne, 'she wouldn't. She had to obey her master, and please you.'

'We decided that Sun would work for me. I needed someone like him, a go-between. I took him back to Shanghai. The girl came with us. So did the rest of his family. She was very shy. She never spoke in front of them. We passed through the Gorges. It was rough, but not too bad. From then on it looked like a clear run. The current was with us. The water was high. We all relaxed. I turned the rudder over to one of the crewmen and went aft to check on Sun. I saw her standing at the side of the boat. She looked funny, strange. I thought she was sick. I took a step toward her, just one step, and she went over, head first. I saw that look in her eyes, just before she did it: she wanted to die. I went in after her. The current carried her away from the boat, and I swam like hell to catch up with her before it pulled her under. She did go under once or twice. I got close to her, close enough to grab her. She cursed me, and scratched at my eyes, I couldn't see for a second, and when I looked again, she was gone.'

Anne said, 'Sun shouldn't have done that to her. Her position was unnatural, uncomfortable. You treated her well, but he was still her master, and I'm sure his family treated her badly, with disdain. She was disturbed by it all. And then you took her far from her home and her family. Shanghai is the other side of the world to girls like that. A different country. You were taking her away from everything she knew. Of course she was frightened.'

'I wouldn't have hurt her,' Innes said. 'I've never hit a woman in my life.'

'You don't understand. You don't know how strange we appear to the Chinese. They really think we're ugly, and barbaric, and ghostlike. You looked like a demon to her, with your white skin and hairy body and eyes as blue as a blind man's. She would never have become accustomed to you. She was an ignorant girl, superstitious, frightened of shadows. The prospect of going to Shanghai with you truly terrified her. But any white man would have had the same effect. I remember once when I was very small, I wandered away from the mission compound in Nanking, where we lived. My amah wasn't watching me closely and I seized my chance at freedom, I guess. I

173

found myself a couple of streets away, in a poor section where I had never been before. Suddenly there were Chinese all around, watching me. I wasn't frightened, because the mission Chinese I knew had always been kind to me. I must have spoken to them. They began to point and back away. And then one of them threw a stone. It hit me on the head.' She pushed the hair back from her hairline to reveal a crescent-shaped scar about an inch and a half long. 'I remember I was so astonished that I didn't even cry. I was small, only about five or six, but someone in that crowd thought I was a demon or a ghost and wanted to chase me away.'

'What happened then?'

'I hardly remember. I think my amah found me and whisked me away to safety. But don't you see, they attacked me because they were afraid of me. What that girl did had very little to do with you. It would be wrong of you to take all the blame for that. Or for Josepha. You couldn't know the way her mind worked. She thought that if she disobeyed you and had a child, you would beat her, or throw her out, let her starve. It was sad, stupid, and wasteful, but not your fault. I think if you hadn't taken her in, someone else would have. That's what she wanted, someone to take care of her. I suppose that's what we all want.'

Innes said, 'I wanted her because she looked like Kit.'

'Kit?' Anne frowned.

'You saw it yourself – you must have seen it. I wanted her to dress like Kit, walk like her, talk like her – not that there was ever any chance of that. I even tried to make her drink and smoke cigarettes. I changed her hair, her clothes.'

Anne said, 'Then those weren't Kit's things in her closet.'

'They were copies. Perfect copies. Jewelry, underwear, nightgowns – everything.'

Anne was astonished. 'But – why?'

'Because I couldn't have the real one. I know, we're married. But it never went right, not from our first night together. I don't know what I expected. There were a few days between the time she talked to me about it and the

174

time we got married when I couldn't believe my luck. I wanted her – didn't every man in Shanghai want her? – and I turned around one day and there she was, saying, "Do you want to get married?" It was too easy. I should have known she was up to something.'

Anne said, 'I don't understand. She proposed to you?'

'That's right. But she hated my guts even then. She told me so later. She was interested in my money, sure. But she's no more interested in the money she could make for herself. She has a genious for attracting investors, rich men. One look at her and they pull out their checkbooks. She could bring a lot of new money into the company, but she's not interested. She's done some entertaining for me – part of the deal before we got married was that she'd be my hostess – and she's hooked a couple of big ones. I offered her a percentage. She laughed in my face. It's part of the game she plays. She never gets excited. Always bored, always cold. I can't get near her unless she wants something. The rest of the time she treats me like I had the plague. A woman like that can make life hell for a man. Make him think he isn't a man at all.'

Anne wished he wouldn't talk like this, wished she could think of something to say that would make his fears and his misery evaporate. Magic words, secret signs. Where were they? What were they?

'I'm sorry,' she said. 'I didn't know.'

'You want to talk about a woman disappointing a man? Well, Kit is the champ. She can take the wind out of your sails faster than anybody, and she doesn't have to do anything so dramatic as dying. All it takes is a word, or a laugh. God, I can hear that laugh of hers in my sleep. You know that it doesn't matter what you have, how hard you've worked, you're nothing in her eyes and you'll always be nothing. You think you've left it all behind, the nothingness. You climb the ladder, higher and higher, then you look up and there it is, staring you in the face. I thought Josepha could make it better. She was like Kit, without any of Kit's coldness. When I was with her, I could almost forget which woman I'd married. She made me feel good again. Right. Now she's gone.'

He ground the heels of his hands into his eye sockets.

His shoulders shook. He made an ugly, rasping noise. It was a sob.

'Oh, no.' Anne watched, horrified and helpless at this display of despair. 'No, don't.' She sat beside him and put her arm around his shoulders. 'Please, Jamie. It will be all right. Everything will be all right, I promise. Don't worry, Jamie. Please.'

He whirled, clasping his arms around her waist, and pressed his face hard against her breasts. The sudden movement caught her by surprise and she sat frozen for a moment, then she folded her arms around his shoulders.

'There, Jamie,' she murmured. 'Poor Jamie, don't be sad. It's all right, you'll see. Hush. Hush, now.'

She smoothed his hair and rocked gently. She relaxed a little and settled back with him into the curve of the sofa arm. He was very quiet. She wondered if he was asleep. She stroked his forehead rhythmically and lightly.

The weight of his head on her breasts felt so good, so right. It had been a long time since she had held anyone. In the early days of their marriage, Gilbert had suffered her affectionate displays with poor grace, and now he never touched her at all. She was grateful now that she could comfort Innes, offer him something he seemed to need.

She knew Innes. She could read him as plainly as if he had a window cut in his skull so that she could observe the workings of his brain. He was surprisingly vulnerable, because he was romantic. Women always disappointed him, because the woman didn't exist who would fit his dream. It was a pity. He had dragged himself up from nothing and he had no one to share in the heady joy of his success. Women like Kit sneered at his origins; women like Josepha took what he gave them without caring who he was or where he came from. His mother was dead. There was no one to be proud of him.

She felt suddenly angry. Unconsciously her arms tightened around him. She wanted to berate God, to shout, 'Why won't You let anyone be happy?' But of course it wasn't God's fault. Weak people, like her, and proud people, like Gilbert, and foolish people, like Innes, wouldn't let themselves be happy. Kit pretended not to

176

concern herself with happiness, and perhaps that was the secret: don't let yourself care too much, or want anything so badly that you feel cheated if you don't get it.

Chen sacrificed personal happiness for the shimmering ideal of the general good. Revolution doesn't engender happiness, only dim hopes. Father Jacquinot had seen too much misery to believe in happiness. Like success and failure, happiness had no place in a peasant's vocabulary. Priests were too shrewd to promise happiness here on earth. That would come later, after death, they said. Typical clerical lies. She had heard her father tell those same lies hundreds of times.

She traced the whorl of hair on the top of Innes' head. The side of his face that was turned up to her was eroded, weathered by worry and the Yangtze sun. Deep creases, pale from being pressed into a squint, fanned out from the corners of his eyes.

His body radiated welcome warmth, and she realized that she had felt cold. Locking your arms around another human being was the most pleasant sensation in the world. You gave comfort and gained comfort. She closed her eyes and wished for someone to love. A child, the child she had given up. Her daughter would be eight years old. She wanted someone who would love her uncritically and unreservedly, someone who didn't care that she couldn't make coffee or that she left her stockings slung over the foot of the bed. If only Gilbert would give her a child. Small chance of that. He was bored, and cold, like Kit. He had looked like a dead man in his white coat, perhaps more like an angel. Too good for her. Saintly. She was too much, even for a saint.

When she awoke she was alone. She wondered for a moment if she had dreamed the whole nightmarish evening. Then she saw the half-empty scotch bottle, the glass, the soiled coffee service. A cigarette still smoldered in the ashtray. Innes had been gone for only a few minutes. She slumped down and buried her face in her arms, and she hoped fervently that she wouldn't have to see him again.

Josepha died on a Wednesday. The next day Father

Jacquinot telephoned Anne to tell her that the funeral would take place on Friday morning, and that Monsieur Innes' car would call for her at eight o'clock. She protested that she didn't need a lift, since she always left for school on her bicycle at that hour anyway, but he repeated his message and hung up.

Gilbert never mentioned what had happened at the Aldershot. He treated the whole business as an embarrassing aberration that he would prefer to forget, rather as if Anne had drunk too much and disgraced herself at a party.

At breakfast on Friday he barricaded himself behind the *North China Daily News*, as usual. As she was about to leave the house, Anne said loudly, 'Josepha Chang's funeral is this morning.'

He put down his paper and looked at her. She was shocked at how worn and haggard he seemed. Poor man, suffering from overwork and no sympathy at home. She felt a pang of guilt. He opened his mouth to speak and closed it again with an almost audible snap. What was there to say?

Innes hardly said a word during the drive to L'École des Filles. Anne suspected he was hung over. She herself felt emotionally hung over, and she was grateful for his silence.

The little chapel was brimming with flowers, almost as if a wedding were about to take place. The flower-bedecked coffin stood at the foot of the center aisle, in front of the altar. It was topped with a wreath of exquisite red roses that could only have come from Innes.

The senior girls filed in, all dressed in white. They cast curious looks at Innes, seated beside Anne in the front pew, and nudged and whispered to each other. Anne was certain that they knew all the juiciest details of their former classmate's demise. The nuns and the students chanted the funeral liturgy in Latin; Father Jacquinot sang the Mass in his lusty bass-baritone. Innes seemed familiar with the pattern of behavior at Mass, and rose to his feet and fell to his knees with the rest. Anne, the uninitiated Protestant, was always half a beat behind everyone else.

Father Jacquinot thoughtfully repeated his brief remarks in English for the benefit of the sole non-French-speaking person in church, James Innes.

The ceremony was beautiful but impersonal, Anne thought. Anyone could have lain under that blanket of flowers. Father Jacquinot's references to a 'dear child' seemed to have very little to do with the Josepha she knew. What had set her apart from the others? She was mischievous, full of laughter, eager to please, eager to love. She never complained about her crippled feet, although she was in pain most of the time. Sexually experienced, she had a quality of innocence that many genuinely innocent girls lacked. Nothing could make her believe there was anything dirty or bad about sex. She would have felt no shame at being Innes' mistress, and she would have given herself to him freely and joyously. Anne had no doubt that her death left an aching void in his life. Not just because he had lost his Kit surrogate, but because love like Josepha's was rarer than rubies.

And yet Anne had wanted to change her. So had Innes. How foolish they both were.

In one of those exotic juxtapositions so dear to the hearts of travel writers, a seven-tiered pagoda loomed over the Roman Catholic cemetery at the southwestern edge of the city. The mother superior of the order of Les Filles de Sainte Thérèse and the principal of the school attended the brief service at the graveside with Innes and Anne. After they had all tossed a flower onto the coffin and turned their backs on the grave, the two nuns spoke warmly to Innes and thanked him for coming. Anne wondered if they knew just how Josepha had died, or if they still believed that Innes was simply Josepha's employer at Innes & Company. Doubtless he had given them a generous check to cover the funeral expenses. That would explain their gracious manner.

The nuns had their own car and a driver to take them back to the school, in a western suburb of Shanghai. They insisted that Anne take the rest of the day off and go home to rest. Still protesting that they didn't have to treat her like an invalid, she rode off in the Rolls with Innes and Father Jacquinot, who had accepted a lift as far as Aurora

University, where he had a noon lecture. He admired the Rolls enthusiastically, and relaxing against the plush seat he closed his eyes and murmured without envy, 'Ah, it is wonderful, the comfort that money can buy.' He would never have owned such a car himself, but he didn't begrudge Innes the trappings of wealth.

Innes handed around cigarettes. Both Anne and the priest accepted and his lighter flashed three times. Anne had a sudden vivid picture of the three of them sitting silently in the back of the car, moving their hands to their lips and expelling puffs of smoke in an uneven rhythm, like the components of a bizarre machine. She had a sudden mad urge to laugh, and suppressed it with difficulty. She had seen people laughing hysterically at funerals, and knew that it was just a sign of strain and a manifestation of grief.

Father Jacquinot said, 'I observe, Monsieur Innes, that you are familiar with the rites and ceremonies of the Catholic Church.'

'I was an altar boy when I was a kid. I haven't been in a church since my mother died. Funny, how it comes back.'

'Ah, you never lose the habits that are instilled in you in childhood. Tell me, Monsieur, do you play chess, by any chance?'

Innes said he had never had time to learn.

'Be careful,' Anne cautioned. 'He'll offer to teach you. Those lessons will degenerate into theological discussions. He'll have you back in the fold before you know it.'

'Oh, Anne, how can you say such a thing?' Father Jacquinot sounded hurt. 'I didn't succeed in making either a decent chess player or a Catholic out of you.'

'You had your chance to make me a Catholic, and you decided that I wasn't good enough,' she retorted. 'And as for chess – I beat you once, remember?'

'Yes, when I had a fever of a hundred and four degrees! A baby could have beaten me. But you should keep up your chess, Anne. It would clear your thinking, and make you more patient and logical.'

'I'm afraid I have no talent for logic or patience. Or religion, for that matter. But Mr Innes has a flair for strategy. I think he would make a very good chess player.'

180

'I suspect that Monsieur Innes finds life more amusing than any game,' said Father Jacquinot, smiling at Innes. 'Chess is for armchair warriors like me.'

'I never heard a Jesuit call himself an armchair warrior before,' Innes remarked. 'I think you're right, Anne. He's up to something.'

The two men laughed companionably. Anne experienced a little flutter of nerves when Innes said her name. She decided to get out of the car with Father Jacquinot at Aurora and not let Innes take her home. She didn't want to be alone with him.

The car stopped suddenly. They were surrounded by people. Sanjay sounded the horn impatiently but no one moved. They heard the unmistakable crackle of firecrackers.

'Let's get out and see,' Father Jacquinot said. He opened the door himself and jumped out spryly. Anne and Innes looked at each other and exchanged warm, indulgent smiles. She thought, I'm glad they like each other. 'A funeral, Anne!' Father Jacquinot appeared at the open door. 'Come and look. Hurry!'

He surged through the crowd, Anne and Innes following in his wake. Sanjay left the car, too, in order to keep a close watch on Innes. Crowds were always dangerous, although it was unlikely that an assassin had gone to the trouble to arrange a funeral just to waylay his employer.

They had been stopped on the western approach to the French Concession. The streets were clogged with people eager to see the colorful entertainment of a parade. Father Jacquinot pushed through to the front of the throng.

An enormous papier-mâché dragon, his eyes rolling and his flame-colored body striped with green, bore down on them. Firecrackers popped, sending up puffs of smoke like bullets biting the dust. The dragon was followed by a score of banner carriers in elaborate costume. They were made up to look like ancient warriors with red cheeks, fiercely slanting eyebrows, and billowing mustaches. They wore hats like multitiered pagodas and suits of fake armor, with shoulder plates that shot out like wings, heavy gauntlets and breastplates, and cardboard scabbards with wooden swords. As they marched they gave out blood-curdling yells that made the more timid elements of the populace cringe and back away. Behind them came the musicians, similarly guised. The drummers rolled out an uneven one-two-pause rhythm that somehow marked time for the marchers. Horn players and violinists provided a wailing continuo; percussionists with wood blocks and cymbals rapped out a counterpoint to the drums.

'Are you sure this is a funeral?' Innes had to speak directly into Anne's ear.

'Oh, yes,' Anne said. 'Look at the banners. His name was Feng Tung-chen. He was a warlord, very powerful, very rich. He had many wives and children, including sixteen sons. See, here comes the casket.'

The coffin was draped in white. It sat on a bier as big as a barge which rested on the shoulders of fifty men, all dressed in white, the Chinese funeral color. Little paper and cloth runners lettered with black characters fluttered around the edges of the bier like a grass skirt. They named the deceased and his ancestry. Hired mourners wearing white followed the casket. Their screeches and moans were high-pitched and nerve-shattering, like a thousand fingernails being drawn slowly over glass.

'Pretty noisy,' Innes remarked.

'A Chinese funeral is just like any other public celebration,' Anne said. 'The noise and the bogeymen are supposed to scare away demons.'

Father Jacquinot pointed and began to speak excitedly in French. Anne craned her neck and lifted herself up on tiptoe.

'Oh, look,' she said to Innes. 'Those dancers – right behind the coffin.'

The dancers were also costumed in what looked like Chinese operatic dress, but for classical heroines. They wore brilliantly colored gowns with long, flowing sleeves, and high headdresses decorated with artificial flowers and hundreds of tiny mirrors that showered the crowd with tiny rainbows. Their faces were painted, but not fearsomely like the musicians and banner carriers in the vanguard. Rather they looked like the maidens in ancient Chinese paintings: smooth-faced and demure, lovely pleasure-givers. They swirled their arms gracefully over their heads, and they dipped and turned, lifting their legs in high arcs on every fourth step, when the cymbals clashed. Every motion was slow and deliberate, smoothly choreographed to mesh with the music, which was just barely audible over the howls of the mourners.

'We are very fortunate,' Father Jacquinot said. 'He was very important – one seldom sees such grand funerals anymore. And these beauties – I have not seen the like for many years. This is truly wonderful!'

'Those are the enticers,' Anne told Innes. 'The dragon and the firecrackers and the fake warriors are supposed to scare away the demons, but there are always good spirits hovering over us as well. The enticers are supposed to attract them. Maybe they'll bring a little good fortune to the living.'

'They have certainly enticed me,' Father Jacquinot said, stepping out into the street. 'I think I shall follow them for a little while. Adieu, both of you.'

He raised his arm in farewell and disappeared, swallowed up by the excited onlookers. Anne and Innes were shunted to the rear of the mob. The area around them cleared as part of the crowd opted to follow the funeral and the rest returned to their various occupations.

'Nice guy,' Innes said.

'He's wonderful,' Anne said. 'The only real friend I have in Shanghai.'

'One friend,' Innes smiled. 'Kit must have a thousand and one.'

'I'm probably fussier than Kit in that respect. I may not care what I look like, or how I live, or what I say, but I won't call every half-wit who knows my name my friend.'

They walked back to the car. Even in flat shoes Anne was nearly as tall as Innes. A stray hairpin dangled from a wisp of hair over her left ear. Her old raincoat still bore stains of Josepha's blood.

Anne said, 'I'll leave you here. Thanks for the lift.'

'I thought you wanted to go home.'

'No, not really. We're not far from the university now. I have some things to do there.' She hoped he wouldn't ask questions. She couldn't think of a thing she needed to do at Aurora.

She shoved her hands deeper into her coat pockets and gave him a weak smile. 'Well, goodbye.' She started to move away.

'Wait a minute, Anne.'

She stopped. He came closer. 'I haven't thanked you for your help the other night.'

'You don't need to. She was my friend.'

'I didn't mean just Josepha. You helped me, too. I can't believe – you're nothing like Kit.'

'So I've been told, many times,' she said stiffly. 'It's usually a veiled insult. Or maybe not so veiled.'

'No, I don't mean it that way. I wish – she were more like you.' He thrust out his hand. She hesitated, then gave him her own. He held it for an uncomfortably long moment. 'I'd like you to think you had two friends in Shanghai. If there's ever anything —'

I've really got to go,' she said nervously, withdrawing her hand and stepping back a pace. 'Goodbye, Mr Innes.' She turned and fled, before he could say more.

So he wanted Kit to be more like her. Well! That was a first, and about as meaningful as anything a man said under the influence of grief, excitement, and too much scotch.

Anne read the attached card before she opened the box. It said, 'Thanks again.' The signature was a scrawled 'Jamie.' The blood rose to her cheeks and she felt warm. 'Oh, really,' she muttered. 'How absurd.' She wondered if she should send the box back unopened. But what if it were something innocuous, like flowers? Flowers, in a broad, flat box as big as a table? She lifted the lid and pushed aside a layer of tissue paper. Inside lay a new coat, a fine trench coat with an English label, the kind Garbo might wear in a film. 'Oh, really,' Anne said again.

She couldn't help herself. She had to try it on. She walked around the living room, and wandered into the bathroom to admire herself in the cracked mirror over the sink. The coat fit perfectly. Innes must have a very efficient secretary who shopped for him: 'She's about so high, not too heavy, but she has big tits.' She couldn't believe he had chosen it himself. She tweaked the cuffs and tightened the belt. It was nice, the nicest thing she would ever own. Too bad she had to return it.

She sat on the edge of the bathtub and tried to imagine the conversation: I can't possibly accept, but thank you very much. Why in hell can't you? She winced, and decided she would refuse the gift by messenger instead of by phone. She would enclose a note with the coat and that would be the end of it.

She went back to the living room. She was holding Innes' note in her hand when Gilbert came in, and she shoved the paper into the pocket of her coat. Not that she had anything to feel guilty about. The intimacy she had shared with Innes hadn't been remotely sexual, but the memory of her impulsiveness that night embarrassed her. She had been so eager for any kind of closeness. It was pathetic. Humiliating.

Gilbert set his black doctor's bag down on the table near the door and peeled off his overcoat.

Anne said, 'You're home early. I thought you had surgery this afternoon.'

'I got it assigned to someone else. I've reassigned all my patients, too. We're leaving.'

'What do you mean? For the States?'

'No, for Chengtu.' He sat down on the couch and tilted his head back. 'I talked to Dr Morrison today. I'm not happy here.'

Stab of guilt. 'Yes, I know.'

'You think I hate the Chinese,' he said defensively, 'but I don't. I don't hate anyone. It's this city – I can't bear to live here anymore. It's a cesspool. Corrupt, ugly.' Beautiful, destructive.

'You think God doesn't know Shanghai exists,' Anne said. 'There's important work to do here.'

'You can stay, if you like,' he said, closing his eyes. 'I won't force you to come with me.'

'That would look awfully bad.'

'You don't care about that.' His tone was bitter, accusing.

'Yes, I do care, Gilbert. Please don't be – Of course I'll go. What did Uncle Billy say?'

'Not too much. He understands how I feel. We're leaving tomorrow. He's booked us on a steamer that leaves at nine in the morning.'

'So soon?'

'It can't be soon enough.' He sounded weary, bored, uninterested in the adventure ahead of them.

How he had changed. He wasn't the same Gilbert who had come ashore six months ago, so full of enthusiasm and hope. What had happened to him? He married a woman he didn't love.

'We don't have that much to pack,' he said. 'You can say your goodbyes by telephone.'

'My job,' she said. 'They'll have a hard time finding someone to replace me.'

'They'll cope. The Aldershot will cope. You can do all the explaining you want – by letter from Chengtu.'

Anne walked to the window and looked out at her roses. Perhaps she could take a couple of plants – no, that would be silly. There were roses in Szechwan.

'We'd better get started,' Gilbert said. 'That's a new coat, isn't it?'

She turned. 'Yes, in a way. Actually —'

'It's nice. About time you got yourself something decent to wear. At least you won't turn up in Chengtu looking like a refugee.'

She fingered the little card in her pocket. 'No,' she said. 'At least I won't disgrace you. I suppose it came just in time.'

Chapter Seven

Their guide shouted encouragement. Gilbert grasped Anne's hand and pulled her up the last steep step. They stood at the top of a mile-high precipice halfway up the western face of Mount Omei, about a hundred and fifty miles southwest of Chengtu. They had spent the night at an inn at the foot of the sacred mountain. Their guide woke them well before sunrise and they started their climb by lanternlight.

Now the rising sun broke over the top of the mountain and spread its orange blaze over the valleys and mountains in the distance. One large snow-covered peak towered above the rest. The fiery brightness of the sun on its slopes made it look like a volcanic cone bathed in lava.

'Is that Tibet?' Anne panted. 'And Everest?'

'No, it's still the Tahsueh chain. That big one is Minya Konka. We'll climb it someday. It's only twenty-five thousand feet.'

Anne shook her head. 'You go. Take plenty of photographs.' She collapsed on a low rock. 'I don't know where you get your energy.'

Gilbert said severely, 'I don't smoke cigarettes.'

'Neither do I. Much.'

They laughed together. Gilbert sat next to her. Their arms touched but he didn't pull away, as he might have done in the past.

'This is nice,' Anne said. 'We've never had a real holiday before. We'll be married two years in August.'

'I'll be able to take a real furlough in another couple of years. We'll go home. My mother is dying to meet you.'

'And I can meet Louise,' Anne teased, 'and her two remarkable babies. She certainly didn't waste any time pining away for you.'

'She knew I wasn't worth it.'

'Don't expect me to argue with you about that.'

'I won't. I'm glad you stuck it out.'

'So am I. Besides, every couple has difficulties at first.

All the ladies' magazines say so.'

'Really? Where do you get to read ladies' magazines?'

'Reverend Masters' wife's sister sends her a whole slew from Boston every month. Must cost a fortune in postage alone. When Dinah's through with them she passes them on to those of us who aren't so fortunate in our sisters.'

Gilbert jerked spasmodically. Anne looked at him, concerned. 'Cramp in my calf,' he explained, rubbing the false affliction. They had been in Chengtu nearly two years, and he still experienced sharp jolts of feeling whenever he thought about Kit. Guilt? Longing? He wasn't sure. He still couldn't believe he was really free of her. Every day he prayed his thanks.

They picnicked by the side of the path, near a Buddhist shrine. Pilgrims passed on their way to the summit: monks in saffron-colored robes, their heads shaved, prostrating themselves on the ground at regular intervals; rich men from Chungking, riding in sedan chairs and surrounded by servants; peasants from the countryside, coming to pray for a good harvest, a good marriage, a son.

They shared their sandwiches and flask of tea with their guide, a youth from the village of Omei whose brother lived in San Francisco.

'I go someday. Everybody is rich there. Everybody drives car.'

Anne and Gilbert smiled at each other and didn't disillusion him. In the afternoon they rested a little, then explored the eastern face of the mountain below the frosty rime of clouds at the peak. The day was clear, the humidity low, and they could see far beyond the hills and the Min and T'o rivers to the level plain that surrounded Chengtu. It was a sprawling patchwork of brilliant greens and golds, dotted with villages and clusters of bamboo forests, crisscrossed by canals and rivers. Before sunset they climbed to the summit, above the clouds, to see 'Buddha's Glory.' The waning sun at their backs cast their own long shadows on the blanket of clouds below them. They waved their arms; their shadowy counterparts did the same within golden halos of sunlight.

To stand high above the clouds, Anne thought. It's worth the climb, worth the waiting and the worrying.

Their sudden departure from Shanghai not only forced them into close proximity; it necessitated closer communication. There were a thousand details to attend to. At the last moment Dr Morrison asked them to take along a supply of serums and other medicines which the staff of the University Hospital at Chengtu had requested. They had to guard these items plus their own possessions. Their steamer broke down just east òf the Gorges, and Anne had to hire a barge and some trackers to haul them upriver to Chungking. Since Gilbert's Chinese was feeble and always seemed to fail him in critical moments, the burden of organization fell on Anne, who handled everything with calm efficiency. She paid their laborers the right amount each evening – enough for food but not enough for opium, arranged for rooms and meals, kept a watchful eye on their valuable cargo, soothed tempers, and attended to Gilbert's comfort. He realized that she was really an old China hand. She had grown up helping her mother deal with just such problems. He knew he would have been helpless without her.

American Methodist and Baptist missionaries had established the West China Union University in Chengtu, the capital of Szechwan Province. They were joined by English and American members of the Society of Friends, and Canadian Methodists. Each denomination maintained its own dormitories and athletic fields around the periphery of the university compound, which was located a mile from the south gate of the ancient walled city. All contributed teachers to the colleges located at the center of the campus. The hospital and medical schools were part of the university.

The white community was small, less diverse and more close-knit than Shanghai's. Anne likened it to a pond, in which ripples from a disturbance at one end reached them all. They all felt the turbulent winds of the unsettled political situation in China. Two months before Anne and Gilbert's arrival, an English Quaker physician had been attacked by a band of ruffians. He died soon after. Officials of the Nationalist Government blamed the Communists, the Communists blamed the Nationalists, and both cast a share of blame on the deceased, a newcomer to China who had unwittingly wandered into a neighborhood well outside the guarded university compound. There were no gunboats to protect whites in Chengtu. They were vulnerable, more exposed than they would have been in treaty ports like Chungking or Shanghai.

The Lawrences moved into an apartment on the tree-shaded campus, which boasted an interesting assortment of classically styled Chinese and modern red brick buildings. Their flat in Shanghai had been furnished, so they had accumulated very little in the way of necessities. Anne spent her first week in Chengtu haunting second-hand shops and bargaining with Chinese merchants. The members of the medical faculty held a surprise shower for them and gave them linens, blankets, dishes, and towels to help fill in the gaps.

They had been in their new home less than a month when Gilbert gave the little cough that always preceded one of his portentous announcements.

'Dr Masters asked if we would be in church on Sunday. I said yes. I want you to come with me.'

Anne said, 'You shouldn't have promised for me. You know how I feel about it.'

'Yes, but think how it will look —'

'They'll get used to it. Don't worry, they won't shun you just because your wife is a little strange.'

'But what shall I tell them?'

'Tell them the truth, that I don't believe in it, and that the hypocrisy of most Christians sickens me.'

His face reddened. 'I know I have no right to ask for favors. You didn't have to come here at all. But I would appreciate it if you would do just this one thing for me. I won't ask anything else of you.'

She thought for a long moment, and sighed. 'Since I'm here primarily to save your face in front of your fellow missionaries, I suppose it's my duty to keep on saving it. All right, I'll go. But if Masters' sermons are as boring as his conversation, I won't promise to stay awake.'

Repeating the pattern of their Shanghai days, Anne slept on the couch in the living room. One day their amah remarked to Gilbert that they would have a hard time making a baby if they didn't share the same bed. That night as Anne was unfurling her blanket, Gilbert said, 'This is silly. The bed is plenty big enough for two. There's no need for you to sleep out here.'

Anne, to whom the amah had voiced an identical observation, gave him a sour smile. 'More face-saving?'

'Not at all. I just —'

'It's all right. My back was giving out anyway.'

The pain of her frustration and loneliness was even sharper now that he was so near and yet so unapproachable. The void inside her throbbed; her empty womb seemed to expand, engulfing every part of her body and her mind so that she felt possessed by aching emptiness. Often, after Gilbert had fallen asleep, she shut herself up in the bathroom and made frantic love to herself. These sessions brought no relief, not because she felt wicked but because they made her situation seem even more hopeless and ridiculous. But at least their amah was content, and she watched Anne closely for signs of pregnancy.

Anne held herself aloof from the other white women. She resisted the temptation to form close friendships. She was a poor liar and prevaricator, and she knew every time she spoke her mind and voiced her opinions of joss-pidgin-men and the white man's folly in China, not she but Gilbert would suffer. So she avoided her neighbors, and refused their invitations to coffee parties and luncheons. She spent long hours by herself, exploring the city and its environs. After a few weeks she decided she must find herself something productive to do, and she announced to Gilbert that she was going to resume nurse's training. The Director of Nursing was going to let her pick up the first-year course in the middle of the term. Gilbert was skeptical.

'Going to take another stab at it? I think you're wasting your time. Why don't you teach? I'm sure the university would be glad to have you.'

'They don't need another English teacher. Besides, I think I can do it now. I've learned to be like you, not to care about people too much. Nursing is better than teaching: your efforts bear instant fruit. Your patient either lives or he dies.'

Gilbert made a face. 'A peculiar reason for going into medicine.'

She shrugged. 'I'm a peculiar person.'

She found the course in midwifery most exciting. Assisting at the birth of a baby was painful for her at first because it evoked so many sad memories, but at the same time she was thrilled, and she felt that every child she helped deliver belonged, in some way, to her.

At her supervisor's suggestion, she put together an illustrated talk for Chinese women on feminine hygiene, birth control, and childbirth. She was frank, amusing, and informative, and the talk was a great success with the University Hospital's obstetrics patients and with the women who came to the outpatient clinic in Chengtu.

The head of the medical school wanted her to take her lecture into the countryside, and suggested she accompany Gilbert and his nurse on their weekly visits to outlying village clinics. Gilbert couldn't refuse, and grudgingly arranged for her transportation. One afternoon his regular Chinese nurse became ill at the last minute and no replacement could be found. He and Anne traveled to the village of Bihsien by ricksha. She would assist him, translate for him, and try to gather an audience for her talk.

Gilbert's patients were all poor peasants, with the sweat and grime of their fields and paddies still on their skins. Because Chengtu was located in the middle of a fertile plain irrigated by river waters that spilled down from the mountains, few people ever starved. At least missionaries in Szechwan didn't have that horror to contend with.

Anne helped him treat an infected bound foot, a scalp laceration, a skin cancer, and a bad case of malaria. All the whites regularly dosed themselves with quinine pills to prevent malarial infection, but it was prevalent among the peasants. She watched him closely. He was gentle, deft, a fine doctor. But every time he touched a Chinese, he flinched ever so slightly. He still despised them. Anne hoped she would never again be called upon to assist him professionally.

They were both silent on the ride home. She knew that if she opened her mouth to say anything, even to remark upon the coolness of the evening or the song of a thrush, a torrent of bitterness would come pouring out. She decided, as they rocked over a deserted stretch of road among low hills, that she would have to leave him and return to Shanghai. She could no longer endure the strain of presenting a contented face to the world.

Suddenly the ricksha was surrounded by ragged soldiers carrying rifles. Their ricksha coolie gave a yelp of terror, dropped the shafts of his vehicle, and ran. A shot rang out and he fell on his face in the dust, twitched a little, and lay still. One of the brigands stepped between the shafts and began to pull them along, into the hills.

'No, wait, don't do this. You will get no ransom from us,' Anne shouted. 'We are poor. We are only missionaries. No one will pay to redeem our worthless lives.'

The soldiers paid no attention. They left the track and climbed into the foothills of the Taliangshan Mountains. The ricksha lurched and pitched as the terrain grew rougher, and from time to time two of their captors had to push from behind. Gilbert and Anne clutched at each other to keep from falling out. Darkness fell quickly in the valley, but their pace didn't slacken even after the last vestiges of pink faded from the sky.

Hours later they arrived at a camp surrounded by a bamboo fence. A lookout shouted to them, and one of their men shouted back. A gate swung open. The ricksha stopped and they climbed out, trembling, happy to feel the ground under their feet. The air was cold, heavy with the smell of cooking mutton, rotting straw, animal manure. Rough hands pushed them toward a hut built of mud bricks and roofed with thatch. The only light inside came from burning wicks floating in bowls of tallow. Men at the doors pointed rifle muzzles at their backs. A groan came from a low bed in the corner.

The man on the bed was broad and bald. His head and face were shiny with sweat.

'You will forgive this rudeness,' he gasped. 'I have had to resort to unorthodox methods —'

Anne and Gilbert exchanged worried glances. They both smelled the stink of gangrene. Anne said, 'Don't talk. We will try to help you.' They drew back the blanket that covered him from the waist down. His left leg was swollen, festering.

'When did this happen?' Gilbert asked in his halting Chinese.

'Five days ago. A fall in the mountains. Not even a bad one. Ridiculous, is it not?'

'We must take you to Chengtu at once,' Gilbert said. 'You should be in the hospital. You may need surgery.'

'No!' Their patient was adamant. 'Yen T'ing-chang will slaughter me. Do you think I want to offer myself like a goat tied to a tree? No!'

'Who is Yen?' Gilbert asked Anne in English.

'Local warlord, one of those who has joined forces with Chiang Kai-shek, supposedly to help him exterminate the Communists. It's just an excuse to get more arms to help him wipe out his own rivals.' She said in Chinese, 'We understand that you do not wish to leave the safety of your camp. But we are not prepared to help you. We have no supplies, no medicines. We will not betray your position to anyone, but we must go to Chengtu and bring back what we need.'

'No. You cannot leave here. No one leaves here!'

The guards at the door shifted nervously. Anne thought of the dead coolie and told Gilbert, 'If we don't obey, they will kill us. We'll just have to do what we can.'

'But we can't possibly save him. We'll probably have to amputate, and even under ideal circumstances he wouldn't have much of a chance.'

'I don't see that we have a choice,' she said, casting a look over her shoulder.

'Even if we manage to save him, they won't let us go.'

'Perhaps not. But the Chinese are not entirely without honor.'

Gilbert had some chloroform in his bag, and Anne dripped some onto the handkerchief which she held over the warlord's nose and mouth. He began to snore sonorously. Gilbert probed the shattered leg and the man moaned in his drugged sleep. The guards made threatening noises and Anne hurriedly explained to them what they were doing. Gilbert demanded more light, and a dozen more tallow lamps were produced.

194

'We're going to have to take it off.'

'Can it wait until daylight?'

'I don't think so. It's probably too late already. The infection has reached the thigh. The sooner the better.'

Anne informed the guards, one of whom turned out to be the warlord's oldest son. She asked for a saw or an ax or a stout knife with a very sharp blade. Someone found a good knife, and honed it until it was as sharp as one of Gilbert's scalpels. Their request for a fire to boil a caldron of water was denied: the flames would betray their position to their enemy warlord or to Nationalist planes. So they sterilized their instruments in the flames of the tallow lamps, and disinfected themselves with alcohol. The inside of the shack grew stifling. Anne blotted perspiration from Gilbert's forehead.

The warlord's son carried away the amputated limb. He would bury it and mark the place so that after the warlord's death his spirit could be whole again. Gilbert packed the wound with a sulfa drug and bound the stump.

'Nothing to do now but pray,' he said.

'I need some air.' Anne went outside. It was almost dawn. One of the guards had some homemade cigarettes and she asked for one. The Chinese had never seen a woman smoke before and they laughed and jostled each other. She was too exhausted to take any pleasure in their joking. Gilbert joined her.

'I think we got it all. He's in pretty good shape otherwise. He might pull through.'

'Won't it be wonderful,' she said, 'to be able to tell people that you operated on a warlord under the most primitive conditions, without proper lights or instruments or medicines, and that he lived. Another illustration of what a marvelous technician you are.'

'What brought this on?' he asked.

'You don't care about that man. You don't care about any of them. They're like bacteria on a petri dish, aren't they? Just a collection of ailments, of organs and arteries, encased in yellow skins.' She smoked the vile cigarette furiously, defiantly. 'It would be different if they were white. Then they'd be people, real people. And you'd have to be decent to them because if you treated them like you treat the Chinese you wouldn't have a patient left. I don't know what you want from us,' putting herself firmly on the side of the Chinese. 'I don't know why you stay. Why don't you just swallow that damned pride of yours and go back home? You're not interested in helping them. And I can't imagine what you want from them in return. You just want to show the world how noble and saintly you can be.'

'Really, Anne, I don't think this is the time or the place —'

'Oh, I beg your pardon. I'm sure I wouldn't want our esteemed physician to lose face in front of a ragtag bunch of bandits. When their wives berate them in public, they beat them bloody. I guess I'm lucky to be white, to be married to a civilized man. Please excuse my thoughtlessness.' She took a last drag on her cigarette and smeared it out in the dirt with her toe.

'You're just tired. We both are. We've had a long day.'

'You can spare me the bedside homilies, Gilbert. Not that it's particularly relevant at this point, as we may never get back to Chengtu at all, but I'm going back to Shanghai. I'll hop the next boat or camel or sedan chair. I don't care if I have to walk. I just can't take any more.' She covered her eyes with her hand.

'But you can't leave,' Gilbert said, shocked by the prospect of having to cope in China without a go-between. 'Please, Anne, give me a chance. I know I've been horrible to you. I hate myself for it. But don't make any decisions now. Please, wait until we get back.'

'I didn't decide just now. I've been thinking it over for a long time. And then back in Bihsien, watching you treat those villagers – it was sickening. I thought maybe the Chinese had stopped being foreigners to you. You've been in this country nearly a year, after all. I thought the distance had narrowed. But you were so cold. As cold as ice. Your loathing for them was written all over you. And they could see it. Did you think they couldn't? I've never been so ashamed in my life, ashamed of being white.'

'I can't help myself,' he said miserably. 'I get down on my knees every day and ask God to break down this wall of pride and make me see them as His children. But –

nothing. I've tried, you'll never know how hard. I'd wear sackcloth and take up a tin cup and live among them like a beggar if I thought it would do any good.'

'It's not pride,' she said. 'You're just afraid of them. That's why you hate them.'

'Anne, if you left me I'd be lost. The others don't know what a fraud I am. I don't know how much longer I can keep it up. I need you, Anne. I need you to keep me sane.'

'Give it up,' she said, facing him squarely. 'It's no disgrace. This life isn't for everyone. Missionaries have killed themselves rather than admit failure. There was one when I was a child. He hung himself in the chapel he'd built with his own hands. Is that what you want? Go home, Gilbert. I'll give you a divorce. I don't want anything from you. But I can't bear living like this anymore. I won't let you use me as a smoke screen. I feel like a mask hiding a grotesque face. We're not married. We're just pretending. And it's killing me, Gilbert. I want children and a good relationship with a man and a place in the world, just a small place, but I'm not getting any of that. You're hurting me, and you're hurting yourself, too. Please, Gilbert. Let's just admit defeat, cut our losses, and stop the charade.'

He shook his head slowly. One of the guards called to them from the hut and he turned and went inside. Anne sagged against the wall, then slid down into a crouch and rested her head on her arms. She felt hollow, aching, desperate.

They stayed in the warlord's encampment for four days, taking turns nursing the man, changing his bandages, watching for infection. On the third day the warlord stumped around on crudely fashioned crutches. His fever was gone and his strength was returning. On the fourth day he ordered his sons to carve him a new leg. Gilbert warned him not to put pressure on the wound until it was completely healed, in a month's time or longer, but the warlord laughed and told them he didn't need their advice any longer. He ordered his men to take them back to the Chengtu road.

They stood beside the ricksha. The warlord's men had

gone. 'Well, shall you pull or shall I?' Anne asked wryly. They were both sweat-soaked and dusty, ready to drop.

'Let's walk.'

The other missionaries, who had found the dead ricksha man and feared the worst, gave them a warm welcome. Anne felt herself sliding back into the charade she hated. When they were alone that night she dragged her trunk into the middle of the living room and she began to gather up clothes and books.

'I can't believe you're really doing this,' Gilbert said. 'What shall I tell them?'

'I don't care.' She knelt in front of the trunk and began to load it. 'Tell them I have an inoperable cancer. Tell them my mother is dying. Tell them I ran away with a coolie. Tell them whatever you want.'

'I don't want you to leave, Anne.'

'Of course you don't. I've been very useful to you, haven't I? But frankly, Gilbert, you have been of no earthly use to me. Don't worry, you'll get along. There are always plenty of women around who love to take in poor, abandoned husbands. It's a weakness that knows no cultural bounds. You won't starve, or freeze to death at night.'

'That's not fair,' he bristled.

'I don't have to be fair. I'm not your wife anymore.' Tears ran down her cheeks and plopped onto the books in her lap. She blotted them quickly, knowing that moisture would mildew the paper in the heat of the Shanghai summer.

Gilbert crouched down beside her and put his hand on her arm. 'Anne, please, can't we talk?'

She shrugged him off. 'Oh, leave me alone, Gilbert. You haven't been able to speak civilly to me for ten months. You haven't touched me. You can hardly bring yourself to look at me. But as soon as I tell you I want out, you relent. Don't you have any shame at all? Do you think I can't see what kind of game you're playing?'

'I know what you think of me. You despise me. I despise myself. You can call me whatever you like – it's all true. I can't explain what made me behave toward you as I did. You never deserved that. You're fine, and good. Whatever happened in the past doesn't matter – I always knew that – but I couldn't go back. I must have been mad. I feel like I've been bewitched, under a spell.'

'Oh, Gilbert,' Anne sighed. 'Please don't.'

'No, I have, really. I've lost my grip, Anne, lost sight of everything that used to have meaning for me. You've seen how it is: I'm not even a decent doctor anymore. I just don't care. I've lost touch with my God, and with myself. The only thing that's kept me alive is you. You're so strong. Yes, I've been using you. I had to, to keep afloat. But I couldn't touch you. I felt like I was living inside a glass cube. I could see and hear people, and they could see me, but I couldn't feel anything for anyone. I think I must have been crazy. Nothing like this has ever happened to me before. But it's over now, I know it is. Things will be better from now on, I promise.' He put his hands on her shoulders and repeated softly. 'I promise.'

She clapped her hands over her ears. 'I don't believe it. I don't believe it. I'm leaving you and I'm not going to change my mind.'

'Don't go, Anne. Stay just a little while longer. If you find out that I've been lying, then you can leave. But don't go now. Stay. Stay.'

His arms encircled her waist. Her hands fell limply into her lap. 'I wish I could trust you.'

'You can, Anne, I swear it. Stay. Please stay.'

Her head fell back on his shoulder and he kissed the curve of her neck. She smelled like tea leaves and roses and the soap their amah used on their clothes. He opened her blouse and fondled her breast. She shuddered, and the tension left her body. They fell back onto the piles of clothes she had gathered and he mounted her and dragged her skirt up around her hips. His body remembered what it was like to love a woman, and he shut off his thoughts and obeyed his instincts. Gasping, she clung to him, and moved with him.

When it was over he tried deliberately to conjure up Kit by saying her name inside his head. *Kit. Kit.* Nothing happened. No image appeared, no laughter sounded in his ears, no nagging hunger twisted his insides. He was safe, free at last. The danger was past, and he could begin to live again. His enslavement to her now seemed like temporary madness. He was sane, whole, saved from damnation.

'But you don't love me,' Anne murmured.

'Of course I do,' he said gently. 'Come to bed now. We can put this stuff away in the morning.'

They made love again and he fell into an exhausted sleep. Anne crept out of bed and went into the living room. She took a cigarette out of the pack she had begged from one of the Chinese biology teachers that afternoon, and she smoked while she surveyed the ruins of her plans. Yes, she would stay. There was nothing for her in Shanghai, and as long as there was the merest chance of happiness here, with him, she would stay.

She felt cold, and pulled on her trench coat, which was draped over the opened lid of the trunk. She poked her hands into her pockets, and her fingers closed around a worn screw of paper. Innes' note. She had felt it a hundred times, fingered it unconsciously, or perhaps even consciously, while reminding herself that here was one person in the world who appreciated her. She unfurled it now, for the first time since leaving Shanghai. 'Thanks again. Jamie.' She could imagine his hesitation before he signed. 'Jim' would have been breezy and informal. But 'Jamie' belonged to her.

She twisted the paper again and held it over the saucer she was using as an ashtray. She lit the end and blew gently to make it flame, and watched the red edge of fire devour it slowly, layer by layer.

Anne lost her awe of Gilbert, and with it her fear of failing him. She told herself they had weathered the typhoon together and that their marriage was stronger for having been tested. They were more relaxed with each other, and more comfortable around other people. Anne tried to guard her tongue and to keep her most radical opinions to herself, but in every other respect she felt that she could walk normally again instead of tiptoeing. She attended Sunday service when she felt like it, and stayed home when she didn't. Gilbert didn't make excuses for her.

They arrived in Chengtu in January 1934. In August, heavy rains in the mountains swelled the rivers that nourished the plain. Floods destroyed crops, displaced peasants, killed their livestock and their children. When the waters subsided malaria and typhoid broke out, touching even the whites, who were forced to remain in Chengtu that summer, because their mountain retreats were inaccessible. Anne and Gilbert worked closely together. She saw that he, too, was losing his fear of failing, and that he was drawing closer to the people he served. They came home exhausted every night, ate and undressed and fell into bed without speaking, but their silences no longer vibrated with unspoken hostility and resentment. They would never be lovers, Anne thought, because they weren't in love with each other. But respect and friendship provided a very comforting substitute for passion. She felt that happiness lay cradled in the palm of her hand, as sturdy and as fragile as an eggshell. Gently handled, jealously guarded, it could last for a long time, perhaps forever.

At the end of 1934 Chiang Kai-shek's dogged pursuit of the Communists forced them into retreat. The remnants of the Red Army broke free of Chiang's stranglehold and began the Long March to Yenan, in Shensi Province. In the course of the next year Mao Tse-tung and his followers would travel over five thousand miles, through some of the harshest country in Asia. Anne eagerly read accounts of the retreat in the Shanghai newspapers her father sent, which always arrived in Chengtu weeks after publication. She thought about Chen. Was he with them? Could he survive? He had always been underweight, frail. Thousands of more robust men were succumbing to cold, hunger, attacks from savage tribesmen in remote areas. She asked herself if she really cared whether he lived or not, and she knew that she did. No matter what he had done, what he had become, he would always be part of her.

Early in 1935 renewed activity by the Communists that remained in Szechwan created new difficulties. Chinese students and employees of the university were not so much conscripted as impressed into military service in Chiang Kai-shek's armies. That spring saw a Red Scare, a witch-hunt. The Board of Trustees expelled any student they suspected of having Communist sympathies. Anne finished her nurse's training in June, graduating with highest honors. She was offered a position on the obstetrics staff of the University Hospital. She refused, in protest against the Board's high-handed and unfair treatment of certain students. In April, whites were advised to evacuate the city, which seemed to be the object of a new Communist thrust. Anne and Gilbert decided to stay. A flood of refugees from areas overrun by the Reds had reached Chengtu. Many needed medical attention. All needed shelter and food. The Communists never reached Chengtu. Nationalist Army reinforcements arrived and the siege never materialized.

Japanese aggression in the North continued to mount through 1935. Thousands of tons of duty-free goods, including opium, poured into China through Japanese-held territories like Manchuria. The Chinese economy suffered. In Japan the militarists seized control of the government, giving rise to rumors of war.

'Sometimes I wonder if the whole world is coming apart at the seams,' Anne said, poring over a month-old copy of the *North China Daily News*. It was June 1936.

'It's always looked like that,' Gilbert said. 'More people can read about it these days, that's all. Oh, the Masters asked if we'd like to share the bungalow at Mount Omei again this summer.'

'That sounds nice. Look, here's a picture of my father. He addressed the Ladies' Anti-Cultural and Vicious Gossip Circle last week. I mean, six weeks ago.'

'You're making that up.' Gilbert looked over his shoulder.

'Just part of it. See, here's his picture. I wonder why Mother didn't send a clipping. I hope she's all right. Maybe we ought to go to Shanghai this summer. We've been away nearly two and a half years.'

Gilbert said, 'I don't particularly relish Shanghai in the summer. I'm sure they're all right, Anne. Her letters are cheerful enough, and so are your father's.'

'That's true. I suppose you're right.'

'Of course I am.' Relieved, he sat back in his chair. 'Maybe when autumn comes —' he said vaguely.

'You know we can't leave after school starts. It's so hard to get away.' She folded up the newspaper carefully. She would pass it along to one of the other missionaries, who would in turn pass it on, until there was nothing left of it. 'It was a beautiful day today, wasn't it?'

'Perfect. Real June weather, just like home. We've had a lovely spring.'

A cricket chirped under their pillow. Two nights ago they had heard a nightingale. Maybe it would come again. Anne sighed contentedly and rearranged the roses in the bowl at her elbow. Her roses were spectacular this year, the most beautiful she had ever raised.

They ate a light supper, then left the campus by the south gate and strolled along the narrow road into the countryside. The wheat in the fields on either side was already tall; heads were beginning to form. A flock of geese padded across their path in leisurely fashion. The goosegirl was far behind, in no hurry to catch up. They stopped to converse with the farmer who sold them eggs. The man proudly introduced his oldest son, a boy of nine who stood shyly in his father's shadow.

The lowlands beyond the wheatfields had been flooded and planted with rice. Anne and Gilbert saw a crane swooping low over a rice paddy, and reminded each other that cranes bring good luck. As they started home, the soft breeze from the north carried the thump of the evening drum from the walls around Chengtu, and the music of temple bells.

'We're happy here, aren't we?' Anne said as they walked along. They didn't hold hands; Gilbert wasn't demonstrative, and the Chinese frowned upon public displays of affection. But Anne felt that their spirits were touching. 'We're luckier than my parents. They had a much harder time when they started out. I was born as soon as it was decent for me to be, exactly nine months to the day after the wedding. They had been in China only two months. And Father was gone most of the time. He had some idea that he would set up a chain of street chapels in little towns and visit them each once a month.'

'Sounds like a good scheme. What happened?'

'Oh, he'd leave a place and come back in a month to find that it had burned down, or become occupied by a family with ten children and a dozen in-laws, or that the person who was going to permit his house to be used for meetings had died or gone away. It was frustrating. He worked for nearly seven years out here and made all of six converts. I remember the night he counted them up – the real ones, not just the rice Christians who came hoping for a handout. He sat at the table and cried, and my mother said. "But Jesus himself only had twelve when He died. What's wrong with six?" And Father cried harder and said that was all very well, since Jesus had labored for only three years.'

They laughed sympathetically, aware of the bitter truth behind the tale: it was hard to make a place for the white man's God in China. Anne thought the whites should give up trying to force the Chinese to accept a religion that didn't suit their culture, and confine their efforts to teaching humanities, science, and medicine. Gilbert insisted that China could and should be Christianized, but even he admitted that it would take time.

An airplane droned overhead. They looked up, shading their eyes against the rosy glare of the sunset. 'Maybe we could fly to Shanghai,' Anne suggested.

Gilbert said rather sharply, 'It would cost more than either of us makes in a year. Perhaps you should go visit your parents by yourself.'

'No, I don't want to do that. They're so fond of you – they'd be happier if you went without me.'

'There's no chance of that,' Gilbert said sincerely.

They reached their apartment. Gilbert picked up his black bag. 'I want to run over to the hospital for a few minutes. Mrs Wong isn't doing too well. That surgery took a lot out of her.'

A long time afterward he looked back on that serene, rather ordinary evening and thought that it was the last truly peaceful time he had known. He remembered small details vividly: the blue skirt and white blouse Anne wore, the snag in her hose, the touch of sunburn she'd picked up on her nose and forearms because she always forgot to put on a hat when she gardened. He remembered how comfortable their sitting room seemed, like a burrow or a rabbits' nest, cozily lined with newspapers and cushions and brightened with flowers.

He saw his patient, gave the nurses on night duty special instructions, and walked back to the apartment as the light was fading. He passed little clusters of students, boys engaged in hot, presumably political argument, girls giggling, skipping a little as they walked. It might have been a cool evening on any American campus, the week before graduation. Pressures on the students had eased; there was a sense of resolution and satisfaction in the air. He encountered the Methodist theologian who lived in the house next door and walked the rest of the way with him. They bade each other good night, exchanged insincere invitations to drop over sometime, and entered their respective dwellings. Later Gilbert wondered how he could have proceeded so normally with such a cataclysm in the offing. Shouldn't there have been a warning in the atmosphere, like the drop in pressure that precedes a storm? Unlike disease, disaster strikes without symptoms.

He opened the door. They never locked it until they went to bed, and then only because a university memo had advised it. He went inside, dropped his bag on the table by the door, and stood for a moment relishing the comfort of home. Then he heard the laughter and his heart froze. He felt like a fugitive who has been living under an assumed name in another part of the world, whose past has finally, inevitably caught up with him.

Anne came out of the kitchen to greet him. 'Oh, Gilbert, the most exciting thing has happened! You'll never believe it – such a surprise!'

Kit appeared behind her and smiled slowly. 'Hullo, Gil. I'm such a lousy correspondent I thought I'd treat you to some delicious Shanghai gossip firsthand.'

'She flew in from Chungking. Can you believe it? On that same plane we saw going over on our way home.'

He smiled weakly. If he'd known who was on that plane he'd have wished it into a death spiral. 'Quite a surprise,' he croaked. 'We were just talking about going to see you.'

'I'll bet it wouldn't have amounted to much more than

talk,' Kit said. 'You can't fool me. You missionaries can never tear yourselves away from the needy.'

'We were having tea in the kitchen,' Anne said. 'I'll bring it out. Sit down, please, Kit. Isn't this wonderful, Gilbert? I got home, and then there was a knock on the door, and there she was. I didn't know whether to laugh or cry.'

Or scream.

'Kit's brought all kinds of things for us – soaps and books and even a phonograph! And Uncle Billy sent a shipment of medicines, too. Kit asked someone at the airstrip to take it to the hospital.' She chattered away happily, alone in the kitchen. Gilbert watched Kit warily. She smoked nonchalantly, and cast him an occasional amused glance.

'I brought Anne a few things no woman should be without,' Kit said, turning the full power of her gaze upon Gilbert. 'French perfume, silk stockings, and the most gorgeous silk negligee. She'll be irresistible, I guarantee.'

'Can't you see me in a negligee?' Anne called out. 'I'd spill something on it the first day, I just know it.'

'You're not supposed to wear it during the day, Mouse,' Kit said, not taking her eyes off Gilbert, 'and definitely not in the kitchen. I brought along some champagne, too. Just to celebrate. Even Gilbert won't refuse a toast at a reunion like this.'

'I'll go ask the Porters for some ice,' Anne said, emerging breathlessly from the kitchen. 'I won't be a minute.' She set the tea tray down on the table in front of the couch and started for the door.

'No!' The word came out too loudly, almost in a shout. The sisters looked startled, and Gilbert cleared his throat noisily. 'I'll go. You entertain your sister, Anne.'

'Oh, you don't need to entertain me,' said Kit, flopping down in a secondhand easy chair that Anne had re-covered. All at once the little room lost its charm. Anne's attempts at decoration looked cheap, makeshift, pathetic. 'I'm not company, I'm family, remember?'

Anne said, 'Oh, no, you're an honored guest. Our first! Oh, Kit, I can't believe it. There's so much to tell you, and show you. How long can you stay?'

'Until you throw me out. I needed a change – the season was simply exhausting this year – and I decided a dose of small-town life would agree with me. How are the summers here, as beastly as Shanghai?'

'Worse,' Anne said cheerfully. 'But we were thinking about getting a bungalow in the mountains. Last year we shared one with the Masters – he's president of the university this year – but maybe we could get one for just the three of us. It's so beautiful up there, Kit. Even you'd like it. How are Mother and Father ? I was concerned —'

Kit reassured her that their parents were well, although her mother seemed a little frailer and her mind was beginning to wander.

'But she always was a little fuzzy. You know.' She flipped her hand in an evasive gesture.

Anne nodded sadly. 'And Mr Innes?' she asked hesitantly. 'How is he?'

Kit laughed. 'Mr Innes is just dandy, as far as I can tell. Richer than ever, thanks to me. I throw marvelous parties for rich people and persuade them to invest in Innes & Company. If I'd been a man, I'd be president. I can do anything. He and Daddy have reconciled, sort of. Innes gave the church a whopping gift, and Daddy couldn't bring himself to refuse it. We all dined together a few weeks ago. It was funny. Both of them on their company behavior. But he and I don't run with the same crowd. We never did. You know these modern marriages – hello and goodbye.'

'You look wonderful, Kit,' Anne said warmly. 'I wouldn't have believed that you could get more beautiful.'

Gilbert, slinking toward the door, stole a look at Kit while she lit cigarettes for herself and Anne. She had lost a little weight. The bones in her face were more defined, as delicate as a child's. He realized with a shock that she had been little more than a child when they met, a girl just out of her teens. She was really a woman now.

She was wearing a two-piece beige suit with a pleated skirt and a tight-fitting jacket with a peplum. She had tossed aside her blond straw hat and shaken out her curls, which were lusher and longer than ever. She crossed her elegant legs and waggled her foot slowly. The movement mesmerized Gilbert. He felt a little dizzy.

She looked up and their eyes met through a haze of cigarette smoke. 'Hurry up with the ice, Gilbert. We girls are dying of thirst.'

'Porters – ice,' he mumbled, and slipped out the door.

Surrender, the game is up. He remembered a gangster film he had seen years ago in the States. The fugitive, barricaded inside a deserted building, peppered his pursuers with bullets, until one of them lowered himself by rope from the rooftop and shot him in the gut. You never knew where your enemies were coming from.

He felt nauseous and faint. He sat on the front steps and dropped his head into his hands. He could hear the duet of female voices: Anne's low and breathless from excitement, Kit's higher-pitched and musical. Two temple bells. Temple belles and a hollow gong, himself. He wanted to laugh, but tears rushed to his eyes. So much for that bad case of complacency, Dr Lawrence. Dr Kit always did have a ready remedy for it.

What next? He could go to Dr Masters, friend and counselor, confess all, and ask for sanctuary and protection. He could fall asleep in a rice paddy, face down. He could hail a passing yak and flee to the mountains of Tibet.

Or he could be a man and face the danger squarely, telling Anne the truth so that Kit wouldn't have any power over him anymore.

Just then he heard Anne say clearly, 'We're happy here,' and he jumped. Had she really spoken, or had it been a vivid memory?

The condemned man dragged himself over to the Porters' house, satisfied their curiosity about his guest, acquired some chips from their ice block, and started home. As he drew nearer his step quickened. He realized with despair that he couldn't wait to see her again.

* * *

Cat with a capital *K* and mouse with a small *g*, Gilbert thought. Every time he turned around he seemed to see her standing there, arms folded across her waist, claws

208

retracted, one hip hitched higher than the other, her eyes bright with the knowledge of how the chase would end. Every once in a while she would bat him playfully with her paw, just to let him know that she was in control.

'You haven't asked about my health, Gilbert. I'm looking pretty well, don't you think? You'll be happy to know that there won't be any more abortions. I had a lovely little operation at the Aldershot. I persuaded this sweet little German doctor to persuade me that having children would be disastrous to one of such a small build. What was his name? Stupid me, I can't remember.'

'Schmidt,' Gilbert said dully. 'He always liked women.'

'Oh, yes, Smitty. How could I forget?' She lay back on the couch and stretched her arms above her head. Her breasts rose under the silk of her blouse. They, too, had gained definition. Gilbert looked away.

'What do you want from me?' he demanded. She couldn't have been more seductive if she'd stripped off all her clothes. Maja clothed, maja naked. The same pose, the same smile, evocative and haunting. 'Why don't you go away? Why don't you leave us alone?'

'I have left you alone, for two whole years. More. But I seemed to hear a distant voice calling, "Kit, Kit!" I was sure it came from the west. Sorry if I was wrong.'

He couldn't assault her, couldn't insult her. If he said anything damning or hateful, she just laughed at him and hurled back a barbed dart that smarted for a day. He felt as though he were trying to fight his way through a swarm of hornets with only a croquet mallet to use for self-defense.

He tried to juggle bodies so that he was never alone with her. But Anne behaved thoughtlessly, disappearing into the bathroom or running to the market or dashing over to a neighbor's to borrow something. All of a sudden Gilbert would find himself face to face with Kit, who licked her lips.

He stayed long hours at the hospital, fabricated tutorial sessions with phantom medical students, scheduled his surgery during mealtimes. Anne clucked that he was working too hard. Kit preened her whiskers.

He told everyone on campus that his sister-in-law Mrs

Innes was visiting from Shanghai. Many of them had read about her in the social columns of the Shanghai newspapers, and all of them knew about Innes, the archetypal godless plunderer, the adventurer, the kind of man who spread sin faster than the missionaries could clean it up. Invitations poured in, and Gilbert pressed Anne to accept them all. They dragged themselves from one shabby faculty apartment to another, engaging in stultifying conversation, playing bridge, drinking nothing stronger than tea. Kit watched him over the rim of her cup and purred.

He felt himself backsliding into what he thought of as his Shanghai mentality: criticizing Anne – always easy, even when one wasn't under a strain – loathing the Chinese, praying, scheming. He couldn't bring himself to make love to Anne, not while Kit was in the apartment, sleeping on a cot in the study on the other side of the wall from their bedroom. Anne was hurt, puzzled. 'Overwork. Too much socializing.' Gilbert would mutter when she reproached him with a look. Excuses were so easy to come by these days: abundant, and cheap.

He waited for Kit to become screamingly bored and announce her departure. Three weeks passed during which they engaged in nothing more exciting than a boating excursion on the Min River. The three of them attended commencement exercises together and sat in the front row. Dr Masters said the invocation without taking his eyes off Kit. Gilbert thought, another victim. Kit cheerfully helped with household chores like mending and gardening. She attended luncheons and bridge parties and morning gatherings of wives. She went around freely, without her hosts, who were otherwise occupied. The other women adored her. Her presence in their little community added a measure of glamour and exoticism to their otherwise dull lives, and Gilbert knew that if he even whispered part of the truth about her, they would encircle and defend her with their last breath, and stone him for a heretic.

Dr Masters pressed them for a decision on the Mount Omei bungalow.

'Tell them we'd rather be off by ourselves,' Kit said. 'If

it's a question of money —'

The noose tightened. Feverishly Gilbert began to list all the reasons why he couldn't leave Chengtu. Anne swept them away, uncooperative wretch.

'That's silly, Gilbert. You know Dr Wallace promised long ago that he'd take over your patients while you were gone.'

His desperation mounted. He knew what would happen when the three of them reached Mount Omei. He would keep his guard up and be vigilant, but one day Anne, his only protection, would run down to the village to deliver a baby or to help some modern-minded girl get out of the marriage her parents had arranged. She would be gone for a whole day, perhaps a night, and Kit, tired of waiting, would pounce. Her claws would emerge from their sheaths and gather him in. Her smiling mouth would close around him, and the circle of her teeth would tease his flesh.

And then, a miracle. Salvation came in the person of an elderly missionary named Farley Mudd. Reverend Mudd's labors in the vineyards of the Lord had been hampered of late by blinding headaches and frequent blackouts. Gilbert diagnosed, and his colleagues confirmed, a tumor on the brain in a region where surgery could endanger vision and coordination or even life. Their hospital was not equipped to handle delicate brain surgery; the one at Chungking was no better. There was no time to be lost. Gilbert radioed a message to Dr Morrison, who advised him to send the patient to the Aldershot immediately. The Methodist Mission Council agreed to pay for everything, including a nurse to accompany Reverend Mudd to Shanghai and to attend him there. Gilbert was jubilant. Here was an opportunity for Anne to see her mother. He arranged for her to escort Reverend Mudd. Kit, he knew, couldn't very well prolong her visit in Chengtu after her sister left. Reverend Mudd and the two women would fly to Chungking, and from there to Shanghai. Gilbert counted the days, the hours before the plane left.

An ambulance took them out to the tarred strip of land between rice paddies, the Chengtu airport. Reverend

Mudd was able to walk, with Anne and Gilbert supporting him in case he felt faint. Kit trailed after them. Suddenly they heard a cry, and turned to see her sitting on the tarmac clutching her ankle.

'Oh, God, I think it's broken,' Kit gasped. Anne reached her first, then Gilbert. Reverend Mudd stood swaying solitarily in the breeze like an aged pine tree.

'Can you make it to the plane?' Gilbert probed the injured ankle none to gently. 'It's not broken.'

Kit gave an anguished squeal. 'God, don't touch it! Just leave me alone, will you? Go on, take care of your patient. He's the one you need to worry about. I can always stay in a hotel and take a later flight.'

'Hotel? Oh, Kit, no,' Anne cried. 'Please, can't you try?'

They helped her to her feet. She couldn't bear any pressure on her ankle and Anne called to a coolie to push over one of Kit's trunks for a seat. The plane's engines started and the few passengers who had gathered around Kit boarded reluctantly. The wind from the whirling propellers tugged at Anne's hat. She clapped her hand to her head.

'For heaven's sake, Mouse, this doesn't make any sense,' Kit moaned. 'You don't want to nurse me and Dr Mudd, too.' Anne protested but Kit was adamant. 'No, really, I can stay here until the next plane out. Gil will take good care of me, won't you, Gil? . . . Oh, God, he's falling!'

Indeed, Reverend Mudd, his buzzing head baking in the July sun, began to teeter. Gilbert reached him just as his knees crumpled, and half-carried him up the steps to the plane.

Kit grimaced at Anne, whose face reflected confusion and concern. 'I feel like such an idiot, Mouse. At the last minute, too. What a mess! But don't worry about me. I'll be along when I can. I might even stay a few extra days in Chungking. Did I tell you Boo and Potsy have moved there? They're awful bores, but they'd be so hurt if I didn't stop in. You run along. Kiss Mummy and Daddy for me and don't worry about a thing. Have yourself a wonderful holiday.'

'Oh, Kit, I'm so sorry.'

'It's not your fault, Mouse. I'm not usually so clumsy: I hope I haven't caught it from you.'

Anne smiled wanly. Gilbert reappeared. His face was grim. 'Mudd is looking a little green, Anne. He'll probably lose his breakfast.'

'Oh, Gilbert, I don't want to leave you.'

'I don't want you to go,' he said with perfect honesty. 'But don't worry, please. I'll look after Kit. I'll strap that ankle up and put her on the next plane out.' His kiss was surprisingly warm, and he held her in a fierce embrace. 'Goodbye, Anne. Give the old boy a shot of Adrenalin if he looks like he's going to fade out on you. Anything to get him to Shanghai.'

She nodded and clung to him, then embraced Kit quickly and ran to the plane. Gilbert watched it taxi down the runway and lift off drunkenly.

Behind him Kit lit a cigarette. The hiss of the striking match sounded like the whisper of a falling blade.

'It's not serious,' he said, pinning the elastic bandage to itself. 'You can probably even walk on it. To the next boat.'

Kit crossed her legs and lifted her skirt to admire his handiwork. 'Lovely,' she said. 'You really know what you're doing.'

'I used to think so.' He helped her off the examining table. She stood close to him, her palms pressed against his chest. He stepped away abruptly and she stumbled and caught the edge of the table for support. 'There's a ricksha waiting to take you home.'

'Aren't you coming?'

'I have a patient. A real patient.'

'I take it back. You're a brute. Well,' she looked around, 'don't I even get a cane or a wheelchair or something?'

'I'll send in a nurse. Don't wait up for me.'

He lingered at the hospital as long as he decently could without arousing suspicion. He bade everyone good night, but instead of leaving he dodged into an empty room and fell asleep on the bed. He was awakened hours later by a puzzled nurse who needed the bed for a patient. He muttered a shamefaced excuse and looked at his watch. Three in the morning. Surely she was asleep. He could go home.

He smelled the smoke from her cigarette and saw a moving pinpoint of light like a firefly darting in the darkness. He waited for his eyes to become adjusted to the blackness, but there was no moon and no light from the outside and he remained blind and helpless. He heard a creak and a rustle as she got up from the couch, and he watched the eye of fire moving toward him like the bright trajectory of an executioner's bullet. She paused and crushed out her cigarette. How could she see where she was going? But of course, cats can see in the dark.

He had seen patients die with looks of surprised pleasure on their faces, because they expected the end to be agonizing and found instead that it came quietly and sweetly, like sleep. Her aim was unerring. She found his mouth and gave him her tongue, and at the same time she led his shaking hand to the warm wetness between her legs. He whimpered a little, from remembered terror. He wanted her right then and there, but she slipped out of his arms. She left her hand in his, and she led him, like a blind man, to the bedroom. Each second of delay was torture, and when he found himself on top of her he became a starving man admitted to the feast. He battered her until she sobbed. He punctuated each thrust with curses, hideous words that he had never uttered in his life before this moment.

They lay in a pool of sweat and semen that felt hot and sticky, like sacrificial blood. He watched the immediate future playing itself out on the darkened screen of the ceiling, like a film: visits from concerned neighbors who brought sympathy along with their jellies and blanc-manges; no hints of disapproval – the sisterly bond is sacred – or suspicion, only entreaties for Kit to remain as long as she wished; a glimmer of envy and longing in Dr Masters' eyes – how well Gilbert knew that feeling; hours at the hospital where he hated every task that kept him away from her; baleful looks from their amah and houseboy; the moment at the end of the day when he found himself alone with her; long nights spent thrashing under the ghostly froth of mosquito netting; more schemes – accompanying the invalid to Chungking so that they could steal a few days in a dirty hotel, away from prying eyes and wagging tongues. Lies, excuses, humiliations.

He slid out of bed and stumbled into the living room. He was restless, enervated, shaking with exhaustion yet unable to slow the racing of his heart and brain. He tried to view his case clinically: how would he prescribe for a patient with similar problems? A sedative, of course. Nothing so drastic as morphine, but something gentle that would induce sleep. He thought of the bottle of opium grains in his bag. He prescribed opium occasionally for tubercular patients whose racking coughs could lead to hemorrhaging. He would prepare a weak tincture and dose himself, just this once.

He lit the lamp near the couch. A bottle of local wine stood on the table. It was half empty. Kit was obviously weary of teetotaling. He fetched the small vial from his medical bag. He sloshed a little wine into her glass, sprinkled a few grains of the white powder into the wine, and swirled the glass around until they dissolved. He drank the potion down in a single swallow. He shuddered – he didn't like the sugary-sweet wine – and lay back on the couch.

Laudanum. From the Latin *laudare*, meaning 'to praise'? Oh, most worthy of praise. What had he ever done to be worthy? He had become a healer; if not a life-giver then at least a life-prolonger. But from what he had seen of life, he was more to be censured for that than praised.

An orange glow filled the room. The sun brimmed on the horizon, painting out the darkness, bringing warmth that bathed hurts and banished pain. He found himself on the edge of a precipice. He realized that it was the summit of Mount Omei. What a fine dream, he thought, and touched his fingertips to his eyes to make sure he was asleep. He felt the moist convexness of his pupils between the bristle of his lashes. He was awake! The mountaintop was clear but at the same time shrouded in clouds that looked like wads of cotton. White puffs with red-hot edges billowed around him. The mountain was silent. Miraculously, he found that he could look through the clouds as well as at them. He saw more clouds, in vast rows and swelling ranks.

He lifted his head. In the distance he saw a golden door like a sheet of fire. He stretched out his arm, and his arm grew like a magic vine. His fingers brushed the cool smoothness of the door, which had no latch. It was just a shining plane, its edges softened by a fringe of clouds. 'I wish it would open,' he thought. The door fell away into space and he stood inside the threshold and saw a thousand golden doors lining a long corridor. Behind each door, he knew, was an endless corridor lined with golden doors. He smiled wisely and retreated. The single door closed over him and he hurtled backward, through a century of clouds, and landed in the soft arms of the mountain. Clouds rushed together to protect and covered him like a blanket. Wherever a cloud touched his body, it felt like a kiss.

Chapter Eight

Reverend Mudd's head: shaved, cleaved, relieved of its extraneous matter, stitched, swathed in bandages.

Anne chewed her pencil. What did it resemble? Not a fruit: too colorless and unappetizing. Not a baseball: too irregular shaped. Not a swaddled baby. Definitely *not* a baby. Hmm. With a black veil draped over his head he would be the image of Mère Supérieure. Yes, of course, the bandages looked just like a nun's coif.

'— like a nun's, coifed but without the veil,' she wrote, and frowned. Gilbert had probably never seen a nun up close. He wouldn't appreciate the allusion. She applied her eraser. A mummy, perhaps?

Reverend Mudd mumbled thickly. Anne put down her writing materials and leaned over the bed. He licked his lips and made a sound which meant 'thirsty.' She supported his shoulders and helped him drink. He said, 'Bless you, bless you,' in his sick old preacher's voice, and she murmured soothingly and resettled him.

Anne had been back in Shanghai a month. The Methodists asked her to work as Reverend Mudd's private duty nurse for as long as he needed care. His surgery had gone well, but his recovery was progressing slowly; he was old and worn out from thankless years of helping people who tolerated him but who didn't really want his help. The month passed without a single letter from Gilbert, although she had written him over a dozen, one every other day. Perhaps the Communists were active in Szechwan again. In times of trouble – war or marital discord – communications always suffered first. Kit hadn't returned from Chungking yet. Most likely she had found society there, and Boo and Potsy, less boring than she expected.

Anne spent some of her free time with Father Jacquinot. They talked about Chen, and the Communists, and the Long March, which had taken such a terrible toll of lives. She told him about the painful early months of

217

E.–H

her marriage, and admitted that he had been right in advising her to be truthful.

He said, 'Regretting what is past is as futile an exercise as worrying about the future. I will not reproach you for your folly, and I will not permit you to reproach yourself. I am thankful that you have found happiness, and that we are frends again.'

Reverend and Mrs Fox spent July and early August in the hills near Hangchow, but they returned at the height of the August heat because Reverend Fox felt he couldn't neglect his duties any longer. Anne wondered how dutifully he was behaving towards Olga Kerensky these days.

The night nurse arrived at four. She and Anne coversed in whispers about their patient's condition, and Anne prepared to depart. The other nurse said, 'I almost forgot. Dr Morrison wants you to stop and see him on your way home tonight.'

Uncle Billy blustered some pleasantries, then got down to business. 'I've had a letter from Gilbert, Anne. I wondered if you could tell me anything about it.'

She frowned. 'I don't know. I haven't heard a word from him myself, and it's been over a month.'

'You'd better read it yourself.' He handed over a stained sheet of lined notebook paper.

As she read the letter, her frown deepened.

'But I don't understand – he wants to leave Chengtu! "I no longer feel useful, or adequate, or equal to the enormous task that confronts us all in China." That's all wrong! He's happy there, Uncle Billy, I know he is. He's doing so well – everyone thinks so. What does it mean?'

'I tried to get a message through to him by radio. They couldn't locate him. I think he may already have left Chengtu.' He gave an embarrassed cough. 'There wasn't any trouble between you, was there? I'm sorry, Anne. I have to ask.'

Anne shook her head. 'I don't understand,' she repeated in a small voice. 'He must be ill – I've got to go back!' She stood up, tensed and ready to run back to Szechwan.

'Hold on, hold on. I'm sure it's nothing serious. Just a misunderstanding of some kind.'

'But he could be lying lost and hurt somewhere!'

'Folks don't get lost in China,' Dr Morrison assured her. 'Too many people wandering around who would find them. We've had no reports of any hostile acts toward missionaries in that area. We just have to sit tight and wait. He'll be along any day now. This is the time he usually takes a little break, isn't it? I'll bet he just wanted to see you. He couldn't afford to fly, so he took the slow boat. You know what kind of trip that is, this time of year when the river's so stirred up. I didn't mean to upset you, child. I just thought you might have had some other news. We'll watch and pray together. I wouldn't recommend that you abandon your duties with Reverend Mudd at the Aldershot; work is the best cure for worry. You go home and talk it over with your father. He'll have some words of comfort for you. That's a father's job, isn't it?'

Leonard Fox said, 'I'm sure I don't know what to tell you, Anne. There might have been another letter before this one – you know how undependable the mails are. There's sure to be a reasonable explanation. Gilbert isn't the kind of man who'd just pick up and walk out on a job. There, ah, wasn't any serious trouble between you, was there? I know that marriage isn't easy, and sometimes little annoyances get blown out of all proportion.'

'That's what Uncle Billy said.' Anne drew herself up. 'Everybody seems to think that this is somehow my fault.'

'No one's saying anything of the kind,' her father said soothingly. 'But it's the obvious thing to ask when a man disappears.'

'I'm sure if we were having troubles, we'd come straight to you for counseling,' Anne said. 'You're such an expert on rotten marriages and how to cure them.'

'That's not fair, Anne.' Reverend Fox's tone was sharp. 'I know you're upset, and I understand. But you've never given me a chance to explain.'

'Well, why don't you explain now?' she said, folding her hands in her lap and assuming the skeptical look of a juror. 'I'd like to hear your explanation. Go on, I have plenty of time. Just what kind of excuses can you invent?'

'I don't have to defend my actions to you,' Leonard said, his face reddening.

'Ah, so you can't explain. I'm not surprised. I know what I saw. I know how you've treated Mother all these years, and I know how you treated me. Yet you have the gall to accuse *me* of being a bad wife.'

'I did no such thing. You have no right to take that attitude. I did what I thought best in your case, and I still think I was right. And as for your mother, you don't know what goes on between a man and wife, even if they are your parents. You're so sure I wronged her, drove her to —' He stopped.

'Drug addiction.' Anne supplied the words. 'And there is no nice word or pretty euphemism for what you did to her. It's called adultery.'

'I forbid you to talk to me like that! I have a right to choose my friends without your demeaning our relationship with filthy innuendos.'

'Innuendos,' Anne sneered. 'Are you telling me that my muopic eyes deceived me? Maybe I was wrong? Perhaps the two of you were really engaged in some innocent pursuit, like curing each other's hiccoughs?'

Anne always thought that the events of that afternoon would make a fine scenario for a farce. She, newly returned from Switzerland and still smarting from an avalanche of sorrows, rushed to her old friend's apartment. Olga, who had been a willing mother surrogate, sympathetic and encouraging and understanding of the peculiar situation in the Fox home, seemed oddly cool and restrained. Anne, feeling the chill, left the apartment. She forgot to take her umbrella, and she returned as soon as she discovered her loss. She entered the apartment without knocking. She saw her father, who might have been hiding under the bed or in the broom closet while she was there, locked with Olga in tight embrace. End of farce, end of friendship. She realized that only Olga could have betrayed her to her father. Only Olga could have revealed the contents of her letters and persuaded him to put a stop to her relationship with Chen. And she knew why her mother continued to hide from reality behind a shimmering wall of dreams.

'I refuse to discuss anything with you,' Reverend Fox said angrily. 'I don't know why we can't behave like mature adults. Every time we try to talk, it degenerates into a brawl. You never let me tell me side. You're self-righteous and superior and I'm sick of it, just plain sick of it.'

Tears smarted in Anne's eyes. 'It wouldn't be so bad if you didn't parade your virtue in the pulpit. But to preach against concubinage and then —'

'She is not my concubine! She is my dear friend, nothing more. Our love is innocent, and pure, and I won't let you insult her. How dare you preach to me! You, with your filthy Communist lover – that murdering monster!'

'Leonard! Anne! I can hear you shouting upstairs. What will the servants think?'

'Mother.'

'Marian.'

Mrs Fox wore a flannel nightdress with long sleeves that would have been much too warm for anyone but an invalid. She looked wan and unsteady on her feet.

'You shouldn't be out of bed, Mother,' Anne said, putting her arm around her mother's waist. 'I'll take you upstairs.'

Marian said sadly, 'You mustn't be so hard on your father, dear. He has had to put up with a lot from me. I've never been the wife he deserved.'

'I think you'd better go back to bed before you catch a chill,' Anne said grimly.

'No.' Her mother stood firm. 'I won't go until you apologize to your father. What happened between us is not his fault, and it's certainly not your business. Go on. Say you're sorry.'

'Mother —'

'Do as I say. Apologize at once.'

Anne said stiffly, 'I'm sorry, Father.'

'And now you, Leonard. It was wrong of you to interfere in Anne's affairs. I don't want to hear any more argument between you. You apologize, too.'

'I'm sorry, Anne,' Leonard Fox muttered.

'I wish this rain would stop,' Marian Fox said as Anne

escorted her upstairs. 'It makes tempers so short.'

Anne helped her mother into bed. Marian asked for her medicine. Anne hesitated. 'I can't bear to watch you killing yourself, Mother. You don't eat enough to keep a bird alive, and you're prone to all sorts of infection.'

'Don't preach, dear,' her mother sighed. 'I've had enough of that from your father over the years.' She drank down her potion and lay back on her pillows. She said, 'I used to dream about Leonard after we were first married. He was standing up in a pulpit, preaching. And there were two little feet sticking out from under the pulpit. My feet. Or maybe I didn't dream that at all. Maybe I just imagined it. Still —'

'Please, Mother, you're tired. Try to sleep.' Anne didn't want to listen to her mother's drugged ramblings. She felt guilty because she didn't have the courage to deny her mother the opium she craved, and because she couldn't make her mother happy without it. She couldn't make anyone happy. Not even Gilbert. Especially not Gilbert. Worry gnawed at her. What had happened to him?

'Leonard meant well, I know, but he was always very critical of me. He didn't like me to wear bright colors, or too many frills, or pretty hats. He didn't like it when I sang at home – he said it was inappropriate behavior for a minister's wife, that I had to set a good example. As if the Chinese could be taught by my poor Christian example,' she said with a wistful laugh. 'I hardly saw enough of them to make any difference. But Len took his work very seriously in those days, and he thought that every little thing would have an effect on his success or failure. He drove himself so hard those first years – you remember, he was hardly ever home. And as if he didn't have enough to worry about, he was saddled with me. I was no help to him at all.'

'That's not true, Mother,' Anne said. 'I've often heard him say how helpful you were to him then.'

'I tried so, but I never could learn to speak to those people. I was quite terrified of them then. Day after day, walled up with a child and a servant who didn't speak English. It was horrible. Nothing to do. No one to talk to, only the baby. I was so sick and lonely.'

Anne wanted to say, 'No, you were happy. I was that baby, remember? It should have been enough, just to have me.'

'I knew when I married Len that he wanted to serve the Lord in China. It sounded so exciting, and important. But once we were here – so horrid, so ugly. And he hardly said a kind word to me. He never spoke, except to criticize. I know I shouldn't have minded – he was tired all the time, and I was so useless. Being married to a minister is so hard. If you make one slip, it reflects not only on you, but on your husband and on God. And then I met Frank, and he thought I was wonderful and beautiful. His own wife was shy, and rather dreary, I'm afraid. But Frank said that I always looked like I was on my way to a party. He like that.'

'Frank?' Anne said before she could stop herself. She didn't want to probe into the past, even though it belonged to her, as part of her heritage. She wasn't the kind of person who plunged recklessly down dark alleyways just to see where they led.

'I fell in love with him, of course,' her mother said. 'He was a missionary, too. Married, with three children. I told myself I couldn't help it, but that wasn't true. I just wanted some excitement, I think. Everyone was hurt by it. They went back home, and I heard later that they were divorced. Poor Leonard was devastated. He really believed that I loved him as much as he loved me.' She spoke in a drowsy drone that was compelleing yet horrible, because it reduced the past to a matter-of-fact recital of human weaknesses.

She sighed. 'I felt very lonely after Frank left. I didn't know if I could go on anymore. But I owed it to Leonard to put a good face on things. I didn't want to hurt him anymore. I was a little afraid of myself. I wasn't quite sure who I was.'

'Is that when you started taking your medicine?' Anne asked quietly. 'After Frank left?'

'Something like that,' Marian said vaguely. 'It's all so long ago. I just don't know what's the matter with me. I guess I don't care enough about anything or anyone.'

'No,' said Anne, not wanting to believe her mother's cold self-appraisal. 'You care too much.'

'Like Kit,' her mother said sluggishly, like a record winding down. 'I worry about Kit. She's too much like me.'

She closed her eyes and sighed deeply. Anne wasn't sure if her mother had fallen asleep or if she had simply wandered into the dream she preferred to reality.

Anne crossed the hall to her own room and threw herself wearily across her bed. She heard her father come upstairs and go into his own room. Should she go in and speak to him? No. Nothing had changed. The knowledge that her mother had wronged him long ago couldn't make her forgive all the wrongs he committed since then.

The rain stopped. The strong wind that had been blowing from the southeast died down and the house grew quiet. Anne dozed off, and awoke at two in the morning feeling rumpled and hot and irritated. She turned down her bed and started to undress. There was a soft knock at her door. Wang, their houseboy, stood in the darkened hallway.

'Missee come,' he said softly. 'Sistah sick.'

'Sister?' she grumbled, rubbing her eyes. 'I didn't know you had a sister, Wang. Whenever you need an extra day off, it's your mother who gets sick, remember? I don't understand.'

'Sistah sick,' he repeated. 'You come now.'

Anne knew that argument could be futile. She sighed resignedly and picked up her nurse's bag – smaller than Gilbert's, but useful in emergencies. She followed Wang down the stairs and out of the house.

It never occurred to her to be frightened, even though every now and then one heard horror stories about quiet houseboys who ran amok and dismembered their white employers with axes. Wang had been with them for over twenty years, since they came to Shanghai. He and Anne battled good-naturedly, but she loved and trusted him. She didn't know very much about him, only that he lived on a shabby overcrowded street in Chapei with his wife and children and numerous other relatives. He knew how to read and write – unusual for a house servant – and he spoke Chinese with a Manchurian accent.

A ricksha stood in the driveway in front of the house. Wang stepped between the shafts. 'You come,' he said, gesturing with his head for her to get in.

'I will not,' Anne said, aghast. 'I will not let you pull me through the streets! You're no ricksha coolie, Wang. It's ridiculous. Look, why don't I just get the car —'

'No cah. You come now.'

She tried reasoning with him, first in English and then in Chinese, but he remained obdurate, his face impassive, his tiny eyes unblinking. Muttering to herself, Anne stepped into the ricksha. Wang lifted the shafts and started off at a trot down the driveway. Later she realized that a white woman walking or riding in a car with a Chinese of the servant class might provoke slight interest, while a woman riding in a ricksha drawn by a Chinese would go unnoticed. They went south, into the French Concession, not north into Chapei. Evben at that hour there were still lots of people about, strolling, loitering, talking in small groups, laughing, drifting in and out of bars and nightclubs. At every intrsection Anne saw unusual numbers of Nationalist soldiers and uniformed French policemen.

They crossed the Avenue Joffre and the Rue Lafayette and turned into a narrow street behind the Old City. Wang stopped the ricksha and Anne stepped down. He led her down a winding alley and through a doorway into a pitch-black vestibule. Wang knocked three times on the inner door and exchanged words in whispered Chinese with the man who opened it. The servant gave Anne a little shove, propelling her inside, then backed away and disappeared. The door closed behind her. The new man carried a flashlight. He led her up a steep flight of stairs, lighting each tread for her. They negotiated a twisting corridor and some more steps, then went into a shabbily furnished bedroom. Her guide moved the bed and tapped twice on the streaked papered wall. There was an answering tap, and a cleverly concealed panel swung inward. The man said in Chinese. 'You go in now.'

Anne had to bend to her waist in order to enter. The room was small, furnished with a cot, a table, and three hard chairs. The air inside was stiflingly hot and close. A shaded light bulb dangled from the ceiling. The sole window in the room had been blacked out, covered by a square of heavy fabric that was stretched taut and tacked down on all sides.

The secret door closed gently behind her. A voice said in English, 'Good evening, Anne. It is very good of you to pay a visit to an old friend.'

His face was in shadow, but Anne knew him. 'Chen Ping-ho.'

'Yes, Vhen Ping-ho. Do you remember how some of our friends in Paris used to call me Pierre? You never did that. You always used my Chinese name. I appreciated that. Will you sit down? The chairs are rather uncomfortable. You might prefer the bed.'

She shook her head wonderingly and sank into the nearest chair. 'Chen,' she repeated in a whisper. He walked around the table and sat across from her. He was wearing a long blue cotton gown, a Chinese gentleman's at-home attire.

She scrutinized his face. She was shocked at how different he seemed from her memories of him, and yet how familiar. His face had lost all youthful fleshiness; the hand of a sculptor might have carved out the new hollows at his temples and under his cheekbones. He still wore his hair brushed straight back from his high forehead, and it was as sleek and black as ever, with no signs of gray. His eyebrows were thick and straight, without any curve except a slight upward turn at the outer ends. His eyes seemed larger, set deeper in their sockets. He was a Manchu, a northerner, taller and fairer than the average Chinese from the South or the Yangtze valley. His thin cheeks were covered with a sparse beard.

He stroked his chin ruefully and said, 'A pathetic attempt at disguise. My face is too well known, thanks to the press.'

'This place – you are in hiding.'

'That is so. The life of an outlaw is not at all romantic or luxurious as you can see. There is a price on my head. Five thousand dollars U.S. I suppose I should be flattered.'

'Secret doors, coded knocks. Like something out of a

226

boy's adventure book,' she said. 'So Wang is one of you?'
She felt hot, cold, numb, aching. Was this a dream, like
one of her mother's opium fantasies? Her mouth was dry;
she tasted ashes.

'An old and loyal party member.'

'But the newspapers said you were in Yenan. Why —?'

'I am ashamed to say that I permitted myself to be lured
here. Chiang Kai-shek suggested a meeting; he thinks that
the time has come to forget our differences and turn our
attention to the invader, the Japanese. I wanted to believe
he was sincere. I decided it would be worth taking the
risk.'

'But he'll do anything to exterminate you, all of you!'

'His proposition certainly had merit. He has driven us
into exile, boxed us in so that we are powerless to defend
our country. His own armies are too ill-equipped to fight a
conventional war, but guerrilla tactics would work against
the Japanese, and thanks to his persecution of us, we are
masters of guerrilla warfare. It seemed worthwhile to take
a chance. Unfortunately Chiang had no intention of
discussing anything with me. He merely wanted to
maneuver me into a position where he could assassinate
me. His hatred of me is strong; we worked closely
together during the early days, before he betrayed Sun
Yat-sen and the revolution.'

'He says that you betrayed the Kuomintang, not he.'

'He would say anything to conceal his shame and
consolidate his own power. Fortunately my men discovered the ruse, but not before I became caught in Chiang's
finely spun web. He knows that I am in the city, in the
French Concession. His agents are combing all buildings
systematically and watching the streets, the railroads, and
the docks. This house was searched yesterday. They didn't
discover this room, but to be safe I hid on the roof.'

'Why not under the floor, like those people you
murdered?' she said in a hard voice.

'So, you are angry with me for that. You don't believe
that any cause is worth dying for.'

'No, I don't believe any cause is worth killing for.'

'Traitors are like cancer cells. If you don't cut them out,
their poison will spread through the whole body. I could

not let the man go unpunished, and I needed to make an example of him to discourage anyone else who was tempted to betray us. You think me cruel, and ruthless. So I am, but only because I have to be.'

'I didn't want to believe it,' she said. 'I didn't really believe it, until this moment. How you've changed.'

'No. I have always been committed to revolution. And so were you, at one time. Were you really so naive that you thought it could be accomplished peacefully?'

'You were so gentle. I never once saw you behave violently. You were passionate, yes, but never cruel. You hated the very idea of cruelty and violence.'

'I still hate it,' Chen said. 'You think I felt nothing when I gave that order? I am not a heartless butcher, in spite of those rather extravagane appraisals of me in the press. But I will do everything in my power to wrest control of this country away from the warlords and the generals and the imperialists and give it to the people. That is my mission, and it always has been.'

Anne was silent. She couldn't look at him. He was not the man she had loved. He was grotesque, an obscene impersonator, an imposter. She felt furious with him for violating her memories of him.

Yet she knew she wasn't being fair. She was like a mother who wanted her child to stay small and dependent forever. Selfishly, Anne wanted Chen to stay the same, like an effigy or a moron, not growing, not changing, remaining forever gentle and loving, a man who talked revolution but didn't make it.

She said, 'We had a daughter. I gave her up. They said they would find a family for her.'

'That's good,' he said after a long pause. 'She will be happier in another country. China has never been kind to children of two races.'

'Their half-breed bastards,' Anne said dully. 'Father Jacquinot says you are married now.'

'Yes. My wife is in Yenan at present. She is a fine woman, a devout party member. We have no children. She was beaten by British policemen in the riots in '25.'

'I am sorry.'

'I am not. I have many sons and daughters in the

228

revolution.' He leaned back in his chair. 'You look well, Anne. You haven't changed, have you? You're still passionate and idealistic. You still want to believe in love.'

'You make it sound so trivial.'

'I don't mean to. But romantic love has no place in my life anymore. It belongs to the past, like youth and Paris. It belongs to the time when I believed in the perfectability of man and the possibility of evolution and nonviolence. I have come many miles since then.'

She said, 'What do you want from me, Chen? You certainly didn't bring me here to reminisce about old times.'

'No.' Unconsciously he folded his slender artist's hands into a parody of prayer. 'Your sister is married to the shipowner, Innes. He is an experienced smuggler, an expert at evading soldiers and Customs officials. One of his ships is sailing to Port Arthur in two days. I want you to persuade him to take on a little extra cargo: me.'

'I'm not sure I can.'

'He owes you a favor. You helped him bury his mistress.'

'You know everything, don't you?' she said bitterly. 'Of course, you have a spy in my father's house. Aren't you afraid that I'll betray him – and you?'

'No. No matter how much you hate me now, and hate what I do, you loved me once. You won't betray me.'

'You're so sure of yourself, and sure of me. All right.' She stood up. Her cheeks were burning. 'I'll let you make a fool of me. I suppose I can always get word to you through Wang.'

'I'm sorry it has to be this way, Anne,' he said. 'The times we live in – I don't like using the people I love, but I have no choice.'

'Goodbye, Chen,' she said, turning her back to him. His use of 'love' in the present tense had been deliberate, calculated to break down the last vestiges of her resistance. He was always clever, a skilled manipulator.

She tapped on the wall. Her escort was waiting on the other side. He removed the panel to allow her to pass through, closed it again, restored the bed to its accustomed place, and lighted Anne's way down the stairs.

Wang was curled up inside the ricksha, pretending to doze. A few yards away a bored Nationalist soldier stood smoking a cigarette.

'Wake up, you lazy good-for-nothing,' Anne said loudly. 'Do you think I want to stay here all night?'

'Yes, missee. No, missee.' Wang hopped out of the ricksha and bowed her in. She settled herself – complaining about the lumpiness of the seats and warning him that he'd better nottry and overcharge her – and he started to pull her along. He shouted at the soldier to make way. The man stepped aside, paying no ttention to the white prostitute on her way home from a quick visit to a customer.

* * *

'The guns are Russian, of a very reasonable quality. I cannot imagine how they found their way here – the Russians are rather inefficient at time, I fear – but Chiang Kai-shek's armies are always badly in need of weapons. I think he would be willing to pay a good price for them.'

'The Russians woudln't like the idea of their own guns being turned against them,' Innes said, leaning back in his chair. 'Although I suspect the idea would amuse Chiang. How many guns?'

'Twenty-five cases,' Sun said. 'And fifty cases of ammunition.'

'That's a pretty big shipment. Naturally you can pick them up very cheaply?'

'Yes, very. Only one hundred thousand, U.S. The Generalissimo would pay at least three times that much. It is a once-in-a-lifetime chance. I suspect the weapons were destined for the Communists anyway. We would be doing this country a service, simply by keeping them out of Red hands.'

'That's what I like about you, Sun,' Innes said, snapping the lighter under his cigar. 'Your selfless devotion to your country.' A billow of smoke enveloped Sun, who sat opposite him in the inner sanctum of Innes & Company. Sun steeled himself and suppressed a frown of distaste. 'But I don't want to deal with Chiang Kai-shek any more than I'd want to deal with the Reds. He's as crooked as the Great Wall. And besides, his money's no good.'

'My dear Mr Innes,' Sun permitted himself an indulgent smile, 'the Generalissimo's brother-in-law, Mr H. H. Kung, directs the Bank of China. And Mr T. V. Soong himself has assured me of the solidity of the government's financial position in this matter.' His smile widened. 'They are prepared to pay cash.'

Soong was another Chiang brother-in-law, China's Foreign Minister.

'Sun, the best way to deal with governments is not to let them know you have anything they want. We sell them guns. They want more, and they want them cheap. If we don't play along they make life difficult. It's not like handling Tu; we can't kidnap the Mrs and hold her until Chiang decides to behave himself. Tu has a bunch of thugs, but Chiang has armies. I just don't want to get involved with him. He can't be trusted to play straight. Soong is just as bad. And as far as I can tell, Kung is a moron with a knack for making himself rich, like a lot of other men in this town. He says what he's told to say, and he does what he's told to do. I wouldn't trust any of them from here to that window.' He cocked his thumb over his shoulder at the panorma of Shanghai shimmering below them in summer haze.

'May I infer from your poor opinion of my associates that you also do not trust me?' Sun asked coldly.

'You can infer anything you damn well please, Sun. I don't have to approve of your playmates; I just don't want you bringing them home with you.'

'I think you are making a mistake,' Sun said guardedly. 'This is an excellent opportunity to ingratiate ourselves with the only men who wield real power in China. I see it as a first step in a long and profitable relationship. We will let them have these Russia guns very cheaply, to pique their appetites. And then we can continue to supply them with arms. Why not? You have connections in America and Germany. You have plenty of cash, and an excellent line of credit. You even have your own means of transport readily at hand. One must always look to the future. If this government falls, our position will be precarious. We must do our part to protect ourselves.'

'Our postion will be more precarious if the government falls and we've sided openly with Chiang and his crowd. I want to stay out of it, is that clear? Don't worry about Chiang. He'll get his guns. But not from us.'

'This puts me in a very awkward position,' Sun said, licking his lips.

Innes' eyes narrowed. 'You've already made some deal with Soong, haven't you? Well, you'd better unmake it.'

'You need not involve yourself or the company,' Sun said. 'I would handle the entire transaction myself, but I simply don't have any ready cash right now. Just a small personal loan – a hundred thousand is nothing – and you will get it back immediately, doubled. I will pay one hundred percent interest. That's a hundered thousand profit apiece. No one will ever know.'

'Someone always knows, when you're dealing with that kind of money. Sorry, Sun. You've been living pretty high, haven't you? Concubines, big cars, nice new mansion in Frenchtown. The girl at Radcliffe. Big bets on the dogs and ponies. But this is one bet you're going to lose, my friend.'

Sun's face reddened. He had always hated this man, but never more than now. The gross, ungrateful animal. The smug pig. Innes would be nothing without him, Sun Yu-sing. He wanted to spit in the man's face, curse him, rail at him. How dare he refuse to grant a simple favor! How dare he sneer at Sun's expenses, which were surely no less excessive than his own. Innes' refusal to lend him the money was unreasonable. He was thick-skulled, ignorant, a savage.

The pirates who were hiding the guns below Woosung wouldn't wait forever. Neither would Chiang Kai-shek, who needed the guns desperately to fight the Communists and who had been promised them by his brother-in-law, Soong. Soong himself would be furious to find that the deal had gone sour. He might even prompt Kung to start calling in Sun's loans.

Sun would have to finagle the money out of Innes & Company somehow. Innes kept an eagle eye on his operation, and although he generally winked at Sun's systematic squeezing, he would certainly miss one hundred thousand. Sun's position was intolerable, and it was Innes' fault.

The buzzer on the intercom sounded. 'Sir, Mrs Anne Lawrence is here to see you.'

'Who? Sure, send her in.' Innes flipped the switch, happy for an excuse to ease Sun out of his office. 'Sorry, Sun. I'd like to help you out. If it was any other kind of deal I'd consider it, but not guns, and not to Chiang.'

'Of course, my friend,' said Sun, smarting at the high-handed dismissal. He rose to his feet and bowed with exaggerated politeness. 'I understand your position. I am sorry to have taken up your time.'

Charlie Fong, Innes' private secretary, ushered Anne into the office. She was wearing a skirt and blouse, both of which were faded and ill-fitting. Her hair was wound into a clumsy chignon at the nape of her neck, and the humidity had raised soft tendrils around her face. As usual her glasses rode far down on her nose. She wore flat shoes and carried a battered leather purse that bulged with books, papers, and assorted paraphernalia.

Innes stood up and introduced Sun, who nodded coolly and excused himself. He followed Charlie Fong out of the office, and waited while the secretary notified the garage on the Bund to send over his car.

Sun studied Charlie Fong carefully. Spectacled, pale, serious-minded, the young man was, Sun knew, fiercely loyal to Innes. As a boy he had stowed away on the *Eastern Star*, on one of Innes' last runs up the Yangtze. He was starving, homeless and Innes had seen to it that he was fed and clothed and cared for. Innes had financed his education, and given him a responsible position with the company. Charlie Fong was the key, of course. Innes trusted him absolutely, and he was in a position to work magic with the books. But he was incorruptible. He didn't gamble, didn't smoke opium, didn't patronize the clubs in Blood Alley. He was the kind of young man any father would be proud to have as a son-in-law.

Sun smiled to himself and thought of his daughter, Ai-ling, or Eileen, as her American friends called her. Newly returned from an extravagantly expensive education in America and a tour of the great capitals of the world, beautiful, modern-minded, she was the perfect match for a snob like Charlie Fong, who thought himself too good for any humbly born Chinese girl, despite his own humble origins. He would be flattered by the attentions of a lovely aristocrat. Yes, Ai-ling could be useful. She would not refuse a request from her father to amuse his business associate. She might be quite modern in some respects, but she was still an obedient Chinese daughter.

Charlie Fong said, 'Your car is ready, sir.' Sun thanked him and went out. He was smiling as he left the offices of Innes & Company.

Anne said, 'I hope I didn't interrupt anything.'

'Not at all. Sun and I were through anyway.' Innes sat down and waved his hand at the chair Sun had just vacated. 'I heard you were in town. Nice of you to stop by.'

'I should have called you long ago,' Anne said apologetically. 'I guess you haven't heard anything from Kit?'

'She wired from Chungking about a month ago. She wanted money,' he shrugged. He pushed a box of cigarettes toward her. She took one. 'Well, Anne, you look fine,' he said with practiced heartiness, holding the lighter for her.

She winced at his insincerity, but murmured, 'Thank you.' She glanced around the office, at the mirrored wall and the shelves of artifacts, the ancient temple rug, the huge windows. 'This is all very grand. I've never been inside this building before.'

'A fitting monument to my stolen wealth,' Innes grinned. 'Go on, admit it: you hate it.'

'I don't,' she said unconvincingly. 'I'm sure you gave jobs to a great many people while you were building it.'

'Sure I did. And my compradore kept half of everything I paid them. That's how it goes in Shanghai.'

'Yes, that's how it goes.' She squirmed in her chair. Innes waited. 'I've seen Sun Yu-sing before,' she said, making conversation. 'His daughter studied violin with my

234

old teacher here. A lovely girl, very talented.'

'I wouldn't know. I haven't seen her since she was a kid. Sun manages to keep her out of my reach.' There was an expectant pause. 'Well,' he said.

'It must be obvious by now that my motives in coming here are not altogether pure,' Anne said, taking a long pull on her cigarette.

'That's right. You've been killing yourself trying to be nice to me. What's up?'

'I – that is, a friend of mine— I feel rather embarrassed coming to you like this.'

'Come on, out with it. I must be your last resort or you wouldn't be here.'

'A friend of mine,' she said vaguely. 'He's had some troubles with the government, the police. He would like to leave Shanghai, but they're making it rather difficult.'

'Your friend must be pretty important. Chiang's goons have been turning this town inside out. They've interfered with my shipping. Who is he?'

Anne shook her head. 'It doesn't matter. I mean, if you can't help. He thought you could find a place for him on the ship that's leaving for Port Arthur tomorrow.'

Innes shook his head. 'Chiang's men and the Customs boys have been sticking their bayonets into cotton bales and opening every trunk big enough to hold a baby. It would be tough even to pass him off as part of the crew. They're checking papers and faces. Would they know him?'

'I'm afraid so,' she said, despair pressing down on her like a weight. 'He – we thought that since you had been a smuggler, you might think of a way. I didn't realize it would be so difficult. I'm sorry I bothered you. Thank you for your time.' She clutched her purse to her chest and started to rise.

'Wait a minute, wait a minute,' Innes said. 'What's the rush? I'll help you, Anne, you know that. Just sit down and let me thick about this a little.' Her face was drawn with worry and he grinned reassuringly. 'Hey, take it easy. There hasn't been a Customs man born who could catch Jim Innes with the goods.' And almost as though he'd thought about it for weeks Innes outlined his plan. 'I have a boat, a thirty-foot cabin cruiser with an engine that can outrun anything the Customs Service has to offer. The *Bombay Rose* sails at ten o'clock tomorrow night from Woosung. She'll be fully certified and inspected and given a clean bill of health from the proper authorities before she weighs anchor. That means that any cargo she picks up once she's out to sea will be safe from scrutiny. The cruiser's anchored right here in the yacht basin. She's the *Jo*. Look, you can see her from up here.'

Anne followed him to the vast window that took up one whole wall of the office. 'That one, just next to the ferry dock. She's flying my flag.' He said fondly, 'Fine little craft, the *Jo*. Small and sleek and fast. Tomorrow night we can take a little outing, you and me and your friend. There's a handy little compartment next to the bilge pump where we can stow him in case we're stopped and searched after we're under way. We head downriver to the mouth of the Yangtze and wait for the *Rose*. I'll fix it up with the captain – he's OK. We rendezvous just north of the Great Yangtze Bank; the currents are weak there, because of shifting sandbars. We put your friend aboard, and that's that.'

'How do we get him on board without arousing suspicion?'

'A combination of squeeze and guts. The Customs agent on duty at the yacht basin tomorrow night will probably be my old friend Sean Casey. I'll send down my greetings with a bottle of rye when he comes on duty at six. He won't let Chiang's toughs interfere with his old pal Jim Innes – not that anyone would believe that the high priest of capitalism was helping out an arch-Communist villain like Chen. Where is he now?' he asked smoothly.

Anne's mouth dropped open. 'Oh,' she said weakly. 'You know.'

'I hear things. You really didn't expect me to believe that Chiang's boys would be turning out Shanghai's pockets looking for some renegade missionary who didn't believe in infant baptism,' Innes said. 'But if Chen turns up tomorrow night looking like a refugee from Yenan, even Sean Casey will smell a rat. Can you get some clothes to him?'

'Yes. I'll send someone over with a parcel wrapped up to look like laundry. He's grown a beard,' she offered helpfully.

'A beard?' Innes said. 'Is that so? Well, that sounds promising. I tell you what, we'll rig him out in a turban and a tux. He'll look like a little maharajah out for a night on the town with his friends. Can't you see him turning up in Yenan all decked out in a monkey suit and pearl studs, just like some babe's Parsee sugar daddy?' He guffawed loudly.

Anne was a little annoyed by his levity. 'It seems to me you're enjoying this whole thing entirely too much, Mr Innes,' she said stiffly.

'The Chinese have a saying, Anne: "enjoy each woman and each adventure as if it were your last."'

'I've lived in China all my life and I've never heard that before.'

'You travel in the wrong circles, then. Listen, it's the guts more than the squeeze that will get you out of most tight spots. Your pockets can be full of gold, but if you act like a felon and can't tell a decent lie, they'll bury you. The bigger the lie, the happier they are to swallow it. You know that.'

'I'm afraid I don't. I'm the world's worst liar.'

'Well, now's your chance to study with a master. Here's the plan: when you leave here, go to Sam Wong, the tailor on Nanking just two doors up from Wing On's. I'll call and tell him to expect you; you help him with the sizes. Can you do that?' Anne nodded. 'Have him send the monkey suit over to you; you don't want to be seen carrying it around. Then run over to Maurice's salon and he'll fix you up with some glad rags and the rest of the getup. You have to look like you're out for a night on the town, too.'

Anne saw a devilish gleam in his eyes. 'I'm sure that part isn't really necessary,' she said. 'I do have a gown I can wear.'

'If you want my help, you've got to do this my way, Anne,' Innes said seriously. 'I don't want you looking like a missionary's daughter on her way to a lantern show and lecture on the savages of Upper Borneo. Jim Innes

doesn't run around with that sort of woman. Understand?
We don't want to make Casey suspicious.'

She said, 'Why do I get the feeling you're up to
something?'

'Because I'm always up to something,' he said cheerfully. 'That's what it's all about. Plenty of time for lying on
your back and doing nothing when you're dead.' He saw
the doubtful look on her face and laughed. 'You don't
know what to think, do you? You don't know whether to
love me or loathe me.'

She said, 'Whatever people feel for you, I'm sure it's
one or the other, and nothing in between.'

'You're right about that. Ask Kit. Ask Sun.' He shook
his head. 'Looks like things are pretty well weighted on
the side of loathing, huh? Well, let's have a little drink to
the success of our adventure.' He went over to the
refrigerated bar.

'Nothing for me, thank you.'

'That's right, you don't like the taste.' He sloshed some
scotch into a tumbler and drank it down, then rejoined her
at the window.

'The city looks almost beautiful from up here,' Anne
said softly.

'It is beautiful. Like some women – faces that would
stop traffic, but between the sheets—' He cleared his
throat and glanced at her mischievously.

'You're trying to shock me,' she sighed without looking
at him. 'It won't work. I'm quite immune. Missionaries'
wives and missionaries' daughters aren't exactly cosseted
and mounted on pedestals in churches, you know. We
know what goes on.'

'That's good. I wouldn't want you to start loathing me
in earnest before tomorrow night. We're going to have to
look like good friends, and since you're such a bad liar—'

'What made you come to Shanghai, Mr Innes?' she
asked, shifting the subject away from herself.

'That's the kind of question that's usually followed by
"Why don't you go back where you came from?"' Innes
said.

'Sorry. It's none of my business, I know. I'm just
interested in what brings people here, what they expect,

what they find.'

Innes said, 'I got here in '23. After the war I drifted some. Got mixed up with some rough boys in Boston. Really rough. Like everybody else in the States, they were getting rich from Prohibition. I thought I could, too. But the little guys don't get rich. They just get smeared underfoot, like insects. I had a few friends, a little organisation of my own. I thought I could move in for a fair share of the pile. I was lucky to get out of Boston in one piece. I shipped out on a merchant ship bound for San Francisco. But the boys from Boston had long arms, and so I shipped out again, for Shanghai. Id heard stories – Blood Alley, the opium dens, the women – sailors talk a lot to relieve the boredom, and I didn't pay too much attention. But when I got off that ship, I knew I didn't want to get back on again. There she was, sprawled out all over the delta, flat and stinking of heat, just waiting to be straddled, to be taken.' He smiled, remembering. 'What a woman – not beautiful, but eager to please. Cheap. Willing.' He looked down to the Bund and across the Whangpoo to Pootung. 'I've been in this town thirteen years. Thirteen, and still lucky.'

'I hope your luck continues,' Anne said, stepping away from the window. 'I want to thank you.'

Innes shook his head. 'Wait until it's over, and Chen's on his way to Port Arthur. Plenty of time for thanks later. I'll pick you up at eight o'clock tomorrow night. Yu'll take me to Chen.'

'The street was being watched.'

'They won't stop the Rolls. It's the last car they'd expect to see him in. If anybody tries, we'll run 'em down,' he said with relish.

With his sleeves rolled up and his hair uncombed, surrounded by the fruits of his conquest and with the conquered city lying docilely at his feet, he looked like a swashbuckler of legend, Anne thought, who didn't realize that his era had passed.

* * *

Half an hour before sunset the following evening, the

Rolls glided to a stop at the yacht basin on the Bund. Sean Casey strolled over to greet his old pal Jim Innes as he emerged from the car.

He slapped Innes' shoulder. His face was flushed and his eyes slightly glazed. 'Good evening and God bless you, Jim, for being such a fine and generous soul,' Casey said. 'Thanks very much for the bottle. But you wouldn't be tryin' to corrupt a public official now, would you?'

'Of course I would,' Innes said cheerfully, throwing his arm around Casey and leading him away from the Rolls. 'Why else would I be sendin' down a bottle if I didn't want you pie-eyed when I took the *Jo* out tonight?'

'Ah, Jimmie, you don't want to be takin' her out this night,' Casey waggled his head. 'There've been gale warnings up for three hours now; I wouldn't let me own wife out on a night like this, and me wantin' to see the last of her. No, boy, you'd better stay on land. You wouldn't be wanting to risk your fine lady's life, now, would you?'

'Indeed, I wouldn't,' Innes said solemnly, 'but the lady has a hankerin' for sea air tonight, don't ask me why. Besides, I've never yet seen the gale I couldn't handle in this little boat. She's as light as a cork, and we'll skim right over the tops of the waves, as safe as can be.'

'You're not thinking of takin' her out to sea!' Casey gasped.

'No, no, only for a short run to Woosung. I want to show my friends here the new ship I'm outfitting.' He dropped his voice. 'And I don't want the lady's mister to know where we're going,' he said meaningfully. 'He's a fearful old bugger, jealous as they come.'

'Who's the wog?' Sean asked, glancing at Chen, standing with Anne by the side of the car. 'Not her boyfriend!'

'Not yet, but she's workin' on it hard enough, and it's my guess that she'll hook him before the night's out. He's even richer than I am, Sean, if you can believe that. A real maharajah. A prince! You know these women – impressed by royalty, even the scrawny little pipsqueaks who'd be of no more use to them in bed than a baby.'

'Ah, their love runs only as deep as your pocketbook,' Sean said sorrowfully. 'But she's fine-looking, Jim. I don't know how you do it, pickin' up with the beauties, and you bein' as ugly as Satan himself.'

They laughed. Anne smiled at them and said something to Chen, who grinned. They were both gorgeously dressed, aloof, a little bored by their surroundings, impatient for their new escapade to begin.

'Ah, she's something special, all right,' Innes said warmly. 'There's no more beautiful woman in Shanghai this night.'

When she came out of the manse on Bubbling Well Road and stepped gracefully into the car, he couldn't speak for a whole minute, and then he could only repeat, 'I don't believe it. I just don't believe it.'

'Isn't this what you wanted?' Anne asked innocently, trying not to fidget self-consciously like a schoolgirl on her way to her first dance. 'Your frined Maurice is quite a miracle-worker. You should have seen my father's face when I came down the stairs: it was like yours is now. His mouth fell open and he just stared.'

'For once your father and I agree about something,' Innes said. 'There's just one thing you forgot.' He reached over and took off her glasses.

'Oh, no, I can't see!' she protested, groping for them. Her eyes were gray-green, wider than he would have thought. The transformation was complete.

He laughed. 'You don't need to see. I'm nothing to look at, and I'll be doing enough looking for both of us. Besides, I need these for Chen. I've never seen a Parsee with slanty eyes.'

'I can't believe you're not nervous.'

'Why should I be nervous? You're not going to turn into a missionary maiden at midnight.'

'That's not what I meant. I do wish you'd stop staring.'

'I can't help it. I won't be the only one staring tonight.'

His frank admiration embarrassed her. 'It's only tinsel,' she sniffed. 'Fluff. It doesn't mean anything.'

'I've always been a man with a liking for a little fluff and tinsel,' he said, extending his cigarette case.

She fumbled as she tried to remove one. 'I'm sorry, but I can't see very well,' she said.

'Let me.' He lit two cigarettes and slipped one between

her fingers. 'Did you tell your father who you were stepping out with?'

'Oh, yes. I thought he'd faint. He probably thinks you're going to seduce the second of his precious daughters, as though you hadn't done harm enough the first time around.'

Innes leered. 'That's not such a bad idea.'

Anne resisted the urge to drape her shawl across her boson. Her gown was dark green crepe de chine, the most daring thing she had ever worn. Two thin silver straps held up the bodice, which plunged in front to a point just below her breasts, and to her waist in back. The top was trimmed with shimmering silver leaves, and a trailing silver vine down the side outlined her figure to her ankles. She carried a lightweight silver shawl, as well as her trench coat for the boat, and a tiny beaded bag. Maurice's hairdresser had drawn her hair softly back from a center part and woven it into numerous small braids, which he then fashioned into an intriguing nest at the nape of her neck. A pin with a silver leaf gleaned above her left ear, and a similar pendant dangled between her breasts.

She guided Sanjay to the house where Chen was hiding. They stopped at the end of the alley, which was too narrow to permit the passage of a car.

Innes said, 'You go in and get him. Sanjay will keep watch outside. Don't forget, act friendly, lover-like.'

'I won't be able to see a bloody thing,' she grumbled.

He handed back her glasses. 'Give these to Chen. Make sure he puts them on before he comes out. Sanjay will be your guide dog. Go on now, the coast is clear.'

Chen's attendant led her up the stairs and into the secret room. Chen was ready. The suit fit him perfectly, but the blue turban was swirled ineptly around his head.

'This is all wrong,' she said after they had gaped at each other for a moment. 'You'd better let me do it.'

'You may tell your friend Innes that I do not find fancy dress charades amusing,' Chen said as she unwound the ten yards of fabric and began to wrap his head again.

'You can tell him yourself. He's waiting downstairs.'

'Can I take anything with me?'

'No. I need some things for you in the car. Everything

you'll need, and some money. The ship goes straight to
Port Arthur, but you'll have to get through Manchuria
somehow.' Manchuria was Japanese-occupied.

'I'll manage.'

She finished winding the turban and looked at him
critically. 'You'll do, unless we're stopped by a real
Parsee.'

She gave him her glasses before they opened the door to
the street and tucked her arm through his. Both virtually
blind and helpless, they stepped out of the house, and
Sanjay led them back to the car. A Nationalist soldier
appeared at the end of the alley. He glanced at the Rolls,
but seemed to take no notice of its occupants.

Inside the car, Chen removed the glasses and he and
Innes eyed each other suspiciously. Innes said, 'When we
get to the dock, act like good friends. Gossip a little, laugh
a lot. Act a little bored. Anne, you know how it's
supposed to look – just think of Kit. Don't say a word to
Casey unless it's absolutely necessary. I'll explain things to
him. When we board the *Jo* , just stay out of my way until
we're well away from the shore. Clear?' His passengers
nodded. He grinned at Anne. 'Scared?'

'No,' she said, giving him a somewhat blank smile. She
couldn't focus on him at all. She was surprised to discover
that she really wasn't frightened. Her faith in Innes was
absolute.

On the other side Chen sat upright, stiff. From the
windows he could see knots of Chiang's men, armed,
watching for him. The web was fine indeed. He wondered
if Innes could get him through, or if he would die on the
streets of Shanghai, costumed like a degenerate dandy.
Chiang would exhibit his gun-riddled body in a conspicuous place, where it would be the object of scorn and
ridicule.

Innes signaled to Chen and Anne to follow him down to
the *Jo*. Anne forced herself to walk slowly, sensuously,
swinging her shoulders as well as her hips. Casey's eyes
popped. He barely looked at Chen. Sanjay followed with
Anne's coat, a blanket, and a wicker hamper containing
clothes for Chen. He handed the hamper to Innes,
already on board, and Anne cautioned them not to

jar the champagne.

'Don't you worry, darlin',' Innes said, helping her into the boat. He passed his arm around her waist, and dropped his hand down to caress her rump. He grinned at Casey. Anne smiled up at him provocatively. Casey himself helped to steady Chen as he climbed into the *Jo*. The rising wind whipped up the water, and as the cruiser tossed, the gap between the hull and the dock narrowed and widened dangerously.

'Watch it, Prince,' Casey said. 'You almost went in that time. Those glasses of yours don't seem to be doin' much good.'

Chen thanked him in a musical voice that was a perfect approximation of a high-caste, British-educated Indian's. He fussed like an attentive escort, draping Anne's coat around her shoulders, settling himself next to her on the cushioned seats at the stern of the cruiser. They put their heads together and cooed like lovers. Innes started the engine. Sanjay threw off the ropes and Innes backed the *Jo* out into the Whangpoo.

Just then a squad of Nationalist soldiers ran onto the dock. They shouted and waved their arms. Casey brandished his swagger stick and ordered them off British territory. One of the soldiers aimed his pistol at the *Jo*.

Anne started to duck. Chen gripped her shoulder. 'Don't,' he said. 'It will only confirm their suspicions.' He raised his hand and waved a buoyant farewell to Chiang's men. Casey knocked the marksman's arm up as he fired and the shot spent itself in the air. Sanjay absented himself from the fray, and the *Jo* slipped downriver, toward the Yangtze and the sea.

Innes opened the throttle and they skimmed through the water. 'Nice send-off,' he shouted approvingly over the engine's roar. 'Wouldn't want you folks to be bored.'

The shower of spray drove Anne and Chen into the small cabin. They sat side by side on one of the two berths. Innes stood at the helm at the front of the cabin. It was too noisy to talk. Chen unwrapped his turban, and Anne balled it up and stuffed it into the hamper. She said in his ear, 'You can change when we drop anchor. There will be plenty of time.'

As they neared the place where the Whangpoo poured into the Yangtze, the water became more turbulent. Both rivers were high from typhoon rains and the current was strong. The little boat bucked over the choppy waves. Anne and Chen clung to the sides of the berth to keep from being pitched to the floor.

Innes called back, 'If you think this is rough, wait till we get out to the mouth. Can you swim, Chen?' Chen nodded. 'If it's too choppy out there, we might not be able to get close enough to the *Rose*. They'll drop a ladder over the side, but you might have to swim for it.'

The squall worsened. Innes slowed the engine and squinted into the gale. His high-powered searchlight played over the water in front of them. The usually busy Whangpoo was clear; even the sampan people who scavenged for edible garbage had fled to shore.

Anne felt cold in her thin gown, even with her coat belted tightly around her, and she edged closer to Chen. Their hands touched. Impulsively he grasped hers. They looked at each other for a long moment, wishing they could speak, grateful that they couldn't. Anne sighed and dropped her head onto Chen's shoulder. He smoothed her hair with his free hand, and planted a soft kiss on her forehead. Innes glanced around. His eyebrows rose.

At eleven o'clock, the *Bombay Rose* dropped her anchor into the shallow waters near the Great Yangtze Bank. The gale churned the sea into twelve-foot waves. Innes dragged his own anchor and cautiously approached the freighter, which swept the sea with its searchlights. Once the lights found the *Jo*, they stayed with her to help guide her. Innes pulled nearer. The *Rose* loomed over the little cruiser, dwarfing it. A ladder slithered down the hull of the ship and touched the sea. The *Jo* pitched wildly.

Chen changed rapidly into cotton trousers and a padded jacket, and Anne jettisoned the hamper, which contained his hated costume. He wore cloth shoes and carried five hundred U.S. dollars and the equivalent amount in Japanese yen in a rubber pouch next to his skin.

He waited tensely as the space between the two boats narrowed. He shouted to Innes, 'Don't take her any closer. I will swim.'

Innes said, 'Don't be a fool. The sea's too rough. I can take you right up to the *Rose's* belly.' He wrestled with the wheel. The moving shadows on Chen's face made him look savage and strange. 'It's too dangerous.' He lurched over to Anne, who stood clinging to a handrail near the door. He leaned close to her and said in Chinese, 'I have thought of you often, and I will continue to remember with pleasure the times we shared together. We will not meet again.'

She said, 'I pray that God will keep you safe, and that your work will prosper.'

Chen cast a backward glance at Innes, intent on maneuvering the *Jo* closer to the freighter, and darted out of the cabin. Anne called, 'Chen!'

Innes looked around, saw that Chen was gone, and said, 'That damned fool! Which way did he jump?' Anne pointed to starboard. Innes jerked the *Jo* immediately to port, so that the fierce lash of the wind and the water wouldn't hurl the little boat into the swimmer. Anne joined him at the wheel and they anxiously scanned the patch of sea illuminated by the *Rose's* searchlight. When the *Jo* rode the crest of the waves, they could see a dark head bobbing in the trough below them, but when the boat fell with the suck of the sea, they lost sight of him. Innes opened throttle, pulled back, then turned his own searchlight on the water below the dangling ladder on the side of the *Rose*. Although the ladder was weighted, the rolling of the ship and the tearing of the waves caused it to flap wildly. Only luck would bring it within reach of the exhausted swimmer. They waited for agonizing minutes, and finally saw a figure crawling spider-like up the rope strands to safety. The captain of the *Bombay Rose* ordered his searchlights extinguished, and he sounded the ship's horn twice to signal mission accomplished.

'That's it,' Innes roared. 'Now let's see if we can get this tub back to Shanghai.' He gave Anne a delighted grin.

'Thank you,' she said, and even though he couldn't hear her voice, he understood.

On the way back they had to fight the Yangtze current as well as the gale. Two hours later they saw the lights of the Bund. Innes cut his engine and eased the *Jo* into her berth. As they emerged from the cabin, they were blinded by a powerful bean of light.

'Weather's a bit rough to be taking a pleasure cruise, isn't it, Mr Innes?' a harsh British-accented voice demanded.

'Best kind of weather for sailing, Kendall, you know that. Where's Casey?'

'In hospital, nursing a cracked skull. There was a bit of a brawl here this evening: my men and some Nationalist soldiers. But you wouldn't know anything about that, would you?' The voice was sarcastic. 'Poor drunken Casey thought he was defending the integrity of the British Empire.'

'That's too bad. I'll tell my secretary to send flowers,' Innes said. 'Kendall, I'd like you to meet Mrs Lawrence.'

Anne offered her hand. 'How do you do, Mr Kendall. I've heard a lot about you. Mr Innes has told me how much he admires the fine work carried on by you and the men of the Customs Service.'

'I'll bet he has,' Kendall growled. 'You two haven't seen anything of Chen Ping-ho, have you?'

'What did he say, darling?' Anne asked Innes. 'Something about a jumping hoe?'

'The Shanghai Butcher, honey. You've heard about him. He carved up a bunch of people in the French Concession a couple of years ago.'

'Gracious! Do you mean they've let him out of jail!'

'No, but only because they never managed to get him into jail. Sorry, Kendall, I haven't seen your Commie friend tonight.'

'I would certainly like to know what you were doing out on a night like this,' Kendall said.

Anne looped her arm through Innes'. 'Why, Mr Kendall, haven't you noticed how hard it is for two people to be alone in Shanghai?' she purred.

'I think I'd like to take a look at your boat,' Kendall said stubbornly.

'Help yourself,' Innes said. 'But you'll have to excuse us, Kendall. We're a little wet, and a lot hungry.'

He and Anne strolled up the dock to the Bund. Behind them Kendall and his men crawled over the *Jo*. 'Poor

Kendall,' Innes said. 'He has to save his face a little. It's not the first time I've made a fool of him.'

Anne swayed suddenly and he put his arms around her. She shuddered violently and he pressed her close to his chest, giving her his strength and warmth. 'It's all right now,' he said softly. 'It's all over. It's tough, when you're not used to it. I remember the first time I saw battle, in the Argonne. Took me three hours to stop shaking afterward. But it gets easier. Why, the next time we help one of your undesirable friends out of a jam, you'll be just as cool and calm as I am – although you couldn't have been better tonight. I was proud of you. A brilliant actress, and you don't even get seasick.'

'Yes, I do,' Anne said, without lifting her head. 'I just forgot. There was too much else to think about.'

He laughed. The tremors that shook her were weaker, but he didn't want to release her yet. 'Tired?' he asked. Her head moved against his shoulder. 'Hungry?' She shrugged. 'You haven't eaten a thing today, have you? Let's go, then. We're going to step out. You look too good to waste. I want to show you off a little.'

She looked up. 'Oh, no, I look just awful! I couldn't possibly —'

'You look fine,' he said sincerely. She smelled like the sea, and the soft tendrils around her face were beaded with salt spray. 'Just fine. Anyway, we're not going to one of Kit's fancy joints. Have you every been to Gert's?' She shook her head. 'It's a little bit of home: a bit of Brooklyn, a bit of Chicago, with a touch of San Francisco thrown in. Besides, it always gives Gert a laugh to see me decked out like this. She calls this tux my funeral outfit.'

Anne strained slightly against the pressure of his arms and he released her. 'I'm afraid I rumpled your shirtfront,' she said.

'You and your sister are two fof a kind,' he said. 'You both know how to take the starch out of a man. Where did you learn to move like that, from her? I thought Casey was going to burst his britches.'

Anne made a face. 'I've always been as plain as mud – that's Kit's phrase – and when I was young I used to wonder what it would be like to be beautiful. So I'd lock myself in my room and dab on a little lipstick and pin my hair up, and I'd try to imitate the girls I saw in the street, or at the theater. I discovered that it's all a pose. There's nothing real about that kind of beauty. I decided that I didn't want any of the things I could get by looking like that, and I stopped trying.'

'You wanted to make sure your man loved you for yourself,' Innes mocked gently.

'Yes. Is there anything wrong with that?'

'Not a thing. I suppose Gilbert isn't taken in by tinsel and fluff?'

'No. He doesn't notice what I wear. At least he never says anything. He noticed this coat, though.' She fingered the lapel. 'I didn't tell him where it came from. I should have thanked you.'

'Thanked me for what?' Innes said. She realized that he didn't recognize the coat. Of course, it had been a minor task delegated to his secretary, as she suspected. Charlie Fong had probably even penned the enclosure: 'Thanks again. Jamie.' She felt like a fool.

Gert was an enormous black woman who had come to Shanghai as nursemaid for an American family. When they moved on to a new diplomatic posting, Gert stayed behind and opened a restaurant, on the corner of Avenue Edward VII, where Blood Alley met the Bund. She served steak and fried chicken and potatoes in portions too big for a lumberjack to finish, and packed whatever remained in bags, for her customers to take with them. A flock of beggars always gathered outside Gert's doors and clamored for the leftover food. Any patron who refused to take his bag was not welcome a second time.

She greeted them warmly, enfolding Innes in a vast hug and beaming at Anne. 'Lord, ain't she pretty! You ain't had her in here before, Jimmie.'

'Mrs Lawrence doesn't frequent low-class dives like this,' Innes said.

Gert guffawed. 'What's she doin' with you, then, if she's so fussy?'

'We're related. She doesn't have a choice. How's Billy tonight?'

Billy was a musician and drug addict washed ashore in

Shanghai and salvaged by Gert, Innes told Anne later.

'Not too bad tonight. I'll get him to sing for you later. I swear I don't know what I'm gonna do with that boy. He was all clean last week, and now he's startin' somethin' again. Sleepin' all the time and hardly eatin' a thing. I don't know where he gets the stuff, but Lord, in this town I guess you can get dizzy just breathin' the air. I can't keep my eyes on him all the time. You folks sit here. You look like you got talkin' to do.'

She seated them in a booth in a corner. The tables were covered with red-checked cloths. There was a layer of sawdust on the floor. Innes asked their waiter for a couple of brandies and two steak platters. Anne protested that she didn't think she could eat, and Innes explained how Gert's system operated.

'I've never heard of anything like that,' Anne said. 'She's wonderful, isn't she?'

'None better,' Innes agreed. He leaned across the table and lit her cigarette. 'She's a pretty good businesswoman, too.'

'You own this place?'

'No, I just staked her. She came up to the office one day, told me what she wanted to do, and said that she'd heard I had more money than anybody else in town. I haven't been sorry.' Their brandies arrived. Innes downed his in a swallow and asked for another. Anne sipped. She felt calmer. 'Tell me about Chen,' Innes said casually. 'You were lovers, weren't you?'

Anne sat quite still; her fingers tightened around her glass.

'I could tell by the fit of his tux,' Innes went on. 'No woman can guess a man's size that closely unless she's slept with him.'

'That was a long time ago,' she said. 'Well, aren't you surprised? I'll bet you didn't expect the dreary Miss Fox to have a past.'

'Don't get excited, Anne. I didn't mean anything. But you can't blame me for being curious.'

'I don't owe you any sort of explanation,' she said. 'What do you want me to do, tell you what a silly little fool I was? I'm not sorry it happened. I'll never be sorry. I had his child, too, and I'm not sorry about that. You and my father and Gilbert, you're all the same. You can't stand the idea that any white woman would want a Chinese lover. My father even called him a coolie. Chen, a coolie! He's more brilliant and sensitive than the three of you put together, but because you're white, you think you're so damned superior. I wish —' her voice shook with anger '— I wish I'd never asked you to help me.'

Now wait a minute, Anne. I'm not making any kind of judgment. I don't like the guy; I don't like his methods and I'd sure as hell hate to see this country with him and his crowd in charge. What happened between the two of you is your business. It's just that — I saw the way you looked at each other. He's a lucky guy.'

Anne bit her lip. 'I'm sorry. I didn't have to bite your head off like that.'

'I shouldn't have said anything. I just don't want you to get hurt.'

'No, that part's all over. Even the memories don't hurt anymore. We were so young, so naive. He was as big a dreamer as I was. We had our lives all planned out. He was going to teach at one of the universities in the interior, and I was going to raise our children and play my violin for them, and somehow we were going to change the world peacefully, eliminate suffering without causing more. He was repelled by violence then. He was a party member, but he disagreed with a lot of what they said. He thought that the key to change was in education. I believed in him. I trusted him to know what was right. Politics meant very little to me. I was only a musician, after all. And I loved him. I knew my parents would understand and approve. Christians don't make an issue of race, you know.' Her tone was bitter. 'But my father was more interested in what the people here would think about him than he was in my happiness. All children reflect on their parents, but a minister's children are like little mirrors that have to be kept highly polished and spotless at all times.'

'What happened?'

Anne told him about her father's unexpected arrival in Paris. 'I was sick at the time. Flu. I hardly knew what was happening. He talked to me, and talked. I was weak and

251

feverish and I couldn't come up with a single argument in defense of what I had done. He made it sound as though falling in love with a Chinese would destroy the social order. Father's persuasive powers were at their zenith. He trotted out every ruse he could think of, including telling me that my mother had had a breakdown when she found out about Chen and me. He said she was on her deathbed, and that what I had done would probably kill her. When I got back here, I discovered he had lied to me. She was the same as always, doped to the gills, no better or no worse than usual. She only understood about half of what was going on, and she didn't care about that. Her only concern for the past thirty years has been having enough laudanum to get through the day.'

'I'm sorry,' Innes said. 'I didn't know about that.'

Anne moved her finger around the rim of her glass. 'Chen and I were living in a little room near the Sorbonne. It had been a rough winter, and I suppose I had let myself get run-down. He had gone to Marseilles for a few days, to workers' meetings, but he planned to be back before the baby came. It was just bad luck that he wasn't there when Father turned up. He would have saved me. Before I knew what was happening, Father and I were on our way to Switzerland, to a very exclusive clinic some friends in Shanghai had told him about. The baby came early, and I had a bad time of it, and Father and the people there persuaded me to give it up. I wasn't in any condition to take care of myself, much less a child, and I did it. I still wish I hadn't. I'll never forgive myself. I didn't even have a chance to say goodbye to Chen. I left a note in our room, and I wrote to him from the hospital, but he didn't answer. I found out later that he'd gone to Shanghai after the May Fourth Uprising. I didn't see him again until the day before yesterday.'

Innes remembered that day in 1925, when Chinese students rioted in front of a Japanese factory to protest the abominable working conditions there. Japanese police fired on the mob, killing several. The incident sparked off what would have become a full-scale revolution had it not been for foreign gunboats and superior military strength. As the latest in a long series of humiliations of the Chinese by outsiders, the May Fourth Uprising aroused intensely bitter feelings against all foreigners in China, in particular the Japanese. Two years later a series of strikes forced business in Shanghai to a standstill. Everyone said the strikes had been conceived and coordinated by Chen Ping-ho.

'I wish I could make you understand what he was like in those days,' Anne said softly. 'He was interested in so many things – art and music, history, literature. He was a wonderful painter and calligrapher. I still have all of the drawings he did for me, and some poems he wrote and illustrated. I suppose I should have thrown them away long ago, but I couldn't.' She finished her brandy. Innes signaled to the waiter to bring another. 'We lived in the same street, and I'd see him from time to time in the cafes. Then one night I heard him speak at a students' meeting. A lot of my friends were Marxists – everyone was in those days – and I tagged along. I had never heard anyone talk as he did about the misery the whites had brought to China, certainly not my father or any other missionary. I wanted to tell him how I felt, but I was too shy. Someone introduced us and told him I was from Shanghai. He said something to me in Chinese, and my mind went completely blank. I stared at him like a fool. A month after that, I played in a chamber music recital, in a church near the Pantheon. He was sitting near the front. I could feel him watching me, all through the performance. Afterward he told me that he thought I played well, and he asked me to have coffee with him. We talked for hours. We felt the same about so many things. Falling in love with him was so easy. There was a kind of grace about him, about everything he did. He always reminded me of a hero in a Chinese legend, one of those warriors who calms himself after a battle by composing an ode or a song. He thought I was beautiful,' she said with a wistful smile.

'I'd have to agree with him,' Innes said.

She flushed. 'I wasn't fishing for a compliment.'

He laughed. 'And I wasn't nibbling your bait. I'm beginning to change my mind about Chen. He can't be all bad if he fell in love with you and you fell in love with him.'

She shook her head. 'He's changed. There's a hardness in him that wasn't there before. I believed in him then, because I assumed that his answers were the right ones: Sun Yat-sen's revolution followed by a socialistic state. But I just don't know anymore. I've seen what the Communists have done to the countryside, and what the Nationalists are doing in the name of preserving the country from the Communists. The ones who have suffered most are the innocents, the people. It's always the way. It doesn't make sense.'

'Not much makes sense,' Innes said. 'You have to decide what's important to you, and forget the rest.'

'No, it doesn't work that way for me. Even when I make decisions, they're wrong somehow.'

'Only because you're trying to make everybody happy but yourself. If you start trying to figure out what makes sense to everybody else, you'll never get anywhere.'

She said, 'I envy you. I'll bet you've never regretted anything you've done in your entire life.'

He said without smiling, 'You'd lose money if you bet on that.'

Their food came. Anne discovered she was famished. 'I'm embarrassed,' she said, pushing her empty plate away later. 'I've eaten more than you have.'

'I won't tell. Another drink?'

'I'd better not. You really don't want me to drink too much; I start talking and I can't stop.'

He laughed. 'Not too different from when you're sober. Look, here comes Billy. We'll dance instead.'

'Oh, no, I can't,' Anne said quickly. 'I'm a terrible dancer.'

'You'll hurt Gert's feelings,' he told her. 'She got him off his opium couch just for you.'

Billy sat down at the upright piano at one end of the room and began to play a slow rendition of 'Ain't Misbehavin'.' He sang, more to himself than to his audience, in a voice that was like an old man's reminiscence, hazy yet compelling. A few couples came together on the small open space in front of the piano. Innes stood up and reached for Anne's hand. She held back, then followed reluctantly.

'You've been warned,' she said darkly.

'That's right. I have no one to blame but myself.'

She was stiff with nervousness and stepped on his feet. He laughed and tightened his arm around her waist. 'Come on, you can do better than that. Don't be scared. I won't bite.'

She smiled and relaxed then, and followed his lead easily.

'See, I was right,' he said in her ear. 'Any woman who can move like you—'

'You're not going to let me forget that, are you?'

'I sure won't forget it anytime soon. Poor Casey won't either. He'll say the sight of you walking along that dock was worth a few bumps on the head.'

'I hope he's all right.'

'Don't worry. The Irish have skulls like lumps of pig iron. I'll check in on him tomorrow, make sure he has everything he needs. A long-legged woman and a bottle of rye will have him on his feet in no time.'

'You keep trying to shock me,' she said, amused. 'It won't work, you know.'

'You'd better not bet on that one either,' he advised her.

Alcohol and the lateness of the hour made her reckless. 'Oh, I don't know. I've seen and heard just about everything there is, as far as human nature is concerned. I think I'm fairly immune to shock by now. I'd take that bet.'

'You're on.'

'Well, I'm waiting. Say something shocking.'

He shook his head. 'No. I get to choose my own time and place. I have to feel inspired.'

'I keep getting the feeling that you're trying to put something over on me,' she said warily. 'I had the same feeling the other day in your office, and I was right. You told Maurice to dress me in the sexiest dress he could come up with, didn't you?'

Innes said, 'You'll never get a jury to convict me. They'd give me a medal instead.'

Billy finished his song to enthusiastic applause. He smiled vaguely and saluted Anne and Innes, then swung into 'My Honey's Lovin' Arms.'

His voice was thin and dream-soaked, like her mother's. Anne stopped dancing abruptly and said, 'It's late. I have to work tomorrow.'

'Sure,' Innes said. 'I understand.'

Looking into his eyes, she thought for a moment that he did understand.

At the door they encountered Albert McClure, the Reuters man, and a Junoesque blonde of uncertain age. Anne stiffened. The woman was Olga Kerensky.

'Jim Innes, just the man I was looking for!' McClure said. 'What's this I hear about a rumpus at the yacht basin? One of England's finest landed up in hospital, too. Ah, this must be the mysterious lady in the case. Introduce us, Jim.'

'My wife's sister, Anne Lawrence. Al McClure, professional snoop.'

'Now, Jim, I'm not trespassing on anything that isn't public domain. So you're Kit's sister! I'm going to have to revise my opinion of missionaries' daughters.' His eyes flashed appreciatively. 'This is Madame Kerensky, folks. Olga, these are my friends, Jim and Anne.'

'I know Anne,' Olga said warmly. 'You look marvelous tonight, my dear.' Anne didn't reply.

'Now tell me about the bloke in the turban,' McClure said eagerly. 'Rumor hath that it was Chen Ping-ho, of all people. Well?' He looked expectantly from Anne to Innes to Anne again. 'Did you aid and abet the fugitive? Three of you left on the *Jo*, but only two of you came back. I find that curious, and fascinating. I also find it fascinating that one of Jim's ships sailed from Woosung at the same time. 'Fess up, kids. Old Al can smell a story a mile away.'

'Oh, Albert, Anne would never have anything to do with that filthy Communist,' Olga said imperiously. 'What an absurd notion! Come, let us have our supper and permit these dear people to be on their way. Anne looks rather tired,

I'm afraid. Come along.' She tugged at his elbow.

McClure said dramatically, 'Apron strings. I feel the creeping stranglehold of apron strings!'

'Oh, Albert, don't be silly.'

* * *

Sanjay, lounging against the side of the Rolls, leaped to attention when he saw them. Anne wondered when he slept. When did anyone sleep in Shanghai? The Bund was as busy and noisy as daytime, and it was nearly three in the morning.

'She saved our skins,' Innes remarked as the car turned up Nanking Road. 'You know her?'

'Oh, yes,' Anne said wearily. 'Sometimes I feel that there are really only thirty people in Shanghai, but I keep seeing the same ones over and over.'

The car pulled up in front of the manse. Innes walked Anne to the front door. 'Would you like to come in?' she said. 'My parents are asleep, I'm sure. I'll make coffee.'

'No thanks, I've had your coffee.' They laughed. 'Your father would have the place fumigated if he knew I'd been inside.'

'I thought you two had become reconciled. Kit said—'

'She rigged up something, just so she could make fools out of both of us. She persuaded me to make a generous donation to the church – too generous for him to refuse. It nearly killed him, but he took the money. She brought us together at dinner one night. I thought your father would choke on every bite. Your mother didn't seem to know there was anything going on. I didn't know then—' He pulled out his cigarette case. 'Here, one for the road.' He clicked his lighter. 'I'd like to hear you play the violin sometime. I don't know anything about music, but I'd be willing to learn.'

'No,' she said quickly. 'I don't play anymore. I wasn't ever that good. I couldn't have made a career as a soloist. My teacher in Paris said I could probably get a job in a theater orchestra. He didn't mean it kindly, but I almost cried with relief when he said it: "Mademoiselle, I'm afraid you are not of the caliber to be a concert soloist." I'd been terrified that I wasn't good enough to play in public at all, that I had no business even touching a violin, wasting my teachers' time. I think he felt a little sorry for being so blunt, because he said that if I worked very hard, I could probably get a job with a minor symphony someday. He didn't understand how happy he'd made me, just by telling me that I could earn my living making

257

music somewhere.'

'So you haven't tried to play since then?'

'Why should I?' she demanded. 'Music was something that gave me pleasure. It belonged to a special time when I was happy. I don't have to torture myself by trying to recapture something that's gone forever. I used to have dreams about losing my baby, only in a lot of them it wasn't a baby at all, but a violin. They're the same size, almost. I can't do it. I just can't!' She broke off and made a rueful face. 'I'm sorry. I didn't mean to treat you to a sample of my hysterical behavior. You don't know what a mess I am, practically a mental case. I spent some time in a sanitarium after it was all over. That was my flirtation with madness. The people there reminded me of my mother, only they didn't need opium to help them run away. You ought to choose your company more carefully, Mr Innes.'

'I thought we were friends,' he said. 'Jamie.'

She felt a nervous flutter under her ribs. 'Everyone else calls you Jim.'

'You're not everyone else. I remember the night Jo died. You held me and called me by my mother's name for me. I was surprised. You looked like an old-maid schoolteacher, but you weren't afraid to hold a man in your arms, even a man you hated. I revised my opinion of you that night. I've revised that revision tonight. You, Mrs Lawrence, are guilty of not being what you seem. You're hiding something. I wonder what it is.'

'What a lot of nonsense you talk,' she said crisply. 'I'm not afraid of anything. And I certainly didn't hate you then. You just – I mean, it was all so mixed up – you needed someone,' she finished lamely.

'That's right.' He braced one arm against the doorframe and leaned closer to her. 'It was lucky for me you were around.'

'I really ought to go in. Our voices might wake Mother – she's a light sleeper. It's been quite a day, hasn't it?' she said with a nervous laugh. 'But now Cinderella has come home to roost – there's an awful mixed metaphor for you.' She took a deep drag on her cigarette. She wanted to distract his attention, make him think about something other than that awful night, the way she acted then, the way she looked now. 'Funny, I haven't thought about Gilbert at all. He might be dead, or hurt, and I haven't thought about him. That's a loving wife for you.'

'What's the trouble? Can I help?'

'No. I shouldn't have mentioned it. I can't burden you with any more of my problems.' She ground out her cigarette. She wished he wouldn't stand so close, crowding her, surrounding her. She could hardly breathe.

'What's a brother-in-law for?'

'Dr Morrison had a letter,' she began and related the contents to Innes. 'We don't know what can have happened to him. I wish Kit were home. Maybe she could tell us something.'

'I'll see what I can find out. I have people working on the river, and in Chungking. Don't worry, we'll get a line on him.'

'You always sound so confident, like you can do anything,' she said with envy.

'I can do anything,' he said softly. 'Watch.'

He placed his hands alongside her face and kissed her. Her mouth was sweet and soft, and she smelled of the sea. He pressed closer, deepening the kiss, and her lips parted slightly. Her breathing was strong and deep, and the pulse in her body matched his own. He was aware of the hardness of her pelvis and her pubic bone, and the softness of her belly and her breasts. His desire rose quickly, and he pushed hard against her so that she could feel it. She gasped, and he filled her mouth with his tongue. He caressed her shoulders, and cupped his hands around her full breasts.

She stiffened and jerked away. He stepped back. Breathless, they stared at each other.

Innes swallowed, and said with a shaky laugh, 'I was going to show you how easily I could win that bet we made back at Gert's. I have a feeling the joke's on me.'

She groped behind her for the door handle. 'I've got to go in,' she said in a throaty whisper.

'No, don't,' he said. 'It's still early.'

'Please, Jamie, I have to. It's late. So late.'

She ducked inside and closed the door firmly in his face.

He didn't move for a long time, then he turned and walked slowly back to the car.

Chapter Nine

'Hullo, Mouse.' The voice that came over the phone sounded crisp and cheerful.

'Kit! Where are you?'

'In the Innes mausoleum, of course. Where else?'

'But where have you been? Where's Gilbert?'

'In Chengtu, I guess. At least that's where I left him, ages ago. I've been having the most marvelous time in Peiping. Met the loveliest English couple – diplomats. I brought you something wonderful. You must come over and see it at once.'

'But Kit, Gilbert's not in Chengtu.' Despair settled over her like a fine mist. 'He's gone. Something has happened and I thought you would know —'

'I don't know a thing. He was perfectly all right when I left – was I glad to get out of that town! Listen, come over for a drink. Don't worry. He probably went to the mountains with the Masters.'

Anne hung up. She knew he wasn't in the mountains. It was the second week of September. The new term at the university had just started without him. Where was he?

One day in mid-November, Reverend Mudd died quietly in his sleep. Anne, sitting by his side, wasn't even aware that he had stopped breathing. She had expected it – the tumor had been malignant – but the end was still a shock. He had been her sole reason for staying in Shanghai. Ordinarily she would have been free to return home, to Chengtu, but she had no home there without Gilbert.

He had been missing for over three months. Letters from Dr Masters confirmed that Gilbert had indeed left the university in early August without saying a word to anyone. He never gave the slightest indication that there was anything wrong. Kit stayed on campus for a week after her accident, to everyone's delight, and a few days after she departed, Dr Lawrence simply vanished. From the tone of his letters, Dr Masters couldn't believe that

Anne was as ignorant of her husband's state of mind as everyone else in Chengtu.

One of the nurses called her to the telephone as she was leaving the hospital.

'This is Dad, Anne. Can you come home? Gilbert's here. One of Innes' river steamers picked him up in Itu, in Hupeh Province.'

She went into the nurses' lounge and cried until she felt calm. She didn't want to greet Gilbert with a display of hysteria.

'He's got worms, a touch of dysentery, malarial fever, and some bad infections on his hands and feet,' Dr Morrison diagnosed. 'Nothing that can't be cured.'

'Jesus humbled himself and became man,' Gilbert muttered, thrashing on sweat-soaked sheets. 'We act like gods here, but we ought to humble ourselves, too. Jesus saved them because he was one of them. They will listen if you become one of them.'

'It's only fever talking,' Uncle Billy said. 'Don't you worry. I'll look in tomorrow.' He left the room and went to reassure Marian and Leonard.

'What happened, Gilbert?' Anne asked, grasping his hands and kneeling beside the bed. 'Tell me what happened. You left the university. Why did you do that? You can tell me.'

'You won't understand,' he said irritably through lips cracked by sickness and harsh sunlight. 'Nobody understands.'

His eyes, bright with fever, glowed like a saint's. His hair had been so long and matted that she had had to cut it off, and his body was malnourished, broken, and bruised. Two of his ribs had been fractured, and two fingers. His hands and feet were deeply scarred and bruised, thickly calloused and stained with filth. Most mysterious was the broad red scar on his forehead. He looked, Anne thought, as if he'd been broken on the wheel.

'We are all God's children. Who am I to set myself above God? I had to purify myself, cleanse myself. I was not worthy to serve Him. Can't you understand that?'

'Of course,' Anne murmured, understanding nothing.

He said, 'At first they were frightened of me, because they thought I was mad. They set upon me and beat me and stole my money. But that was good. I was so proud, so arrogant. I thought that I could set out on my journey of purification with money, when they had none. They took my clothes. They took everything. I slept in the fields, and begged for my bread. Everywhere I went I told them about the Lord and His love, and they began to listen. They began to listen, Anne! I had worked so hard healing their bodies that I never gave a thought to their souls. But God showed me my error. He led me out of the darkness, and He cleansed me of all my sins.'

She gazed at him dumbly while the well-worn Christian epithets for suffering dribbled out of his mouth. She had noticed how many people, when they were unable to endure the depths of sorrow, wrapped themselves in jargon and hypnotized themselves with familiar ecclesiastical phrases. To her ears the words always sounded false and trite and dangerous, because they distorted reality. Suffering was the lot of humanity, not its salvation. It was something to be overcome, not welcomed.

She wouldn't have expected Gilbert to be one of those pathetic self-deluders. Nor would she have expected him to crucify himself in the name of salvation. Few Presbyterians ever developed a martyr mentality, unless they martyred themselves by hard work.

'I knew I wouldn't starve,' he said. 'God wouldn't let me. I wandered into villages. Sometimes they drove me out and set their dogs on me. But sometimes they let me stay, and gave me a bowl of rice, because they said I was a holy man.'

Anne nodded. Begging monks were nothing new to the Chinese.

'I labored for God. For the first time in my life I worked with my hands. I wanted no pay. I plowed their fields and carried the night-soil to the plants. I helped with the harvest. I worked hard, and they fed me and gave me shelter. But those people are very close to God, even though they don't know it. It's the people in the cities and towns who have no time for God. So I went to work on the river, where I could go from town to town. I became a tracker.'

He said it proudly. Anne caught her breath. Most of the barges on China's river were drawn upstream by men, linked together by ropes like teams of draft animals. As they strained against the cruel current, they bent over so far that their bodies were almost parallel to the ground. They wore the ropes across their foreheads, where bone instead of flesh absorbed the strain.

Trackers were a rough lot, hardened and cynical and rootless, without homes, without families. They spent their wages on opium, which dulled the pain in their battered bodies. They didn't live long. They were lower on the social scale than coolies. Gilbert had announced with pride that he had been a tracker. She thought her heart would burst with pity.

A week later she called Innes to thank him for his help.

'I should have known that you'd find him.'

'I wish it could have been sooner. My men said he was in pretty bad shape. How is he now?'

'Better. He's even talking about going back to Chengtu and his work there. He seems almost normal again. He says those three months were like a dream. But he has the scars to prove they weren't.'

'Jesus,' Innes breathed. 'It's rough on you, isn't it? Listen, would you like to come up to the office? We can talk —'

'I'm sorry, I can't,' she said too quickly. 'I just wanted you to know how grateful we are. All of us.'

It was ridiculous, she knew, but she didn't want to see him again. A frivolous kiss in the moonlight on the front porch does not grand passion make, but all the same —. She wasn't so much afraid of him as of herself. She had thought about that idiotic kiss, and about Innes, entirely too much. It wasn't right. After all, he was her sister's husband.

Marian Fox was reading to Gilbert in the sitting room one sunny morning when Kit breezed in, kissed her mother, and sat down to tell them about her adventures in Peiping and most recently Hong Kong.

'I'm getting to be quite a gypsy,' she said, crossing her

legs and swinging her foot. Fascinated and horrified, Gilbert stared at that foot. Swish, swish, moving like a pendulum, marking off the seconds. Kit broke off her recital. 'Golly, Mums, where's Wang? I'm dying for a drink.'

'I'll go ask him to make tea, dear,' Marian said helpfully, rising from her chair. Gilbert wanted to plead with her not to go, but his tongue felt as though it was wrapped in a flannel sock. Helpless, he watched her leave the room.

Kit said, 'Well you've had some adventures yourself, I hear. That's what I like about you, Gil, your spirit of adventure.' Her tone dripped sarcasm. He couldn't speak. He watched her mouth, red-painted and pulsating like an open, bleeding artery. 'You can't blame me for running out on you. You weren't worth very much those last few days. You know what opium does to the old libido: puts it right to sleep. Just ask Daddy. Are you still doping?'

He shook his head. 'I ran away from it.' He spoke thickly, like a stroke victim who has had to learn to talk again. 'It was wrong. God showed me the way.'

'Good old God,' Kit said. 'Listen, take my advice. Stay away from it. Nothing ruins a good man so fast as dope.' She grinned suddenly and touched his arm. He recoiled. Her hand felt like a burning iron. 'Cheer up. You're looking a little seedy now, but you'll be ready for play soon. Maybe I'll take you and Anne to Hong Kong. Now there's a town!'

Marian returned. Kit removed her hand and began to chatter again. Gilbert still felt her touch like a brand on his arm. He wondered if it would wash off. It would leave a mark, like a stain. He had endured the torments of hell in order to purify himself, and now she had tainted him again with her sin

After Kit left he began to shiver violently. Marian called to Wang and together they got him upstairs.

'I'll call Billy,' Marian said in a panic.

'No!' Gilbert grasped her hand. It was like holding a silken bag full of brittle sticks. 'Don't leave me, please. Mother – may I call you Mother?'

'Of course you may, Gilbert. I am your mother,

in a way.'

'You're my mother, but you won't help me,' he said accusingly. 'I'm in pain, and you can save me, but you won't. Why won't you help me?'

Marian was confused and distressed. 'But of course I'll help you, Gilbert. I'll do anything for you, you know that. Just tell me, dear.'

She felt flattered. She hadn't been a mother – or a wife – for a long time, but her instincts hadn't deserted her. She felt a rush of warmth for him. Everyone else in her family was so busy. For years the activities of her household had passed her by. No one cared about her because she couldn't be useful to them anymore. Liberation from usefulness had only made her more isolated and afraid. But now someone needed her. She was a mother again.

'What can I do, Gilbert?'

He ran his fingers over the ridges on the back of her hand, strumming the bones and tendons nervously. She leaned over him. She smelled of lavender and tea leaves.

He said, 'I am in pain. Can you understand that? In my soul. I can't stand it anymore. I want some medicine. Your medicine. Do you understand? That wonderful medicine that takes away all pain.'

'Yes, yes,' she said in an excited whisper. 'You're right, it will help you. You're a doctor, you know how wonderful it is. I'll bring it right away, Gilbert. Of course, it's exactly what you need.'

'We can't tell anyone,' he said anxiously. 'It's just this once, because I'm in pain. Once never hurt anybody. But don't tell anyone. Don't tell Anne.'

'I promise, dear.' She patted his hand fondly. 'I won't tell. It will be our secret, yours and mine.'

At first Gilbert's recovery was steady. His appetite and strength returned. He seemed alert and calm and eager to resume his work. Therefore when Anne saw signs of regression she was concerned.

'He's lost some of the weight he'd gained,' she told Dr Morrison. 'He's been unusually restless lately, and he's had trouble sleeping.'

'That's normal at this stage,' Dr Morrison assured her.

'He ought to be allowed to backslide a little after such consistent improvement. You can't expect his recovery to proceed in a straight upward line without an occasional dip and plateau now and then. Listen, one of our doctors has a villa near Hangchow. You both need to get away for a while. You're exhausted, and Gilbert could use a change of scene. I'll arrange it.'

They stayed in Hangchow a month. Gilbert seemed calmer away from Shanghai, and he began to improve again. He and Anne walked in the parks, explored the temples, and revisited the places they had seen on their honeymoon. They spent increasingly longer periods of time away from the villa as he gained strength, even renting a rowboat for a day and picnicking on the shore of one of the lakes.

If he seemed preoccupied or distracted, Anne told herself it was because he was trying to make sense out of what happened, and setting a new course for himself. Sometimes he wanted to talk, and he'd launch into a long rambling discourse on the meaning of his Soul's Journey, as he called it. She forced herself to listen patiently. The need to talk was part of the healing process, wasn't it? She herself had run to Olga when she returned from Switzerland, because there was so much she needed to talk out. When Olga failed her she had found Father Jacquinot, who saved her sanity.

They returned to the manse on Bubbling Well Road. Anne didn't want to burden her parents further, but they protested that Gilbert was no trouble at all, and that it would be cruel to move him before he was fully recovered. Even Gilbert insisted that he felt quite comfortable there and that he didn't want to leave.

Anne took a job at the Shanghai General Hospital. She refused Dr Morrison's offer of an easy shift at the Aldershot. She had been willing to work there as long as Reverend Mudd was alive, but she had always despised their policies and had no wish to remain after he was gone.

She worked from four in the afternoon to midnight. Every night when she came home, she looked in on Gilbert. They had separate rooms. Gilbert stayed in Kit's own beautifully decorated boudoir because he was often wakeful at night and disturbed her own rest. He had rebuffed the only intimate overture she made, with the excuse that he wasn't ready yet. She knew he would have to make the first move, and she waited, somewhat impatiently, and tried to ignore the gnawing ache inside her.

One night she tapped on his door and peeked in to see if he was sleeping. His bed was empty, even though the lights in his room were burning brightly. She wasn't concerned. He was probably in the bathroom. Then she heard voices next door, in her mother's room. She smiled. The two night owls were keeping each other company. She opened her mother's door softly.

'— starts in my feet, like I was sinking into feathers, and works its way up. I can feel it sucking me under, but when it reaches the top of my head I find that I'm on top of the mountain,' Gilbert said dreamily.

'Yes, yes, I know that feeling. Wonderful.'

He sat at the foot of his mother-in-law's bed. Marian was lying down, her thin body hardly raising a ripple under the covers. She saw Anne first, and hissed, 'Gilbert!' Gilbert was holding a glass in his hands. He looked up guiltily and the glass slipped through his fingers. The contents spilled on the beige rug.

'What's the matter with you two?' Anne asked slowly. She approached the bed. Neither of them moved. She stooped and picked up the glass. She recognized the color and the smell as her mother's medicine. She said calmly, 'I'd better clean this up before it stains the rug.' Then her hands began to shake and she dropped the glass as if it had burned her. It landed with a soft thud and rolled under the bed. She looked at Gilbert, who wouldn't meet her gaze. 'How could you?' she whispered. 'How could you?' She turned to her mother, who closed her eyes. 'Mother – Why? Why?'

She backed away from them. Her mother said, 'You don't understand. You have never understood.'

'You seduced him with your poison,' Anne said in a horrified whisper. She could feel a scream of anger building inside her. Her voice rose in a crescendo. 'Isn't it enough for you to kill yourself? Do you have to kill him, too? Why couldn't you leave him alone?'

Gilbert said, 'No, it's not her fault. I begged for it. It wasn't the first time. In Chengtu, after you left. I needed it then, and I thought I could run away from it. But I can't. It's not your mother's fault.'

'Oh, my God,' Anne croaked. The room tilted sharply. She knew she was going to be sick, and she ran into her mother's bathroom and slammed the door. When she came out, Gilbert was gone. She left the room without speaking to her mother, and without glancing at the stain on the rug.

She lay huddled on her bed. Her door opened and her father said, 'Anne? I heard the ruckus in Mother's room. I got Gilbert to bed. He told me what happened.'

She didn't move.

'I wish I knew what to say.'

'You might tell me you sympathize,' she said bitterly.

'I do, Anne. With all my heart.' His voice choked. She knew he was crying.

'The two of them,' she said, 'with their heads together, sharing their dreams – it's sickening. It's almost funny. He really fooled me. And Uncle Billy, with his little speech about dips and plateaus. That's a doctor for you – so sure he's right that he'll ignore any symptom that doesn't fit his diagnosis. We can't stay here.'

'I know that. I'll help you find a place.'

'I couldn't understand it. He didn't mind having me around, but he didn't want me to touch him.'

'No,' her father said. 'They don't.'

Anne and Gilbert moved into an apartment in the French Concession, on the Rue Pere Robert not far from the Jesuits' residence. It was just another space furnished with other people's smells and other people's ghosts, not unlike their old place near Soochow Creek, except that here they were on the third floor and had no garden. Anne didn't care; she had no wish to grow flowers when she herself felt as barren and desolate as the Gobi Desert.

Gilbert said, 'I know you're angry with me. I don't blame you.'

'I thought we were happy. Why didn't you tell me you

269

were troubled? Not to tell the truth is the same as lying.'

'We were happy,' he said dully. 'It wasn't anything you did. It's just me. I'm weak. I know that. Your mother and I are alike, both weak. I can't explain it. Anne, I don't want Dr Morrison to know about this.'

'I can't tell him he's a fool and an incompetent without giving him a reason.'

'Please. He's always been good to me. He thinks I'm better than I really am. He even told me that what I did was brave, courageous. I'd be ashamed if he knew the truth. Please, Anne. I'll give up the laudanum, I swear it. I'll never touch it again. I only took it once, because I had such a terrible pain in my back, I won't even think about it anymore.'

She had noticed lately that when he told a lie he tried to look appealingly lost and boyish. 'All right,' she said. 'I won't tell him.'

In December 1936 Chiang Kai-shek was kidnapped in Sian, Shensi Province, by one of his own generals, who was reluctant to embark on the Sixth Extermination Campaign of the Communists while the Japanese were penetrating farther and farther into China. The world waited for news of Chiang's release or death. Finally he was freed, to general rejoicing. In light of the fact that the scheduled campaign against the Communists never materialized, everyone assumed that some kind of conference between Chiang and Communist leaders had taken place, and the two groups had agreed to postpone their mutual warfare and act jointly to repel the invader.

So, Anne thought, Chen got his meeting with Chiang after all. Unless all-out war with Japan erupted, most of the country would enjoy a respite from killing. She knew how clever and persuasive Chen could be, and she had no doubt that he had been a chief architect of the truce, if not of the whole scheme. Ironically, China owed the cessation of its internal warfare to one of its greatest imperialist exploiters, James Innes. It was a great story. It was a shame Albert McClure would never ferret it out.

In 1937 Chinese New Year fell in early February. For

weeks before the actual day the firecrackers rattled in Shanghai's streets. The din made Gilbert nervous, and he reacted to each noisy crackle as if it were gunfire.

Anne knew he was still taking laudanum, although she never found any in the apartment. She was away a good part of the day, however, and he was free to come and go. He wouldn't have any trouble obtaining the stuff. His appetite was poor; like her mother, he seemed to be fading into ghostliness. Even his hair was pale, and it matched the parchment tone of his flesh. He walked the floors at night, and her own sleep suffered. He never touched her, and most of the time he hardly seemed aware of her presence in the room.

'Why is Shanghai so noisy?' he fussed one night as a long string of firecrackers popped under their front window. He put his hands over his ears. 'I can't sleep anymore. I hear them all the time.'

'It will be over soon,' she said. 'The New Year starts in just a couple of days. Things quiet down after that.'

'No, it's never quiet. I remember the music and the laughter. She brings the noise with her. The fox-fairy. It's her way of distracting me, so I won't know the difference.'

'What are you talking about, Gilbert? Fox-fairy?'

'Don't you remember Mr Weston's story? She looks like the woman you love, exactly like her, but she's really a demon. Mischievous and cunning, like a fox. Only it's not true about the tail. That part is just fantasy.'

Anne tilted the lampshade so she would have more light on her mending. It cast an oblique shadow on Gilbert's face. She said, 'It's all fantasy. Just a fable made up by some old man who couldn't keep up with his young wife. Naturally, if she had been human, he wouldn't have had any difficulty, so he had to persuade himself and everyone else that she was really a mischievous spirit who looked like his wife. And so the fox-fairy legend was born. Or perhaps the legend was invented by a husband who caught his beloved in bed with another man and didn't want to believe the evidence of his own eyes. I can think of lots of —'

'Will you stop mocking me!' Gilbert said furiously. 'You make fun of everything I say. You're always contradicting me, laughing at me. Don't deny it. You go to the hospital every day and tell everyone that I'm bewitched, and you all sneer at me, because there's nothing more pathetic than a man bewitched.'

'Oh, stop it, Gilbert,' she said crossly. 'It's not you, it's the opium talking. Get a hold on yourself. Can't you hear how you sound? No one laughs at you, honestly. Everyone who knows you loves and respects you.'

'I don't know why you're lying to me,' he said testily. 'I'm not a fool. I know what she's like. She's told everyone about me. They have to believe her, because she's a demon. If they're not careful, she'll bewitch them, too. You see how clever she is. You're her sister, and even you can't tell them apart.'

'Are you talking about Kit? Oh, Gilbert, that's silly. Kit's not a fox-fairy, really she's not. I admit she's bewitching – I've seen her in action – but she's quite human, I assure you.'

'That's exactly what I mean,' he crowed. 'Not even you can tell the difference between the real one and the demon! At first I couldn't understand how I could love someone who was so cunning and evil, and then I remembered the fox-fairy, and I knew that there were two of them. Good and evil, don't you see? I thought at first that she was good, but then later, when we were alone, she took control of my mind and forced me to do things I didn't want to do. I couldn't help myself. I had no strength to resist her, and not even God could help me, because I was consorting with demons.'

Her needle slipped and plunged into the ball of her middle finger. She sucked the wound and staunched it with her handkerchief and thought, It's the opium talking. He's hallucinating. He doesn't know what he's saying. It's all a dream. He's in the middle of a waking dream.

Yet she was aware of a hardness within her, like a core of ice. She was afraid.

'Oh, so you were in love with Kit,' she said calmly. 'He's not responsible for what he's saying. Don't believe a word he says.

'Oh, yes. Since the very first time I saw her. I couldn't think of anything else. I know now that the demon had

272

possessed me, and that's why I couldn't forget her. I thought I could escape her by marrying you, but it didn't work. She wouldn't leave me alone.'

'And you went to bed with her?' Anne hated herself for asking the question, and told herself that the answer, when it came, was sure to be a lie.

'Yes. She always wanted that. In my hotel, that was the first time. And after we were married she made me come to her house, and we met in other hotels.'

'And what about Chengtu?' Well, what if he did fantasize about sleeping with Kit? Was he so different from every other man in Shanghai? 'Did you sleep together while she was staying with us?'

'No, only once, just after you left. But I took opium and she couldn't touch me after that.' He smiled proudly, because he had outwitted the fox.

'I don't believe you,' Anne said. 'It's all a dream, isn't it, Gilbert? Just another beautiful dream? Please, tell me the truth now. Try hard. Concentrate, just for a moment. You and Kit never – you weren't really lovers —'

'It wasn't Kit,' he said maddeningly. 'I told you, it was the spirit.'

She stood up shakily. 'I have to go out for a little while. You'll be all right.'

Why are you doing this? she asked herself as she ran toward the Innes mansion on the Avenue Joffre. Kit will only laugh at you. It's ridiculous, a drug dream. Don't ring the bell. Turn around and go home again. You don't need Kit to tell you you're making a fool of yourself. Don't go in there.

She found herself face to face with the houseboy. 'Is Missee Kit at home?' He bowed her in. He seemed surprised about something. She realized that she wasn't wearing a coat. It was damp and bitterly cold outside, but she hadn't noticed.

In a trance, she followed the boy upstairs. Kit turned around from her dressing table and greeted her gaily. Anne wanted to cry with relief. She was the same old Kit, irreverent and informal, calling her Mouse, asking for a cigarette then finding her own under a discarded dress, chattering about the dinner party she was giving, sipping a martini as she put the finishing touches on her makeup.

'I had to come,' Anne said, twisting the handkerchief she had wrapped around her finger. 'I know you'll laugh. I'm embarrassed to repeat it, really. But Gilbert said that you and he had been lovers. Isn't that silly? I don't know why I ran over to tell you, because it isn't true. It can't be true.' She was trying to convince herself, begging for the truth, hoping for a lie.

'What? Gil? Of course it's true, Mouse. What did you think, that he married you because he loved you? Don't fret though. It's all over and no harm done.'

'No harm done,' Anne echoed. The ice in her core spread its coldness quickly.

'He's a dear boy, but immature, don't you think? No realistic notion of women at all.' She didn't meet Anne's anguished gaze, but inspected herself critically in the gold-framed cheval glass in the corner. Her gown was long-sleeved, with a high bodice and low back. It clung to her slender form like a shining snakeskin, and every square inch glittered with sequins, like silvery scales.

'He was a virgin when we met.' Kit moistened her fingertip and touched it to her eyebrow. 'Didn't you ever wonder when and where he was initiated? Or by whom? You didn't think it was that dreadful girlfriend of his, what was her name?'

'I can't remember.' She's doing this deliberately, hurling the truths at me like stones.

'He hated the idea of my divorce, and he married you because he thought you were virtuous, and safe. What a marvelous joke, on both counts. You were sullied, my dear, and he found out that he couldn't hide from me. All the time you were sleeping on the couch, he was sleeping with me, Mouse.'

'Why are you doing this?' Anne felt a sudden irrational rush of pity for her sister. 'Why do you want to hurt me like this, Kit? I've never done anything to harm you, ever.'

Kit swung her shoulders. 'Why not? It was fun. It didn't hurt anybody, not really. It had nothing to do with you. It was Gilbert, always running like a scared rabbit, thinking he could get away. He was horrid to me. He called me all sorts of names. No one had ever treated me like that, not even Richard – and he had a good reason to be nasty. But the British are so wonderfully civilized. Do you know why Richard and I got divorced? Because he came home from riding to his ghastly hounds one day and found me in bed with his father. You see, I don't discriminate. I'll break up anyone's family, even my own.' Her laughter had a hollow sound.

'But you're not like that,' Anne said lamely.

'You don't know what I'm like,' Kit said, facing her. 'No one knows what I'm like. You only think you do. You think you have me right where you want me, all tied up in a neat little package. Gilbert, Innes, Richard, even Daddy. They all want something – a wife, a goddess, a trophy, a loving daughter – that doesn't have anything to do with me. Me. I don't have to fit myself into anybody's mold. I do what I want. I live my own life and I don't play by anybody else's rules.'

Anne felt as though she had been eviscerated and stuffed with sawdust. She stared at Kit through unblinking glass eyes.

Kit stubbed out her cigarette. 'Quite a speech, wasn't it? You'd better run along, Mouse. I've got some high-toned guests coming any minute and you won't fit in.' She sat at her dressing table and brushed her hair vigorously.

'You destroyed him. You almost killed him. Don't you care about that?'

'I didn't do anything. I just gave him the opportunity to do what he wanted to do. You know these sex-obsessed Puritans. They're all just dying for a taste of the apple.'

'He called you a demon. A fox-fairy.'

'Did he? That's good. I wouldn't have thought he had that much imagination. Cheer up, Mouse. If it hadn't been for me, he wouldn't have married you at all. Looking at it that way, I did you a favor.'

Anne had no desire to weep or laugh, to shout or lash out in anger. She was surprised at how empty she felt. She said, but only because she didn't want to slink away silently, 'I'll never forgive you for this.'

Just as she reached the bottom of the stairs the

houseboy opened the front door and Innes strode in.

'God, it's raw out tonight.' He peeled off his overcoat. He saw Anne then. 'Oh, hullo. Coming to Kit's party? She's got a couple of live ones lined up for me to meet.'

'Be sure to tell them what a fool you've made of me,' she said tonelessly. 'It's a very funny story.'

'What are you talking about?'

'You knew. And you didn't tell me. You let me go on thinking everything was all right. Not to tell the truth is the same as lying.'

She frowned and shook her head, trying to clear it a little, then she brushed past him. The boy held the door and she went out into the frigid darkness.

Innes stared after her, a puzzled scowl on his face. On his way to his room to change into evening clothes, he tapped on Kit's door.

'What's the matter with Anne? I just ran into her.'

Kit shrugged. 'Some trouble with Gil. You know how she gets. Upset over nothing. Hurry up and change, will you?'

'In my own good time,' he said stubbornly.

'Look, I arranged this little party as a favor to you – not that I owe you any favors,' she said, fastening on an earring. 'The least you can do is cooperate. I'm not going to entertain these morons by myself. If you're not downstairs when they come, I'm not staying.'

'You're in an even bitchier mood than usual tonight,' he remarked. 'Maybe it would be a good idea if you did leave.'

'You need me, Innes. These Texas Bible-beaters wouldn't even spit in your direction if it weren't for me. If you want this deal to go through, you'd better be nice to me. I can ruin it for you.'

'You ought to try being a little more like your sister,' Innes said. 'I don't know anybody who hates her, but I can think of a thousand people who —'

She screamed an obscenity and hurled a large jar of cold cream at him. He ducked and backed out the door.

'Shanghai is like an island,' Innes told the Texan, who had a hard time concentrating on what his host was saying while his hostess's very attractive naked back was turned in his direction. 'Out there governments rise and fall. There are wars in the interior. But here it's business as usual, no matter what happens in the rest of the country. As long as our guns are bigger than theirs, we can keep right on going, and that will be for a long, long time to come.'

'But the Japs bombed this city in '32,' the Texan said distractedly.

'They bombed the Chinese sections and left the international settlements alone,' Innes reminded him. 'The Japs have a big stake in Shanghai, too. They're linked to every other good-sized business here, through banking and real estate connections. They can't hurt us without hurting themselves. No, they'll restrict their aggression to the North. That's where the richest mineral deposits and resources are.'

Kit flashed them a smile and a wink and moved to the other side of the room.

'How much money do you have in banks abroad?' the man asked shrewdly, giving his full attention to Innes for the first time.

'Not a cent,' Innes said. 'Not a red cent. I do business in China, and I bank in China. My money's as safe here as it would be in Switzerland – and the way Hitler's acting up, it's probably safer.'

The Texan nodded, impressed. Innes smiled to himself. Things were going nicely, very nicely indeed. Just then the houseboy appeared at his elbow to tell him that he had a telephone call. Innes excused himself and went out to the hall.

'This is Leonard Fox, Mr Innes. Have you seen Anne, by any chance? I came to call, expecting to find her home. Gilbert has no idea where she's gone, and it's getting late. I am rather concerned.'

'Anne? Yes, she was here a couple of hours ago, but she left.' Innes was impatient to get back to his guest. 'Listen, if I see her, I'll tell her you're looking for her.'

He hung up and rejoined the party. Kit had invited a throng of other guests so that the Texans wouldn't realize they were being singled out for special attention. He rubbed his hands. It was about time to turn Mr Texas over to Kit and get to work on Mrs Texas, a burly woman who had been dressed – according to Kit – by a slipcover manufacturer.

'Houston's a great little town,' Innes said warmly as he tried to maneuver Mrs Texas around the area of the sitting room that had been cleared for dancing. It was like trying to push a wheelbarrow with a square wheel. 'I was there in '19, just after the war.'

'Oh, were you in the war, Mr Innes?'

'Yes, ma'am. Got wounded in the Argonne. I won't tell you where else I was wounded.' He grinned and she slapped his shoulder and bellowed delightedly.

Mrs Texas began to talk about her son, also wounded in the war. Innes moved the talk back to Houston again, and from Houston to Shanghai, another great little town. The houseboy informed him that he had another telephone call. Irritated, Innes told him to take a message and not to bother him again. The boy vanished and reappeared a moment later to say that the caller insisted on speaking to Mr Innes. Innes apologized to his lady, who smiled sympathetically.

'This is your good friend Casey, Jim. Sorry to bother you, but I thought you'd like to know that your lady friend is on board the *Jo*. I tried to get her to come out and let me take her home, but she wouldn't. I gave her a blanket. She doesn't have a coat and it's bloody cold out here.'

'What in hell are you talking about?' Innes growled. 'What lady friend?'

'The one who was with you the night I got my head bashed in. The one with the jealous husband.'

Anne. Innes blew out his breath. 'I'll be right down. Thanks, Casey.'

He cursed silently. So much for that nice check drawn on a Texas bank. He found his guests, expressed regrets and warm hopes that they would meet again, and left the party. Kit ran after him.

'And just where do you think you're going? You're not leaving me alone with those sodbusters. I won't stand for it. I warned you —'

'Your sister is in some kind of trouble,' he said, pulling

278

on his overcoat. 'I've had a call from one of the Customs men. I'd better see what it's all about.'

'Anne? Oh, really, how could she! Don't pay any attention. She overdramatizes everything, you know that.'

'No, I hadn't noticed.'

'Well, she does. I know her better than you, don't I? The best way to deal with her moods is to ignore them. Come on, you can't leave now. Those two are eating out of our hands.'

'You charm them. I have to go.' He walked toward the door.

'I won't be here when you get back,' she said shrilly. 'I told you that. These people can just entertain themselves!'

'Don't try to play your little blackmail games with me, Kit,' he said stonily. 'Do as you damned well please. You always have.'

Innes shined Casey's flashlight around the interior of the cruiser's cabin. Anne was huddled at the end of one of the berths. Her arms were clasped around her updrawn knees and her head was lowered. Casey had draped a blanket around her shoulders, but it had slipped unnoticed to the floor. She didn't move when he said her name. He lowered the light and sat beside her.

'Anne, can you hear me? Are you all right?'

'Go away,' she said hollowly from the cave of her arms. 'Leave me alone, will you? I'm not hurting anything here. Go back to your party.'

'Do you want to tell me what this is all about? Your father called. He's worried about you. Gilbert's worried.'

'Gilbert's only worried about where his next dose of laudanum is coming from. He doesn't need me. No one needs me. Go away.'

'You can't stay here, Anne. You'll freeze. Come on, let's go.' He put his arm around her shoulders.

'Don't touch me!' she cried, pulling away from him. 'I'll get off your precious boat. But leave me alone. You're just like her, aren't you? Everything you say is false, and you don't do anything unless it benefits you in some way. You don't care about anything but yourself and money and pleasure. You chew people up and spit them out. You destroy them and you don't care. But I won't let you destroy me, do you understand? You can't hurt me anymore. You can't even touch me.'

'I don't know what you're talking about, Anne. I thought we were friends.'

'You've never had a friend. If you died tomorrow no one would cry, no one would even care. Kit would be a merry widow with so many lovers that she'd have to give out tickets so there wouldn't be any pushing or shoving at the bedroom door. You use her and she uses you and you both use everybody else. You have a perfect marriage, made in hell. You had a good time after I left tonight, didn't you, laughing so hard you could hardly stand? I could hear you, all the way down here.' She wrapped her arms around her head again. 'I could hear you laughing.'

'Nobody laughed at you,' he said firmly. 'Come on, let's talk this over someplace else. It's damned cold here.'

He put his arms around her and tried to raise her off the berth. She struggled with him and scratched at his face.

'I won't go! I won't let you touch me! Leave me alone! Leave me alone!'

She broke free and hurtled across the cabin to the wall near the door. She struck it full force, frontally, and slid slowly to the deck. Her clawed hands were raised above her head, and they gouged the paneled wall as she went down. Her nails left deep white scratches in the varnished wood.

She sobbed and said, 'Why didn't you tell me? You should have warned me, Jamie. You should have given me a hint. I never guessed – I'm such a fool. He always acted so strangely – and he was sleeping with her all the time – never touching me, never even looking at me. I wouldn't have let her stay with us in Chengtu. I wouldn't have left her alone with him if I'd had any idea at all. You should have told me.'

'I didn't know. I had no idea,' he said slowly. The boat moved gently under them.

'Don't lie to me. I'm tired of being lied to.'

'No, I swear it. I knew there were other men – there had to be – but I didn't interfere with her, and she didn't interfere with me. I guess I should have been more curious.' He gave a short bitter laugh. 'We're in the same boat, Anne, whichever way you look at it. She made a fool of both of us.'

Anne hunched over, clutching her middle. She was wracked by great ugly, tearing sobs. Innes sat down on the berth and watched helplessly. Finally she was quieter, drawing her breath in heaving gasps. He picked up the blanket and put it around her, then lifted her to her feet.

'Let's go. You'll make yourself sick, carrying on like this. They're not worth it, either of them.'

She permitted him to lead her out of the cabin, onto the dock, up to the Bund. Casey was standing there, waiting. Innes said, 'Thanks, Casey.'

'Is she all right, Jim?'

'She'll be fine. Good night. I'll send you down a little something in the morning.'

'No need, Jim. No need. Always glad to help a friend.'

She was so cold she didn't feel her feet moving under her. They crossed the busy street. She turned her face into his body because the glare of lights hurt her eyes. She had lost her glasses, probably left them on the *Jo*. They entered the Cathay through a side door and Innes used his key to operate the private elevator to the penthouse.

She realized where they were going. 'No, can't. Josepha died —'

'She didn't die here,' he said. 'She was happy here. We were both happy.'

He eased her into a chair and pushed a snifter of brandy into her hand. 'Drink,' he commanded. 'I'm going to run a bath for you, as hot as you can stand. If you don't get warm right away, you'll be sick before morning.'

'It doesn't matter,' she mumbled, pushing his hand away.

'It does matter, damn it!' he said, holding the glass to her mouth. She choked, but managed to drink. 'I told you they're not worth it, but you are. Don't give Kit the satisfaction of knowing she's hurt you. That's just what she wants.'

The bath water was steaming, but when she stepped into it and sank down she began to shiver. She moaned aloud. Innes' voice came through the door. 'Are you all right?'

'Yes. Cold,' she stuttered.

'Stay put until you feel warm, then drain the water out and fill the tub up again, as hot as you can stand. If you don't, I will.'

'Yes, I will,' she said. She closed her eyes and leaned her head back. When she drained the tub some minutes later, all her pain and sorrow seemed to disappear in a swirl, along with the water.

Innes heard the taps running and said, 'Can you hear me, Anne? I'm going out for a few minutes. I won't be long. Will you be all right?'

'Yes. Yes, I'm fine now.'

'Good. Make yourself at home. Help yourself to more brandy. It won't hurt you.'

The house on the Avenue Joffre was quiet except for the slippered shuffle of servants tidying away the debris from the party. Innes stood in the drawing-room door and watched them for a moment. He noticed that they carefully set aside any remnants of food, for their own families, most likely. He could almost hear Anne, scornfully condemning the wasteful practices of the *ancien régime*. But that was the old Anne, before her sister and her husband destroyed her happiness and broke her spirit.

Kit was lying on her bed. She was still dressed in her party gown. A damp towel covered her eyes. Innes stood over her.

She peeked out from under the towel. 'Oh, it's you. Texas is going to phone you tomorrow. He's definitely interested. You might thank me. I really laid the butter on thick after you left. Now get out, will you? My head is splitting and I feel god-awful.'

'Anne's not feeling too well herself right now.'

'Oh. So Anne has poured out her sorrows on your manly bosom, and you're having an attack of nobility. Take two aspirin and lie down. You'll feel better in the morning.'

He grabbed her arm and hauled her off the bed. 'It's not funny,' he said through gritted teeth. He seemed enormous, swollen with rage. She felt a spasm of terror. He shook her. 'You couldn't leave him alone, could you? The poor bastard never had a chance. And you still don't feel a thing, do you?'

'What do you want me to feel? Compassion? Remorse? Don't be ridiculous. He had it coming.'

'You never gave her a thought, your own sister.' His pupils were fully dilated; his usually good-humored blue eyes were dark wells of anger. He lifted her easily by her shoulders and then hurled her away from him. She landed on top of her dressing table then sprawled on the floor amid a shower of perfume flasks and makeup pots. 'I've let you make a fool of me long enough. I don't know what was the matter with me. I've let you use me, and laugh at me, and I didn't care. I don't know what I thought I was getting out of this marriage.'

'I'm your showpiece, remember?' she rasped as she struggled to rise. 'Your gold cup, your bronze medal. I'm proof to the world that you've made it. You need me.'

'Shut up!' he roared, standing over her. His voice rattled the windows. 'No man in his right mind needs a woman like you. I've known whores who had more heart than you, and more conscience. You're trash. Beautiful soulless trash. If I had any guts, I'd kill you. I owe the world that much.'

'You're too much of a coward,' she sneered. 'You wouldn't dare lay a finger on me. I'll tell everybody I know. I have a lot of important friends in Shanghai. They'll lynch you and drive you out of town.'

Innes unbuckled his belt. Her eyes widened. 'Oh, no. You won't – don't you dare! No!'

He applied the lash with a vengeance, wanting to flay the skin from her beautiful body. The belt sliced through the air with a terrifying whining song. Kit shrieked and covered her face with her hands. She slithered along the floor, a lovely reptile, trying to escape him. He pursued her relentlessly, laying the whip on her thighs, her buttocks, her shoulders. He shredded her spangled gown. Sequins rained down on both of them like a shower of diamonds. Long red welts began to glow against her soft white flesh.

'Don't kill me! Oh, God, please, don't kill me!'

He stopped himself. He didn't really want to kill her. She lay sobbing and retching in a ragged coil at his feet.

'You're privileged,' Innes puffed, slinging the belt aside. 'I've never beaten a woman before. You'll never know how good it felt.'

Her wails grew louder.

'When you call your fancy friends to tell them what I've done, be sure to tell them why.'

He went to his room and threw some clothes into a suitcase. He wouldn't come back to this house. He would start divorce proceedings immediately; she could keep the mansion as part of her settlement. He had never been happy there, and he would always associate it with the greatest folly of his life.

As he left the house, he could see satisfied smirks on the faces of the servants, who scurried away from the foot of the stairs, where they had gathered to listen. Of course they approved. In China wife-beating was socially acceptable.

Sanjay drove him to the Lawrence apartment. The door was unlocked. Gilbert looked up from the couch.

'I thought it was Anne,' he said groggily. 'Where's Anne?'

'She's not coming back tonight. Maybe she's never coming back.'

'Oh. She's angry with me about something, isn't she?'

Innes couldn't muster up hatred for the man who had cuckolded him. All he felt was scorn, and pity. He went into the bedroom. He found a battered suitcase under the bed and loaded it with some of her things: nightgown, hairbrush, underwear, sweaters, a skirt, and a pair of slacks. Everything was much worn, much mended. He thought of Kit's glittering wardrobe and felt a little sick.

He made Gilbert stand up, draped his own overcoat around him, and pushed him toward the door.

'Where are you taking me?' Gilbert wondered without much interest.

'Old man Fox can look after you for a while. Anne will be taking a vacation. Let's go.'

Together Innes and Sanjay carried Gilbert into the sitting

room of the manse. His head bobbed heavily, like a peony on a slender stem, and he mumbled incoherently. They set him down on the couch, where he listed farther and farther to the side until he was half-lying, half-sitting. He began to snore noisily.

Innes told his father-in-law briefly what had happened. Leonard Fox seemed to shrink under a load of shame.

'I'm sorry,' he said humbly. 'I'm sorry our family has been such a trial to you. Do you think she'll come back?'

'That's up to her, isn't it? She can stay at my place as long as she likes. She's had a rough time.'

'Yes. Yes, she has,' Leonard agreed. 'I wish I had been more help to her.'

'I gave your younger daughter a whipping. A good one. It's something that should have been done a long time ago.'

'Yes, I suppose so. I still can't believe she would do such a thing. Kit. My beautiful little girl. Oh, Kit.' Tears streamed down his cheeks. He looked old, beaten.

Anne emerged from the bathroom. She was naked except for the towel around her middle. She listened carefully. The apartment was silent. Innes had not yet returned. She remembered that the bedroom was to her right, and she groped along the wall for the light switch.

The room was quite different from the last time she had seen it, the night Josepha died. Every vestige of Kit and Josepha had been stripped away. The Chinese rug on the floor was gold, patterned with camels and horses in shades of brown. The drapes were made of dark brown fabric that felt like nubbly sacking. The bed was Chinese, a high black lacquered crate decorated with geometric designs in gold. The coverlet was heavy gold silk with an embroidered border of tiny blue flowers.

A large yellow vase stood on a low square lacquered platform in front of the window. It was decorated with brilliantly colored moths fluttering eternally around its golden glow. She stroked it appreciatively and wished that Father Jacquinot could see it.

She opened the closet door, half-expecting to find something like the perfumed magnificence of Kit's or

Josepha's wardrobe, but there were only masculine clothes in evidence, some slacks and shirts, a couple of sports jackets, an evening jacket, a lounge suit, a black Chinese silk robe with the Innes dragon emblazoned on the back, and a softer white robe made of terry cloth. She chose the white robe, and snuggled into it.

There was a low bookcase on one wall. She knelt in front of it and peered closely at the titles: histories of Europe and China, a few books on shipping and navigation, *David Copperfield* and an English translation of Voltaire's *Candide* – the only works of fiction, biographies of Caesar and Napoleon. A small slender book at the end of the top row caught her eye. The corners were battered into roundness, the red binding was faded and stained. She opened it gently, and saw a flowing inscription in sepia ink: 'For Jamie. From Mother, with all my love. Christmas, 1908.' Feeling like an intruder, Anne put the little book away. She knew that it was the only thing he possessed from his childhood, the only remembrance he took with him when he left his home forever, after her death.

She took the pins out of her hair, and undid her braids. She borrowed one of Innes' hairbrushes and brushed until her arm felt tired. She wandered out to the sitting room. It was a comfortable room, less imposing than Innes' private office at Innes & Company. The white marble fireplace on one wall was topped by a gilt-framed mirror. The mantelpiece and two rosewood étagères on either side displayed Chinese artifacts: bowls, figurines, jewelry. The wainscoting was dark wood; the walls above were white and hung with small paintings. Looking closer, Anne saw that they were all scenes of life in Canton and Macao done by the Anglo-Irish artist George Chinnery during the early days of trade with China, the great age of the taipans. Two sofas upholstered in a dark chintz occupied the space in front of the fireplace, and between them stood a low rosewood table. The great jade bowl in the center of the table was empty. Anne wished she could fill it with flowers.

She went to the vast windows at one end of the room and opened the drapes. Standing in front of the glass, she could see clearly the distorted reflection of her own face, sorrowed and pained. She quickly turned out the only lamp that was burning in the room. The haunted face disappeared and the gentle night engulfed her. Anne had never seen a night sky so thick with stars, some so close that they seemed to be almost within reach, just beyond the glass. Stars glittered above her, and below, and all around. She blinked, stunned at finding herself suddenly transported to such a warm and magical world. Then she realized that she had been watching the lights on the river through credulous nearsighted eyes. She felt a little dizzy and disoriented, and she laughed at herself. The laugh threatened to become a sob, and she pressed her forehead against the cool window glass. She was still living in the real world after all, a world of heat and cold, hardness and softness, love and loss.

She was drained of anger, empty of sorrow, although she felt something akin to sorrow but not as deep – regret. Regret that so much time had been wasted in trying to cultivate love in barren ground.

There was something else. She couldn't quite analyze it at first, then she realized that she felt relieved. Or perhaps a better word was exonerated. She had tried so hard to make Gilbert happy, and she had failed so consistently, and blamed herself alone for the failure. And now she knew that nothing she did could have saved her marriage, because it didn't exist.

'It wasn't my fault, none of it,' she said aloud, with some amazement. 'It wasn't my fault.'

She tried to think dispassionately about her future. She would leave Shanghai at once. She had relatives in the States, cousins, who would take her in until she found a job. She would ask Gilbert for nothing. She was sorry for him, but she felt no responsibility for him anymore. No one could help him until he was ready to help himself.

And what about her friends here? Father Jacquinot? Innes? What about James Innes? Thinking about him sent a shudder of nervousness through her. He was hardly a friend. His acts of kindness had always been performed in times of crisis. A dangerous friend, Mr Innes. Unpredictable. Disturbing. She had always been wary of him, and with good reason. That kiss – Would she never stop thinking about that stupid kiss? Yes, she had to get away. She couldn't stay.

The door opened and light from the hallway pierced the darkness. She whirled around from the window, her heart pounding. Her robe had no sash, and she held the edges tightly together in front of her.

'Anne?' Innes called softly. He tossed his overcoat over a chair and set down the two suitcases. He snapped on the lights. Anne flinched and shaded her eyes with her hand.

'Oh, there you are.' His voice was sharp, edged with anger. 'Are you all right?'

She found that she couldn't answer him. She could only stare blankly at the outline of his shadowy figure moving toward her.

He drew nearer, but he still remained a blur, inscrutable and mysterious. He had shed his dinner jacket. The black fingers of his unknotted tie lay lifelessly on his snowy shirtfront. His hair bristled around his head like a dark halo. His body was rigid with fury.

She tried to focus on his face, and she searched it anxiously for some clue to what he was thinking, the cause of his anger. She cursed her poor vision. She could see the black arcs of his brows, the deep lines around his mouth and eyes, but not the fine lines, nor the revealing set of his mouth. She took a step toward him, and saw that his eyes were dark with sadness.

Watching her, Innes felt oddly confused and disconcerted, as he had on the night of Chen's escape. This was not the pathetic, shivering creature he had brought here an hour ago. White-robed, barefooted, her hair falling around her shoulders in a tawny veil, she was a vision, unearthly and shimmering. Her eyes were not those of a real woman. They were wide and wondering, as innocent as a child's. Without the glasses that brought the world so ruthlessly into focus, they could not see evil or ugliness, only shadow and light, softness and beauty.

But her inner vision was clear. The sight of his pain reminded her of her own sorrow and humiliation. Her eyes lost their childish brightness and became as dull and fathomless as a dead woman's.

'No,' Innes said fiercely, throwing his arms around her and pulling her close to his chest. He had to save her from the despair which was worse than death. 'No.'

She slid her arms around his waist and pressed her face into the hollow of his shoulder. They stood for a long time drawing warmth and comfort from each other. Like a couple of shipwreck survivors, they were content for the moment just to savor the solidness of the earth under their feet. It was enough just to know they were alive.

Innes buried his face in the fresh sweetness of her hair. Her warmth dissolved the icy chill of his rage. Her softness promised a safe harbor, a shelter, a haven. He became aware once again of the possibilities of living beyond simply existing. He lifted her face to his and kissed her gently. She was startled, but the light returned to her eyes. She opened her mouth to speak, but he wouldn't let her. There would be plenty of time later to rediscover speech, and thought, and ambition, and anger. They could talk another time about what had happened, and about what it meant. But now it was time to glory in the survival of their bodies and their spirits.

'I love you,' he murmured, covering her lips with his own. 'I love you.'

'I love you,' she whispered. He kissed her closed eyes, tasting the salt of dried tears. Her head lolled to the side, and he kissed the hollow under her ear, the line of her jaw, the curve of her neck. Her breathing quickened, became as shallow and panting as his own. Her hands moved confidently over his body, learning its contours and its hardness.

Her robe gaped open in front. He pulled it down over her shoulders and it slid to the floor. His hands explored her body, appraising her softness and the rich roundness of her breasts and hips and buttocks. The pressure of his tongue and teeth became more insistent. He sank to his knees worshipfully, and buried his face in the softness of her belly. She sucked in her breath. His tongue reached her wet darkness, and tasted it greedily. She groaned aloud and tried to escape from a pleasure that was too rich to endure. He wouldn't free her, but pulled her down, down on top of him.

They swirled together, gasping, sobbing. She moved under him, rising and falling in increasingly violent waves, using him, offering him her flesh, her mouth. He rubbed his face between her breasts, scratching them with his light growth of beard, cooling them with his tongue. Her excitement built quickly. Her fingers dug into his back, his shoulders. Then she strained against him, moaning, and he rocked within her and released his own fire.

Her body relaxed. Her arms slid away from him. She lay under him, spent and motionless, her eyes closed. She might have been dead, but it was only a parody of death. He could still feel the life surging within her. He himself had never felt more fiercely alive.

He stroked her cheek and her eyes fluttered open.

She gave him an embarrassed smile. 'What must you think of me?'

He laughed. 'You're asking me to think?' He shook his head. 'I think you're the best-kept secret in Shanghai. Beautiful, and wonderful.' He kissed her.

'You don't have to say things like that to me.'

'Things like what?'

'You know what I mean,' she said. 'I was so pathetically eager. As if I hadn't had a man in seven months, which I haven't. I'm grateful.'

'What in hell are you talking about?' He raised himself up on one elbow and scowled at her.

'You. I've lived like a frustrated spinster for so long, just wishing for something like this. You wouldn't think it, would you? Dowdy, dull, and dreary Anne, secretly half-crazed with lust, entertaining the most incredibly erotic dreams. You were in those dreams, you know. Do you remember when you kissed me, the night you saved Chen?'

He nodded. 'Yes.'

'I know it didn't mean anything to you. It was all in fun. But I thought about it a lot. Too much. I was thinking about it when you came in. You must have known. Something must have shown in my face.'

He said, 'Let me get this straight. You think I made love to you tonight because I wanted to be kind to you?'

'Well, didn't you? You couldn't have done anything nicer to restore my battered self-esteem. You felt sorry for me.'

'My God!' he exploded. 'You're the damnedest woman I've ever met. No, I did not —' He broke off. 'You don't have any idea of what you look like now, do you? Come on, I want to show you something.'

He grabbed her hand, hauled her to her feet, and dragged her into the bedroom. There was a full-length mirror on one wall. He positioned her in front of it and stood behind her, his hands on her shoulders.

'Look,' he said. 'What do you see?'

She said, laughing. 'You know very well I can't see anything.'

He pushed her closer to the surface of the mirror. 'Come on, look,' he said. 'I want you to see what I see.'

Through a mist she saw her own nakedness, her hair massed around her shoulders, her long body, thin except for her full breasts and wide hips. Her face was glowing. Innes' hands moved like dark disembodied creatures on her breasts. She closed her eyes and let her head fall back.

'I want you, Anne,' he said firmly. 'Can you understand that? I don't pity you. I don't feel sorry for you. I am not, repeat *not* being kind to you. Only a goddamn minister's daughter could think up something like that.'

'But you —'

'End of argument. Case closed.'

He watched her coming slowly out of sleep. She had been lying on her side; then she twisted her upper torso so that her shoulders and face were turned up toward the ceiling. Her legs were bound up in the sheet and her hair was spread over two pillows. She looked like a beached mermaid.

She must have smelled the smoke from his cigarette, because her nose twitched. She moved again, kicking at the covers.

Innes jerked open the drapes. Gray winter light flooded the room. Anne groaned softly.

'Happy Chinese New Year,' he said affably, sitting on the side of the bed.

'What time is it?'

'What difference does it make?'

She sat up and squinted at him. His powerful body was knotted and scarred, slightly grizzled, and beautifully naked. Anne smiled and flushed slightly. 'Oh, none, I guess.' She drew the sheet up over her breasts and said primly. 'Please don't let me keep you from doing whatever it is you were going to do today. I don't want to be a nuisance.'

'I was going to stay here and make love to you all day,' he said. 'I'm glad to hear I'll have your approval – and your cooperation.'

'You were angry with me last night for taking you away from your party, weren't you?'

'I wasn't in the best of tempers,' he admitted. 'I was worried about losing a half-million-dollar investment. This morning it doesn't seem so important. If I get it, fine. If I don't, I've found something better.' He leaned over and kissed her, then he went out of the room.

Anne lay back again and stretched happily. Her conscience prodded her, and her sense of responsibility stirred into wakefulness, but she ignored them both. She thought warmly and wonderingly about Innes. Dangerous? Perhaps. Unpredictable? Absolutely.

He came in and tossed her white robe on the foot of the bed.

'Coffee's here. Come out when you're ready. Oh, you might need these.' He held out her glasses. 'Casey sent them up.'

She took them gratefully and put them on. 'There, now I feel more like my old self.'

He grinned. 'You sure don't look it.'

She took a leisurely bath, then put on the robe and went out to the sitting room. Innes was on the telephone. He smiled at her and rolled his eyes while he made grunting noises into the phone. She saw a coffeepot on a wheeled hotel cart near the door and poured a cup for herself, then she curled up on a couch and waited for him to finish.

'I'm glad he's so hot. That means it won't hurt if I lie low for a little while and play hard to get. . . . Sure, do what you can to keep him interested, Charlie, but if we lose him, tough. . . . I know I do. Cancel it. . . . Damn, I forgot about that. Yes, I'll be there. Reserve a suite for the whole weekend. I don't know yet when I'll be going up.' He depressed the receiver and said to Anne, 'One more. Desk? This is Innes. No more calls for the rest of the day, and no visitors.'

He lit a cigarette and lounged against the mantelpiece. 'That company doesn't need me. Charlie Fong could run it all by himself, but don't tell him I said so.' He grinned at her. 'How are you feeling this morning?'

'Very well, considering.' Her eyes were bright behind her glasses. 'That was quite a prodigious display you put on last night.'

'Glad you liked it. May I say you inspired me to heights of greatness that I haven't achieved since I was a lad,' he said gallantly.

Anne took a swallow of coffee. 'I made some plans last night, before you came home.' She told him about her cousins in the States. 'I was wondering if you'd lend me some money. Just enough for a ticket.'

'Of course I will, Anne. As much as you want.'

'I'll pay it back as soon as I find work,' she said quickly.

'Sure,' he said. 'You wouldn't want to feel like you were being paid for last night, would you?'

She flushed. 'That's not fair.'

'No, you're the one who's not being fair. You can't wait to leave – after I've been so nice to you. My feelings are hurt. Seriously, Anne, don't rush into anything yet. Give yourself a little time. Give me some time, too. I don't like being treated like a one-night stand.'

'There's no reason for you to talk like that,' she said. 'You've already proved to our mutual satisfaction that I'm not immune to shock.'

'Sorry. I want you to stay, Anne.' He sat beside her and put his arm over the back of the couch, but he didn't try to touch her.

'I know you do,' she said, looking away. His nakedness was disturbing and distracting. 'You'd like me to live here like Josepha did. You want to dress me up and show me off and come here every night when you finish work and make love to me. It sounds like a very nice life, for someone like Josepha who didn't have any brains or ambition – not that I'm exactly loaded with either – but it's not for me. You can see that. I'd die of shame – being acquired and kept on a shelf, or a lacquered stand, like part of your collection. You don't want me, Anne Fox. You can't. I'm simply not the kind of woman you'd want to have around.'

Innes chose his words carefully. 'I'm not an educated man, Anne. I never had any schooling past the seventh grade. But I'm not ignorant. When a man thinks he knows everything, and you can't tell him anything, that's ignorance. Not lack of education, but lack of a willingness to learn. I was guilty of that for a long time. I knew it all, or thought I did. The war didn't shake it out of me – a lot of college men died in the trenches, just a few feet away from me, but I lived. I knew how to survive; what else did a guy have to know? Afterward I knocked around some, and I got tangled up with that bunch in Boston I told you about. That's when I began to get a glimmer of the high cost of ignorance. They were powerful, and they were rich, but they were all as ignorant as hell. I knew they would pay for that ignorance, and most of them have by now; they're either behind bars or six feet under. Because they thought they knew it all.

'It took me a long time to appreciate the full extent of my own ignorance. It happened here, in China. You've met Sun, my compradore.' Anne nodded. 'He treated me just fine, Sun did – I told you about the girl – and at first I thought he liked me. I found out soon enough that he only wanted to use me, and that he really despised me. He thought I was the basest, most uncouth oaf to come down the Yangtze since the Mongols. He thought I was ignorant. And he was right. I didn't know everything. I didn't know anything, except how to crack heads and stay alive in a brawl and make some money running opium. We used each other and made each other rich, but that's another story. The point is, he made me want to educate myself, to find out all I could, about everything. I read, and I listened when people talked, and I learned.'

'I saw your books,' she said.

'Did you? Don't tell anybody. It would hurt my

reputation. If anybody knew that Innes spends some of his evenings curled up with Proust —'

'I didn't see any Proust.'

'I was talking about Yvette Proust, a French girl I know.' He grinned boyishly. 'Let me get on with my story, will you? Where was I? Sun. Sun recommended art as an investment and he helped me start my collection. At first I had to take his word for what was good and what wasn't. I couldn't tell the difference between genuine Ming and the cheap Japanese copies they make in Hongkew. I hated the way he patronized me, but I put up with it, because I knew that he had a lot of valuable information tucked away, information I could use. I learned from him, and from other people. I learned everything I could about dating a piece and appraising it, and I began to see what made a thing beautiful and precious: balance, luster, workman-ship, delicacy. I learned how to tell the real thing from gimcrack imitations. I don't need Sun to tell me what to buy anymore. I use what I know and I trust my instincts. Recently Sun made a couple of bad buys himself, which I advised against.'

'The student outstrips the master,' Anne said. 'But what —'

'You wonder what I'm getting at. There are a lot of beautiful women in this town. Your sister is one of the most beautiful — at least I used to think so. I thought that beauty like hers was quality. We both know how wrong I was. And Josepha: I tried to take a piece of pretty, simple tableware and refashion it into something elegant and fine. That was wrong, too. But I'm learning. There's more to beauty in a woman than a perfect face and a glittering gown. No, you don't look like Kit. I wouldn't want you to. No one loves her. No one ever will. She's cheap, a pretty picture painted on sand. But you — you're quality, Anne. You know how to love. A man could make a home for a woman like you, a real home. He'd have someone to work for, to live for. You are rare, and precious. The man you fall in love with is going to be one hell of a lucky guy. I'm hoping it'll be me.'

'That was very beautifully said,' she said after a long moment. 'Chen himself couldn't have paid me a nicer compliment. Thank you.'

'I don't want to rush you. I'm not trying to con you. But I'd hate like hell to see you leave Shanghai when your future was right here. This is your home. If you want to go away for a little while to think things over, that's fine. I can understand that. But if you do go, promise you'll come back to me.'

'I had it all figured out,' she said. 'Now I'm more confused than ever. I wish I knew what you wanted.'

'Not me. You. What do *you* want? Think about it. Last night I said I loved you. I didn't pull the words out of my arsenal of seduction. I meant it. Did you mean it?'

'I don't know. I thought I did. Of course I meant it. I care about you. But love isn't always enough. We're so different, Jamie. The very first time we met, we had a roaring argument.'

'Our relationship has improved somewhat,' he reminded her with a grin. 'I don't recall any arguments last night.'

'Our philosophies haven't changed since then,' she persisted. 'We'll never agree about your work or your money or China or opium.'

'So we'll agree to disagree about politics, and agree to agree in bed,' he said cheerfully.

'No, it's not that simple. I want more out of a relationship than that, and so do you. We don't have any interests in common.'

'You and Gilbert had a lot of things in common, and it didn't help, did it?' he said. She moaned softly and closed her eyes. 'I'm sorry, Anne,' he said gently. 'I know I have a hell of a nerve, pushing you like this, after what you've been through, but I have to act fast, before you get away from me. I can't see into the future. I'm not saying that we can make something out of this. I only know that I don't want to lose you. Give me a chance, Anne. Give *us* a chance. We need more time together, alone. We need to see where we're going, if anywhere. Look, I have to be in Nanking on Monday. Today's only Friday. We can go up tomorrow, together. If the weather's decent, we could even take the boat over to Soochow, and then follow the Inland Canal to Wuhsi and on up from there. How does that sound?'

She glanced at his swollen member and smiled. 'I think we ought to discuss this after we're both fully dressed, in a place that's open and public.'

'Don't evade the question. Will you come with me, Anne?'

'Don't you see how complicated things would be if we decided that we want to be together?'

'No, I don't see any problems. You'll divorce Gilbert, I'll divorce Kit, and we'll get married. It would be tougher on you than it would be on me, but I'd stand by you, you know that. Your father would get used to it. Kit wouldn't bother us.'

'I don't want to think about that,' she said, ducking her head. 'Please.'

'Then don't. It might not come to that. You might decide that you'd rather spend your life in a convent in Outer Mongolia than be married to a bloated capitalist like me. But give yourself time to find out. We won't talk about it again, if you don't want to. Give me a week, that's all I ask. If at the end you decide you want a ticket for the States, I'll give it to you.' She jerked her head up and he saw that she was about to protest. He said quickly, 'But I'll expect repayment in three months, at a hundred percent interest.'

'One week,' she said.

'You can have as long as you want. But a week will give you time to get over the shock of what's happened and to think more clearly about what you want. I already know what I want. Well?' He waited expectantly.

'Are you sure you're not just being kind? Again?'

He pulled her onto his lap. 'Not kind. Selfish.' He pushed his hands inside her robe and kissed her. She felt a strong rush of pleasure, like a swirling typhoon under her ribs. 'I'll make sure you won't want to leave me,' he whispered fiercely. 'Ever.'

They could hear the faint clash of cymbals and the bleat of horns, the popping of firecrackers and the pounding of drums in the street far below. It was the first day of the New Year. Debts would be settled and contracts made and bitter enmities ended. Dragons snaked through the streets, frightening away demons. Red streamers, the color of good luck and the color of blood, fluttered cheerfully in the chill wind.

Chapter Ten

'I've asked Sanjay to pick up our bags and stow them on the *Jo*. We're lucky, I think we're going to have a break in the weather.'

'I don't see my suitcase,' Anne said, pulling her old coat over the slacks and sweater Innes had brought from her apartment. 'I must have left it in the bedroom.'

'You won't need it,' Innes said too casually. 'I asked Maurice to send over a few things. He knows your size.'

She stood very still. 'You shouldn't have done that.'

'Why not, if it makes me happy to give you things?'

'Because it means that you don't like me as I am.'

'It doesn't mean that at all. I think it's a damned shame that you've had to wear rags all these years. You're too good for that. Why shouldn't you want to look nice now? After all, I'm footing the bill.'

As soon as he said it, he knew it was a mistake. Her eyes grew cold behind her glasses. She shoved her fists deep into her coat pockets.

'I thought you had learned to look for subtler beauties in a woman,' she said stiffly. 'You don't want me to look like Kit, remember? I suppose I could have dressed like her, but I didn't want to. I didn't want to parade around in fancy feathers in front of people who didn't have enough to eat. Yes, my things are old and shabby, but so are theirs. I know why you did this – you don't want to be ashamed of me in Nanking. I don't blame you. In your business it's important what people think. But it's important to me what I think, too. I have to live with myself, and if that means I can't look the way you want me to look —' She turned away, hunched and miserable. 'I wish you hadn't done it, Jamie. But maybe it's for the best. I don't belong in your world. I hate it. I'll always hate it.'

'"My world,"' he echoed scathingly. 'What the hell does that mean? What do you want me to do, sell the company and give the proceeds to charity? Put on a hair

299

shirt and go out into the desert to preach? Maybe you'd like me to become a tracker, like Gilbert. I'm sure you'd be very happy in that kind of world.'

Anne said, 'I'd never ask you to leave Shanghai, to give up what you've built. I know how much this all means to you. But if I don't approve of the way you live, you can hardly expect me to share in it. I'm not accustomed to riches. They make me nervous and uncomfortable. How can I drink champagne when the poor have only contaminated water? How can I eat steak when they're fishing for garbage in the Whangpoo? Yes, I know that you capitalists have done great things for society, and that a lot of people benefit from businesses like yours. But a lot of people suffer because of them, too. How can I make you understand that I don't want anything you have? I won't ask you for anything, and I won't take anything from you. I can't.'

'Why not?' Innes demanded. 'If you needed money to help somebody out, if you wanted to endow a hospital or ransom a singsong girl or save a village from starvation, wouldn't you ask me?'

'I might,' she admitted grudgingly.

'Come on, Anne, wouldn't it give you some satisfaction to spend my filthy lucre on good works and charity? Nice irony in that; I'm surprised you don't appreciate it.'

'You haven't been terribly openhanded before now,' she pointed out.

'Yes, I have, to the hundreds of families in Shanghai that Kit supports: the people who wait on her, dress her, drive her around, play her music. I never begrudged her any of the money she spent. Do you think I would begrudge you?'

'No, but I'm not Kit. She lives her way, and I live mine. I hate asking people for things. I hate waste. I hate flaunting my possessions in front of people who have nothing. I don't begrudge you your jade and your porcelain. I just couldn't possess any of it myself, no matter how beautiful it was. It would haunt me.'

'I'm not asking you to accept a sixteenth-century jade vase. I'm asking you to please me by letting me see you in something that hasn't come out of a mission barrel.

You've done other things to please me. Why not this?'

She said wearily, 'I guess I must leave my principles at the bedroom door. Please don't ask me to compromise them, Jamie. I'm not strong. I'll cave in, just to make you happy, but I won't be happy myself. It's useless, can't you see that? Couldn't we just – not go on?'

'Not go on,' he said. 'We have a little problem, and you don't even want to try to solve it. You just want to abandon the whole thing.'

'There is no solution,' she said stubbornly.

'There is, and we'll find it. Look at this stuff first. Maybe there won't be anything in here to suit your taste.' He opened one of the ostrich-leather suitcases that Maurice had sent with the clothes.

He pulled out a gray wool dress, long-sleeved and modest, with a matching scarf that passed through a loop on the shoulder, two cashmere sweaters, a skirt and a pair of slacks, an evening dress in dark blue crepe that was chic and simple but not revealing, and a camel-colored suit with a dark brown beret and brown accessories. Everything was elegant, expensive, and understated.

'I told him we were dressing the missionary's daughter as a missionary's daughter this time,' Innes said. 'See anything objectionable?'

'No, it's all lovely, but that's not the point.'

'Come and sit down.' He led her to the couch. 'I remember you in that green gown. You looked beautiful, and you knew it, and you liked the feeling, didn't you?'

'It was part of the charade,' she said stiffly. 'I didn't like it at all. I felt embarrassed and ashamed.'

'Liar. You walked differently, you held yourself differently. There wasn't another woman in Shanghai who looked as beautiful as you did that night, and you knew it. Now, I think I've come up with a solution to our problem. When the bill for this stuff comes in, I'll send a check for twice the amount to Father Jacquinot. How does that sound? If you don't keep the clothes, he won't get the money.'

She stared. 'But that's the most devious thing I've ever heard. It's horrible. It's blackmail!'

'I don't know about that,' Innes said. 'It's a solution

'that satisfies everybody.'

'But you're buying me! You're forcing me to take clothes that I don't want, because if I reject them someone else will suffer.'

'I'm just trying to make it easier for you to accept things from me. You tried to blackmail me just now, by threatening to end everything. Is that any different?'

Anne moaned and dropped her head into her hands. 'It's hopeless. I can see us going on and on like this forever. Around and around – and you always getting your own way.'

The buzzer sounded. 'There's Sanjay. Do you want me to pack up this stuff, or do you want to stay here? I won't take you to Nanking without it. We'd both be miserable. If you want to stay, fine, I won't hold it against you. We'll have a nice weekend right here and I'll fly up on Monday.'

'I wish —' The buzzer sounded again. 'I wish I knew why you were trying so hard.'

Innes said, 'I want to see her again, the woman in the green gown, tossing her shoulders and looking the world straight in the eye, without fear or apologies for anyone.'

'But that wasn't the real me,' she said despairingly.

'I think it was. I don't mean the vamping – that was an act. But the boldness, the freedom – that was you. You're like that in bed, and it's no act. You're stunted, Anne. Maybe it's from growing up with Kit. She casts a lot of shade. You're pale where you should be dark, and weak where you should be strong. You've spent your life trying to make other people happy, and it's blighted you. You're afraid of trying to be happy yourself. Afraid of failing, maybe.'

She could feel tears welling up. 'Oh, pack the damned stuff, for God's sake. I'm sick of hearing about it!' She bolted into the bedroom and slammed the door.

He came in a minute later. She was lying face down on the bed, not moving. He sat beside her and put his hand on her shoulder.

'I'm sorry,' she said. 'I just can't bear talk like that – the Dutch uncle routine. I always fall apart. Ask Father Jacquinot. I've shed enough tears in front of him to turn the Gobi green. I know everything you said is true. I'm a coward and I have a rigid Christian conscience and my radicalism is more rebellion than anything else. I'm an awful mess – nearly thirty-one years old and not grown up yet. I don't know why you bother with me.'

'You won't believe this, but I'll say it anyway: I'm in love with you.' He cradled her in his arms and wiped away the tears that smeared her cheeks.

She said, 'You mentioned mission barrels. Every time I hear the word "charity", that's what I think of, boxes of used clothes, most of them fit only for rags, twisted shoes, lifeless straw hats, faded dresses that reek of camphor balls and mildew. We had to be grateful for those things, things the people back home were only too pleased to be rid of. That was charity, and I hated it. Mother made the best of it; she was a wonder at turning dresses and redesigning them so that the wear didn't show. But I couldn't forget where those dresses came from. I still can't buy anything decent for myself, even though I know it's really all right and I won't be robbing anybody by doing it. I'm shocked at the cost and I can't help thinking how that money could be used for something more worthwhile. You can't escape the past, can you? The lady in the green gown will always be a Presbyterian in her soul, a missionary's daughter. I can't stand it.' She hiccoughed.

Innes said, 'I never noticed that Kit had any scruples about accepting charity, and she was dressed out of the same mission barrels.'

'Not really. By the time she came along, we had moved to Shanghai and Father had the big church here, with its flock of rich taipans. The quality of life really improved for the Fox family. I think Father must have hated the poverty, because he blossomed out once we were here – new suits, a car, lots of servants, manicured fingernails.' She snorted disapprovingly. 'His family wasn't rich like Mother's, you know. He had to work hard for everything. He went to school on scholarships, and he worked full time all the while he was in the seminary, just so he could buy books and clothes. How he must have hated it. Shanghai must have seemed like paradise to him.'

'Sounds like your dad and I are a lot alike,' Innes said. 'You're still trying to show him that you don't approve of him.'

'I suppose I am. Kit wouldn't wear anything old or ugly, even when she was small. And of course they didn't want her to, precious baby.' She couldn't keep old jealousy and new bitterness out of her tone.

'The Chinese know how to accept gifts graciously,' Innes said. 'Josepha never made me feel like a fool because I wanted to give her things.'

'Is that how I make you feel?' Anne asked sorrowfully.

'Yes. You're going to have to work very hard to make it up to me,' he told her, brushing the tip of her nose with his lips.

She put her arms around his neck and kissed him. 'Can I start now?' she asked in a warm whisper.

He laughed and hauled her off the bed. 'No. Time and tide wait for no man, remember? Let's go to Nanking.'

They walked to the yacht basin. Sanjay followed a few paces behind. Anne began to understand that Sanjay's function was not restricted merely to driving Innes' cars. Sean Casey stood about thirty feet from the *Jo* and watched their approach uneasily. With him was Kendall, the chief inspector of Customs.

'Day shift, eh, Casey?' Innes greeted him. 'Tough luck – with the boss looking over your shoulder, you'll have to behave yourself.'

Casey managed a weak smile, and Kendall said, 'I understand you're taking a little trip today, Mr Innes. What might be the purpose of that, I wonder?'

'Business combined with pleasure, as usual,' Innes said. 'You gentlemen remember Mrs Lawrence, don't you? We had a hankering to see Soochow, if that's all right wth you.'

'February is an odd month to go boating,' Kendall remarked. 'But I suppose you want to be alone,' he said with a cool glance at Anne, who flushed slightly. 'Nevertheless, I find this sudden departure suspicious.'

'Kendall, you'd find it suspicious if I pissed into the river. Now would you mind letting us go aboard – I have some opium I'm in a hurry to deliver.'

Casey rolled his eyes. Kendall's nose worked like a

rabbit's. 'I thought as much,' he said. 'I think we're going to have to examine your boat thoroughly before we let you shove off, just to make sure you're not violating any rules.'

'Come off it, Kendall,' Innes said. 'You know damned well that I'm not carrying anything illegal. You're just subjecting me to one more petty annoyance because your men let Chen slip through their fingers. I had nothing to do with that, as Mrs Lawrence here can attest. But ever since that night you've been a real nuisance, going over my ships with a fine-toothed comb, delaying my sailings, holding up my cargo. Look, why don't we just shake hands and call it quits. Or maybe I ought to make it worth your while. Five hundred's your standard bribe, isn't it?'

Casey groaned aloud. Kendall flushed to the visor of his cap. 'I intend to give your boat and its contents a thorough examination, personally,' he said tightly, his hand going to the pistol in his belt. 'If you make any attempt to interfere with me, I shall have you arrested for obstructing an officer in performance of his duty. Casey!'

He turned on his heel and strode down the dock to the *Jo*. Casey said, 'You shouldn't have insulted him, Jim. He's been makin' my life miserable these few months. I'm thinkin' of turnin' in my badge.'

Innes patted his shoulder consolingly. 'Don't worry, old man. Ride out the storm – it won't last.'

'He's a bugger,' Casey sighed. 'Watchin' me like a hawk, changin' my shifts every other day. I'm losin' sleep, man. It's awful.'

'Casey!' Kendall roared from the deck of the *Jo*. 'Hurry up, man. You're not being paid to socialize with known criminals.'

'Ouch,' said Innes. Casey shrugged and walked with dragging step toward the boat.

Kendall disappeared into the cabin. Innes said, 'Maybe we ought to stand over him and watch every move, just to make him nervous.'

'I'm sorry you've been having trouble,' Anne said. 'It's my fault.'

'There you go, taking the blame for something that —'

There was a loud explosion, like a thousand firecrackers

going off at the same time, and the *Jo* rose out of the water and expanded balloon-like in the air before she disintegrated. Innes threw himself at Anne and covered her with his body. Debris showered them: bits of wood and glass and metal, pieces of clothing, and ·bloody fragments of Inspector Kendall. A billowing black cloud spread over the yacht basin.

'Gasoline,' Anne said. 'He must have lit a match.'

'Like hell,' Innes said, raising his head. 'I can smell the gelignite. Where's Sanjay?' He looked around.

'I saw him running, just before the explosion, in the direction of the Cathay.'

'Listen to me.' Innes helped her to her feet. 'Go back to the penthouse, lock yourself in, and wait for me. Don't let anyone else in. Anyone, understand?'

She nodded and hesitated for just a moment before hurrying back to the hotel. A crowd of people, with Sikh policemen in the vanguard, surged toward the docks.

Innes ran over to Casey, who lay face down on the dock. Blood streamed from cuts on his face, but he was breathing. Innes helped him stand.

'Jesus, Jim,' Casey breathed. 'I think I've shit my pants.'

'I'm not surprised. These cuts don't look too bad. Look, get someone to take you to the hospital. I've got to find Sanjay.'

Innes pushed through the mob of curious onlookers and ran across the Bund to the Cathay Hotel. No one seemed to be watching for him, lying in wait. Why should they? He was supposed to be dead. He took his gun out of his holster and put it into the side pocket of his jacket. He went into the hotel through the main doors. The lobby-sitters were crowded in front of the windows to watch the excitement. Sirens wailed. A woman noticed him and screamed. He touched his fingers to his face. They came away black and red, from soot and blood.

He took the stairs to the servants' rooms at the back of the hotel. The door to Sanjay's room was ajar. Innes kicked it open all the way and looked in. The door of the wardrobe was hanging open, as were the dresser drawers. Items of clothing lay scattered on the floor. Sanjay had fled in a hurry. He had expected to have more time to pack.

Innes ran down to the garages on Peking Road, a short block away from the Cathay. The Rolls was in its usual slot, but the smaller Daimler was gone. Peking Road itself was clogged with rickshas and pushcarts at the northern end; Sanjay must have gone in the other direction, out onto the Bund. Innes looked to the right and didn't see any sign of the car, but he noticed that traffic was massed at the entrance to the Garden Bridge that spanned Soochow Creek. A traffic policeman was trying to keep the way clear for the fire trucks and ambulances that were on their way to the yacht basin. Innes saw the Daimler, wedged between a lorry and a half-dozen rickshas. He approached cautiously, but when he was within ten feet of the car his eyes met Sanjay's in the sideview mirror. Sanjay leaped out of the car, just as the policeman waved at the traffic in front of him. Horns blasted at the abandoned Daimler and the ricksha drivers cursed.

Sanjay raced across the bridge. Innes followed. He didn't dare shoot because there were too many people in his way. At the other end Sanjay paused. He knew that what he did next was critical. In front of him stood the apartment house known as the Broadway Mansions. A man could easily lose himself in its maze of stairs and corridors, but any building could be a deathtrap. The American Consulate was back on the other side of the bridge. There was a gate at the rear of the grounds. Freedom lay on the other side of that gate, but he would have to recross the bridge. His hesitation cost him precious seconds. Innes narrowed the distance between them. Sanjay headed for the Consulate, and sprinted between the pair of astonished Marines who guarded the entrance to the grounds. The guards tried to stop Innes, who pushed them roughly aside and raced after his quarry.

The gate was locked. Sanjay rattled it frantically, hoping to break the lock with the force of his will. He retreated a few steps, took a running leap, and tried to clamber over the top. He couldn't make it. He clung there for an agonizing moment, clutching at the high spikes that were just a little too high, and cast a frantic look over his shoulder. He saw Innes emerging from behind a massive banyan tree and he heard the shouts of the Marines who were pursuing them both. He dropped back down, landing on all fours, and dove into a clump of oleander. Innes saw the glint of sunlight on gun metal and threw himself face down as a bullet passed over him. The embassy guards took cover.

Innes approached the bushes cautiously, keeping himself as low to the ground as he could. He fired into the shrubbery, and Sanjay leaped to the side, his gun pointed at Innes' head. They fired simultaneously. Innes' shot found its mark, and Sanjay threw up his arms and reeled back.

Panting, Innes lifted the fallen man by the collar of his uniform jacket.

'Who did it? Who bought you, Sanjay? Tell me!'

Sanjay looked at him. Hatred glimmered in his dying eyes. Innes shook him. 'Who?' he demanded again. 'Was it Tu? Sun? Who?'

Red froth bubbled out from between Sanjay's lips, and a hollow rattle sounded in his throat. Innes released him and stood up. A cordon of Marines closed around the two men.

Anne heard Innes' voice on the other side of the door and went weak with relief. He came in, covered with soot and sweat. His step was tired, dragging. His mouth was drawn into a bitter, ugly line.

'Sanjay's dead,' he said. 'I shot. I had to.'

'You're all right,' Anne said. 'That's all that matters.'

He went past her without looking at her and poured himself a stiff whiskey. 'Somebody bought him. I thought I could trust him. I shouldn't have. I can't trust anyone. I wish I knew who got to him.' He quaffed the whiskey and poured another. He drank it less quickly, and sat wearily on the couch. Anne stood behind him.

'I'm sorry,' she said lamely. She put her hands on his shoulders and kissed the top of his head.

'You can't let your guard down for a minute,' he said angrily. 'You're only safe in a cell like this, barricaded behind locked doors. I shouldn't have brought you here. I had no business exposing you to the kind of danger I live with, a gun under my armpit twenty hours a day. If it hadn't been for Kendall's stupidity, we'd both be dead now.' He slumped forward, elbows on his knees, and dropped his head into his hands.

Anne drew him back gently and rested his head between her breasts. She rubbed his forehead with easy strokes, and massaged his neck and shoulders.

'I know all about your guns and your guards and the dangers.'

'I can't let you stay with me. You'd be crazy to stay. You wouldn't be free to come and go. There's always the chance that you'd be kidnapped, or killed. I don't care about myself – I've lived with that kind of danger for years. I even like it. But I care about you too much to let you —'

'Why don't you let me decide about my future,' she said. 'I'm aware of the dangers. If I choose to risk them, that's my business. Lots of women live guarded lives here, because they must. If they can get used to it, so can I.'

'If only I knew who paid him off. Tu? Sun? But Sun has nothing to gain by killing me. He can't run the business by himself. He wouldn't. He's too scared. I'm the front man, the target. That's the way he wants it.'

'What about Tu?'

'We're holding his father, in Hong Kong. We've had him for three years. Maybe Tu misses his old dad.' Innes gave a sour laugh.

'It won't ever end, will it?' Anne said. 'As long as you are who you are.'

'No, it won't end,' he said harshly. 'So you'd better get out while you can, before things get more complicated.'

'Please don't talk like that.' She came around and sat close to him, and dabbed at his dirty face with her handkerchief. 'Besides, you can't throw me out yet. My week's not up.'

'If I cared about you, I'd put you on the next boat out of here,' he growled.

'If I cared about you, I'd refuse to go.'

He caught her in his arms and held her so tightly that

she couldn't breathe for a moment. 'You're good for me, better than I deserve. I never worried about Kit. I paid for her guards, and I never gave her a thought. But you – I'd worry about you night and day. And kids, if we had kids – no, it wouldn't be fair, to them or to you.'

'But what about you?' She gazed into his eyes. 'How do you want to spend the rest of your life: growing more and more isolated, just waiting for the end, the critical moment when your guard slips? Living for yourself, and pleasure, and the accumulation of money and power? Love means sharing, halving the burdens and doubling the triumphs. If we decide that we want to be together, it will be because we've both weighed the risks and decided that it's worth it.'

He said, 'You're taking this very calmly.'

'Oh, I'm at my best when someone is in trouble. You know that.'

'Cool as ice,' he grunted. 'One might think you played with bombs in your crib.'

'Being a white in China is a lot like playing with a bomb, a bomb with a delayed fuse. When I was a child I heard about missionaries who were slaughtered for no other reason than because they were white. I had nightmares about it, because it could have been us, my family, me. Since then I've seen death over and over again. It's too familiar to be frightening. Do you know,' she smiled suddenly, radiantly, 'my first reaction was relief, because I knew I wouldn't have Maurice's clothes to worry about anymore.'

Innes laughed and kissed her, again and again. Warmth enveloped them both, shutting out fear and anger. Minutes later he said, 'You have dirt on your nose.'

'It wasn't there before you came in.'

'What next? After you've made love to me and scrubbed my back, I mean.'

'Do you have to do something else about this? Talk to Sun, or the police?'

'No. I can't do anything more. Both Tu and Sun are too smart to leave traces, and any information I might have gotten from Sanjay is gone. The police weren't happy about the shoot-out, and apparently it put the consul off his lunch, but they've finished with me for the time being. There will have to be a hearing, but not for a week or more.'

'Then let's take the three o'clock train to Nanking. We'll spend the rest of the day making love in our hotel room, and we'll spend all day tomorrow being tourists. I'll take you to Dr Sun Yat-sen's mausoleum.'

'Take me to the home of the architect of the Chinese Revolution, who advocated expelling all whites? You will like hell.'

They returned from Nanking on Wednesday night. Innes had to spend the next day at his office, catching up on urgent business. Most pressing was his need for a new driver and bodyguard, and he hired two men, one a Russian and the other a Pole. As he hoped, they took an instant dislike to each other. Innes knew that he could play one against the other in order to ensure the loyalty of both.

After he left the penthouse that morning, Anne went out for a walk. She strolled to the park that overlooked the junction of the Whangpoo River and Soochow Creek. The wind from the sea was bitter, and there were fewer people than usual about. She found a vacant bench in the sun and sat down to watch the traffic on the creek.

She felt curiously at peace with herself, even though she knew that certain problems would demand solutions before too long. But for the present, she stashed them on a shelf in the back of her mind. She thought about Innes: alive and energetic and ambitious, bent on proving that he was as good as or better than the other taipans in Shanghai, who were mostly university-educated and well-born. He was strong, self-assured, shrewd about people. He had certainly told her some hard truths about herself. Yet he had blind spots, too; Kit, Sanjay. He wanted so badly to be loved. He didn't realize how badly.

Living with him wouldn't be easy. They hadn't much in common. They were poles apart ideologically. She would have to make more compromises and concessions than he. His various projects consumed his attentions and left very little time for the demands of another person in his life.

She knew she would hate living behind gates, always guarded, always vulnerable.

But hadn't life with Gilbert been like that in a way? She had hidden herself away behind a false front, guarded her tongue and her desires, and she had still been appallingly vulnerable to hurt.

At least she and Innes would be walled up together, like lovers of legend. She thought of him, naked and powerful, the two of them coiled around each other like a couple of shining snakes, and she felt a wonderful scooping sensation in her middle. That was the real miracle, that he thought her beautiful, and desirable, that he wanted her.

'Good morning, Anne. May I join you?'

She looked up, startled from her reverie. Olga Kerensky, swathed in black rabbit fur dyed to look like ermine, lowered herself onto the bench.

'I can't very well refuse,' Anne said, drawing her coat aside. 'This is a public place.'

'Ah, we are making progress,' Olga said brightly. 'At least you didn't jump up and run away the moment you saw me.'

'How is Mr McClure?' Anne inquired.

'Quite well, thank you,' Olga smiled. 'You won't believe this, but he and I share an interest in classical music. In fact we met at a performance of the Shanghai Philharmonic – execrable, by the way. Albert is quite passionate about Beethoven.'

'How marvelous for you. My father never appreciated Beethoven properly. I don't know what you found to talk about.'

'Albert has asked me to marry him,' Olga said, ignoring the jibe. 'I am strongly tempted to accept.'

'Marry! But what about Father?' Anne asked, surprised.

'You can't always have what you want in this world, you and I both know that. Your father and I have been very close. But he will never marry me as long as your mother lives, and I wouldn't want him to leave her.'

'A laudable sentiment,' Anne sniffed.

'I am getting older,' Olga said softly. 'I feel history pressing in on me again, and it terrifies me. I don't want to be caught by it, as I was in Russia in 1917. The horrors I saw then – no, I couldn't bear it. I am a refugee without a passport. I must stay in Shanghai until I die, unless I marry someone like Albert. It is a shallow and not very noble motive for marrying, but I will make him a good wife, and perhaps prolong his life for a few years. It is amazing, I think, how love can transform a man who has thought himself worthless. My love helped your father through a difficult time. That seems to be my function in life – loving and redeeming men.'

Anne gazed stolidly at a sampan passing under the Garden Bridge.

'I did not betray you to your father, Anne,' Olga said, facing her. 'I don't expect you to believe that. The letter from the concierge of your hotel, telling of her nasty suspicions and reminding your father of his duties, no longer exists. But I never revealed one word of the things you told me in your letters. I disapproved of your father's actions. I told him so then and I have told him so since, many times. I know we can't be friends again, but I don't want you to go on thinking that I wronged you. I didn't.'

Anne shrugged. 'It doesn't seem as important now as it did once.'

'Your father has told me what happened between you and your husband. I am most dreadfully sorry.'

'So am I, but that won't change anything.'

'Are you going to go back to him, and try to patch things up?'

Anne's eyes flashed angrily. 'Did my father send you here to talk to me?'

'No, he did not.' Olga pulled herself up regally. 'I am not your father's spy, or his secret agent. How could I possibly know you were going to be here this morning?'

'Well, when you do see my father, you can tell him that I don't want to patch things up. The marriage was bad, wrong from the start. In fact, I'm thinking of staying with Kit's husband, Mr Innes. He loves me and wants to marry me, and I just might go ahead and let him. Father can put that in his pious preacher's pipe and smoke it.'

'Innes,' Olga murmured. 'An interesting man. Yes, I can see why you are attracted to him. He is everything your Gilbert is not, no? And your father detests him. Innes. He has found something in you that he needs very much, something he has been missing. I am a little surprised at that, only because I wouldn't have given him credit for having sense enough to recognize quality when he sees it. I only hope —' She stopped abruptly and plucked the fur in her lap.

'What?' Anne prompted her.

'I hope you aren't doing this,' Olga said hesitantly, 'the two of you, perhaps without knowing it, to get a sort of revenge on your sister and your husband.'

'That's horrible,' Anne said, shocked. 'We never – no, it's just not true!'

Olga stood up. 'I am happy to hear it. But we don't always know why we act as we do. Goodbye, Anne. I hope we shall meet again, very soon.'

She strolled north toward the Garden Bridge. She walked slowly, lifting her face to the sun, savoring its warmth.

Anne felt a sudden chill and she covered her face with her hands. 'No, it isn't true,' she said. 'It isn't true!'

She returned to Innes' penthouse. She had been quite comfortable there, but all of a sudden she felt out of place, wrong. She looked at herself in the bedroom mirror, against the backdrop of the golden vase, the beautiful bed, the lush carpet. But she was still Anne, homely, rabbity behind her glasses, unsure of herself, destined to live with soaring dreams and plodding reality.

The telephone rang. It was the desk, announcing Dr Lawrence and Reverend Fox. Could they come up? She gave her consent, and hung up. Strange. Just an hour ago she could have faced them bravely, told them both that she wanted to be left alone, to live her own life. But now – the buzzer sounded and she opened the door resignedly.

'Just what in hell do you think you're doing, writing me a goddamned note like you were thanking me for a lovely weekend?'

Innes loomed large in the Lawrence apartment, his eyes like ice chips, Anne's note compressed in his fist.

'I just thought it would be simpler if we didn't meet

314

again.' She turned away from the door and tossed the sweater she had been holding into an open trunk. 'I wrote down everything I had to say.'

'Because you didn't have the guts to tell me in person. But I'm like a lot of uneducated people. I don't always believe what I read. Would you mind repeating it, to my face?'

Anne said woodenly, 'I appreciate your help, and your kindness, but I have responsibilities and duties that I must attend to. I shall always remember fondly – but you don't want to hear that part again.'

'You're right, I don't. Where's the prodigal husband?' Innes asked, looking around. 'He ought to be here, giving you a warm welcome home.'

'He had some errands to run.'

'Looks like you're going on a trip. Sure, he has to make sure he has enough opium to tide him over. Where to? The States ? With a little honeymoon stop in Hawaii?'

'Please don't be like that. This wasn't an easy decision for me to make.'

'How in hell am I supposed to be?' he demanded. 'I come home, after spending just three hours away from you, and I find this – this *thing* sitting prominently against the bottle of my favorite scotch. Nice touch, Anne. Is that a hint that I drink too much? Why didn't you just leave it on the pillow?' He balled up the paper and pitched it into a corner.

'I'm sorry you're unhappy about this. So am I. But my week was nearly up. I couldn't stay with you indefinitely. I need work to do. I need to have a purpose.'

'Loving me isn't purpose enough for you.'

'Gilbert and my father came to see me. Gilbert really wants to start over. Dr Morrison has found him a position in a small Methodist mission in Paoting, about a hundred and fifty miles south of Peiping. He'll be the only doctor there. He's promised to stop taking opium. He knows he won't be able to quit cold, but he thinks he can taper off eventually.'

'And you believe him? You're a damned fool. You know damned well you can't believe anything a dope fiend tells you.'

'I believe he'll try. He doesn't know how difficult it will be. But with his work, and his faith, and my help, he can do it.'

'And you want to bury yourself with him,' Innes said disgustedly. 'I thought you were supposed to be smart. But this is just downright stupid.'

She sat down wearily and closed her eyes. She could feel him glaring at her malevolently. 'We both knew I couldn't stay with you forever, didn't we? I mean, we're not right for each other, Jamie. The time we had together was wonderful, perfect, but it wasn't real. It was just a dream.'

'You're dreaming now if you think he'll stop doping. He needs that opium to help him forget Kit, and he won't get over her anytime soon. Oh, you'll have a fine time, waiting for him to get back to normal and notice you again. Maybe you can take up knitting. And who knows, maybe he'll fall in love with you, in another five or ten years.'

Anne took off her glasses and pressed her fingers to her eyes.

'I don't understand you,' Innes said in a softer voice. 'I thought we were happy together.'

'We were, for a week. But I don't belong in your world. Remember, I told you that. And I was right.'

He sat next to her and grasped her hand. 'What happened while I was gone? What did they say to you?'

'Only what I'd been thinking but was afraid to say aloud, even to myself. You and I were both hurt by what happened. Yes, you, even though you thought you didn't care what Kit did. We thought that by —' she swallowed '— by coming together, we could hurt them back. It was a kind of revenge.'

'Revenge! That's the craziest thing I've ever heard. The thought never entered my mind.'

'But that doesn't mean it couldn't have been there anyway, in the subconscious.'

'Freudian horseshit,' Innes snorted. 'I can't believe you'd swallow that stuff.'

'I think it's true,' she said stubbornly. 'We don't always know why we act as we do. We could hardly have planned a better revenge, could we? Divorce them, marry each other, try like hell to make it work. But it wouldn't have worked. We just don't belong together.'

He was silent for a long moment, then he said, 'You're a damned coward. Gutless. You can't stand the thought of being happy, can you? Any more than you can stand the thought of being well dressed and well fed and comfortable. You think you're not worthy, and so you'd rather crucify yourself.'

'I can't be happy if I don't do what I believe is right,' she cried. 'I ignored my responsibilities, the consequences of my actions. Gilbert left first, and Father and I talked. We both talked, he didn't just sermonize. He admitted that he was wrong about Chen, and he apologized for interfering. It was the first time he'd ever said that. He didn't try to pressure me, not like Paris. He just said that Gilbert needed me, and that he wouldn't live if I stayed away any longer. I knew it was true. Gilbert is weak. In the past he has relied on me for everything. But you're not weak, Jamie. You're strong. I'd be excess baggage in your life. You don't need me. You don't need anyone.'

'I do need you.' He tightened his grip on her hand.

'No, you don't. I'm nothing special. I'm as ordinary as mud. I know I'm not really beautiful. It doesn't make any difference how many times you say it. You're just trying to persuade yourself that I'm as good a catch as Kit, don't you see? It's three o'clock now. By four o'clock you'll have found somebody to take my place. Someone who will fit into your life better than I could. And besides – no, never mind.'

'Go on, get it off your chest. We've gotten this far, it would be a shame to stop.'

She said, 'I'm afraid of what will happen when you get tired of me. You're not accustomed to being faithful. You never developed the habit, because you didn't have to. Kit didn't demand fidelity from you, and she didn't deserve it, and so you never stopped living like a bachelor. You've always been able to indulge every whim and desire. I'm not condemning that, or saying that it's wrong for you to be that way. But if you were ever unfaithful to me after we'd made a commitment to each other, I couldn't forgive you. Can you understand that? I think I could get used to everything else – the way you make your money, your attitudes about opium – but not that. Never that. Not after what's happened. It would kill me.'

His hand slipped away from hers. He said, 'So you're willing to overlook Gilbert's little peccadillo – adultery with your own sister – but you're not willing to forgive me for sins I haven't even committed yet. Oh, that makes a lot of sense.'

'I wouldn't expect you to understand. I can almost forgive Gilbert. You know Kit, how hard she is to resist when she wants something. Once I get him away from her, he'll be all right. He'll never look at another woman.'

Innes stood up. 'So you'll stick with the sure thing instead of taking a chance. That's like staying with a sinking ship because you're too scared to go down the ropes to the lifeboat. I guess I know where that leaves me.'

'I'm sorry, Jamie,' she said miserably.

'You'll be sorrier,' he predicted. 'He doesn't love you, Anne. He didn't even notice you were gone. The only ones who got thrown for a loop by what happened last week were you and your father. Gilbert came crawling to you today because your father was standing behind him, nudging his ass with his toe. Your old man is scared to death that the people in his congregation are going to find out about this mess. He set this whole thing up to save his own face. He doesn't care about you or your happiness. Neither does Gilbert. He knows he behaved like an ass, but if you can make it all better, that's fine with him. You're just like your father; the only consequence that worries you is scandal, what people will think when they find out that you've shacked up with Wild Man Innes.'

'That's not true. I've never cared about what other people thought, never.'

'What about Kit? I can hear her laughing now; the Mouse and the Ape, what a combination! You don't want to stick around to hear that. You know what the Chinese say – of the thirty-six methods of escape, running away is the best – and you're really a master at escaping when things get tough, aren't you, Anne? You ran out on Chen, leaving him the same kind of shitty note you left me. You ran out on Gilbert. Now you're running out on me. I'll say it again; you're gutless.'

Her cheeks were crimson. She quivered with anger. 'Just what are you trying to prove by baiting me like this? That you can change my mind or make me cry? I know I'm taking the path of least resistance, the easy way, but that doesn't mean it's not the right way. You don't think you're alive unless you're doing something torturous or dangerous. But I'm not like that. If wanting to avoid complications and guilt and pain means I'm cowardly, then I guess I am. How could I expect you to understand? You've never paused to consider a consequence in your life. You never think about the effect of your actions on other people. You just plunge in, take what you can, and the hell with everybody else. You don't even care what you're doing to me now. By leaving you first, I've wounded your silly masculine pride. You think you can talk me into coming back.'

'I could get you to come back to me easy,' Innes said scornfully. 'I'd just have to shove a morphine needle up my arm, or get jailed for something, or get my foot blown off by a bomb. You'd come on the run because you don't feel alive or needed unless you're helping the afflicted. You and Gert are the same kind of woman. You hitch yourselves up to cripples because cripples don't make demands. You can run the show, have your own way, feel like a saint and a martyr, and then stand back and blush modestly when everyone tells you how noble and wonderful you are. It's bullshit. You're afraid to deal with a man as an equal, because you know you'd lose. You don't feel really comfortable with a man unless he's using your chest as a crying pillow.'

'If you don't get out of here right now, I swear —'

'You'd do what?' Innes jeered. 'You would have liked it better if I came in on my hands and knees, wouldn't you? Then you could play the noble-wife-giving-up-her-lover scene to the hilt, and tell yourself all the way to Paoting that you'd done the right thing by sacrificing true happiness for the higher joy of nursing the handicapped. But instead I came in roaring like a Dutch uncle, and you

319

hate it, because you know I'm right. You're making a first-class ass out of yourself.'

'I do hate it,' she said shakily. 'I hate you!'

She ran into the bathroom and locked the door. At once he began to batter it with his shoulder. The whole building shuddered. The floor trembled. Amazed and frightened, she watched the wood splinter around the lock. The door burst open with a crash. 'Don't you come near me!' she screamed, pulling the shower curtain in front of her like a shield.

Innes put his arms around her and dragged her out of the bathroom. She didn't relinquish her grip on the curtain and the whole rod pulled out of the rotten plaster and fell noisily into the tub.

'You're not playing the scene right, Anne,' he panted. 'I didn't get my dainty farewell kiss, the one that's supposed to remind me on rainy days of how sweet and gentle and bullshit self-sacrificing you are.'

'Let me go, damn you,' she said, struggling. 'Get away from me!'

'No, I plunge in and take what I want, remember? I think I ought to give you a little something to remember me by. You and I may be finished, but I haven't said goodbye to the lady in the green dress yet, have I? She deserves a special farewell all her own.'

He pinned her up against the wall in the narrow hallway with the length of his body. He tried to kiss her, and she jerked her head aside. He pinched her jawbone between thumb and forefinger and ground his mouth against hers. She couldn't lift her hands above the elbow and they fluttered impotently against him. She was aware of his free hand dragging at her skirt.

She thought, My God, he's going to rape me. The idea so astonished her that she stopped fighting him. 'Not this way, Jamie,' she said breathlessly. 'Please, not this way.'

'Yes, this way.' He ripped open her blouse and tore at the cups of her brassiere. The straps cut into her flesh. He unfastened her skirt and pulled it down over her hips, then lifted her in his arms and carried her into the bedroom.

He shoved his shoulders under her knees and penetrated her so deeply that he encountered the hardness of her cervix, like a closed fist. He moved inside her and coldly watched her excitement mount. He knew that her brain and her body were separate and distinct, and that if he couldn't appeal to her reason, at least he could master her flesh. The fistlike resistance softened and seemed to envelop him. He felt something inside her, gently gripping and releasing him. She screamed and thrashed violently. He shoved her legs aside and covered her completely, and they rocked together. Her fingernails raked his back. Finally, violently, he exploded inside her. He collapsed on top of her, his heart bursting, and he could still feel her muscles tensing and relaxing, like a kiss.

Her cheeks were wet with tears. He said, 'I'm sorry, Anne. I had to. I had to show you. Come with me now. Come home.'

'No,' she whispered. 'No! Get away from me!'

He stood up. She turned on her side and hid her face. He stared at her for a long time and said in a rasping voice. 'Go to hell, Anne. I'm sorry I wasted my time.'

A long time passed, two minutes or two hours. She heard Gilbert come into the apartment and call her name. He paused wonderingly in front of the wrecked bathroom door, and entered the bedroom.

'My God, Anne, what happened? Are you hurt?'

'No. It was just a typhoon. An irresistible natural force,' she said thickly, not lifting her head from her pillow.

He sat gingerly on the side of the bed and touched her shoulder. She shrugged him off. 'You're hurt. Was it him, that man, Innes?'

'It's none of your business what happened, Gilbert,' she said angrily. 'I don't owe you any explanations. I don't owe you anything, after what you've done. Just count yourself lucky that you got your slave and nursemaid back. You don't have to go home and admit disgrace and defeat. I saved you from that. We can pick up and go on as though nothing had happened, as though you had never fornicated or committed adultery with my sister, as though I —' She broke off.

'So you're going to reproach me for that,' he said in a defeated voice.

'Why not? Did you think I'd have the good taste not to mention it? I'm so sorry to disappoint you, Gilbert dear. But maybe you're right. Maybe we should treat the whole thing as a bad dream, an opium dream.' She lifted her head and smiled strangely. 'Not such a bad idea, is it? Life is just a soft and lovely opium dream. I've really been missing something, haven't I? Fix me a laudanum cocktail, will you, Gilbert? I want to see what I've been missing.'

'Oh, Anne.' He gazed at her helplessly.

'What kind of doctor are you? You won't prescribe for heartbreak, you can't diagnose despair, and you don't have a treatment for loneliness. You're a fraud, a quack!'

'Please don't talk like that,' he fretted. 'I don't know how to help you. I wish I did. But I can't help anyone. I can't even help myself.'

He dropped his head into his hands.

She looked at him. She knew why the Chinese called white people ghosts. He was a ghost, a quivering apparition, without substance, almost without form. Nebulous, empty, sad, having only a past and no future.

'We are a pair, aren't we?' she said with a bitter laugh. 'A couple of ghosts, doomed to wander the earth together, wailing and rattling our chains. We won't have children. Ghosts, can't reproduce. You'll depend on me more and more. You'll become my child, and we'll both have what we want, no earthly life and no earthly worries. A ghost mother, and a ghost child that never grows up.'

'Stop,' he pleaded. 'I don't like it when you talk like this, Anne. It frightens me.' He threw himself down next to her. He lay inside the curve of her body, next to her breasts. She felt a sudden strong urge to hold him close, to comfort him, but she resisted it. Instead she rolled off the other side of the bed and said without looking at him, 'I'm sorry, Gilbert. I won't do it again.'

Chapter Eleven

Kit swirled her ermine coat angrily. 'Oh, don't be such an old stick, Bink,' she snapped. 'It's early yet.'

'But I don't want to dance anymore,' Binky whined. 'I'm too tired, Kit, really—'

'Then I'll just go to the Delmonte by myself. I'm quite sure I can find someone to dance with me there.'

Before he realized what was happening, she jumped into her car and slammed the door, and her chauffeur pulled away with a roar. He was left standing on the crowded sidewalk in front of the Flamingo. Binky sucked his fleshy upper lip and wondered if he should follow. He decided that he was really much too tired, and that she would be quite all right alone.

He sighed. She was so difficult lately; hard to please, impatient, and with a mad compulsion to be doing something every minute. Binky missed the leisurely lunches at the Country Club and the easy flow of conversation over cocktails. These days all she wanted to do was drink and dance, which meant that he had to follow her from one noisy club to another until he was ready to drop from exhaustion. Well, it would do her good to learn that he wouldn't dance to her tune all the time. He hailed a ricksha and went home.

The chauffeur saw Kit safely inside the Delmonte, and stationed himself outside the door. He was an enormous White Russian named Ivor, perhaps the only man in Shanghai who was immune to Kit's charms. His job was easy, if a little boring. She always went to well-lighted busy places where there was little danger.

Kit paused for a moment just inside the door and surveyed the crowd. No familiar face caught her eye. The headwaiter, recognizing her, led her to a good table and asked if she were expecting anyone.

'Anyone and everyone,' she said with an airy wave of her hand.

She glanced around. It seemed to her that her entrance

had attracted less attention than usual. Was it the gown, she wondered? That Grecian draping was lovely, but perhaps she was too petite to carry it off. She'd have to give Maurice a good talking-to. What was he trying to do, make her a laughingstock? She checked her face in the small mirror of her compact. Even though the light was soft and flattering, she decided that she definitely looked drawn and old.

She knew she needed to rest, but she couldn't rest. She couldn't sleep. Whenever she tried to sleep, she had the most horrible nightmare in which she was being attacked by an enormous black bird. It descended on her, screeching. Its talons looked as large and lethal as pitchforks. She didn't need a psychiatrist to tell her that the dream symbolized Innes' attack on her, but knowing what the dream meant didn't make it go away.

She drank her scotch neat, even though she hated it that way. She was drinking more and more and it was hurting her looks and not helping her to sleep. She still dreamed, no matter how much she drank. She dreamed even while she was awake and sober.

A couple came off the dance floor and sat at the next table. Kit had seen the woman before and knew she was a professional bar girl, one of those who worked at the Delmonte on a regular basis. But even if she hadn't recognized the woman she would have known her profession. The cheap gown, the home-styled hair, the worn shoes, the glazed tiredness in her eyes gave her away. Kit stared openly, and wondered for the millionth time what life was like for a girl like that. Were the men rough or were they gentle? Did she enjoy having strange men make love to her? Did she work for a pimp, or for herself? Could she refuse to sleep with a man if he didn't appeal to her? Did the men ever beat her? Did she want to quit, save her money, get a respectable job? Or was she happy being a prostitute?

A porcine German wearing a pea-green suit with a tiny swastika pinned on the lapel came over to her table and bowed. He asked if he could join her. Kit gazed at him coldly and said, 'No, I'm waiting for someone,' and he went away.

It was true, she was waiting for someone. But who? A friend? She had no friends, only companions in gaiety who were as shallow and lighthearted in their loyalties as she. She saw no one for a whole month after the beating. Even though the marks disappeared after only a week, she felt that anyone could tell just by looking at her how Innes had humiliated her. She didn't return phone calls, and visitors were turned away at the door. After being rebuffed by the houseboy a few times, her friends simply stopped coming.

She wasn't waiting for a lover. The thought of being touched by a man frightened and excited her, but so far fear prevailed. She would have to choose carefully, wisely.

Was she waiting for her father, perhaps? He hadn't called or tried to see her since that night. He believed the poisonous lies Anne told him. Anne was the reigning favorite now.

She wasn't waiting for her husband. She felt a spasm of nervousness in her bowels and finished her drink in a single swallow. Innes hated her. He wanted to kill her. She had never been frightened of anything before, but the knowledge that he hated her enough to kill her terrified her. She knew that if she didn't do something to save herself, one day he would whip her until there was nothing left of her, until she was dead.

Someone was speaking to her, an attractive dark-haired man with heavy-lidded brown eyes. Not a Chinese. '—once a year and I always hit the Delmonte because the prettiest girls are here. Mind if I sit down?'

The bar girl at the next table gave her a jealous look. Her own companion was greasy, sweating, rumpled. Kit said, 'Please do. Where did you say you were from?'

'New York. I'm in the rag trade – that's a pretty fine gown you're wearing, if I may say so. Made here? The fabric, I mean. I'm a fabric buyer.'

'I'm sure I don't know,' she said distractedly.

There was a slight commotion at the doors of the club and a ripple of excitement passed through the room. A wedge-shaped body of people entered. They were all Chinese. At their core, flanked by two pearl-faced concubines and surrounded by sturdily built Cantonese bodyguards, was Tu Yueh-sen, the head of the criminal Green Dragon Society and, according to some, the most powerful man in Shanghai. Kit had seen him on several occasions, and had laughingly observed that he looked the most powerful ratcatcher in Shanghai. But tonight he impressed her differently. He seemed to have gained strength and stature.

'Would you mind leaving now?' Kit said to the New Yorker.

'What? Wait a minute, I haven't even had a drink yet.'

'They serve drinks at other tables, too,' she informed him. 'I don't want you to sit here anymore.'

He called her an impolite name, which she didn't hear. All her attention was concentrated on Tu, seated with his party at the most prominent table in the room. Kit fished in her purse for her fountain pen and wrote in bold letters on the Delmonte's wine list: 'I think we can be of service to each other. Kit Fox Innes.' She underlined her married name twice, and signaled to her waiter.

'Would you give this to Mr. Tu and tell him that Mrs Innes presents her compliments.'

She sipped her second drink and forced herself not to look over at Tu's table. In a few minutes the waiter returned with an invitation from Tu to join his party.

Tu didn't stand when she approached, but gave her a bored, sleepy look. He smoked without removing his cigarette from his mouth. Ash sprinkled the front of his suit. His tiny eyes, narrowed against the smoke, looked even tinier, like a pig's eyes. One of his bodyguards made room for Kit. She sat down and smiled brightly.

'Are you surprised that I wanted to see you?' she asked.

Tu shrugged. 'Maybe.' He said something in Shanghai dialect to one of the girls, who tittered. The cluster of bodyguards grinned in unison.

'I am the wife of Innes,' Kit said. 'I understand you and he don't get along very well. I have heard that you would destroy him if you could.'

'Maybe,' Tu said to the accompaniment of titters.

'Don't you understand English?' Kit demanded, annoyed.

'Maybe.' His crowd laughed, and one of the guards

leaned over Tu's chair and quickly translated what Kit had said. Kit thought she saw a flicker of interest in the tiny eyes.

She said, 'Tell him that Innes has angered me, and that I, too, would like to destroy him. I can be of help to you, perhaps.'

Tu listened while the man murmured in his ear, and said a few words.

'He says you must drink with us, and have some food with us. There will be time for talk later.'

'Yes, of course,' she said happily. She opened her purse to get a cigarette. A large hand stayed hers long enough for its owner to have a peek inside. She displayed the contents of her purse willingly, and coolly offered to let the man search her. This provoked laughter from the group. A smile flickered on Tu's impassive face. A waiter hovered and she ordered scotch. One of the guards asked her if she wanted to dance. She consented. To her surprise, Tu rose with her. He was a terrible dancer, stiff-legged and jerky, but she smiled gamely while he shoved her around the floor. The people of their table grinned encouragingly, and applauded heartily when Kit and Tu sat down.

She drank two more scotches. Her fears seemed less menacing, now that a possible solution was at hand. She had made a powerful friend, and she could look forward to peaceful slumber. Once Innes was dead she would be free of nightmares, free of the terror that haunted her. She knew what she had been waiting for.

Tu stood up, indicating his readiness to leave. He spoke to her. His interpreter said, 'You will come with us, please,' and she nodded.

She was absorbed into the inner circle and the party moved toward the doors, past an honor guard of bowing waiters. Ivor, the chauffeur-bodyguard, saw her emerge with Tu's party. He shouted to her and tried to push through the phalanx that surrounded her. One of Tu's guards made a graceful movement with his arm. There was a sharp crack, and Ivor whirled around, clutching his belly, and pitched forward into the gutter.

Kit thought with alcohol-induced calm, 'Oh, they've

shot him.' She slowed slightly and turned around, but strong arms propelled her forward and pushed her into the back of a waiting car, not the same one in which Tu had ridden off.

Kit knew that Tu ran his organization from the French Concession. The police there were notoriously corrupt and boasted several convicted criminals among them. Opium laws went unenforced there. They passed the Innes mansion on the Avenue Joffre and headed west toward the suburb of Ziccawei, where the famous Jesuit observatory was located. Their driver pulled up in front of a pair of massive iron gates and spoke to an armed watchman, who opened the gates and waved them through. The car drew up in front of a boxy Western-style mansion with a red-tiled roof. There were no trees or foundation plantings close to the house, nothing that could give cover to an assassin. Lights blazed from every window, but the place was eerily silent.

Kit experienced a thrill of excitement. She was actually inside Tu's headquarters, the seat of his enormous power, his storehouse of treasure and women. Her escort, the guard who spoke English, took her up to a small parlor on the second floor.

Tu was already there, lying on his side on a low couch. One of the concubines who had been with him at the Delmonte was preparing an opium pipe. She knelt between the couch and a low table, on which burned a small spirit lamp. She placed a particle of raw opium on the point of a needle and held it over the flame. When it hissed and bubbled, she transferred it to the bowl of a long pipe, which she presented ceremoniously to Tu, who inhaled the thick white smoke in three noisy puffs. The girl took the pipe back and repeated the procedure. The room was silent except for the sizzle of cooking opium and Tu's greedy sucking.

Kit looked around. The furnishings in the room and in the rest of the house were all Chinese-style, gaudy and new rather than antique and elegant. She experienced a twinge of disappointment. She had expected something grander.

She said eagerly, 'I think we should kill him tonight. It

328

will be so easy, now that you have my help. Just one thing, don't be too quick about it. I want him to suffer. You understand?' She looked from the man on the couch to the guard standing impassively at her side. 'Well, come on, what are we waiting for?'

Tu grunted. The guard, a burly Cantonese with a bald head and long serpentine mustaches, said, 'Wait.'

'But I don't want to wait,' she said impatiently. 'I've waited long enough. Look, I know where he is right now – he's at the penthouse in the Cathay. He'll see me, I know he will. And you'll be right there with me. Tu must come, too. I want Innes to see him, to know what's happening. He won't suspect a thing at first, and then—'

Tu murmured. The guard translated. 'He says to be quiet.'

'Why should I be quiet?' she demanded loudly. 'Do you want my help or don't you? I'm not going to wait around here all night until he decides to get off his couch and do something. You do need me if you want to destroy Innes. You'll never be able to get close to him without me.'

'You will stay, until we are ready.'

'But I don't want to stay. I'm ready now, and if you're too doped and too lazy to cooperate, I'll just be on my way.' She swung her ermine coat capelike around her shoulders.

The stocky guard shook his head. 'Too much hurry. Whites always hurry. Wait.'

'I won't,' she said. 'Kindly order a car to take me home. I can see that I'm wasting my time.'

She stalked toward the door. The guard moved quickly and silently to intercept her. He stood in front of her and spread out his arms as if ready to embrace her.

'Kindly get out of my way,' Kit said imperiously. 'I want to leave now.'

The bald head rolled back and forth but the small black eyes never left her face. 'You stay,' the man said amiably. 'Smoke opium, maybe.'

'I will not. If I want to smoke opium, I can do it in my own house.'

He grinned, displaying an assortment of chipped and yellow teeth. He stepped close to her and touched her cheek. She slapped his hand away and stood her ground.

'Stop that,' she hissed. 'Chinese filth. How dare you touch me.'

He laughed and grabbed her wrists. He was shorter than she, but his fingers were made of steel. His face moved closer and closer to hers. His breath was foul. She could see that his teeth were rotting and black. Sweat gleamed like dew on the dome of his bald skull. She knew from experience that resistance would only provoke a painful demonstration of his masculine potency, so she closed her eyes and went limp in his arms. Her coat slid to the floor. Laughing, the guard pushed her down, onto the blanket of ermine.

'I don't give a damn if Tu cuts her up into little pieces,' Innes growled. 'I've already started divorce proceedings. She's not worth a thing to me. Too bad about Ivor, though. He was a good man.'

Sun said, 'I fear you do not appreciate the broader implications of this matter. Your wife has many friends in Shanghai, and so does her father.'

'I know, I know,' Innes said, bowing to the inevitable. 'We're going to have to play ball and hand over his father in order to get her back. Bloody hell. We haven't had any trouble with Tu for three years – that old man was our only insurance – but now all hell's going to break loose, just wait and see.'

'Most regrettable,' Sun murmured. 'But we can devise another deterrent, I am sure.'

'Maybe we can plant a bomb on his yacht,' Innes suggested acidly.

'Ah, yes, your boat. That was unfortunate.'

'Regrettable, you mean. What's your theory about that bomb, Sun?' Innes narrowed his eyes. 'Did Tu buy Sanjay, or did someone else?'

'You are not suggesting that perhaps I had something to do with it.' Sun sounded shocked. 'I assure you I did not. I detest violence, you know that. In incidents like that, there is always the chance that innocent people may be hurt.'

'One was. Kendall. Terminally hurt.'

'Very true. But that was extremely advantageous for you, was it not? Perhaps you yourself planted the bomb, and tricked him into searching the boat, in order to rid yourself of a nuisance.'

Innes laughed and Sun joined in. 'You're slick, Sun,' Innes said. 'You're crooked and you're slick.'

'I flatter myself that I can still be useful to you from time to time.' Sun rose to his feet and bowed his head. 'I will make the arrangements for the exchange. I hope they have not abused your wife too terribly.'

'I wouldn't care if they had,' Innes said. 'She deserves everything she gets.'

'She's asking for you, Mr Innes,' said the doctor at the Aldershot. 'I've sedated her, but I don't think she'll be able to rest until she's spoken with you.'

'Did they hurt her?' Innes asked.

'I think she was raped,' the doctor said with an embarrassed cough. 'But she wouldn't talk about it – became hysterical when I tried to examine her. Mostly it's shock. Terrible thing to happen to any decent woman. Men like Tu should be exterminated.'

Innes refrained from adding, And so should women like Kit. He went into her room. A white-veiled nurse gave him a simpering smile and left them alone. Kit looked deathly pale, almost invisible against the white sheets.

'You want to see me?' he said gruffly.

Her eyes were open, but she didn't look at him. He thought she hadn't heard him. He repeated his question. She moistened her lips and said. 'You didn't want to ransom me, did you? You wanted to leave me there.'

'What do you think?'

'You did. You don't care about me. No one cares about me. My father hasn't even come to see me.'

'He's in the mountains with your mother. I sent a man with a message. He'll be here.'

'He used to love me, but he doesn't anymore. I thought parents were supposed to love you no matter what you did. Nobody loves me now.'

'I guess there are some things even fathers can't forgive.' He didn't want to feel sorry for her. Pity would

331

open the door to forgiveness, and other things. He didn't want to backslide into her traps and snares.

'I did this on purpose – to kill you,' she said. 'I wasn't really kidnapped. I approached Tu at the Delmonte. I knew what I was doing. I just didn't expect him to be so awful.' She closed her eyes. 'I was a fool. I thought I could get him to do what I wanted. I have a way with men, you know.'

'It doesn't matter now,' Innes said. 'It's over. You could have been hurt a lot worse. You were lucky.'

'Yes. It wasn't so bad. No worse than the night you— This wasn't the first time.'

'What do you mean? You've seen Tu before?'

'No, I tried to kill you once before. Sanjay. I told Sanjay what you did to me, that you whipped me. I told him to put a bomb in your car or boat. He knew all about bombs.'

Innes stared. 'You did that? I don't believe it.'

'He was in love with me. He was sweet, although for an Indian he was awfully ignorant about the *Kama Sutra*. I was surprised.'

'But you could have killed Anne, too. Didn't you think about that?'

She moved her head on the pillow. 'No. I didn't think about anything, except how much I hated you. See, aren't you sorry you didn't leave me with Tu?' Innes didn't answer. She said, 'I guess that makes me a murderer. Or murderess.' She gave a sleepy little laugh.

He said, 'You don't even care, do you? You're only sorry that your scheme didn't work, either time. But you're not going to try again,' he added grimly.

'No. There's not much point. I'd only fail. I'd make a good Lady Macbeth but a terrible Lucrezia Borgia. End up poisoning myself, most likely, or blowing myself up. You shouldn't have shot Sanjay. Wasn't his fault. You should have shot me.' She sighed deeply and muttered to herself. The sedation had taken effect.

He looked down at her. 'I wish I had, damn you.'

'The girls don't like it when you high-class broads come in here slummin'.'

'But you don't understand, I don't want to be paid for this,' Kit told the dance hall manager. 'I just want to work here for one night, that's all. I lost a bet to one of my friends. I'll give the other girls whatever tickets I collect, you can tell them that.'

The Flamingo was still fairly empty at eight o'clock at night. A few of the girls had taken their places at the tiny tables. They powdered their noses, adjusted their seams and straps, fingered curls, sipped cold tea from champagne glasses, smoked cheap cigarettes. The Filipino musicians climbed wearily onto the bandstand, dragged their chairs into position, and tuned and tested their instruments. The drummer produced a few thumps and cymbal shimmers, the pianist replied with an arpeggio, the saxophonist added a riff and a wailing cadenza.

'Don't you think I'll be good for business?' Kit asked, producing her most dazzling smile. 'Give your place a little tone, you know. Come on, just one night.'

'All right,' the man said grudgingly. 'I'll take you over to meet the girls. If they don't want you around, out you go.'

The looks that greeted her were hostile and cold. She opened her cigarette case and offered it around, gave them a friendly smile and said, 'Hello. My name's Kit.'

'Look, one of those society dollies come to see what life is like at the bottom,' said a bored Eurasian girl.

'Why not?' Kit shrugged. 'Wouldn't you like to see what it's like at the top?'

The girls laughed. The atmosphere thawed a little. Kit told them the lie about losing the bet, and said she would divide the tickets she got among them.

'Not good,' said a tall Russian girl. 'I think we draw straws, and one of us keeps all.'

This appealed to their betting instincts. The Eurasian girl won. She said, 'You sit with me. Maybe I get lucky with you sittin' here. My name is Iris but I change to Isis. I tell them I am Egyptian. Good, eh?'

The band played 'Lulu's Back in Town.' The Russian girl said, 'You good dancer? Dance with me. I want to see.'

Kit hesitated. 'I've never danced with a woman before.'

333

'Slow nights we dance with each other. Passes time.'

The Russian assumed the lead. Kit followed easily and the girl nodded approvingly. 'You are rich?' she asked.

'My husband's rich,' Kit told her. 'But we're getting divorced.'

'That is stupid. If I had rich husband I would not divorce, never. I would not divorce even poor husband.'

'He beat me, and I cheated on him. We don't exactly get along.'

'Husband should beat wife who cheats. You are very stupid.'

'I don't think so. I think I'm smart for getting out. Marriage isn't for me.'

'Is not smart to end up in place like this. Feet tired, eyes burning from smoke, back hurting. I would trade places with you in a minute, you bet. You go back to him, smile pretty. You pretty lady. Tell him you love him. He will believe that is true. Ask him to forgive.'

'I wouldn't dream of it!' Kit said, outraged. 'Why should he forgive me and not the other way around?'

'Because he has the money,' the Russian said sensibly. The dance ended. Tourists and sailors had begun to drift into the club. 'We must work now. I give you advice – go home to your husband. This is stinking life.'

Kit said, 'No, it's not. I like it here. I like talking to you.'

'Only because this is one night, and when it is over, you go home to fancy house, plenty servants. We go to stinking little rooms. No servants, no showers even. Do not be stupid.'

Albert McClure said, 'Working late, Jim? You know what they say about all work and no play.'

'What do you want, McClure? I don't have any news for you. Just the usual. Innes & Company is getting richer all the time.'

'Happy to hear it.' McClure lounged in the chair opposite Innes' vast desk. Innes finished signing a stack of letters and Charlie Fong took them away. 'You might congratulate me, old boy. I'm married. To Olga, the Russian you met that night at Gert's.'

'I suppose you're old enough to know what you're doing,' Innes said. He pushed the silver cigarette box toward his visitor. 'My own experience with matrimony doesn't permit me to recommend it.'

'Kit's a beauty, Jim. You're the envy of every man in Shanghai.' Albert McClure added with a meaningful cough, 'Or at least you will be until the rest of them find out what she's been up to.'

'I don't give a damn what she's been up to,' Innes said. 'We're getting a divorce. She goes her way, I go mine. Finished.'

'I'm sorry to hear that. I like Kit. Something of the little girl lost about her.'

'Would you call a prowling female tiger a little girl lost?' Innes demanded. 'She knows what she wants and she can damn well take care of herself.'

McClure said, 'She's been dancing for money at the Flamingo every night for the past month, since Tu let her go. Sure, I know about the exchange. You've doubled your own guard since then. But you don't have Kit guarded at all anymore. Don't you care what happens to her?'

'No, I don't. Any complaints?'

'It's none of my business.' McClure shrugged. 'But it doesn't look right for a taipan's wife to be picking up tickets at a dime-a-dance joint.'

'She's not going to be my wife much longer. Besides, what's wrong with the Flamingo? As long as she's dancing with sailors she's not doing something worse, like trying to murder someone.'

McClure perked up his ears. 'What's that? So she's been plotting and planning against you, has she? Ah, Jim.'

Charlie Fong entered the office without knocking. He leaned over the back of Innes' chair and spoke in a rapid whisper into his employer's ear.

Innes' scowl deepened. 'Here's some real news for you, McClure. There was a shoot-out today near the Marco Polo Bridge in Peiping. The Japs are saying it was an act of provocation. Looks like war.'

McClure stood up. 'I'd better get back to the office. Your sister-in-law's up near Peiping now, isn't she?'

'South. Paoting.'

'I know the place. Terrible hole. Mountainous. But there's a lot of coal there and the location is important – fifty miles from the Great Wall and right on the railroad. The Japanese have shown a lot of interest in that area. You know, they weren't very nice to white missionaries in Manchuria. Burned them out, raped the women. You should see their soldiers when they come into a village: the officers bring their own meat, but the men take whatever's handy. White or yellow, makes no difference to them. Even sows, I've heard. Real ones, the four-legged kind. Poor kid. I hope she's all right.'

Innes nodded. McClure went back to the Reuters office in the North China Daily News building down the street. Innes said to Charlie Fong, 'See if you can get hold of any of our people who have been working near Paoting. Find out if anything's happened to the missionaries there.'

'But the Japanese are not at war with the whites,' Fong said. 'Surely Mrs Lawrence is safe.'

'She wouldn't want to be treated like a white,' Innes said. 'If there's any trouble, she'll side with the Chinese.'

The mountains around Paoting were rocky and treeless. Small villages and farms clung to the slopes like hopeful fleas to a starving dog. There was a saying that even a goat would starve in the Taihang Mountains. The farmers planted winter wheat and corn in minute patches no bigger than the space taken up by a parked car. If the summer rains were heavy, they harvested just enough to live on through the winter. In seasons of drought they either starved or migrated to the coastal city of Tientsin or to Peiping, where they joined thousands of other beggars from the parched and war-ravaged countryside.

The mines near Paoting had been active for a thousand years, but primitive methods had left a large reserve under the ground, waiting for the age of mechanization. A Japanese company had bought the rights to the Paoting mines from the local warlord, and a whole village of miners had sprung up just a few miles from the old walled Chinese town.

The Methodist mission was also located outside the city,

in a small walled compound about a mile from the south gate. Four white missionaries, Reverend and Mrs Forrest and Dr and Mrs Lawrence, lived there with several Chinese Christian families. The largest building in the compound was the chapel, which also served as the schoolroom and hospital, when necessary. If it chanced to rain during Sunday service, or when school was in session, the occupants engaged in a noisy search for seats between the leaks. The mission was reasonably self-sufficient, with its own well, though the water even when boiled was vile-tasting, and a cistern to capture rainwater for drinking. There was a miserable-looking vegetable garden, a pig yard, with a single resident since plague had carried off the rest during the winter, and a rutted playing field for recreation. Anne had seen a lot of missions in her life, but never one so grim and impoverished as Paoting.

Reverend Alva Forrest was seventy-five, an evangelical preacher of the old blood-and-thunder school. With his small Chinese printing press he turned out tracts by the thousand, written in the same bombastic vein as his sermons. The fact that most of his flock were illiterate didn't deter him. Still, he was a competent administrator and a dynamic speaker, and Anne was somewhat surprised to find him relegated to what undoubtedly was the bleakest bastion of Methodism. She expressed her curiosity to her father, who hinted in his next letter that the good preacher owed his decline to a rather un-Methodical fondness for the grape.

Until the incident at the bridge on July 7, 1937, the people at the mission had cooperated with the Japanese mine workers, whose superiors traveled to Peiping frequently and brought back needed books and medicines as well as mail. The arrival of a Japanese regiment in the area a few weeks before the shooting provoked some interest but no concern. The soldiers were there, the missionaries were told, to protect the mines from Communist saboteurs, known to be active in the area.

Spring crept up on them almost unnoticed. The barren hills offered no peonies, which Anne loved, no wisteria, no iris, only a few anemic-looking violets which she refrained from picking, in the hopes that they would seed themselves in the rocky soil. She had brought some narcissus bulbs with her from Shanghai, and she sprouted them on a saucer of white gravel indoors when the weather was still bleak and blustery outside. Her father sent a rose bush, but it had provided a tasty snack for Reverend Forrest's pride and joy, his hog Samson. There was very little visual evidence that the seasons changed at all in Paoting. In summer as well as winter the winds that blew out of Mongolia filled the air with clouds of yellow loess dust, and on the worst days everyone walked around with handkerchiefs tied around the lower portions of their faces. The dust sullied even the snow.

One day about a week after the incident at Marco Polo Bridge, Kate Forrest ran into the Lawrence cottage. 'What can we do? What can we do?' she wailed, flapping her withered hands helplessly. 'Some soldiers just came and arrested Mrs Chan!'

'Chinese soldiers?' Gilbert asked, wiping the perspiration from his face. It was only early July and the temperature was already in the nineties. How would they ever survive August?

'No, Japanese. I don't understand. Oh, I wish Alva were here. Can't we do something?' Reverend Forrest had been preaching in neighboring villages. He was expected to return that evening.

'I'm sure it's nothing to worry about,' Anne said calmly. 'I'll go see what I can find out, shall I, Gilbert? Mrs Ling's baby is due at any time. You don't want to be tied up with these bureaucrats when she sends for you.'

'I'll come with you, dear,' Mrs Forrest said. 'I can't imagine why they took her away. I tried to ask them, but they didn't speak Chinese and they didn't speak English and I didn't know any Japanese. Do you know any Japanese?'

'A little,' Anne said. 'But their superiors speak English. Don't worry, we'll find out what we can. Mrs Chan will be home for dinner.'

An hour later Mrs Forrest returned to the mission, alone.

'I think there's some sort of war going on,' she told Gilbert. 'They asked Anne a lot of questions. She said she wouldn't answer any of them until they freed Mrs Chan. They said that Mrs Chan was a Communist spy, can you believe it? Anne told them that was ridiculous, and so did I, but they weren't interested in me. They told a soldier to take me home. Anyway, there's a curfew in the town, eight o'clock. Can you imagine? Oh dear, what if Alva isn't back by then?'

'If there is war, there's nothing we can do about it,' Gilbert said. 'It's our duty not to take sides. I'm sure Anne will be fine, and Alva, too. And Mrs Chan.'

He spoke distractedly. The boy had not yet returned from Paoting with the opium he had ordered. The old sweet hunger had been sneaking up on him for three days now. It was like the longing he used to feel for Kit, only more persistent. He had often succeeded in banishing thoughts of Kit by hard work or prayer, but nothing could quell his craving for opium. It started in his middle and worked its way upward to his brain and outward into his fingers and toes. If he waited long enough, he could feel himself beginning to vibrate, like a tuning fork. That was when the draft of laudanum gave him the greatest pleasure. And today would be the day, if only Mah Foo would come back.

He tried to quit, as he promised Anne, but it was more difficult than he imagined. Then he realized, to his shame and relief, that he really didn't want to stop. He had never felt more competent, more capable, more alert. Opium had given him new wisdom and intuition, and a new understanding of the workings of God and the universe. He tried to explain these things to Anne, but she refused to listen and gave him looks of such deep reproach and sorrow that he could see pain shooting from her eyes like glowing rays. The rays stung him like a thousand acupuncture needles. Sometimes he could hear her crying in the night, on the other side of their bed. He wished then that he could drown in her tears, and he swore that he would give up the opium. He prayed for the strength to conquer the poison that had conquered him. But in the morning the hunger was keener than ever. He delayed dosing himself for as long as he could, but at the same time he knew that delay heightened ultimate delight, and he anticipated that enhanced pleasure even as he swore to himself that he would forgo it forever.

Reverend Forrest, a lean and vigorous septuagenarian, returned late that afternoon. His wife told him about the morning's excitement and the rumors of war, and he went immediately to Paoting to see what he could learn. He came back two hours later, just before curfew, with more details of the Peiping incident but no satisfactory explanation of Anne's prolonged detention at Japanese headquarters.

'It's as bad as it can be. If Chiang Kai-shek hasn't declared war yet, he soon will, everyone says so. Our Mrs Chan's son was involved in a scrape with some soldiers yesterday. Nobody hurt, but with the current climate it's not surprising that they're looking for trouble. I insisted on seeing her, but they wouldn't let me. When I asked about Anne, they said something about her being a spy, about all of us being spies for the government. It's all nonsense, of course. I think they're just trying to throw a scare into us now so that we won't trouble them later.'

'Oh, how dreadful,' his wife moaned. 'We must take down that picture of the Generalissimo near Samson's pen, Alva.'

'We'll do no such thing, Kate. We must stand above the fray. We're here to do the Lord's work, not to involve ourselves in man's folly.'

'It's ridiculous, all ridiculous,' said Gilbert irritably. The boy still hadn't returned, and Mrs Ling's prolonged labor and the impending curfew made it impossible for him to leave the compound himself. Why, why had he been so stupid and let his stock get so low? He could have sworn that he had enough to last, but when he went to his cupboard for his dose, the bottle was empty. Of course! It was Anne's doing. She and the Forrests were collaborating, plotting against him, siphoning off his supply, stealing from him. He would have to be more careful in the future and make a secret stockpile, somewhere where no one would find it.

'What can we do, Alva?'

'Nothing more tonight. They escorted me home and left two guards stationed at our gate. It's nearly eight and they won't let anyone in or out again.'

Gilbert groaned aloud. Mah Foo would not return.

'Oh, poor Gilbert,' Mrs Forrest said. 'I know you're just sick with worry. So am I. I blame myself. I shouldn't have let them send me away. But Anne was so calm, and she said it was all a stupid misunderstanding and that she'd be home in a little while, and then they made the guard take me home. But I should have insisted. I should have stayed with her.'

'Don't be a fool, Kate,' Reverend Forrest said. 'No sense in all of us wasting our time at Japanese headquarters.'

Mrs Forrest tried to persuade Gilbert to eat, but he had no appetite. She cast her husband worried looks, as she used to when their children were small and couldn't eat. After supper, which they insisted on sharing with Gilbert at his cottage, Mrs Forrest took out her knitting and her husband began to scribble the first draft of a new tract on the evils of warfare. The clicking of knitting needles and the scratch of pencil on paper were amplified in Gilbert's ears. His nerve endings were tingling, beginning to burn. He wanted to scream at them to leave him alone and take their din elsewhere.

He remembered then that he had a small stock of morphine in the dispensary. An injection of just a couple of cc's would still his craving and calm him a little. He wouldn't take much, just enough to hold him over until morning, when Mah Foo brought his opium.

He glanced slyly at the Forrests. No good. They would never let him out of their sight. They knew. Anne had told them. They were part of her scheme to destroy him.

There was a knock at the door. They all jumped. It was a little girl, telling them that Mrs Ling's baby was finally ready to come.

'I'll help, dear,' said Mrs Forrest, grateful that a distraction had presented itself. 'Alva, you stay here, just in case Anne comes back.'

'I don't think I need any help,' Gilbert said crisply. She would watch him like a hawk, he knew. She certainly wouldn't leave him alone in the dispensary long enough to prepare an injection for himself. 'I don't really anticipate any difficulty with this baby.'

'Oh, no, I want to come,' the maddening woman said. 'I think there is no more beautiful sight in the world than a baby coming into it! Anne feels the same way, I know. We've talked about it. Even though God's plan for her doesn't seem to include children of her own, she takes such pleasure in other people's. It's wonderful, and after all, you never know. I had a cousin who had her first at age forty-five. Can you imagine?'

He knew that she would chatter all the way to the infirmary, all the way through the delivery, all the way home again. And her keen old eyes would never blink, never stray from him.

'Why are you holding Mrs Chan? I insist that you release her at once.'

'She is a Communist, a spy. We want her to tell us the names of the other Communists here, and then we will free her.'

'Ridiculous. You might as well ask me for the names. I know as much as she does.'

'So, you are a Communist! You admit that you have been spying for the Communists?'

'Yes, as much as Mrs Chan has. What are you going to do about it? You can either release us both, or imprison us both. Take your choice.'

While they talked, there was a volley of gunshots. A smile creased Colonel Noguchi's smooth brown face. He led her out to the yard in front of the building the Japanese army had commandeered as headquarters in Paoting. Mrs Chan's riddled body oozed blood onto the sand.

'This is the fate of spies and traitors,' he said. 'Now will you tell us what we want to know? Who are the Communists in this area?'

Anne said, 'I only know one.'

'Ah. We make progress. Who is that?'

'Myself. Do I get a blindfold and a last cigarette?'

'This is not a matter for joking. You are a spy! You are all spies! You speak Chinese, for one thing—'

'That doesn't mean anything. You speak Japanese. I

342

was born here. You wouldn't expect me to speak Swahili.'

'Bah. You are sympathetic to the Chinese, are you not? A missionary ought to remain neutral, but you have taken sides. This quarrel is none of your affair.'

'I am sympathetic to anyone who has been exploited and oppressed. No nation has the right to oppress the peoples of another. China is—'

'There is no such thing as China!' the colonel sneered. 'China is not a nation, has never been a nation. China is a geographical designation, nothing more. A polyglot collection of races who have never been unified.'

'They soon will be unified, in their hatred of you.'

'Nationalist propaganda. Lies! We are not oppressors, we are liberators.'

'Yes, I've just seen how you liberated Mrs Chan from this vale of woe.'

On and on it went, until the colonel spat at her feet in disgust and ordered his guards to take her back to the compound.

There were two of them, simple soldiers, peasant lads from the Japanese countryside, both a head shorter than Anne. Anne felt no fear of them; they were no different from the Chinese peasants with whom she had grown up. They escorted her through the winding streets of Paoting, and through the south gate to the road that led to the mission. The full moon shone brilliantly in the clear mountain air. The stars looked like spatters of white paint on deep blue velvet.

One of the guards pushed her roughly, and she lurched into the man on her other side, who muttered angrily and shoved her back, into his companion, who laughingly returned the shove. Anne protested, in the few words of Japanese she knew. They jeered at her, and pushed her back and forth until she stumbled and fell, scraping her knees on the rocky roadbed. They hauled her to her feet and made her walk in front of them, and they kept kicking her and trying to trip her up. She spoke angrily to them. They laughed. She stopped dead and refused to go farther until they desisted. They became irritated, and one of them slapped her face. She cuffed his ear, and he howled with pain. His mate lifted his rifle butt and swung it at the back of her head.

She was aware of tiny hands tugging at her clothes. A man wriggled between her legs, and pumped madly. She thought, This is as different from love as chalk is from cheese. The first man finished and made way for the second, who slapped her face and tried to awaken her. She feigned unconsciousness and waited for the onslaught to end. Finally they took her arms and made her stand, made her walk. They half-dragged her to the gate of the mission compound. They exchanged words with the two sentries. The foolish woman fell down a ravine; we thought we'd never get her home. The gates creaked comfortingly, and they shoved her inside. She sprawled on her face in the dust. She could hear Samson snuffling a welcome from his pen, just a few feet away.

Kate Forrest exclaimed to Alva about Mrs Ling's wonderful baby boy. Alva, seated at the table, hunched his bony shoulders high around his ears. He had learned long ago that that position helped to block out at least some of his wife's noise. Gilbert paced the floor. Thankfully Anne's absence gave him an excuse for nervousness and preoccupation.

They heard a weak voice, and Anne appeared at the open door. The three stared at her. Her clothes were torn and filthy, as if she had been rolling in the dirt. There was a streak of dried blood at the corner of her mouth, and scrapes on both knees oozed blood down her shins, into her shoes.

'Hello. They finally let me go,' she said in a queer strangled voice. 'My escorts were – less than gentlemanly.' She slumped against the wall and covered her face with her hands.

'Oh, you poor child,' Mrs Forrest murmured, going to her. 'We'd better get you to bed right away.'

'Wouldn't it be funny if I got pregnant? What would happen then?' Anne dropped her hands and gave a short bark of hysterical laughter. 'I suppose the Methodists would throw me out!'

'No such thing,' Reverend Forrest said in a reassuring boom. 'Whatever is God's will, we must accept. What happened tonight is God's will.'

'Gilbert,' Anne said frantically. 'Where's Gilbert?'

He stood in the farthest corner of the room, his hands shoved deep in his pockets, a scowl on his face. So, she had come back to police him herself.

'Oh, the poor man is paralyzed with shock,' Kate Forrest said. 'Isn't it awful, dear? Come into the bedroom, Anne. I'll help you get cleaned up.'

'No, thank you, Kate,' Anne said, trying to keep the hysterical tone out of her voice. 'I think we'd better be alone. I'll be all right. Gilbert will take care of me.'

'Come along, Kate,' Alva Forrest said, taking his wife's arm. 'Anne's been through enough for one day, she doesn't need you jabbering in her ear. Gilbert will look after her now.'

When they were alone, Anne said, 'The Chinese here at the mission will be gone by tomorrow. They've been told that we're spies, and they're forbidden to consort with us. The Japanese shot Mrs Chan. I saw her. They said she was a traitor and a spy. They'll probably put her body on display in town, as a warning. It's a good way to deter resistance.'

Gilbert said nothing, but glared at her.

'You're angry with me, aren't you? It wasn't my fault. I didn't enjoy it. Oh, God.' She ran outside and Gilbert could hear her vomiting. He didn't make a move to help or comfort her.

Anne came back into the cottage. The mellow light of their lantern made her wince. Putting her fingers to her face, she discovered that her eyes were beginning to swell shut. Her glasses were lying smashed and twisted on the road between the mission and Paoting. Fortunately she had a spare pair.

'A blight on my beauty,' she said with a shaky laugh. 'Too bad. I guess I'll have to stay home from the ball.'

'The key,' Gilbert said. His mouth felt dry. 'The key to the drug cabinet in the dispensary. Where is it?'

'You know I always keep it with me,' she said. 'Oh, I see. You needed something today and you couldn't get to it, is that it? I'm sorry.'

'You took it away on purpose,' he said angrily. 'You're

trying to torture me, aren't you? And Mah Foo, you told him not to come back today, didn't you? Didn't you!'

'I don't know what you're talking about,' she said wearily. 'What's the matter with you, Gilbert?'

He came closer, into the circle of lantern light. His pupils were dilated, and he was trembling all over. She understood.

'It wasn't deliberate,' she said. 'Honestly, Gilbert. Here's the key, in my pocket.' She felt in the pocket of her dress. 'It's gone. It must have fallen out when—' She gnawed her lower lip. 'I don't have it anymore.'

'I don't believe you. You're lying to me again. Give it to me, Anne. Give it to me!'

He lunged at her and tore at her dress. Already weak and battered, she didn't try to resist him, but let him search her pockets. It was the first time he had touched her in months.

'I don't have it,' she repeated dully. 'I swear I don't have it.'

'Liar. Liar!' he growled, pawing at her.

He was sweating profusely. His hair was dripping and his clothes were drenched. He looked as though he had just stepped in out of the rain.

She said, 'You'll just have to break the lock off, won't you? Don't worry, you can tell the Forrests the Japanese did it. I won't contradict you. But I won't lie for you anymore.'

'You knew this would happen,' he panted. 'You brought me out here just to torment and shame me, to make me suffer. You stole my opium, and then you told the Forrests to spy on me. Well, didn't you?'

'No, Gilbert, I didn't.'

She felt hot and dirty and defiled, and she had a sudden beautiful vision, not of a crystal-clear mountain stream, but of the immense bathtub in Innes' penthouse. She saw Innes himself, naked and powerful, swollen with desire. What a fool she was, chaining herself to a drug addict, burying herself in the most desolate place on the continent, when she could be soaking in scented water in a green marble bathtub, and making love.

She pushed past Gilbert and went into the section of the

one-room cottage that had been curtained off as a bedroom. She stood in front of the washstand in the corner, and poured some water into the basin. She brushed the sand and bits of dry grass out of her hair and pinned it up, then stripped off all her clothes and tossed them into a corner. They were filthy and torn, not damaged beyond repair, but she would burn them anyway. No thrifty impulse would stop her. She would burn everything she wore She wished she could strip off her skin and burn it, too.

Gilbert wrenched the curtain aside and glared at her. She ignored him, and vigorously scrubbed her thighs and crotch. 'Filth,' he spat out. 'Slut.' He ran stumbling out of the cottage.

She pictured him groping in the darkness of the dispensary, trying to rip the cabinet door right off its hinges and failing, blundering around in search of a tool with which he could break open the hasp of the lock. He would succeed on the first try, because his desperation would give him strength. His fingers would close eagerly around the vial of morphine and he would grip it tightly, lest it fall out of his trembling hands. Then he would suck a couple of grains of morphine into a syringe. He might stand near the door or window where the moonlight could illuminate his work. He wouldn't take time to swab his arm with alcohol, but he would plunge the needle right through his sweaty, dusty skin into the vein just inside the elbow.

If he took too much, he would die.

'I don't care,' Anne said, brushing away the tears that stung her bruised eyes. 'I'm not going to cry for him anymore.'

'I am very sorry, gentlemen, but we cannot make ourselves responsible for every missionary in China who chooses to work outside the treaty ports where they would come under our protection. Dr and Mrs Lawrence were aware of the tense political situation in the North when they left Shanghai. I'm afraid there is nothing we can do.'

The American consul leaned back in his chair and waved a rattan fan under his chin. Some of the breeze he stirred up reached Innes and Leonard Fox, sitting opposite him on the other side of the desk.

'But the Japanese are holding them illegally,' Reverend Fox argued. 'We have no quarrel with them. They have no right to imprison American nationals.'

'A state of undeclared war exists between China and Japan at the moment, and it is your daughter's misfortune that she and her husband happen to be caught in the middle of the hostilities in Paoting.'

Innes stood up. 'I can't listen to any more of this diplomatic bullshit,' he snorted. 'You're not telling us you can't help, Hopkins, you're telling us you won't. There's a difference. You just don't want to step on any goddamned diplomatic toes.'

'We have received many requests for aid and intercession since the Marco Polo Bridge incident two weeks ago,' the consul said stiffly. 'I have given everyone the same answer: there is nothing we can do. Perhaps you can speak to the Japanese consul on their behalf?'

'We already have,' Leonard Fox said wearily. 'They say they know nothing about it. But we heard from two different sources – the Methodist bishop in Peiping and from one of Mr Innes' mining engineers who was working in that area – that the Chinese in the mission have all left and the whites are still living there, under guard. They're virtually prisoners. It's outrageous!'

'I quite agree, but unfortunately—'

'More bullshit,' said Innes. 'Let's go. I told you this was a waste of time. These embassy guys are a bunch of gutless sissies.'

'I ought to warn you, Mr Innes, that if you undertake any sort of rescue effort on your own, the government of the United States will not make itself responsible for the outcome, and if you embarrass your country in any way, you will be liable for prosecution under the statutes and laws—'

Innes said another word that made Reverend Fox wince, but which he echoed heartily inside his head.

'What next?' Leonard Fox asked as they left the consulate.

'We've tried your way to get them out, and it didn't

work. Now we'll try mine.'

'You're not really going to try and rescue them.'

'Why not?'

'Because if you fail, it might only complicate things further. The Japanese will retaliate. Anne will suffer for it.'

'The Japanese have already accused her and the others of spying for the Communists. How long do you think they're going to let spies live?'

'You can't mean they would execute them,' Reverend Fox gasped. 'But it's unthinkable!'

'You don't need a firing squad to carry out an execution. You can just seal people up inside a walled compound and let them starve to death. Relax. If I do go in, I won't be alone. And I won't fail.'

The car dropped Innes and one of his bodyguards at the Innes Building and took Reverend Fox back to the Bubbling Well Presbyterian Church. As Innes entered the office, Charlie Fong looked up from the telephone.

'One moment, please.' He covered the receiver with his hand. 'Your wife, sir. Shall I tell her—'

'I'll take it in here,' Innes said, striding toward the inner office. 'Innes,' he said into the phone.

'Hullo, it's me. Long time no see, and all that. Look, I wanted to talk to you about this settlement. It's very generous.'

'I've never known you to complain about my generosity before.'

'I'm not complaining, darling. Far from it. How about coming over for a drink and a little dinner tonight? Nothing fancy, and no crowd scene. Just the two of us, man to man, so to speak, and strictly business. What do you say? Eight o'clock all right?'

'OK. Eight o'clock.' He hung up. What in hell did she really want? Was it a trick, another attempt to kill him?

'What I really want to talk to you about is this house,' Kit said after they had exchanged cool greetings. She walked over to the bar in the corner of the drawing room and sloshed colorless liquid into a couple of stemmed glasses. 'Martini all right?' she asked, handing him one. He could tell from her speech and the stiff way she carried herself that this wasn't her first drink of the day. Her gown was dark green jersey, and it fit her like a second skin. At least she wasn't carrying any concealed weapons.

'I want to sell it,' she said, arranging herself gracefully on an overstuffed couch and motioning for him to sit. He remained standing. 'It's much too big for me, and I can use the money for other things. I was wondering if you'd take care of it for me.'

'It's your house,' Innes shrugged. 'Or at least it will be, as soon as the divorce goes through. Any lawyer will be happy to handle the sale for you. On the other hand, this isn't the best time to unload real estate. China's at war with Japan, in case you hadn't heard. Any kind of political unrest tends to depress land values.'

'How knowledgeable you sound,' she marveled.

He shrugged. 'It's part of my business.'

'I'm impressed. Then you think I'll do better if I hang onto it for a while longer?'

'Sure. Chiang will make a few concessions and things will settle down. The Japanese can't possibly hope to conquer China. It's just too big. They just want to secure Manchuria and the North. They won't go any farther.' He drained his glass. 'Appeasement is in the air.'

'Right here, as in the rest of China?' Kit asked with the crooked smile that had so excited him in the past.

'Why not? I don't hold grudges. The marriage was a bad idea from the start.'

'I suppose it was. We worked well together, though don't you think? I made very good bait, and you were a skilled angler. Too bad we didn't get along.'

'No harm done,' Innes said.

'How about regrets?'

'Aside from the most obvious one, no.' He gazed at her thoughtfully.

'You mean, you can sum them all up in "I never should have married her in the first place."'

'Something like that.'

'I don't like people to hate me, Innes,' she said, twirling her glass by the stem. 'I've done some thinking lately. I can be an awful bitch, but I'm not a bad person, not really.

I know – that business with Sanjay and Tu – but I was a little crazy for a while, I guess.' She looked up at him. Her eyes were vague, innocent, startlingly like Anne's. Of course, she was probably a little nearsighted, too, but she was too vain to wear glasses. 'I'm not trying to apologize for anything. I've never done that in my life. But I feel – I'm not ready to rush into this divorce.'

'Why not? You rushed into marriage.'

'I was younger then, and inclined to be impetuous. I've lost some of that, I think. I've become more cautious.' She extracted a cigarette from the lacquered box on the table near the couch. Innes leaned forward and clicked his lighter. 'You've been moving heaven and earth to get Anne out of Paoting, haven't you? The grapevine even says that you're going to stage some sort of spectacular rescue all by yourself.'

'Does the grapevine say just how I'm going to do it? I could use some ideas.'

'So it is true. You're in love with her, aren't you?'

'Do I have to be? Maybe I just don't like the idea of her sitting up there in Paoting with a division of Japanese soldiers stationed outside her door.'

'That's not good enough.' Kit shook her head. 'No, you must be in love with her. A couple of years ago you wouldn't have bothered doing anything like this for her. You thought she was ugly, and a little crazy, didn't you? But things have changed. Either the Mouse has subtle attractions that I'm not aware of, or she's brighter than I thought. You're quite a catch. I could use some tips – how did she do it?'

'She didn't do anything, as I recall. In fact she wasn't very happy about it. She couldn't wait to get away.'

'Oh, Anne's got lots of conscience,' Kit said. 'Too much. But I can't believe you find that radical-religious mumbo jumbo of hers interesting, and she's not much to look at. What is it that attracts you, then? I know, she must be good in bed.' Her tone was snide.

'Better than you ever were,' said Innes, walking to the bar and refilling his glass.

'Touché. Well, I was never much impressed with you, either. You added new meaning to the word "manhandle."

351

Tortured innocents like Gilbert were more to my taste then. But one's tastes can change.'

'I guess so. I hear you've been taking lessons in taste from the sailors in Blood Alley. Just be careful. You never know what you'll pick up from men like that.' He sat on a chair across from her.

Kit laughed. 'I don't sleep with them, darling. I just dance with them. It's fun. Different.'

'You always did have a peculiar idea of fun.'

'I like to pretend I'm a working girl. You used to go to the Flamingo and places like that, didn't you? In the old days. The girls are sweet. Simple and straightforward and uncomplicated.'

'Just like you,' Innes observed. 'You never cared about anybody else but yourself. That's about as simple and straightforward and uncomplicated as you can get.'

'Is that so terrible? You've never been overly concerned about anyone else but Jim Innes, have you? Everything you've ever done has been calculated to promote yourself, make yourself rich, make yourself respectable. Marrying me, buying this house, entertaining the Shanghai Four Hundred. You don't need to come on like Daddy to me, all preachy and goody-goody, because I don't believe it. I know you too well. What I really don't understand is your peculiar attraction to Anne. Maybe you feel sorry for her. She's been through a lot, but it was all her own doing, after all. Nobody told her to fall in love with a Chinese, or get knocked up, or marry a man who didn't love her. Honestly, Jim, she's not for you. She's so serious and stuffy. Don't get me wrong, I'm fond of Anne. She's my sister, after all, and I think it's too bad we're on the outs. But you'd be terribly unhappy with her, even more than you were with me.'

'I wouldn't think that was possible,' Innes said softly.

'Now, don't be a meany,' said Kit. She pushed her lower lip into a pout but her eyes were smiling. 'You're not the same as you were three years ago. Neither am I. We don't need to call it quits just because we've had a few minor misunderstandings, do we? I know, it was awful of me to chase after Gil, but he chased me, too. And then you chased after Anne so that makes us even, doesn't it?

352

Look.' She left the couch and sat on the arm of his chair. She toyed lightly with the hair at the nape of his neck. 'I'm going to do something very unusual for me, Jim. I am going to overlook the terrible way you treated me, and I'm even going to ask you to overlook my dreadful sins. I think we have a lot more in common than you realize. We're a lot alike – independent, free, bold. You liked that in me once. I like it in you.'

'So it's not appeasement, but reconciliation I smell,' Innes said. 'I wondered what you wanted from me.'

'Are you surprised?' She leaned closer to him.

'Not at all. You can't stomach the idea of losing a man to Anne. You wouldn't let Gilbert go, and now you won't let me go. But there's something you don't understand about her, Kit.'

'Please don't tell me how wonderful and witty and perfect she is,' Kit drawled. 'That's something I really couldn't stomach.'

'No, she's not perfect. She's got a lot of crack-brained ideas, and most of the time she looks like hell, and she could argue the ears off a donkey. But think about this. Three men have loved her: Chen, Gilbert, and me. And not one man has ever loved you, Kit. Because you don't know how to love in return. A man can sense that.'

'Gilbert did love me,' she said hotly. 'Lots of men have, lots of them!'

'Gilbert seems to have a knack for becoming addicted to things that are bad for him. Where are all these men who love you now? At the Flamingo?'

She struggled to control her temper and forced herself to smile. 'Of course, you're still angry with me, because I tried to assassinate you. I don't blame you. That was a terrible thing. But you said yourself just now that you didn't hold a grudge, remember?' She fingered the lapel of his jacket. He could smell her perfume. He remembered the way she applied it, spraying it on lavishly with a crystal atomiser, misting her throat and breasts and between her thighs so that her rising heat would lift the scent, mingled with her own, to a man's nostrils and make him quiver like a stallion. 'You used to think I was beautiful,' she said, stroking his cheek with her fingernail. 'Just looking at me used to excite you. Does it still?' Her hand slid down to the bulge between his legs.

'See for yourself,' he grinned.

Deftly she unfastened his belt and opened his trousers. She leaned across his body and kissed him slowly, deeply, letting her tongue flick in and out of his mouth while her practiced fingers closed around his flaccid member.

'See?' he said. 'I guess I'm immune.'

'Oh, no, no,' she whispered. Her eyes were half-closed and her breathing was quick. She seemed drunk with desire. He parted his legs and she slid to the floor between his knees and took him into her mouth. He shuddered and pushed his hands into her hair. She felt him swelling, almost bursting, and moaned happily. She worked her skirt up around her hips. Her legs were bare and she was naked below the waist. She tried to pull him down on top of her but he twisted hanks of her hair around his hands and held her head firmly, thrusting deeper and deeper into her throat until she was gagging, and squealing furiously.

He finished, and released her. She fell back on the rug, choking and swearing at him. Unconcerned, he stood up, cleaned himself off with his handkerchief, fastened his trousers, and buckled his belt.

'Thanks for the invitation to dinner. I guess I didn't realize that I was going to be the main course.'

'You son of a bitch.' She retched, swallowed the bile, and wiped her mouth with her hand.

'In answer to your question, in case it wasn't clear, I'm not in a reconciling mood right now. I don't understand how I could have ever found you beautiful, Kit. Whatever you had once, you've lost it. If I were you, I'd start worrying about the future. Old, ugly, unloved.'

'Get out of here, you—'

'Don't bother to call again if you need advice. I'm paying you plenty. You can afford a good lawyer.'

When she was alone she threw herself flat out on the rug and sobbed. The house seemed to expand around her until she felt like a speck in the universe, swallowed up by silence.

'I don't want to get old,' she whimpered. 'Oh, God, don't let me get old.'

Chapter Twelve

Innes handed Albert McClure a tumbler of scotch.

'You were in Yenan last year, weren't you, McClure? Doing interviews with the big-shot Communists?'

'That's right. Got a nice series of articles out of it. I wanted to turn them into a book, but I never got around to it. I thought as a married man I'd have more time to concentrate on my work, but I seem to have less. Worth it, though. Doesn't seem to matter to me anymore if the world never hears of Albert McClure.'

'I'm glad it's working out,' Innes said, swallowing scotch. 'You got along pretty well with the Reds, didn't you?'

'I'm predisposed to be sympathetic,' McClure confessed cheerfully. 'My old dad was a Communist before it had a name. "Albert, me lad," he'd say, "Don't let the bleedin' rich intimidate you. They wipe their arses like everybody else." I always remember those words, whenever some rich bastard tries to throw his weight around.' He raised his glass in a toast and drank.

'Why, I've never tried to intimidate you, Albert,' Innes grinned.

'You did pretty good giving me the brush-off the night Chen left town.'

'Sorry about that. Maybe I can make it up to you – with a real story. How would you like to go back to Yenan and see how Chen and Mao and the rest of the boys are getting along? Update your story a little.'

'Love to, but I don't see how I can. The Japanese control most of the surrounding territory. I flew in from Peiping last year, but that's out of the question now. I'm not up to repeating the Long March from Szechwan.'

'No, you can still fly. I have a plane you can use, and a pilot who can land on a tennis court in heavy fog.'

'Sounds good. But why do you want me to see Chen again? Or were you thinking of coming along?' McClure's eyes narrowed shrewdly. 'Maybe you need Chen's help.

That little matter of your sister-in-law?'

'You're pretty smart, Al.' Innes saluted him with his glass.

'It's my job to nose out the facts, and if I can't, then to make a good guess. I'm flattered that you want me to join you. It'll make a terrific story. But I don't know that I can be of very much help to you in persuading Chen to do anything. He makes up his own mind.'

'I can do my own dealing with Chen. I won't go up there empty-handed. No, I want you to come along as publicity man. If anything goes wrong with the rescue, you'll have to work up enough excitement in the international press so that the Japanese won't take it out on Mrs Lawrence and the others. They won't make any retaliatory moves against them if they think the world is watching. You can make it look like another Wild Man Innes stunt – that didn't come off.'

'You'll go through with this, whether I'm with you or not?'

'Yes. I'm leaving tomorrow. I'll understand if you decide not to come along. I'd hate to make your wife a widow so soon after the wedding.'

'No, she knows that the profession has its risks. Well, I'd better get my cameras ready. A few pictures won't hurt.' He set down his glass on Innes' desk and stood up. 'I won't mention when I write the story that Mrs Lawrence and Chen were good friends in Paris a long time ago. That fact might be interesting, but it isn't really relevant.'

'How in hell did you find out about that?'

'Olga told me. Swore me to secrecy, bless her,' he sighed. 'I don't suppose I can drop any hints about why Chen owes you a favor.'

'I don't suppose you can,' Innes said. 'That's the trouble with you newspapermen – throw you a bone and you want the whole hog. Thankless.'

'What you ask is impossible,' Chen said with an apologetic shrug. 'I appreciate your concern about Mrs Lawrence, Mr Innes, and I share it, but I see no reason to risk the lives of my men trying to free persons who are in no real danger.'

'I believe they are in danger, and I want Anne out of there, now. You're going to help me, Chen. For her sake, for old times, and because you owe me. I'm here to collect.'

Albert McClure stifled a groan. He would have adopted a completely different tactic with Chen: addressing him as a supplicant, adopting a conciliatory attitude, taking an oblique approach that would cause neither party to lose face. But instead Innes had pulled out his big guns, and blown off his own foot. How in hell could he have gotten along in China all these years without learning the Oriental way of doing things, Albert wondered. Laying your cards on the table just didn't work with the Chinese, who kept their best cards up their sleeves and never played their aces unless they had to. The only give-and-take Innes knew about was, 'You give, and I'll take.'

Chen's face remained impassive while he sipped his tea. The heat of summer had not yet penetrated into the cave dwellings in the hills above Yenan. His home was small, Spartan, clean, with a few touches – a cloth on the table, a vase holding a few mountain daisies – that suggested a woman's presence.

A corn-yellow pagoda bristling with upturned eaves marked their arrival in Yenan. As Innes' pilot flew up the broad valley of the Yen River, his two passengers could see that the steep brown hills on either side were honeycombed with caves. Here the Communists had retreated like bandits after Chiang Kai-shek's relentless purges and the Long March; here they had set down roots; here they had consolidated their power and begun to expand their influence.

The pilot set the plane down on an airstrip in the valley, just north of the town. A pair of guards, armed and wearing suits of blue padding, greeted them and escorted them into Yenan, which resembled a rough frontier outpost: dusty and dry, primitive and ramshackle, bustling with horse and mule traffic and stinking of manure and untanned leather. A train of camels, laden with goods and hung with bells, reminded the visitors that the Gobi Desert lay just to the north.

'Place looks busier than it did last year,' McClure

357

remarked as they passed through the marketplace.

'They're mobilizing,' Innes said. 'There have been reports of some guerrilla activity around Peiping. I'll bet Chen's boys were involved.'

'More than likely. Their strikes seem to have been pretty well planned and coordinated. Nice bit of sabotage on that Japanese arsenal – not just hit or miss. I can see Chen's fine hand at work.'

They waited for three hours to see Chen, who was reportedly conferring with local farmers about their efforts at collectivization. McClure said, 'He doesn't like uninvited guests. Wants us to cool our heels.'

Now McClure thought disgustedly that the whole trip had been a waste of time. Innes had indeed come to Yenan empty-handed, and he would go back to Shanghai the same way.

'I regret that you have come so far only to be disappointed, gentlemen,' Chen said. 'I trust you will accept our hospitality this evening.'

Ignoring the invitation to depart, Innes said, 'Let's talk about this business theoretically for a minute. Paoting's nicely situated strategically. That's why the Japanese are there. They also like the ore they're taking out of the ground. Paoting iron will make plenty of bullets for them to pump into Chinese bodies. It's on high ground, exposed on four sides, easy to defend, easy to hold.'

'And thereby impossible to take,' Chen pointed out. 'Speaking theoretically, if anyone were thinking about slipping in unnoticed, liberating the captives, and slipping out again, I would advise them to give their plan a little more thought. Not even Chiang Kai-shek could supply enough men to storm the area. There is a full division of soldiers garrisoned in the town, and they are all better armed than any comparable Chinese division could hope to be.'

'I wonder just how well they are armed?' Innes said thoughtfully. 'I wonder if they've placed any antiaircraft guns in there yet.'

'I doubt it very much. The possibility of attack by air is remote, considering the impoverished condition of Chiang Kai-shek's air force. Pilots strafing the mines would

358

probably hit the mission, which lies only a thousand feet from the opening of the main shaft.'

Albert McClure thought, So the bastard's looked at the maps and studied the situation. He's interested.

He said casually, 'I don't know, Jim. I don't think we could persuade Chiang to risk his planes. They're his pride and joy. And he doesn't have men who can do the kind of daredevil flying you would need.'

'Well, Albert, I happen to have acquired a couple of planes recently that could easily be fitted with aerial guns. And I have some very decent pilots in my employ, too. Take Tiger Johnson, who flew us in here, for example. He can fly a plane up Nanking Road, ten feet from the ground, without the wing-tips touching a building on either side.'

'Would he be willing?'

'Sure, he's a romantic like me. We romantics can't resist the call of a lady in distress.'

'I can, if rescuing her means risking my own neck. What does that make me?'

'A realist. The realist always looks at the cost, the consequences. He wants to be assured of success before he begins. His head rules his heart, and if you want him to go along with you, you have to appeal to his reason.' Innes studiously avoided looking at Chen. 'But if you can get a realist and a romantic to work together, you'll find that they make a pretty good team.'

'All right, Jim,' Albert said, frowning, 'suppose you do get Johnson to fly in there and strafe the mines. What then?'

'We'll need three planes in all; one to buzz the town, one the mines, and the third the mission. The purpose of the planes will be to keep the ground areas covered long enough for a small party to move into the mission and take out the prisoners. I'll plant some undercover men in Paoting ahead of time, and coordinate the air strikes with bombings on the ground. The Japanese will be in a tailspin.'

'This ought to take some of the wind out of their sails,' McClure said. 'They're feeling pretty cocky now, and you can hardly blame them. They've met with hardly any resistance here, and once China caves in, they can dominate the whole of Asia. No one can stop them. Only guerrilla action can hurt them, slow them down a little until Chiang gets his forces beefed up.'

Innes nodded. 'It seems to me that Paoting would make a hell of a base for guerrilla activity. It's only about fifty miles away from the Peiping-Tientsin railroad, close to the coast yet protected by mountains. I'll offer my own planes to Chiang, if he'll give me the men I need. I could hire my own mercenaries, but I'd have to pull them out again after the operation. There's no point in Innes & Company securing Paoting; it won't do us any good. It would be nice to leave the place in Chinese hands. If not, the Japanese will just retake it.'

They conversed in relaxed fashion, as though Chen weren't even there. Chen hid a smile behind his teacup and listened politely.

'And the rescue itself, Jim?' McClure asked. 'How would you do that? Take them out by air?'

'Can't. There's no place to land a plane anywhere near the mission.' Innes poked a cigarette into his mouth and offered the pack to Chen and McClure. 'I'll spearhead this part of the operation myself. I'll move in with a small party of men right after the plane has pinned down the area. We'll start the air strikes at sunset so that we can get the captives out under cover of darkness. We'll take them through the mountains and down to the edge of the marshland near Lake Kaoyang, where a seaplane will be waiting. I'll need to take someone with me who knows the terrain as well as he knows his own face. We're not going to have any time for map-reading, and those hills are too dangerous to negotiate blind. You know anybody from Paoting, Albert?' He exhaled a billow of smoke.

'I'm sorry to say I don't, Jim.' Albert shook his head sadly.

'I'm sure Chiang can find me a man who knows that area. I think I can persuade him to supply some ground troops, too. They wouldn't be used to guerrilla-type operations and that could be a handicap, but we don't have any other choice. I'll sweeten the proposition a little by offering Chiang something extra, in addition to Paoting itself. I've been in touch with a salesman for a German arms manufacturer, and he's given me a good price on an assortment of grenades, small explosives, repeating rifles, and machine guns. I'll fly them in by the same plane that takes us out of Kaoyang. They'll be there, ready to be picked up when the operation is complete, by whoever helps it succeed. I'm sure Chiang will be happy to have them.'

'Oh, sure he will.' McClure hesitated. 'I have nothing against our revered leader, Jim, him being a devout Methodist and all, but the integrity of some of his associates bothers me a bit. I'd be worried about how much of that fancy weaponry would find its way to the front. I'd hate to think of it falling into the hands of the Japanese, or being used against our friends here in Yenan. That would be a shame.'

'Ah, it certainly would, Al,' Innes said, taking a final pull at his cigarette and stubbing it out in his saucer. 'But I have no choice. If Chiang wants Paoting and those arms, he'll go along with me. I risk the planes, and my own skin, he risks a few men. Sounds fair enough, don't you think?'

'A most equitable arrangement,' Chen said smoothly. 'I am surprised you haven't approached him with the plan. Or perhaps you already have, Jim, with your estimable vaudeville partner Al here to help you, of course.'

'We're just trying our act out on you, Chen,' Innes said. 'I think it sounds pretty good. I haven't approached Chiang with it yet, but I will. I just thought I'd let you hear it first, for old times' sake.'

'It is a rather interesting coincidence,' Chen studied the cigarette burning between two slender fingers, 'but one of the Party's most loyal and trusted men is from a little village just north of Paoting. He is quite familiar with the area. I have heard him say he could negotiate the territory with his eyes blindfolded.'

'Just what we're looking for,' Innes said. McClure nodded. 'I don't suppose you'd be willing to lend him to us? I'm sure he'd fit right in with Chiang's band of cutthroats.'

'I doubt it. He is a man of breeding, and taste, and the highest moral principles.'

'Definitely not Chiang's sort,' McClure said. 'Still, do you think we could talk to him?'

'You are talking to him,' Chen said blandly.

The two visitors expressed amazement. McClure said, 'It's too bad you're not interested in this scheme, Chen. I imagine you even have some Red fifth columnists in Paoting, ready to respond to a snap of your fingers.'

'Many people throughout China sympathize with our cause,' Chen said.

'Sure they do, and I'm one of them. It would make a great story: Reds Rescue Missionaries. You'd make a jackass out of Chiang, who's always been thick with the Christians in China but who hasn't lifted a finger to help the Methodists at Paoting. He has a lot of powerful God-fearing friends abroad. They might rethink their allegiance after this, if we play it up right in the papers. Show them you guys aren't the two-headed monsters he's been saying you are.'

'Ah, the power of the press,' Chen said. 'So important in these swiftly moving times.'

Albert glanced at Innes. It was up to him now, to give Chen a chance to reverse his position and save face gracefully.

'A man rarely gets the opportunity in life to pay his hometown back for what it's given him,' Innes said. 'His province, his neighbors, the people he grew up with – all moaning under the heel of the invader. I can think of no more honorable battle than a fight to free a man's home. If you decide to take Paoting, I hope you'll let me fight with you, Comrade Chen Ping-ho.'

Albert let out his breath. Conciliatory, face-saving. He couldn't have put it better himself.

'It would be an honor to accept your assistance,' said Chen with a paternal smile. He stood up. 'It is late, gentlemen. You are exhausted from your journey. We can discuss the details of the operation further in the morning.' A young woman appeared at the door. 'Comrade Ling will take you to your quarters. I trust you will be comfortable.'

'Well done, old boy,' Albert said when they were outside.

362

The moon hung low over the jagged horizon. Venus gleamed in the silver-veined sky like a bit of Shanghai neon. 'I must say, you had me worried at the beginning. Charging right in like the proverbial bull. I thought you'd lost it. But at the end – a master stroke. I was proud of you. I fancy I played my own part well.' Albert preened a little.

'You were a big help,' Innes said. 'It couldn't have gone better. We had one good break: I didn't know Chen came from Paoting.'

'He doesn't.' Albert laughed. 'He's Manchurian, from Fuhsien on the Liaotung peninsula. Which leads me to ask, just who was manipulating whom?'

'Jesus. This is the guy who can negotiate those mountains blindfolded? I'm depending on him to get us all out of there alive.'

'Oh, I'm sure our friend has something in mind. I hate to say this, Jim, but this is his show now.'

One of us is going to die today, Anne thought coldly, watching Gilbert thrashing on the soiled bed. Either he will or I will. I'll kill him, because if I don't, I'll go mad and kill myself. I just can't take any more.

Gilbert's morphine supply, carefully hidden from the Japanese, had run dry two days before. He scoured the cottage and the dispensary and even the chapel, searching for more. When he didn't find any, he railed at Anne and accused her of stealing from him. He talked all night long. He soaked his clothes and his bed with sweat and urine. Now he declared that he was freezing to death. He lay shuddering under their only blanket while she panted in the ninety-degree heat.

'I know you want me to die,' he said through chattering teeth. 'You don't care what happens to me. You brought me here to die, because you want to be rid of me. I don't blame you. I'm no good, no good to anyone anymore. I'm so cold, so cold. But you don't care. It makes you happy to see me suffer like this, doesn't it? Don't bother to deny it. You despise me. You wish you were back in Shanghai, with your lover, that animal, Innes. You won't even stay around long enough to bury me, will you? You'll go running back to him. You're just like your sister. The two of you. You're beasts. Monsters. You feed on the flesh of men. You destroy them and then you feed on their flesh. You and your sister and your mother, all sluts, whores. You should be rooted out, exterminated, excommunicated. Innes. That monster Innes. This is his fault. He's waiting outside the gate, waiting for me to die.'

If only he were. If only you would.

Her thoughts sickened her, and she shook her head violently, trying to expel them.

'Cold,' he shivered. 'I feel as cold as death.'

'Here, Gilbert, this will warm you.' She held a cup of steaming tea to his lips and tried to coax him to drink. He lashed out at her and his fist struck the cup. It shattered against the wall and tea sprinkled the pounded dirt floor.

She bit back an angry outburst and passed through the curtain to the other half of the room. She sat at the table and dropped her head onto her folded arms. No tears came. She was all cried out. And she felt tired. She hadn't felt so tired in her life.

Reverend Forrest and Kate burst into the cottage. Anne didn't bother to lift her head; she had stopped pretending long ago that Gilbert was just high-strung and nervous.

Instead of inquiring solicitously about Gilbert, as they usually did, the Forrests pulled up stools and sat at the table Anne. sensed that both were humming with excitement.

'Look at this, Anne,' Alva Forrest said, pushing a piece of creased rice paper under her crossed arms. 'I found it in front of the chapel this morning, wrapped around a stone. Someone threw it over the wall in the night.'

'Isn't it exciting, dear?'

Anne read: 'X 14 13.' She scowled. 'I'm sorry, but I don't understand what it means.'

'But it's obvious,' Kate chirped. 'Alva opened his Bible right up, and turned to Exodus, chapter 14, verse 13. Read it to Anne, Alva. I want her to hear the way you read it.'

'I'll read it, woman, if you'll give me a chance.' He cleared his throat and put on his glasses and read in a stentorian bellow, '"And Moses said unto the people, Fear ye not, stand still, and see the salvation of the Lord, which he will shew to you to day: for the Egyptians whom ye have seen to day, ye shall see them again no more for ever."' He closed the book with a pleased snap.

'Don't you see, Anne, someone is coming to rescue us! Deliverance is at hand!'

'No, it's not.' Anne rubbed her eyes. 'It's some kind of joke, just a mission-trained Japanese boy playing a nasty trick on us.'

Kate Forrest was undaunted. 'How can you say that, dear? I don't believe that any Christian boy would fight for them. It was one of our people, don't you see? They're going to storm the walls today and set us free. This message came because they want us to be ready. I don't know what to take – not very much, I'm sure. They'll probably put us in hiding somewhere, like the early Christians. A Bible, of course. And pencil and paper, so that I can write to the children.'

'I don't expect anything to happen until evening,' Alva said. 'There are soldiers back and forth past here all day, watching us and the mines. After the work stops, that's when they'll come.'

'We must be alert and vigilant,' Kate breathed. 'I just hope there won't be any violence or killing. Wouldn't that be horrid, to kill people in the name of the Lord?'

'It's been done before,' Anne remarked. 'Maybe they'll send in a hot-air balloon and float us out. That would be nice. Then Gilbert could go right up into those cloud corridors he's always talking about.'

'You're exhausted, dear,' said Kate. 'You should try and get some rest today. You'll need all your strength.'

'I just don't believe it,' she said numbly. 'I can't. I was all set to —' She stopped herself from saying, 'To die. To kill.' They wouldn't understand.

Gilbert began to wail piteously.

'I heated some bricks in the fire,' Anne said, getting up. 'I'll go get them, if you'll stay with him for a minute. I don't want to leave him alone.'

'I'll tell him about the message,' Alva said, 'and I'll read some other verses to him. I've noticed that the Bible calms

365

him.' He ducked under the curtain. His pipe-organ tones drowned out Gilbert's desperate bleating. Reverend Forrest's Bible verses really did calm Gilbert, because they gave him something to listen to besides his throbbing pain and the chattering of his own teeth.

'Maybe I should launder a few things,' Kate said. 'I guess we should take that little bit of rice that's left. I'm sure none of the people around here have been getting enough to eat. I'm so glad we managed to hide even that much from the soldiers, or we would have starved.'

'We will starve, if your messengers from heaven don't turn up,' Anne said. 'Really, Kate, we shouldn't get our hopes up too far.'

Nevertheless her hopes did rise as she went about her accustomed chores: laundering, weeding the little patch of garden that hadn't been obliterated by soldiers pursuing Samson and the hens. The loss of his hog nearly broke Alva's heart. The pig loved to listen to Bible verses, rehearsals of his sermons, and readings of his tracts. He always grunted appreciatively, and Alva said he was the best audience a preacher ever had.

Anne realized that they all might be killed in an escape attempt, but she decided that she preferred instant death to slow starvation. Their supply of food was dangerously low, and without fuel and bedding they couldn't hope to survive the winter – assuming the Japanese permitted them to live that long. Japanese soldiers had ransacked the mission and carried away food, books, furniture, clothes. All they possessed were the few things they managed to hide.

She had thought about trying to escape, but she couldn't bring herself to abandon Gilbert. Morphine was a crueler mistress than any woman, as he was only now beginning to discover. His feelings of omnipotence were illusory; he didn't comprehend the extent of his own weakness and helplessness. She couldn't leave the Forrests. They were spry and healthy enough now, but they would soon begin to feel the effects of hunger.

In the middle of the morning Gilbert fell into an exhausted sleep. Anne washed her hair and took a hot bath. It might be her last for many weeks, or forever. She couldn't decide if she was grateful to the message-sender, or if she hated him. If he had tricked them, they would all be cruelly disappointed. Even Gilbert, when the idea of freedom penetrated through the haze of pain and confusion in his brain, had expressed excitement. He relished the idea of returning to the real world, where poppy fields stretched as far as the eye could see, and opium-eaters lived beautiful, peaceful lives, free from worry and pain.

But even so, even if the promise of freedom was a lie, the message-sender had given her a rare day. She felt as if she had something to live for. She hadn't felt that way in a long time. For that, at least, he deserved thanks.

They were all too excited to eat. Gilbert woke from his sleep drenched in sweat and burning with a high fever. Alva Forrest, as gentle as a nurse, helped her to bathe and dress him. She had noticed lately how much the poverty of their diet had weakened her. Some nights she lay awake, thinking of heaps of fresh fruit and caldrons of rich bubbling broth.

'We must be ready when the Lord calls us, Gilbert,' the old preacher said sternly. 'We must wash ourselves, and put on clean garments, and wait for His call.'

They gathered in the Lawrence cottage. The long hot hours after noon passed slowly. Alva read aloud from Exodus, interspersing the verses with assertions that he really didn't expect their liberators to come until evening. Kate knitted, and exclaimed over the number of stitches she dropped in her excitement. Gilbert tossed and moaned. Anne pressed cool damp cloths against his forehead. There was no medicine available, not even aspirin. The Japanese had emptied the dispensary on the first day.

'The Lord will swallow up – the veil that shrouds the peoples – swallow up death – forever,' Gilbert mumbled. 'Should I have gone with them? Didn't I do the right thing? Humble myself, had to humble myself. I was right, wasn't I?'

He became distraught, and she tried to reassure him that he had acted wisely, in accordance with his God's wishes. She didn't sleep; she couldn't.

After a while the sun pulled back enough so that the

mission buildings and the walls that surrounded them cast some welcome shade on the treeless yard. Anne thought of other parts of China, lush with bougainvillea and bamboo, studded with willow trees. Trees didn't have a chance to grow in Paoting.

Gilbert fell into a restless sleep. The other three sat outdoors in the shade of the cottage and watched a flock of starlings scratching in the dusty garden. Ordinarily Alva would have chased them away, or tried to trap a couple for food, but this afternoon he left them alone.

They could hear the shuffling feet and bored talk of the pair of guards outside the solid wooden gate of the mission. Every so often, at intervals too irregular to measure, one of the two guards would circle the compound, pausing to urinate against the wall or light a cigarette, and continue on. Just after one of them had completed his circumnavigation, Anne heard a noise, like a snake slithering through dry grass, on the other side of the wall from where they sat. She jostled Alva's arm. He nodded. He, too, had heard the sound. Kate's head drooped over her knitting.

'I could have sworn by my arthritis that it was going to rain today,' Alva said in a voice loud enough to distract the guards and drown out the noise of the skulker outside the wall.

'Poor Alva,' Anne said. 'You're body's getting undependable in its old age.'

Kate awoke with a start. 'What was that? Why, Alva's not old, dear. He's as young as he ever was.'

Suddenly something heavy sailed in an arc over the wall and landed in the dust at their feet. Seeing Kate about to squeal, Anne clapped her hand over the old woman's mouth while Alva sneezed noisily.

'Hay fever,' he bellowed. 'Hay fever. Always get it this time of year. Never fails.'

Anne picked up the missile, a heavy object wrapped in cloth. 'Perhaps we should go inside, if something's bothering you out here,' she said casually. 'I'll make some tea.'

'That sounds nice,' Kate said, recovering her composure. 'I'm even feeling a bit chilly.'

Alva sighed. Kate always overacted.

Inside the cottage, Anne lay the object on the table and unwrapped it. It was a handgun, a revolver nearly as long as her forearm, black and lethal-looking. She gazed at it helplessly.

'What are we supposed to do with this, slaughter the guards and just walk out of here?'

'I'm sure I don't know,' Reverend Forrest said. 'Is there any message enclosed?' They shook out the cloth wrapping and peered cautiously down the barrel of the gun. 'Hmmmph. I know a little bit about rifles – did some rabbit-shooting as a boy – but nothing about revolvers. It's loaded, see the chambers here? I guess all you have to do is point it and pull the trigger.'

'Oh, Alva,' his wife gasped, 'you aren't going to use it! Someone might get hurt! Surely captivity here is uncomfortable, but the Japanese are the Lord's children, too.'

'I know, I know. No, I don't expect I'll try to use it. We will put our trust in the Lord. If it is in His plan to deliver us safely, then we shall be delivered.'

The shadows lengthened. Somewhere outside the walls a lark sang to the setting sun. Reverend Forrest and his Kate sat side by side, hands joined, heads bowed in prayer. Anne stood at the open door and waited.

A heart-stopping scream split the silence. 'Oh, God, it's eating me, it's devouring me, the serpent, the serpent of Satan!'

Gilbert wrestled with his blanket, which had become coiled around him while he slept. He thrashed desperately, trying to free himself. As Anne bent over him, one of his flailing arms caught her on the tip of the chin and sent her sprawling backward, into the washstand. The bowl and pitcher slid to the floor and smashed into each other. Kate ran to help her up.

Anne looked down at the broken pottery. 'If they hadn't fallen together, they wouldn't have broken,' she said. 'The floor's not that hard. But two brittle objects crashing together – Gilbert and me —' Madness and rage welled up inside her. She felt herself sliding away from herself, even as Gilbert was sliding, into the safe refuge of screams that would drown out every other terror.

Kate Forrest said sharply, 'It's all right, Anne. It's not important.' She put her arms around Anne and led her away from the scene. 'Pick up those pieces, will you, Alva?' she said briskly. 'And for heaven's sake, do something about Gilbert. He's beginning to get on my nerves.'

Anne felt the scream rising again, or maybe it was just a shout of laughter.

Just then they heard an unfamiliar rumble, and a crackling noise like lightning splintering a tree.

The women lifted their heads. 'Thunder,' said Kate.

'No,' said Anne, remembering the Japanese bombardment of Shanghai in 1932. 'Guns. And bombs. I think they're bombing the mines.'

Kate ran outside to look. Reverend Forrest, supporting Gilbert, came out of the bedroom.

'The time has come,' the old man said solemnly.

He and Gilbert proceded out of the house. Anne's eyes lit on the gun in the middle of the table. She picked it up and followed the others out into the yard.

The firing seemed to be coming nearer. They heard the buzz of an engine overhead and looked up. A small plane swooped low over the mission. Incredulous, they saw a blue star painted on the underside of the wings.

'It's the Marines,' cried Alva joyously. 'Thank God, they've sent in the Marines!'

The wooden gates burst open. Not American Marines, but the two Japanese guards entered, their guns pointed at the little knot of people standing in the center of the mission yard.

They've been ordered to kill us if there's any trouble, Anne thought. Calmly she lifted the revolver, aimed it, as Alva had said one must do, and pulled the trigger. One guard clutched his stomach and pitched forward on his face. She fired again, and the second man dropped. No more followed them inside. She lowered her arm, and the heavy gun slipped out of her fingers. Alva gave her an amazed look. Kate's mouth worked but no sound came out.

'They were going to kill us,' Anne said. 'I had to do it.'

The plane buzzed the mission again. A voice outside the

370

walls called in English, 'Don't shoot, we're coming in.'
Daylight was fading fast, as it does in the mountains.
Armed men surged through the open gate. The dazed
prisoners moved toward them uncertainly, Anne and the
old minister supporting a sagging Gilbert between them.

'The guards, are they dead?' someone shouted in
Chinese. The plane made another pass, and fired at a
party of soldiers running up the hill from the mines.

'Yes,' Anne replied. 'I shot them.' Two of Chen's men
relieved her and Alva of their burden. They took hold of
Gilbert's arms and dragged him through the gate. For the
first time in a month, Anne and the others found
themselves outside the mission walls. They moved swiftly
down the slope, away from Paoting, shrouded in smoke,
away from the mines.

She heard her name spoken in a voice she knew as well
as her own. She stood stock-still and looked around
frantically. 'Jamie!' she called. 'Jamie!'

Then Innes was beside her, asking if she was all right. A
machine gun nestled in the crook of his arm. His face was
streaked with dirt, and his clothes were stained and torn.
But his eyes were bright with excitement.

'What are you doing here?' she demanded stupidly.

He grinned at her in the thickening darkness. 'What
does it look like I'm doing? Come on, we've got to hurry.
The pride of the Paoting garrison will be here any minute.'

He gave her a push in the direction of the rest of the
party, and he ran off to take up a position on a high rock
near the Paoting Road where he could watch for troops
coming down from the town. There weren't any yet;
bombs exploding inside Japanese headquarters had
thrown the military into a panic, and Communist snipers
stationed on the city walls picked off enemy soldiers who
tried to flee through the gates.

Gilbert stumbled often and finally gave up trying to lift
his feet at all. He kept up a mournful obbligato of moans,
and rolled his head like a dizzy drunken man.

'Is he sick?' a man asked in Chinese. Anne saw to her
astonishment that it was Chen.

'You here, too!' she exclaimed. 'Yes, he has the opium
sickness. He has not had a dream for two days.'

'Then he is seeing fire and dragons,' Chen said. 'I am sorry.'

'I guess I'll wait for my interview until later,' another vaguely familiar voice said. Anne barely recognized the man trotting along behind Chen. His face was smeared with mud and he was wearing a Basque beret pulled down over one ear. A rifle hung over one shoulder and a camera over the other. 'Albert McClure, at your service, remember?'

She shook her head dazedly. 'I wouldn't be surprised to see my own father here at this point.'

There was a rattle of gunfire behind them. 'Quickly,' Chen said.

They plunged down an arroyo on the southeast slope of the mountain. Innes stood guard until they were well under way. A small contingent of Japanese soldiers running up from the mines caught the fire from his machine gun and from Tiger Johnson and his gunner, making their last pass overhead. Innes looked around, saw no evidence that they were being pursued, and followed the rest of the party down the mountain.

They passed a wayside shrine, struggled through thick patches of scrub, and slithered over sharp granite stones that cut through the thin soles of their shoes. Anne was grateful for the protection of her loose trousers and long-sleeved cotton jacket. Chen walked at the head of their party with their guide, a local party member. Innes brought up the rear. Altogether they were ten – five rescuers, four missionaries, and one reporter.

Soon the trail became almost invisible, and they had to pick their way with the help of flashlights masked with squares of blue cloth. The two men who carried Gilbert – one lugging his legs, the other his arms – had trouble negotiating the narrowing passes between outcroppings of rock. Their progress slowed to a crawl.

'Jesus,' Innes said, 'we're never going to meet that plane at this rate. Hold it.'

He ordered the men to put Gilbert down, then he slung the limp body over his shoulders in a fireman's carry.

'Let's go.'

'The serpent – eating my entrails. The serpent has

wings, horns, claws,' Gilbert mumbled as he bumped along on Innes' back.

A plane passed low overhead. One of theirs? It circled and came lower.

'Douse the lights and get down!' Innes shouted. Chen repeated the command in Chinese. A flurry of bullets cut into a rock high over their heads, spraying them with chips of flint. 'They've spotted us. No more lights. Get a move on!'

Fear quickened their pace. They half-tumbled down the steepest parts of the mountain. Anne stumbled frequently and fell flat out once, to be hauled to her feet by Albert McClure. She put her glasses in her pocket; she couldn't see anyway, and she didn't want to lose them. The Forrests helped each other, and one of Chen's men led them over the roughest parts, murmuring instructions and encouragement in Chinese. Chen and their guide moved swiftly over the track, hardly slowing as they forded streams and rounded hairpin turns under rocky crags. Anne pictured them moving like tiny dots over a vast picturesque Chinese landscape: winding around gnarled pine trees, skimming the edges of sheer precipices that fell away into abysses so deep that one could see only a cushion of mist at the bottom.

Gilbert must have fainted, because he remained fairly quiet for the last half of the journey, which was nearly three hours. Anne could hear Innes puffing behind her. She herself could feel the searing pains in his shoulders and back and legs. Why was he doing this? For the hell of it, the sheer love of adventure? Or for her, because he loved her?

Bruised, exhausted, their muscles torn and tendons strained, they hardly noticed that their descent was becoming more gradual. The enemy plane did not return, and a coy moon, gliding in and out of clouds, helped to light their way. At her side Albert McClure said, 'Look.' The pale white light glinted on the silver wings of a seaplane, waiting in a rice paddy half a mile away.

They came to a halt. Reverend and Mrs Forrest collapsed on the ground, their arms around each other. Albert McClure took a long pull from the flask he carried.

Alva Forrest gave him an envious look. Innes let Gilbert slide gently to the ground. Anne knelt by her husband's side. His skin felt clammy and cold to the touch. He muttered incoherently.

Innes turned to Chen. 'Do you want to inspect the weapons before we go? They're in that stand of bamboo.'

'It won't be necessary. Permit me to congratulate you on the success of the mission.'

'Couldn't have done it without you and your people. Thanks.' Innes proffered a pack of cigarettes. Chen shook his head.

'No thanks are necessary. We Chinese like to pay our debts.' Chen gave him a cool nod, and went over to Anne. 'Our meetings seem to have taken on a rather dramatic quality lately,' he said in an amused tone. 'It must be your doing. You always had a love for the dramatic.'

'Oh, certainly, as a spectator.' She stood up. 'But participating in history is too exciting for me. I'll leave that to people like you and Innes.'

'The last time we parted, I said that we would not meet again. I shall not display my lack of prophetic skills a second time. I can only hope that the circumstances will be less precarious, and that we will have a chance to talk at length, as old friends.'

'Yes, I'd like that,' Anne said. She hesitated, then offered her hand. He held it firmly. 'Please take care of yourself. You are still at war.'

'So are you. You killed two of the enemy tonight. You are brave, as well as beautiful.'

Anne felt a flush rising to her cheeks.

'We'd better get moving,' Innes said gruffly.

A passing cloud cloaked them in darkness for a moment. Anne felt Chen's lips brush her own. When the moon emerged again, he and his men were gone.

Innes shouldered his burden again. 'This way.' He led them along the high path between the flooded fields, which would soon be drained for the rice harvest. They had to wade through hip-deep water to reach the seaplane. The pilot helped them up onto the wing and ushered them inside. The lights on the instrument panel provided the only illumination. The cabin was small, hardly large enough to accommodate six passengers, and bare except for a few blankets and parcels of food. Albert McClure passed around his flask of whiskey. Innes drank deeply. Alva Forrest held the flask for a long moment in a trembling hand. Then he passed it on.

Anne held Gilbert in her arms to cushion him during take-off.

'Think he'll be all right?' McClure asked.

'If he wants to be.'

There was no more chance for talk. The engines thundered and the plane began to glide over the shallow water. In the darkness of the cabin Anne couldn't see Innes, sitting in the co-pilot's seat, but she could feel the dynamic force of his will, lifting the plane into the air, carrying them away from the menace, taking them back to Shanghai and safety. Gilbert stirred and cried out once, loudly, as they left the ground. She spoke softly to reassure him, even though she knew he couldn't hear her. Perhaps she was reassuring herself.

They set down about three hours later on the Yellow River just above Tsinan, the capital of Shantung Province, well away from Japanese-held territories. The seaplane taxied up to a pier and the weary passengers disembarked. Looking up the slope they could see the white walls and tiled roofs of a rambling Chinese dwelling. A man in summer whites hurried down to the pier to greet them.

'Jim, thank God! I never thought you'd make it.'

Innes introduced their host, Sam Albright of Asiatic Petroleum. 'We'll spend the rest of the night here, and take another plane from Tsinan to Shanghai in the morning,' Innes told them. 'Nice of you to come down from your mountain retreat for the occasion, Sam. How are Mabel and the girls?'

Servants brought a litter for Gilbert, who had begun to shiver violently.

'I can feel the pain everywhere,' he moaned. 'In my toenails and my fingers. Even in my hair.'

'He'll be screaming bloody murder in a few more minutes,' Albert McClure remarked.

'I should have had a doctor here,' Sam Albright said. 'What's the trouble, malaria?'

'No, morphine addiction,' Anne said tonelessly. 'A doctor couldn't do anything for him except give him morphine or opium, and I don't want him to have it. The cure is started, and he might as well finish it. Just give us a room far away from everybody else, where he won't bother anyone.'

Anne tried to calm Gilbert and get him settled in bed, but he couldn't rest, couldn't even lie down. He complained that his skin hurt wherever it came into contact with something. He jumped at shadows and cringed at the slightest noise. He looked at his hands and screamed because the flesh was being eaten away, and he could see his own bones, stark and white and covered with sheer lace made of nerves and veins. Finally, in a desperate attempt to end his pain, he began to batter the wall with his head. Anne shouted at him to stop, and two of Sam Albright's servants rushed in and helped her restrain him. Albert McClure came into the room.

'Don't mean to barge in, but it sounds like you could use some help. You know, we ought to tie him up before he hurts himself.'

'He'll hate that,' Anne said as Gilbert unleashed a cascade of chilling screams. He thrashed violently, and nearly broke away from the four people who were trying to subdue him.

'He'll hate it even more if he bashes his brains out,' McClure said. He sent one of the servants to fetch a length of cord. He and Anne wrapped Gilbert's wrists and ankles with bandages so that he wouldn't chafe his skin, then they lashed him to the bedposts. He roared angrily, swore at them, threatened them. He called Anne every vile name he could think of, and accused her of adultery with McClure, Innes, and even Alva Forrest.

'You've probably had a bellyful of this,' McClure said sympathetically. 'You ought to get some sleep. Albright has a typewriter I can use, so I'm all set. I think I'll move it in here. I'm going to have to work through the night anyway, to have this story ready by the time we hit Shanghai. I'll keep an eye on him while I work and you can take a rest someplace else.'

He asked a servant to bring the typewriter and a sheaf

of paper.

'That's silly,' Anne said. 'You can't possibly work with this din going on.'

'You're a goddamned whore, Anne,' Gilbert screamed. 'You're the biggest bloody bitch that ever walked this earth.'

'Good thing Innes isn't here,' Albert said. 'He'd bloody the poor bastard's nose for him, sick or not. He's crazy about you. He'd have to be, to do what he did tonight. What a story! Now you listen to me. Newspapermen are used to working under adverse conditions. I've scribbled dispatches in the trenches, with bullets whistling over my head and men dying just a few feet away from me. This is nothing.'

'I don't believe you, but I'm tempted to accept your offer anyway,' Anne said.

'Please help me, God,' Gilbert wailed. 'Oh, God, help me, help me!'

'Albright says that there was a shooting incident in Shanghai a couple of days ago,' McClure told her. 'Two Japanese sailors were killed. The Japanese are demanding retribution. You know what that means: a replay of '32.'

'So there will be a war in Shanghai, too.' Anne said sadly.

'Looks like it. This morning thirty Japanese ships came up the Yangtze. To protect Japanese nationals, the story goes.' He snorted. 'Same old excuse.'

'The world's gone mad, hasn't it?' Anne shook her head.

'No more than usual,' McClure said cheerfully. 'By the way, Olga said to give you her best. We're married now.'

'I'm glad,' Anne said. 'She's a good person. We've had some misunderstandings in the past —'

'I know. She told me,' Albert McClure grinned. 'She's practically one of the Fox family.'

'It's unbelievably sordid, isn't it? Nothing you'd care to write about. Neither is this.' She looked back at the writhing, tormented figure on the bed. 'You won't – you wouldn't —'

'No, I won't. There's nothing newsworthy about a man making a fool of himself like this. I know, because I've been there myself. I don't mind staying with him, though. An occasional night in another man's hell is a good thing. Reminds you to count your blessings.'

'Thank you,' Anne said simply. She went out.

Gilbert strained at his lashings and pleaded with McClure to release him. Albert looked down at him.

'You poor bastard,' he said pityingly. 'I warned you, that first day, remember? But you wouldn't listen. Thought you knew it all.'

Unlike Mediterranean dwellings, which are constructed around a large central courtyard, Chinese residences are comprised of several smaller structures linked together by covered walkways and separated by numerous small gardens. A high sturdy wall surrounds it all, and there are no windows to the outside.

Anne had often thought of China as a series of concentric circles: a walled house within a walled compound within a walled city within a walled country. Within the walled houses lived people whose spirits were walled up by centuries of tradition and prescribed patterns of behavior. Only the most violent spiritual convulsion, like revolution, could break down those walls, which were stronger than any made of brick and mortar.

The moon shimmered on the surface of a shallow fishpond near the main entrance of the residence. The branch of a gnarled willow tree arched over the pool like a high bridge, and trailed long graceful strands of leaves in the water. The green discs of lotus leaves, their slender stems invisible in the darkness, seemed to hover miraculously in midair. Night-blooming water lilies filled the air with heady sweetness. Anne crouched near the edge of the pond and swirled her hand in the water. A golden carp came out of the depths and nibbled her fingers.

A hideous scream shattered the idyll, turning it into a grotesque backdrop for a nightmare. Anne closed her eyes and cupped her hands over her ears. She could still hear his heartrending wails and curses. She knew they would echo inside her head for a long time to come.

A gentle hand touched her hair. Innes. With a cry she hurled herself into his arms. He held her tightly, and said her name over and over again.

'I'm sorry,' he murmured. 'I didn't mean to hurt you that day. I couldn't stand the thought of losing you. I love you.'

'I know. I know.'

She caressed his face. His cheeks were leaner, covered with stubble, and there were deep creases on his forehead and around his eyes, signs of exhaustion and strain.

'You're not going to run away from me anymore,' he said fiercely. 'Wherever you go, I'll find you and bring you back. I don't care if I have to kill every soldier in the Japanese army to do it.'

'I won't run away from you again, ever. I promise.'

They stood for a long time, savoring each other's nearness.

Anne said, 'I shot those guards, Jamie.'

'I know you did.' He held her close.

'I wouldn't have believed that I could do it. I didn't feel anything when it happened, and I'm not sorry now. It was so horribly – simple. I'm blooded now. Part of the war. It's incredible. All I ever wanted in life was to play the violin and grow roses.'

'Really, is that all you wanted?' He smiled.

'I thought so. I was naive, wrong about so many things. I want you now. I'm not wrong about that, am I?'

'No. That's the way it was meant to be.'

'It's so crazy. You and Chen! How on earth did you persuade him to help you? I know he didn't do it for love of me. He's much too sensible to risk his neck for a mere woman.'

'Don't be too sure,' Innes growled. 'That son of a bitch —'

'You're not jealous of him!'

'Damned right I'm jealous. I rigged up this whole thing, put my ass on the line, and he got the first kiss.'

She laughed softly. 'Ah, but you shall have the next hundred thousand,' she whispered, giving him her mouth. She felt him tremble and she pressed closer, promising and demanding more and more.

He lifted her in his arms and carried her to his bed. Their hands moved swiftly and silently in the darkness, undressing each other, caressing and remembering. Her body felt so frail in his arms, ravaged by hunger. He didn't want to hurt her. She laughed softly at his hesitancy and teased him with her tongue and her fingers. Now, now.

Gilbert's screams penetrated the thick stucco walls that surrounded them. The floor underfoot, the air around them seemed to reverberate with echoes of pain and terror. Innes felt the joy go out of her body, and with it all desire.

She sagged limply, despairingly in his arms. 'I can't bear it anymore. I can't.'

'Bitch! Harlot! Jezebel!'

'Don't think about it,' said Innes. 'Don't listen to him. Listen to me. I love you, Anne. I love you. You say it, too – I love you.'

'I love you, Jamie. I love you,' she whispered.

'Louder. I love you, I love you.'

'You'll pay for this, Anne! I'll cut your heart out, by God, I swear I will! You and the monster Innes, two of a kind, two rutting animals! I'll kill you, Anne!'

'Drive away the demons, Jamie,' she pleaded. 'Make them go away, please.'

He enveloped her with his flesh and warmth. She heard the rush of his breathing, the thunder of their hearts, the rustle of flesh sliding against flesh, the crescendo of her own sighs, his shuddering moans. Afterward she pressed her cheek against his chest, and he folded his arms tightly around her to close out the horror. His heart throbbed comfortingly under her ear. The nightmare receded, then went away.

Love drives away demons. Better than firecrackers, better than walking a crooked line.

Chapter Thirteen

Anne heard the false thunder of the bombs just before dawn, when she got up to close her bedroom window against the first gusts of summer monsoon rains. She had been back in Shanghai for only two days, and she had already become accustomed to the constant crackling of gunfire and the boom of heavy artillery. The Japanese fired on the Chinese sections of the city, and the Chinese retaliated by blasting at Hongkew, the Japanese quarter. New bombs would be added to that gruesome chorus.

Both sides were obliged by treaty to respect the neutrality of the French Concession and the International Settlement, but the Japanese, as members of the international community, used their warehouses in the neutral zones to store weapons and ammunition. They insisted that their intentions were peaceful and honorable; they were merely trying to protect their businesses and citizens from the hostile Chinese populace, whose racial hatred had supposedly been fanned by propaganda from Chiang Kai-shek's government. They had used the same excuse for their aggression in 1932. No one believed it then, and no one believed it now.

Japanese planes flew low over the manse, bringing death to Chapei, the Chinese section to the northwest.

Anne didn't go back to bed. There would be a lot to do today: checking in on Gilbert at the Aldershot, helping Father Jacquinot with the refugees who were pouring into the French Concession by the thousand, dealing with reporters who wanted to know more about the rescue. 'Yes,' she would tell them, 'my husband and I are very grateful to Mr Innes. He saved our lives. I am quite sure the Japanese had no intention of releasing us anytime soon.' Dear Mr Innes. Dear Jamie.

They hadn't had a chance to be alone since the morning they left the house on the Yellow River. Gilbert, in the extreme stages of opium withdrawal, had monopolized her attentions during the flight home, and when they landed in Shanghai they were surrounded by reporters and well-wishers. Innes rushed off to his offices on the Bund, and Anne accompanied Gilbert, reported to be suffering from acute malaria and dysentery, to the Aldershot. Then she went home to the manse with her father. She planned to stay with her parents until Gilbert was well enough to leave the hospital, but they would have to move to an apartment. She knew he wouldn't be strong enough to resist the lure of her mother's tonic.

Albert McClure's sensational account of the rescue, interesting despite its exclusion of the most pungent details, had nudged the Japanese aggression off the front page of the *North China Daily News* for a whole day. Anne was amused by McClure's depiction of Innes as a loyal brother-in-law frustrated in his attempts to achieve the release of the Lawrences through diplomatic channels, and his determination to free them, even if it meant striking up an unholy alliance with the rascal Chen. She was always amazed at the way writers could distill chaotic reality into some approximation of order. But then writers could always omit or reshape details that didn't fit, which gave them an advantage over the people whose turbulent lives they wrote about.

The rain poured down, bringing no relief from the August heat. After just a few minutes with the windows closed, the room grew suffocatingly warm. The telephone rang and Anne went downstairs to answer it. A member of the Municipal Council wanted to know if the city could use the church buildings for temporary refugee shelters. Anne asked the caller to wait a moment while she woke her father, but when she looked up she saw him coming down the stairs. He was already dressed.

'It's started,' she said. 'Did you hear the bombs?'

'Yes. God help us all.'

The bombing, like the rain, continued throughout the day. Anne worked at the church, helping her father to set up kitchens to feed the stream of refugees pouring in from Chapei, where their homes had been leveled. Someone told her that the Japanese had dropped a bomb on Great World, an amusement park on Avenue Edward VII, and thousands of people had been killed and wounded. The

382

' hospitals were overflowing with wounded and ambulances refused to pick up more. Reverend Fox turned one half of his church into a makeshift infirmary. Mrs Weston and Mrs Morrison were on hand to help, and even Marian Fox came down to work, and she sat in a corner and rolled bandages and chatted brightly with her two friends, exactly as if she were presiding over a meeting of the Ladies Aid Society.

At one point during the day Anne found herself working next to Olga Kerensky McClure.

'You are surprised to see me here,' Olga said with a smile. 'Don't worry, I am just helping. I knew your father would need lots of extra hands today.'

'Thank you,' Anne said awkwardly. 'It was good of you to come. Your husband – Albert was kind to us. I like him.'

'Yes, he is a good man. I did the right thing by marrying him, I think.'

'Are you going to leave Shanghai, now that you have a passport?'

'It had not occurred to me. Strange. This would be the time to go. The situation here will not improve. But Albert will never leave – the news is too hot, he would say. And I will not leave without him. Where would I go?' She shrugged.

'You love him,' Anne suggested.

'Perhaps I do. It is not the kind of love one experiences when one is young, love that excludes everything else. I had that with my first husband, Kerensky, who was killed by the Reds. This is different even from the love I felt for your father. That was always a little sad, because it had no future, no hope. But Albert needs me. It is very important, to be needed. It gives one purpose. Yes, I know that my students need me, and my friends, but if I died they would find someone to take my place. Albert would not. I think he would die, too.'

'But that's not love at all,' Anne said, thinking of herself and Gilbert and feeling a shiver of fear at the prospect of being trapped forever in a thankless relationship based on duty and guilt. 'It's so one-sided.'

'Not at all. I need him, too. He thinks I am wonderful,

and he tells me so every day. That sort of thing can spoil you very quickly.'

Someone called Anne to the phone. 'It's me, Innes. How are things over there?'

'Frantic.' His voice sent warmth rushing through her. Her legs felt suddenly weak. 'How are you?'

'Busy. The British and American consuls are drawing up an evacuation plan for women and children. That means lining up ships. I've ordered all mine to be kept clear of cargo for the time being. What's that?' There was a watery sound as he covered the receiver with his hand. He said, 'The Japanese just dropped a bomb on the Park Hotel. Damned place is in flames and the trucks can't get to it. Listen, I have to see you. Can you come to the Cathay for an hour, right now?'

'I don't know – no, it's impossible – they need me here.'

'They can spare you for an hour. Make up some excuse. Tell them Gilbert's having fits. Tell them anything. I want to see you.'

'I want to see you, too. I'll try to get over as soon as I can.'

'No, not as soon as you can. Now. My car's waiting for you outside. Take a look if you don't believe me.'

'You're incredible! I suppose if I refuse, your man will come in and whisk me away bodily?'

'That's right. You're catching on to the way I operate.'

She hung up, feeling slightly resentful and exasperated, and at the same time excited at the prospect of seeing him. 'I have to go out for an hour,' she told her father. 'The Aldershot called.' Just a small lie, but all that was needed. Reverend Fox assumed that Gilbert wanted her, and he nodded distractedly and asked her to bring back some medical supplies if she could. She went out to Bubbling Well Road. Sure enough, the Rolls was waiting at the curb.

The Russian driver deftly avoided the streets that were blocked or clogged with debris or corpses or seething humanity, and fifteen minutes later he pulled up at the corner of the Bund and Nanking Road. It was almost three-thirty in the afternoon. He used a special key to summon the penthouse elevator, and Anne rode up alone.

The door to the penthouse swung open before she had a chance to ring the bell and Innes swept her into a suffocating embrace.

'You could have picked a more convenient time,' she said when she was able to catch her breath. 'Don't you know there's a war on?'

Innes' expression was serious. 'That's why I had to see you right away, before we both got too wrapped up in this craziness. We need to talk, Anne.'

'You brought me here to talk?' she exclaimed. 'Oh, dear, that doesn't sound like the Jamie Innes I know. Are you sure you're the right man? My Jamie makes love first, and talks later.' She nuzzled his cheek.

He detached her arms from around his neck. 'Today we talk first. This is important, Anne. I want you to listen to me.' He sat on the couch and drew her down beside him. 'Now that we're back here, it's going to be very easy for you to slip back into your old ways of thinking – duty, honor, country, and all that crap. You're going to get involved in refugee work, and you're going to nurse Gilbert through this crisis, and you're going to spend twenty hours out of every twenty-four thinking about everybody else but yourself. You're not going to think about me very much, either.'

'That's not true, I've thought about you every minute —'

'But you didn't call me. You didn't want to take the time to come here today. You think I don't need you because I'm not bleeding to death in the middle of the street. You'd rather forget all about me until this is over, wouldn't you? And if I just faded away, dropped out of your life, that would be OK, too. You'd feel relieved that you didn't have to worry about me anymore. But I won't. I'm in your life to stay.'

'I think I understand,' she said stiffly. 'You didn't risk your neck for me for nothing. I'm supposed to be properly grateful. I don't even have a choice anymore, do I? I have to come when you whistle, like a trained dog.'

'That's not what I mean.' He held her hands firmly and looked into her eyes. 'We don't have time to argue about this, Anne. You know damned well what I'm talking about. You have to make a promise. Tell yourself that someday we're going to be together. I don't mean right now, or tomorrow, or even next year. I'll wait. I know you're not going to abandon Gilbert while he's sick. I wouldn't want you to. But you have to keep telling yourself that it's only temporary. When he's well enough, you're going to divorce him and marry me. Make that promise to yourself, and to me. Say it aloud. Once you've done that, you won't go back on it. I know you. I'm not going to make unreasonable demands – today was an exception. I won't embarrass you. I won't be indiscreet, and I won't apply heavy pressure. I'll wait until you're ready. I'll wait as long as I have to, if I know you're as committed as I am. You love me. I love you. I just wanted you to keep that in mind. Well, that's it. End of speech. No more Dutch uncle routine. It wasn't so bad, was it?'

She didn't say anything, but regarded him solemnly from behind her glasses. He took them off and tucked them into his shirt pocket.

'You don't want to scrutinize this ugly face too hard,' he said gruffly. 'It's not going to get better-looking.'

'It's not ugly,' she said. 'It's a beautiful face. The most beautiful face I've ever seen. Sometimes, in Paoting, when I thought about you, I'd feel faint all of a sudden and have to sit down. I wanted you so much. It was incredibly strong, a physical thing like hunger or thirst. I was like Gilbert with his opium; I couldn't think of anything else. It broke my heart when I found out that I wasn't going to have your baby. I prayed for that – the first time in years and years that I'd prayed for anything. I do love you, and I want to be with you. I'm just not sure when.'

'That's enough. Don't worry about the rest. Trust me. You don't believe we can be happy, but I know we can. Trust me,' he said again, gathering her into his arms.

'I love you.'

He kissed her warmly. The telephone rang. 'God damn it,' he growled, leaving the couch and striding across the room. 'I thought I said no calls – what's that? Jesus, Charlie – Oh, for God's sake.' He hung up and turned around, his face mirroring irritation and amusement.

'Charlie just thought I'd like to know that the esteemed members of the Shanghai Club voted today to make me a member.'

Anne said, 'And why shouldn't they? You're a hero now. Having you on their rolls would be a feather in their cap – or caps. It's quite an honor, isn't it? Something you've always wanted?'

'They can take their goddamned honor and shove it,' Innes said. 'Sure, I wanted it. Any other man in my position would have been voted in long ago, but those damned snobs pretended that I didn't exist. Innes was a dirty word at the Shanghai Club, not to be mentioned in polite company. They were like you; they hoped if they closed their eyes and held their noses, I'd just go away. And now, just because I rescued a bunch of goddamned candy-assed missionaries, they're fawning all over me. Hypocritical sons of bitches.'

He glared at her. Anne could feel a laugh bubbling up inside her and she chewed her lips and tried to look serious. She couldn't. She started to giggle. Innes scowled ferociously, like a Chinese demon, but the corners of his mouth began to twitch. His face broke into a broad grin, and he threw back his head and roared.

Laughing, Anne lay back on the couch and opened her arms to him, and he flung himself down on top of her.

Anne buttoned her blouse and shoved it into the top of her slacks. 'Speaking as one of those goddamned candy-assed missionaries you rescued, I want to say thank you.'

'You were properly grateful,' he said approvingly.

'I wish we had more time.'

'Someday we'll have all the time we want. Remember, you're committed now. You've sworn a solemn oath.' Innes stood in front of the big window that overlooked the Bund. He stretched and yawned. Anne joined him, and he put his arm around her shoulders.

She said, 'I won't forget. I'll repeat it to myself every day, like a spell: someday Jamie and I are going to be together.' She lifted her face to be kissed.

'See that you do,' he said, obliging her. They heard the drone of an engine and looked up. A plane was approaching from Pootung, on the other side of the Whangpoo River. 'Chinese. Flying pretty low. I wonder if he's going to try to hit the *Izuma*.' Anne knew the *Izuma*, a Japanese cruiser, was anchored in the harbor at the foot of Nanking Road.

As the plane passed overhead they heard an innocuous-sounding whistle.

'Christ!' Innes grabbed her and threw her over the top of the couch, then hurled himself on top of her.

There was a deafening explosion. The Cathay trembled on its foundations, the penthouse tower swayed, and the force of the blast shattered every window in the building and in the Palace Hotel on the opposite corner. Shards of glass struck the inside walls of the apartment, some wedge-shaped pieces impaling themselves in the plaster like demonstrations of a knife-thrower's skills. Vases and figurines toppled to the floor and smashed. Innes cursed and sucked in his breath. Anne knew he had been struck.

The aftershocks and reverberations died away. There was an eerie silence. Anne and Innes lay quite still. Hot damp air rushed in through the shattered windows. Then from twenty stories below them they could hear faint screams and siren wails.

'Oh, God, Jamie. Are we still alive? Are you all right?'

'Jesus, I think so. You?' He rolled off her and helped her to her feet. He winced as he moved, and she looked at his back. Blood oozed out of dozens of tiny cuts. One large shard of glass was embedded in the flesh just over his left shoulder blade. Cautiously Anne pulled it out, and pressed her handkerchief hard over the wound to staunch the bleeding. 'We'd better get out of here,' Innes said.

'No, I want to look at these cuts.'

'No! Later. Come on.'

The electricity had gone off and the elevator wasn't working. They groped their way down the darkened stairs. They met Innes' Polish and Russian bodyguards coming up, their flashlights and revolvers at the ready, as if the bombing were part of a plot against their employer.

By some hideous miscalculation or error, the Chinese bombardier had dropped two bombs at the intersection of Nanking Road and the Bund, perhaps the busiest corner in the city, or in the world for that matter. Watches and clocks, like the large one that jutted out from the corner of the Palace Hotel, were stopped by the shock at 4:27 in the afternoon. The blow fell like a giant hammer striking the earth, smashing everything, opening an enormous hole fifty feet deep and a hundred feet wide. Waves of debris were sprayed for a thousand feet in every direction: bodies and parts of bodies mingled with broken glass and chunks of concrete. During the moment just after the bombs struck, when even those who survived the blow thought they were dead, nothing moved, not even the wind and the rain.

Anne and Innes stepped out onto the Bund as the street started to come to life. A screaming man ran past, half-mad with pain, clutching the stump of his arm. A woman stood forlornly at the edge of the great hole and called out the names of her children. An old man rocked a dead baby in his arms. A dead Sikh policeman hung over the side of a raised traffic kiosk, still clutching in his hand a little flag that continued to wave ludicrously.

The crater left by the bombs was like a huge grave. Inside it everything was peaceful: bloody corpses nestled quietly among the twisted wrecks of cars and rickshas. But there was a mad scramble around the perimeter as some people tried to get away from the horror while others ran to get a closer look at it. Automobile horns blared senselessly and trolley bells clanged. Loose pieces of glass fell from the windows of the two hotels and splintered like great droplets of rain, sending minute glistening particles splashing in all directions.

Anne saw her father's friend Mr Weston staggering out of the Cathay. He didn't seem to be hurt but he was sobbing brokenly. She called to him and asked if he were hurt. He stared at her blankly.

'My birds,' he said. 'The bomb – the windows – my beautiful birds have all escaped. Gone. They're all gone.'

A few feet away from where they were standing, a Chinese woman squatted against the outer wall of the Cathay. She was moaning and clutching her swollen middle. Anne thrust Weston impatiently aside and bent over the heaving woman. She looked up and said to Innes in an awed voice. 'She's going to have a baby. Now, this minute. I have to help her.'

Innes said, 'It's not safe here. Let's take her to the office.'

'No, there's no time. You go, Jamie. I can look after myself, honestly. If you're sure you're all right.'

'There's nothing the matter with me.' He managed a twisted grin. 'This isn't the first time I've been hit in the rear. The boys will take care of me.' He put his hands on Anne's shoulders. 'Be careful, Anne. Please. And don't forget what you promised.'

'I won't. I love you.' She gave him a quick kiss and watched as his guards half-carried him down the street toward the Innes Building. His back was blood-soaked and he dragged his feet a little. She started to follow. The woman beside her groaned.

Anne tore the woman's trousers open and spread them out on the pavement underneath her squatting haunches. The woman strained, and cried out. Anne held her shoulders and shouted encouragingly. The black crown of a tiny head began to emerge. Anne supported the baby's head with one hand while she drew him out into the mad world with the other. In a minute the gummy infant lay squirming feebly on his mother's bloody rags. People swarmed past, not even seeing them.

'The gods have blessed you with a son,' Anne said, lifting the baby gently and giving him to his mother. The cord was still uncut. Tears streamed down the woman's cheeks.

Anne looked around. A wheelbarrow lay on its side just a few feet away, near its dead owner, who had been dashed into the side of the hotel by the force of the exploding bomb. Anne hauled the thing over a pile of rubble and bodies and helped her patient into it. The baby was already sucking at his mother's breast. A muscular coolie stumbled past. Anne grabbed his arm and shouted at him.

'We must help the little mother. Take up this wheelbarrow. We must save the mother and the little one.' The man looked frightened and confused and seemed about to run away. 'Do as I say, and you will be well paid.' Anne tightened her grip on his arm and spoke angrily. 'If you do not obey, you will be beaten. I will tell the Japanese and they will beat you.' Her words gave the man's fear a focus. He couldn't understand the terror that had dropped out of the sky, but he could understand the threat of being beaten. He picked up the shafts of the wheelbarrow. Anne walked beside it, guiding and steadying it as it lurched over the torn and littered roadway.

'The wheel squeaks,' the coolie observed. 'Is good luck.' Anne certainly would have wished it true that squeaking wheels frightened demons.

The Aldershot was just a few blocks away. Anne and the coolie carried the woman and baby inside. The hospital had lost electric power, too, and its darkened lobby was filled with frightened, wailing people. The starched white nurses, usually so dignified and superci-lious, looked harried and helpless. Anne fished some money out of her pocket and gave it to the coolie. Then she settled her charges in a quiet corner and scrounged around for some scissors and bandages and a basin. She tied off the umbilical cord, delivered the mother of the afterbirth, and bathed both mother and child as best she could.

'You have a home?' she asked the woman.

'It is gone. The demons from the sky destroyed it this morning. This is a terrible day, an accursed day.'

'No, you are lucky. You have a fine son. Now you must rest for a while, and try to sleep. I will come back later.'

'Thank you, Ghost Mother.' The woman smiled drowsily.

Gilbert's room was just upstairs. Anne looked in and found him resting quietly, oblivious to the turmoil and havoc around him.

'Dr Morrison has sedated him pretty heavily,' a Eurasian nurse told her. 'He says the worst is over.'

'I'll take him home today and look after him myself,' Anne said. 'You can use the bed. There are people down there who are really hurt.'

She telephoned Innes to ask if he could lend her the Rolls and a driver to take her patients back to the manse.

'Anything, you know that. You're sure you're all right?'

'Yes, fine. And you?'

'Sure. A little stiff. Doc put in a few stitches. What about the baby?'

'It's a boy.' She began to cry. 'And he's beautiful.'

Refugees from the bombed-out sections crowded into the French Concession and the International Settlement. Food supplies there soon ran short. Thousands died of untreated wounds and exposure and disease, and there was widespread looting. In an attempt to stem outbreaks of mob violence in the International Settlement, the Municipal Council instituted a curfew from ten at night until six in the morning. For the first time in memory, the cabarets and clubs were dark. Enforcing the curfew was almost impossible in a city teeming with so many homeless people who had no shelters. Members of local defense leagues and the Chinese Peace Preservation Corps patrolled the streets, along with British police and American Marines.

Chinese businessmen tried to protect their properties by flying British and American flags conspicuously from their rooftops. The Japanese denounced this abuse, and declared that their bombardiers would no longer respect the neutrality of any flag. They dropped their bombs not only on Chinese residential neighborhoods, but on Pootung, the industrial area across the river. The view from the Bund was of a world in flames. The American Cigarette Company, the Sherwin-Williams paint factory, the Simmons Mattress Company, the refineries of Standard Oil and Asiatic Petroleum and thousands of warehouses and smaller businesses were all destroyed. Chinese workers who had lost their homes now lost their jobs as well.

Every day the earth trembled from the hammerlike blows of the bombs. At night the clouds overhead glowed orange with the reflections of the fires below. Star shells flared over the northern sections of the city like indecent fireworks, and tracer bullets streaked like comets across the smoke-blackened skies. Swooping searchlights from Japanese ships pinpointed targets in blacked-out Chinese areas. There was no respite from the killing, even at night. Everyone said that this was the end of Shanghai, even old China hands accustomed to occasional violent upheavals in a country forever at war with some part of itself. Longtime residents as well as tourists scrambled to leave the city. For the first time in its history the Shanghai Club opened its doors to women, in order to register British citizens for evacuation. Every square foot of shipping space on Innes' freighters was crammed with refugees fleeing to Manila and Hong Kong and Yokohama. Passenger lines sold deck as well as cabin space, and the overloaded ships threatened to founder before they even left port. Japanese planes strafed one ship, killing five people, including a respected member of the mission community. Two children were trampled to death in the rush to find shelter from the bullets.

Other missionaries began to depart Shanghai. Leonard Fox vowed to stay, but he tried to persuade Marian to get away to safety. She refused, and became hysterical whenever he mentioned it, and so he relented. He and Anne both knew that the only thing that kept her mother in Shanghai was the fear that she wouldn't be able to procure her laudanum so easily elsewhere.

'Maybe you and Gilbert ought to leave the city,' Leonard Fox suggested to Anne at breakfast one morning. 'There's no reason for you to stay here.'

'Yes, there is, Father.' Anne set down her coffee cup. 'As soon as Gilbert is better, I'm going to divorce him.'

Her father said, 'I see. It's that man Innes, isn't it?'

'Yes, Father. That man Innes. I guess he and Gilbert just married the wrong sisters.' She tried to laugh, but it came out sounding bitter and humorless.

'I just don't understand it,' Fox said softly. 'We were a family once. We were happy. We could talk. What's happened to us? I would never have believed that daughters of mine—' He looked away. 'I suppose we didn't set you a very good example.'

'It has nothing to do with you. Gilbert and I were wrong from the start.'

'We're like a shattered vessel. We don't fit together anymore,' he murmured sadly. 'Your mother is so vague lately. Sometimes I don't think she even knows who I am. You and Gilbert getting divorced. And Kit—' He passed his hand over his eyes. 'My little Kitten, my baby. That's the worst hurt of all. She's notorious. Her behavior is the scandal of Shanghai.'

'Oh, it can't be that bad,' Anne said. 'You know how Kit always loved to scandalize people.'

'No, not like now. You haven't heard, have you? She's a bar girl. She works as a taxi dancer, and she goes—' the words caught in her throat '—she goes with sailors. None of her old friends will speak to her. I tried to talk to her, but she wouldn't listen to me. She's so different. She's not my little girl anymore.' He twisted his big hands together in his lap.

'I'm sorry, Father. For you.'

'You mustn't blame her, Anne. She was born with her mother's addiction. Did you know that? Everything Gilbert has suffered in these past few days, she experienced as an infant. What a horrible thing to do to a child.'

'Not so horrible as what you did to her afterward,' Anne said. 'You never set any limits on her when she was small. She grew up thinking she could get away with anything. Children aren't happy when they're raised like that. Too much freedom is frightening, to a child or a grown-up.'

'Yes, I know, we spoiled her. But it was so hard not to.'

Wang came in to clear away their breakfast plates and to refill their coffee cups. Reverend Fox broke off his conversation and feigned absorbed interest in the morning headlines. Anne wondered for the millionth time why they bothered to hide anything from Wang. He knew it all, and they knew he knew. But the habits of many years die hard, and it was important to keep old patterns of behavior intact. To abandon them would only make chaotic existence even more chaotic and frightening. Wang picked up the tray of soiled dishes and went out.

'I wish you wouldn't leave us now,' Reverend Fox said. 'Gilbert will be all right here, I've spoken to Mother.'

'You're a fool to believe anything she says,' Anne said bluntly. 'You know we can't trust her, and I can't trust Gilbert not to backslide. The sooner we get out of here, the better. I've found a pretty decent apartment on Foochow Road, a few blocks north of the Aldershot. It's over a bookstore, very quiet. With so many people leaving the city, there are a lot of vacancies and I got it cheap. I'll take Lotus with me as amah.' Lotus was the woman she had assisted in childbirth on the first day of the bombings. 'And Wang's brother is coming to work for me, too, to look after Gilbert. Please don't ask me to stay, Father. You know it's impossible.'

'You're different, too,' Reverend Fox said sadly. 'You've become hard, and cynical.'

'No. I've just stopped trying to please everyone all the time. I can't do it, any more than I can make everyone love me. You'll never love me the way you love Kit, and that's all right. I can accept that now. Why shouldn't you have loved her more? She was so beautiful and smart and lively, and I was so dowdy, and so difficult.'

'I'm sorry, Anne. I didn't want to show favoritism.'

'I told myself that I detested you because you were betraying your real mission in China and selling out to the taipans. But I was jealous of Kit, and the way you treated her. I knew I could never be like her, and so I went in the opposite direction and made myself as unlovable as possible. No one could have loved me the way I was then, much less liked me. You barely tolerated me, and I don't blame you. Can you understand, Father? I'm trying to say that I'm not angry with you anymore. You tried to do what you thought was right, and best for all concerned. I know that now. I've made enough mistakes of my own lately, doing what I thought was best. I know how easy it is for a well-meaning person to behave foolishly, and wrongly. I'm sorry it took so long for me to come to my senses. I don't know if we can ever be friends. But at least we can stop brawling.'

Her father reached across the table and grasped her hand. 'Be happy, Anne. That's all any father can wish for his child.'

'I'm going to try. I love Jamie, and he loves me. I still can't believe it, but it's true. I'll be fine, you'll see.'

'And Kit?' he asked hopefully. 'Will you forgive her? I think she feels bad about what happened. If you went to her—'

'No.' Anne slid her hand from under his. 'I won't

forgive her, and I won't see her, ever again. I don't care what happens to her.'

Anne's smiles were falsely bright, and her conversation forced. Gilbert didn't mind; he simply observed these changes in her attitude and recorded them in the cluttered diary of his mind. He remembered Anne in Chengtu, before Kit. She had loved him then, he was sure of it. There was no love in her looks now, only pity, and sorrow, and desperation.

He was free of opium, free of morphine, a free man. His body had not yet recovered from the effects of long dependency on drugs. That would take a year or more, according to Dr Morrison. His appetite was poor, he was skeletally thin, and he suffered from a succession of fevers and colds because his resistance to disease was almost nonexistent. He was impotent, but that didn't bother him as much as his occasional incontinence, which embarrassed him acutely.

Every day he sat by the window and watched the parade of suffering humanity below on Foochow Road: families fleeing the Japanese, their goods piled in carts or on wheelbarrows or in slings on their backs; children wandering lost and forlorn; the wounded seeking shelter in doorways and dying there. He felt strangely removed from the horror, and untouched by it. He knew that Anne involved herself with refugee work. He knew that Lotus and her baby had been left homeless by the bombings, as had their houseboy, Wang's brother. But the noise and the stink and the chaos of war were not much different from the nightmares he had had while he was withdrawing from opium, and perhaps they were even less violent and chaotic. He felt quite at home in a city under siege.

Anne brought him newspapers and books, and she chattered cheerfully, giving him accounts of her day, the people she saw, the rumors she heard. He listened politely, because he didn't want to hurt her feelings, but he wasn't really interested. He wasn't interested in the newspapers, either. He knew all about the war already, without reading about it. He had lived through a worse hell than any indiscriminate bombing could create.

He had no craving for drugs or for anything else. He didn't mind his frailty, because he wouldn't have known how to direct his energies. Dr Morrison had told him he was depressed and fatigued, but he didn't feel sad or tired. The weeks passed. He got no better, and he got no worse. He ate the food Wang brought, drank tea, dozed in his chair, permitted Anne to entertain him. Leonard Fox looked in once or twice a week and read the Bible to him when he ran out of things to talk about. Gilbert had loved the Bible once, loved the lessons, the images, the dynamic flow of words and ideas. But now he found it as boring and meaningless as the *North China Daily News*.

The siege continued for two months. The Nationalist armies claimed nonexistent victories over the enemy, who continued to bomb and shell until all resistance melted away and Shanghai was under Japanese control. Japanese police, or ronin, were stationed at all roads that led into the International Settlement and the French Concession. They harassed and insulted the Chinese who had to cross their barricades in order to get to work, forcing them to bow deeply to the conquerors, but whites were permitted to come and go freely, and to carry on business as usual. Shanghai began to rebuild. The Chinese drifted back to Chapei and Pootung and began to rebuild their homes. The stench of rotting corpses and charred wood became less overpowering. The Palace and Cathay hotels replaced their windows and reopened their restaurants and night-clubs. The Municipal Council lifted the curfew, and Blood Alley blossomed with neon again.

One afternoon Gilbert saw a familiar figure on the other side of Foochow Road from their apartment. Kit. She squinted at the numbers, then crossed the street and entered the building. The buzzer sounded. Lotus ushered her into the sitting room.

'Hullo, Gil. I ran into Albert McClure and he told me you were living here. I came now because I knew Anne wouldn't be home. I'm pretty sure she doesn't want to see me, but you don't mind, do you? No hard feelings. How are you?'

'Fine, thank you,' he said politely. He felt no fear or anger toward her.

'I guess I'll sit down for a few minutes. You don't have anything to drink, do you?' She grinned at Lotus, who hovered watchfully.

'She doesn't speak English, I'm afraid,' Gilbert said. He asked Lotus in Chinese to make some tea. He looked at Kit. He remembered her very well, although he hadn't thought about her for a long time.

She lit a cigarette. She was thinner, he noticed, and she used more paint. Her lips and her eyelids were coated with it, and there were sprinkles of face powder on the front of her black shantung suit. Her hair was curled but unkempt, her shoes dusty.

'What do you think?' she asked cockily. 'Have I lost my looks completely?'

'No,' he said. 'You look all right.'

'Thanks for the compliment.' She dipped her head. 'You're looking pretty well, I guess. I hear you've been sick.'

She was shocked at how much he had changed. His head looked like a skull, with enormous cavities in the cheeks and hollows at the temples and around the eyes. His athletic body was wasted. His once beautiful hands looked especially ugly – large and bony, bulging with knotted purple veins and tendons. His hair was long and lusterless, and he pushed his lips in and out like an old man. She calculated. He was only thirty-four, no more than that.

He lost interest in her and stared out at the street again. She smoked her cigarette to within a half inch of the end and lit another from the glowing butt. Lotus brought tea and poured two cups. The baby began to whimper in another room and she went out again.

'What do you think, Gil,' Kit said sarcastically, 'is it going to rain or not?'

'I don't know.'

'What do you do all day, just sit here and mope? You ought to step out with me, Gil. I'll have you back in shape in no time.'

'I don't think so. I'm not very strong.'

'You used to be a pretty good dancer. Wouldn't you like to dance again? I dance every night. You should see my feet – they're in a shocking state, all calloused and tough. But I don't care. It keeps me off the street.' She laughed stridently.

'I don't think I want to dance,' he said without turning his head.

'Gilbert, look at me. Look at me,' she insisted. 'Don't you know who I am? Don't you remember me?'

'Of course. You're Kit.'

'You were in love with me once, remember? You adored me, and I was fond of you. I still am.'

He sighed. 'I feel rather tired, if you don't mind.'

'But I do mind.' She left her chair and knelt in front of him. She took his hands in hers and looked intently into his face. 'What's the matter with you, Gil? Don't you care about me anymore?'

'I don't know. I haven't thought about you very much.'

'I've thought about you. I really have. We can still be friends, even though—'

He said, 'Oh, God.' His pale face turned scarlet and he turned his face aside. He began to cry silently. The stink of fresh feces reached her nostrils.

She stood up slowly. Without saying another word she picked up her purse and left the apartment. As she closed the door and turned around, she came face to face with Anne, just reaching the landing at the top of the stairs.

'You,' Anne stared. 'You, here?'

'Oh, hullo, Mouse,' Kit said casually. 'I just dropped in for a minute. I didn't mean any harm.'

'Didn't mean any harm,' Anne echoed. 'Then what did you mean? I suppose you came to satisfy your curiosity, to admire your handiwork. Well, what do you think? Aren't you pleased with what you've done? Not much left of the old Gil, is there? Did he impress you with his good looks and his wit? He's absolutely brilliant these days, don't you agree? Or maybe you went to bed with him! That must have been thrilling for you, Kit. About as thrilling as going to bed with a ten-year-old,' she said bitterly. She took a step toward Kit. She felt a cold fury mounting inside her.

Kit edged away, frightened. She had never seen Anne like this before. 'Come on, Anne, don't be that way. I'm sorry.' She tried to dodge down the stairs. Anne gripped her shoulder and pulled her back.

'Sorry? You're sorry? I don't believe you. You're the same little liar you always were. Sorry!'

Kit tried to shrug her off. 'You can't put all the blame on me. Blame Gilbert, too. He knew what he was doing.'

'Liar!' Anne slapped her. The sting brought tears of pain to Kit's eyes. 'Damned little liar!'

She slapped Kit again. Kit didn't try to protect herself. She merely stood and whimpered, 'Stop, please stop.'

'Why should I? You didn't stop. You couldn't leave him alone. You still can't stay away from him.' Each slap seemed to ease some of the tension inside her. Kit tried to slide out of reach, and Anne grabbed her hair and shook her. 'Why couldn't you stay away?' she demanded. 'Damn you, damn you, damn you!'

Kit broke free and plunged down the stairs. Halfway down she caught her heel and stumbled, and rolled shrieking to the bottom. Anne raced down and hauled her to her feet. She began to pound her sister with her fists. Kit wailed, stridently and continuously, like a siren.

'Damn you, damn you!' Anne cried, her voice reverberating through the house, growing louder and louder. 'Leave him alone! Leave him alone!'

The proprietor of the bookseller's shop, who shared the foyer with the apartments upstairs, opened his door and gaped at them. He called to his clerk and together they separated the brawling women.

Kit stumbled out onto Foochow Road and ran blindly across the street, barely avoiding being flattened by a swiftly moving Ford truck. Anne slumped down on the bottom step and buried her head in her arms. Wang and Lotus, alerted by the noise, came down and helped her stand. She sobbed brokenly as they mounted the stairs. All the while she thought, What a terrible loss of face. What a disgrace.

They took her to her bedroom. Lotus brought cool cloths and tea and even her laughing baby. Nothing worked. Anne couldn't stop crying. She lay face down and sobbed until she felt nauseous, but she couldn't stop. She didn't want to. She would gladly have cried herself to death, cried until she drowned in her own tears.

Gilbert watched helplessly from the doorway. 'I'm sorry,' he said. 'I'm sorry, Anne. Please don't cry anymore.'

He sat at the head of the bed and patted her shoulder. She nearly gagged from the stink of his soiled trousers and pity for him and for herself overwhelmed her and made her cry that much harder.

'Don't, don't, you'll make yourself sick, Anne. I'm sorry. Whatever I've done, I'm sorry,' Gilbert said worriedly. 'I'm not good for you. I never have been. Don't cry anymore. I'll go away, Anne. I'll do anything. Just don't cry.'

'Oh, God, I'm so ashamed,' Anne said brokenly. 'I've never acted like that before in my life. I hate her. I hate her!'

'I'm sorry, Anne. I'm sorry.' Gilbert began to sob, too. Lotus wailed in sympathy with her friends, and the baby, frightened by so much noise, started to squall lustily. Wang, certain that their house had been invaded by demons, began to beat on a pan with a heavy metal spoon to scare them away.

All of Shanghai passed beneath Gilbert's window. The color and texture of the parade had changed somewhat since the middle of October when the bombing stopped. Instead of soldiers and streams of frightened refugees, Gilbert saw people once again going calmly about their business. The taipans' cars rolled freely through streets that had been clogged by fleeing humanity. Children made their daily heavy-footed journeys to school and light-hearted journeys homeward. Amahs wheeled prams. Clerks hurried toward their offices on the Bund. Policemen unsnarled traffic jams and patrolled the shady side of the street. Ricksha men trotted along, shouting their warning cries. Vendors hawked. Old men dozed.

Every evening at about eight o'clock, young women who lived nearby began to walk south toward Avenue Edward VII, Blood Alley, where they worked in the clubs. Gilbert recognized them after a while: the husky Russian who always wore a red marabou stole slung around her neck, the petite Japanese twins who dressed identically, the slow-moving English girl who never seemed to be in any hurry to get where she was going, the two French girls who walked with linked arms and chattered volubly and constantly like a couple of magpies. Later, if he couldn't sleep, Gilbert left his bed and returned to his chair near the window. At about two o'clock the girls started to straggle home. When they worked hard and earned only a little money, they limped. When business was slow, they felt energetic enough to walk swiftly. When business was especially good they rode in rickshas. From time to time, they returned home with men.

One evening as Gilbert gazed out at Foochow Road, he saw a familiar figure. Kit strolled along the sidewalk on the other side of the street from the bookseller's shop. She stopped in front of the lingerie shop directly opposite his window, bent to adjust the seam of her stocking, and walked on. She didn't glance up. Gilbert wondered if he should tell Anne, who sat reading in the chair across from him. Her chair was angled so that she couldn't see out the window. He remembered how upset she had been that day after Kit's visit, and he decided not to mention that he had seen Kit on their street.

Kit returned the next evening at the same time, and the next, and every evening after that. Gilbert watched for her. If Anne happened to be standing anywhere near the window, or if she seemed likely to look out at that critical moment when Kit might be passing, he would ask for a cup of tea or a bite of food so as to distract her attention from the activity in the street. If she saw Kit, she would be angry, and Kit might not come again.

At first Kit came alone, always stopping in the same spot, in front of the lingerie shop. She never looked up at his window. One evening a man approached her. They talked for a minute, then moved off together, their arms around each other's waists. From then on she would often pass beneath his window in the company of a man. But even when she was with someone, she found some excuse to pause for a moment – an item in the shop window caught her eye, or her seams needed adjusting, or she wanted her partner to light her cigarette.

At first she appeared only in the evening, at about eight o'clock. Then one night she came a second time, very late, at about two in the morning. She wore an evening gown and a fur stole, and she was with a man in a white uniform, a British naval officer. She and the officer stopped in her usual place, which was well lighted by a streetlamp. She put her arms around his neck and pulled his head down to hers. He kissed her neck, and she looked over his shoulder. For the first time she lifted her face to Gilbert's window. She couldn't possibly have known he was there, watching her from the safety of the darkness, but she looked right into his eyes.

After that she was always with a man. She always stopped in the pool of light from the streetlamp. Gilbert never saw the same man twice, but an assortment of sailors and soldiers, a policeman, a Japanese ronin, a large blond man who talked loudly in German.

Anne usually returned from her work with Father Jacquinot's refugee organization at about six o'clock. One evening late in November, Gilbert watched her cross the street toward the apartment. She stopped and turned around. A man approached her. He recognized James Innes' broad shoulders and dark untidy hair. Gilbert stepped back from the window, behind the lace curtain. He didn't think they could see him, but he could still see them plainly.

They talked. Anne shook her head. Innes shrugged. She cast an anxious look up at Gilbert's window, and seemed relieved not to see him there. She gnawed her finger. Innes touched her elbow and she jerked away. He turned abruptly and started to walk away. She called out to him. He stopped. She ran up to him and stopped short, two feet away from him. He reached out and touched her cheek. She covered his fingers with hers, and pressed her lips into the palm of his hand. Then she backed away from him and darted across the street and into the building. Innes stared after her. From the set of his shoulders and the way he jammed his hands into his trouser pockets, Gilbert could tell that he was angry.

Gilbert went into the bathroom. When he came out Anne was taking off her hat and raincoat.

'Hello, Gilbert.' She forced herself to smile. 'How are you feeling today?' She brushed his cheek with her lips.

It was always the same greeting: the smile, followed by the question, topped off by that miserable kiss. He felt a little sorry for her.

After dinner he said offhandedly, 'Do you ever see Mr Innes, I wonder?'

She closed the book she was reading and looked up. Her heart thumped. 'Well, as a matter of fact, I ran into him tonight, down in the street. Perhaps you saw him.'

'No, I didn't. I must have been in the bathroom. I was just thinking, he's never come to visit me. I haven't seen him since we got back to Shanghai, and that was a long time ago. I guess he's not particularly interested in what happens to me. I don't blame him.'

'That's not true, Gilbert. He always – he asked about you tonight. But he knows you never liked him and he doesn't want to upset you.'

Gilbert said, 'If he hadn't rescued us in Paoting, we would have died. I certainly would have. We have a lot to thank him for.'

'Yes, that's true.'

She felt dizzy, and frightened. What if Gilbert had seen them? She tried to remember how they appeared. It was a perfectly innocent-looking encounter. Except when she forgot herself and called out his name. When he touched her face she had wanted to fling herself into his arms and lose herself there, and she had clung to his hand and kissed it and promised to come to him soon. She was not a willing adulteress. She knew she was a poor liar, and prevarication was beyond her. She hated the idea of coming home to Gilbert directly from Innes' bed, but she wanted him so much, and he was becoming impatient. She swallowed.

'Kit married him to make me jealous,' Gilbert said.

'Yes, I know,' she said in a croaking whisper.

He slumped in his chair and gazed out the window. What was he thinking? She was afraid to ask, and she bent her head over her book.

Reverend Fox read from Isaiah: '"Tremble, ye women that are at ease; be troubled, ye careless ones: strip you, and make you bare, and gird sackcloth upon your loins. They shall lament for the teats, for the pleasant fields, for the fruitful vine. Upon the land of my people shall come up thorns and briers; yea, upon all the houses of joy in the joyous city,"'

The words were beautiful, like rolling thunder. Gilbert glanced out the window and saw the Japanese twins fluttering past, like a pair of lovebirds. He shook his head. Such wasteful, empty lives. He didn't despise them. He pitied them. They didn't realize the high price of frivolity.

Leonard Fox read: '"Woe to thee that spoilest, and thou wast not spoiled; and dealest treacherously, and they dealt not treacherously with thee! when thou shalt cease to spoil, thou shalt be spoiled; and when thou shalt make an end to deal treacherously, they shall deal treacherously with thee. Oh, Lord, be gracious unto us—"' He paused and looked at his watch. 'I didn't realize it was so late. I guess I won't continue with Chapter Thirty-three tonight.'

Gilbert said softly, '"When thou shalt make an end to deal treacherously—"'

'Yes, the Bible is a great source of comfort, isn't it? If only people would turn to it in time of trouble, instead of turning inward and trying to find their solutions within themselves. Well, good night, Gilbert. I'll drop in again later in the week.'

'"Woe to thee that spoilest,"' Gilbert read when he was alone. He read the passage over and over again, then he closed the book and recited it aloud.

Anne noticed at dinner that night that he seemed unusually withdrawn and preoccupied. 'Are you feeling all right, Gilbert? You look feverish.'

'No, I don't think I have a fever.' He poked at his food. 'I'll never be well, will I?'

'Why, of course you will,' she said briskly, trying to convince herself as well as him. 'Dr Morrison's prognosis is very hopeful. It's just that – well, you don't seem to want to be well. That's what really worries me, Gilbert. You have so much to live for. You're such a fine doctor, and you have so much to give. You can go home to your family, and start over, and put this whole nightmare behind you.'

'You mean you won't be coming with me,' he said with sudden penetrating astuteness.

She couldn't lie, but he wasn't ready for the truth. 'I didn't say that, did I? Don't worry, we don't have to talk about it until you're better.'

'I've been an awful burden for you,' he said. 'I don't know why you've stayed with me this long. You could easily find someone else to love you. Even that man Innes.'

Her heart lurched. 'I don't know what you mean. You're not a burden, Gilbert. Please don't think about me. Just concentrate all your energies on getting well.'

'The future has been uncertain for so long, hasn't it?' he said. 'I feel as though I've been far away, and that I've just returned from a long journey. Everything is familiar, yet different somehow. I'm better, Anne. I know what I have to do now.'

'Of course you do. You have to concentrate on getting well and strong, and you have to look ahead.'

'It's a good thing to have a plan, to be able to see the future, isn't it? Otherwise you just drift, and nothing has meaning. Yes, I feel better.'

Kit didn't pass the apartment that evening. Gilbert watched diligently. He was quite sure he hadn't missed her. He forced himself to sit in his chair until nearly four in the morning, waiting and watching. She didn't appear.

When he finally fell asleep, he was restless and cried out: 'Spoiler!' Anne awoke and sat with him until he was calmer. She thought about their conversation with relief and dread. Perhaps he really was better. That meant she could leave him soon. But why had he mentioned Innes? He suspected something. He knew about them. He must have seen them together.

'Maybe I should stay home today,' she said at breakfast. 'You had a bad night. I think you're coming down with something.'

'No, I'm fine. I just had bad dreams, that's all. It would be silly for you to stay home. I'll probably sleep all day anyway.'

'I promised Olga I'd meet her at six,' Anne said hesitantly. Why was lying to him so difficult? 'You won't mind dining alone, will you, just this once? I should be home around eight.'

'Of course I don't mind.' He smiled. 'I'm glad you're going out. You should do it more. You've been penned up with me for such a long time. It won't last, I promise.'

'I'm so glad.' She hugged him impulsively. He returned the pressure. She smoothed his damp hair and kissed him softly on the mouth. It was the first real kiss she had given him in a long, long time.

He grasped her hand. 'I'm sorry, Anne.'

'For what?'

'For spoiling your life. I had no right to marry you. It was wrong of me. I'm not much of a husband. I never have been. I was never much of a man, either. You deserve better. You shouldn't have stayed with me. Any other woman would have left long ago.'

'Don't say that! What a silly way to talk, Gilbert. I stayed because – I care about you. I want to make you well.' It all sounded so lame and unconvincing. 'I don't want Kit to destroy you,' she blurted out before she could stop herself.

'She won't,' he said. 'She won't.'

'I'm sorry.' Anne slipped out of his arms and rolled onto her side. Innes sat up and lit a cigarette. To her ears the rasp of his match sounded accusing, reproachful. 'I shouldn't have come here today. It was a mistake.'

'No, it's my fault,' he said. 'I promised I wouldn't pressure you, and I did.'

'I'd better leave. I'm really sorry, Jamie.' She pulled herself up and swung her legs over the side of the bed.

'Don't worry about it,' Innes said gently. 'I'm not angry with you. This doesn't mean anything, you know that. You just have a lot on your mind right now.'

'I hate deceiving him. It's so unfair. I know, I'm being stupid. He doesn't care what I do, and he practically gave me permission to find someone else. But he knows about us. He must. He saw us that night. He knows I'm betraying him.'

'What difference does it make?' Innes asked. 'It might even be a good thing. It won't be such a shock to him when you tell him you're leaving.' He shifted closer to her and put his arms around her waist. He kissed the top of her shoulder.

'I just wish it were over. I'm so tired.' She leaned back against him and closed her eyes. 'I hate doing this to you.'

'Oh, don't worry about me. I'll just run out and get it from somebody else.'

Anne said miserably, 'I wouldn't blame you if you did.'

'I'm glad to hear it. You'd better hurry up and get out of here. I have to make a phone call. There's a new girl at Ciro's.'

'I wish you wouldn't say things like that, even in fun.'

'Why not?' He lay back, his arms folded under his head. 'You're not jealous, are you?'

'Yes, I'm jealous,' she said, whirling around and throwing herself on top of him. 'I'll cut out her heart, and yours, too. How dare you talk about finding someone else!'

He laughed and gripped her tightly. 'Then let's hear no more talk about leaving.'

The Russian girl was late. She gave her marabou boa an irritated twitch, looked at her wristwatch, and then hailed a ricksha. The Japanese twins passed giggling under the window, their heels clicking like the keys of a typewriter. The French girls chattered. The English girl sauntered past, in no hurry to meet her destiny. The bookseller downstairs rolled up his awning and locked his doors. He and his clerk left the shop together, and strolled south on Foochow Road. But still no Kit.

Gilbert nodded. So she wasn't going to come to him. It didn't matter. He fished in the crack between the seat and the arm of his chair and brought out the small sharp knife he had stolen from the kitchen earlier in the day, when Wang had gone out and Lotus was otherwise occupied. Lotus' baby had watched from his cradle in the corner and gurgled at him. He had smiled at the baby while he sharpened the blade.

Lotus came into the sitting room to take away his

supper tray and he hastily hid the knife. She frowned when she saw that he hadn't touched his food, and scolded him. He told her that he felt tired, and that he just wanted to sleep a little. When she was gone he put the knife in his pocket and slipped out of the apartment.

Evening was drawing in and neon lights blinked on to banish the darkness. The flash and dazzle blinded and confused him for a moment. He passed the open door of a cigar store. A radio inside was turned up full blast and blared forth a Chinese love song that sounded like fingernails scraping on a pane of glass. Gilbert shivered.

Crowds jostled him. All the shops in Shanghai remained open until midnight, seven days a week, and the restaurants and nightclubs stayed open until dawn. The scent of opium mingled with cooking smells and the reek of carrion and the stink of filth. He walked slowly, like an invalid, not hurrying himself or overtaxing his strength. He paused frequently to catch his breath. The evening was cool, but his white shirt and flannel trousers quickly became sweat-soaked and limp. He wondered if he should hire a ricksha, but remembered that he had no money. He could walk the distance. It wasn't far and he had plenty of time.

He crossed Avenue Edward VII, the street they called Blood Alley. It was lined with nightclubs, bars, dance halls. Trumpets screamed out love songs. Girls, painted and plumed like exotic birds, stood in clusters on the sidewalk. He brushed past them without seeing them, and they jeered at him and called him a fool.

Two more short blocks brought him to the old Chinese city. He swerved to the right, taking the broad avenue that used to be a moat, before it was filled in and paved. He had no wish to lose himself in the maze of narrow streets, among so many strangers. He followed Avenue Joffre west, stopping every few yards to rest. Finally he came to the Innes mansion, dark except for a light burning on the second floor.

A new houseboy, sluggish with opium, opened the door. Gilbert said, 'Mrs Innes, please.' The man jerked his thumb at the stairs and shuffled to the back of the house. Gilbert mounted the stairs slowly, hearing the echo of the strong, beautiful words inside his head: 'Woe to thee that spoilest, and thou wast not spoiled.'

He opened the bedroom door. Kit was sitting on the bed, her legs tucked under her, a cigarette burning between her fingers like a stick of incense. The radio in the corner played lively dance music. She was wearing a peach-colored nightgown trimmed with lace, and he could see the dark discs of her nipples behind the sheer panels of the bodice.

He came into the room. The door swung shut behind him. She looked up and smiled warmly.

'Hullo, Gil. I've been waiting for you.'

She stubbed out her cigarette and stood up slowly. Still smiling, she came toward him, and her arms opened to embrace him.

Anne encountered Lotus on the street outside the apartment.

'He is gone, lady,' Lotus wailed. 'I take his supper tray and when I next look, he is not there! Wang says a small knife is missing from the kitchen!'

'Knife?' Anne was puzzled. 'What would he want with a knife?' If he had wanted to kill himself, he could have done it easily, at home. No, not himself. Someone else? Someone else . . . Kit.

She ran down Foochow Road, shouldering her way through knots of shoppers. She pushed aside beggars' outstretched hands, did not hear the angry shouts or see the annoyed looks that her unseemly haste provoked. She darted blindly across streets and into alleys. Her heart bursting, she stumbled up the steps to the Innes mansion and threw herself at the bell. The servant was slow in coming, and she beat at the door with her fists. Finally it swung open. The houseboy's opium-glazed eyes showed no curiosity, just slight irritation at having his dreams disturbed.

'Dr Lawrence! Missee Kit! Where are they?'

He pointed up the stairs. She nearly knocked him down as she ran past. His interest piqued, he followed slowly.

The door was ajar. The only sound was the pulsating bleat of music from the radio. She went in. They were lying in each other's arms. The carpet underneath them was crimson, still damp.

Anne knelt down. Kit's eyes were open. There was a fixed smile on her face. Gilbert had slid the knife into her heart with deadly accuracy, and when he withdrew it, spurting blood covered them both. The knife was still lodged in his breast, just under the sternum. His left hand was entwined in Kit's hair. Both of her hands were locked around folds of his shirt.

The houseboy ran screaming from the house of the dead. Anne stood up and calmly picked up the receiver of the telephone beside the bed. She called the French police and told them that a murder-suicide had taken place on the Avenue Joffre. Then she called Innes at the Cathay.

Chapter Fourteen

'Thank God that's over,' Albert McClure shed his coat and tie. 'I need a drink. I'll tell Lotus to make some tea.' For the first time in his life Albert was motivated to obey his doctor's ban on alcohol.

Olga removed her hat and gloves. She wiped her eyes and blew her nose noisily, and touched her hand to her hair. Then she picked up the violin they had brought home with them and carried it out to the garden.

Anne slouched in a wicker armchair in the shade of a camphor tree. She didn't look up when Olga sat down next to her. She wore the same sexless costume she had worn since the tragedy: loose trousers and a peasant jacket that buttoned up the front. Her hair was neatly braided – one of Lotus' morning tasks – and the plaits hung nearly to her waist. She looked wan and mournful like a spirit that belongs neither to this world or the next, neither to the Orient or the Occident.

'Well, they have finally gone,' Olga puffed. She rested the violin case on her knees and fanned herself. 'I held up very well, meaning I managed not to cry until after they threw us off the ship, and then I couldn't stop. Albert and Jim each donated a handkerchief to the cause. I never seem to have mine when I need it. Your father looked tired but relieved, I think. Your mother didn't seem to know what was happening. She thought they were going back into the interior on a Yangtze steamer.'

'Oh?' Anne watched a beetle crawling up the stem of the red rose bush near the wall.

'Interesting, how people react to shock in different ways. Your mother talks. I remember the funeral. How she talked and talked and I had to take her out of church. All about Kit and how beautiful she was when she was little. Everyone thought she didn't know where she was or that she didn't understand what was going on, but she did. She just didn't want to give herself a chance to think about it.'

'Can you blame her?' Anne said. 'Anyone who tried to make sense out of it would go mad, if they weren't already.'

'Poor Jim,' Olga sighed. 'He thought you had quite lost your mind. You didn't say a word for three whole weeks. I explained to him that it was quite normal for someone who has had a terrible shock not to speak for a long period of time. I have seen it so often – in Russia and here. Women sitting in the ruins of their homes with their dead children in their arms. They cannot speak. They cannot even cry. Sometimes it lasts only for a few hours, sometimes for several days, sometimes for the rest of their lives. Jim was relieved when you finally started talking. We all were. It meant you were beginning to heal.'

The beetle ventured out on a leaf, then changed his mind and climbed upward toward the nodding cluster of buds and blooms at the top of the stem.

'And then I cried for a month. He probably thought that was mad, too.'

'No, men can understand weeping, even though it makes them uncomfortable and nervous. It's the silences they hate.'

The beetle crawled up onto a half-opened bud.

'She was so beautiful, wasn't she?' Anne said softly. 'She had it all, and she wasn't happy. I'll never understand that. She could have done anything.'

Olga said, 'Your sister wasted her talents, because she never had to use them. She never had to prove herself. Gilbert was the same way. Handsome and brilliant and weak. The beautiful ones are often weak, because life is too easy for them. They are never tested. Not like you. You've been trying since you were small to prove to people that you were worthy of their love.'

'I can't hate her for what she did. I think she was always a little lonely and frightened. She filled in the silences and the empty spaces with dancing and laughter and drink and sex, the way my mother fills hers up with talk and dope, and you fill yours with music, and I fill mine with – well, God only knows how I fill mine. At the end, when she wanted somebody to care enough about her to make her stop, no one did.'

413

'Gilbert did,' Olga said. 'I don't think he killed her because he hated her, but because he loved her.'

'I don't believe that,' Anne said. 'It was my fault. I put the idea into his mind.'

'Rubbish,' Olga said sharply. 'People in Gilbert's condition can be very cunning. He had it in mind long before you said anything about Kit. You know what I think, I think he did it for you, to make up to you for the trouble he'd caused and to set you free. He knew you would never leave him, and he wanted you to be happy. He found the quickest solution to all your problems, especially his own.'

'I should have been there,' Anne said for the millionth time. 'I should never have left him alone.'

Olga sighed. 'Regrets are useless. We don't know what lies in store for us. When Kerensky was killed by the Reds, I couldn't comprehend it. We had been so happy. I couldn't believe that it could end like that, so suddenly and horribly. I, too, found things to blame myself for: I should have urged him to leave the country, I should have been more attentive to his needs, I shouldn't have devoted so much time to music. I wanted to die, too. My mother saved me. She made me leave Russia and come here with her, and for a long time I resented her for forcing me to live. But now I'm glad. Life is good again, and this time I don't take the good things for granted. Even terrible tragedies can teach us a lesson.' Anne seemed not to be listening. Olga said, 'Look what your father gave me today, Anne. Your violin. He was going to leave it behind at the manse, and then he remembered that I had given it to you and he thought I might want it.' She opened the case. 'I remember it. A fine instrument. Made by an Italian who lived in Petersburg. Another political refugee. You see, we refugees have our uses.'

She stroked the body of the violin, then lifted it out of its case. 'Sad, to see it so out of tune. I hope it's still usable. The climate here is so hard on the wood.'

For the next ten minutes she tuned the violin, winding the pegs and plucking the strings, then she played a rapid cadenza. 'Not too bad. That's quality for you. It seems a shame that no one has touched it for so many years.

Would you like to try it, Anne?'

She offered the violin and bow to Anne, who recoiled. 'No, take it away. I can't. I can't!'

Olga shrugged and stood up. 'I won't force you, of course. You would feel a little stiff at first, but it would come back. Your fingers would remember. What would you like to hear, a little Bach, perhaps?' She played the Chaconne in D Minor for solo violin, one of the most difficult and dazzling pieces in the violinist's repertoire. Her fingers and the bow flew. Gorgeous music filled the walled garden. Inside the house, Lotus' baby, who had been fretful, gurgled and was quiet. Albert, sipping his tea, smiled blissfully. Even the beetle paused in his rape of the rose to listen. Anne didn't lift her head.

'Ah, a beautiful sound,' Olga sighed when she was finished. 'This instrument has aged well. You are fortunate to have it again.'

'But I don't want it,' Anne said, glaring at her furiously. 'I don't want to touch it, I don't want to look at it, I don't even want to listen to it! Take it away!'

Olga flushed, and reminded herself that violent outbursts were a normal part of grief. Just then Lotus came out of the house, her arms loaded with fragrant pink peonies. 'Tuan Innes send,' she said.

'How beautiful!' Olga exclaimed. 'He knows how you love them.'

'Not really,' Anne said scornfully. 'Charlie Fong has a standing order to send Mrs Lawrence a gift every day. Mr Innes doesn't have to give me a thought from one week to the next.'

'That's not fair,' Olga said severely. 'He cares deeply about you, Anne.'

'He doesn't. He's so busy making money that he's forgotten all about me.'

'You are being ridiculous. Don't you remember what you said to him? "Don't come here, I don't want to see you." You can't blame him for not wishing to put himself in the position of being hurt and humiliated over and over again. He is a proud man. He won't grovel, or follow you around like a puppy. He wants you to make the first move, to give him a sign. Six months is a long time for someone like him to wait. I don't know how much longer you can expect him to be patient.'

'I don't expect anything from him,' Anne said. 'He's perfectly free to do anything he likes – take a mistress, get married. I don't care. We had no right to fall in love. It was all wrong. We can never be happy together, but he's too stubborn to admit it. It's better if I never see him again. And I'm getting tired of hearing you nag me about it.'

Olga suppressed a tart reply. She put the violin back in its case and took the peonies inside to arrange them.

The house was small but cool under the broad overhang of its red-tiled roof. A thick, high wall enclosed both the house and large garden, which was dominated by the ancient gnarled camphor tree. The property was on the outer fringes of the French Concession, close to Aurora University, and thereby convenient for Father Jacquinot, who was a frequent visitor. Olga had brought Anne to the house right after Kit and Gilbert were buried. She knew that Anne and her parents would only feed on each other's sorrow if left together at the manse.

At first Innes came to see Anne daily. She sat silently while he tried to make conversation and finally lapsed into despairing silence himself. When she did speak, she asked him not to come back. He respected her wishes, but he sent a gift every day – wine, cigarettes, flowers, books, a jade bowl, a porcelain figurine – and telephoned Olga to ask about Anne. But whenever Olga relayed his desire to visit, Anne always refused permission.

The beetle began to poke around the top of the rosebud. He found an opening and began to work his way down among the tightly furled petals. Anne frowned. She left her chair, stooped over the plant, and flicked the beetle into the dust. The motion dislodged petals from several spent blooms, and they sprinkled the ground like crimson confetti. Anne picked off the dead blossoms and discarded them. They would only produce fruit and sap the strength of the plant. She noticed that the earth under the bushes was caked hard. When it rained, the water would run off the surface instead of penetrating to the roots. She knelt down and scratched at the roots with her fingers, pulling up weeds, breaking up the brick-hard clumps of soil. The plants were in desperate need of pruning and feeding. They had been neglected for so long because the gardener, unsupervised, confined his efforts to sweeping up camphor leaves and drinking tea in the shade. He had left a small cultivator near the door. Anne fetched it and attacked the crusty earth.

She was still working when Innes arrived half an hour later.

He watched her for a minute. 'Hello, Anne,' he said.

She sat back on her heels and wiped the perspiration from her forehead with her sleeve.

'Pretty hot to be working in the sun, isn't it?' he asked.

'It's not too bad,' she said, rising. He started to help her but she made a discouraging motion with her hand. 'It was nice of you to see my mother and father off this morning. I'm sorry Mother misbehaved. She was frightened.'

'I understand.' He looked around at the wicker chairs grouped under the camphor tree. 'Shall we move into the shade?'

She sat hunched in her chair. Her knees were bony and prominent, like her wrists and elbows. Innes noticed new hollows in her cheeks. Her breasts, unsupported and flattened by the pull of her hands in the pockets of her jacket, looked girlishly small. The braids hanging down her back added to her appearance of childish vulnerability.

'You're looking well,' he lied. 'It's been a long time.'

'Why did you come?' she demanded.

'Olga said you wanted to see me.'

'Well, I didn't. She made it up.'

'Oh. Sorry. Would you like me to go?'

She shrugged. 'If you want to. I don't care.'

'Your father still thinks you should have gone with them. He suspects I'm holding you here against your will,' he said, forcing a grin. 'He can't believe that I'm going to be his son-in-law again.'

Anne said nothing.

'I'm glad you stayed. I'd like to think you stayed because of me.' She didn't reply. 'Did you?' he prompted.

'No. There's nothing for me in the States. There's

417

nothing for me here. It doesn't really matter where I am, and I decided to save Father the passage money and stay.'

'I see.' He put his hands on his knees. 'So you didn't consider me at all. Why not?'

'Because what we did was all wrong. I don't mean that it was a sin. I don't believe that it was. But the whole idea of – us. Pretending we were in love when we weren't.'

'Speak for yourself, Anne,' Innes said, poking a cigarette between his lips and snapping his lighter with unnecessary force. 'I wasn't pretending, and if you were, you put on a pretty good show of believing it.'

'I'm sorry. I don't want to hurt you. You shouldn't have come here. I was going to write to you soon and explain things. I've been composing the letter in my mind for weeks. I know you don't like letters, but I think they're good. You say only what you want to say, without anybody interrupting and arguing.'

'Up to your old tricks,' he snorted. 'I might have known. You don't want to make decisions, so you just let things ride, go on as they are. And if somebody puts on the pressure, you turn tail and run. I'm really surprised you weren't on that ship today. You wouldn't have had to face me again.'

'I've made you angry.' She knotted her hands in her lap.

'Damn right I'm angry. I've tried to be patient, Anne. Wait, wait, Olga said. She'll come around. She'll be all right. But I'm wasting my time. You don't want to live in the real world. You never did. If Gilbert hadn't killed himself, you would have found some reason for staying with him for the rest of your life. You'd rather be a nursemaid than a wife. It's easier. And now that you don't have an invalid to take care of, you're turning yourself into one. Like your mother.'

'That's not true,' she said. A spark of anger flickered in her eyes. 'I'm not like her!'

'Then pick up your bed and walk. Get out of here. Start living again.'

'I will, when I'm ready. But it's too soon yet. You want me to be like you, so obsessed with making money and showing everybody that you're as good as they are that you don't have time for feelings.'

418

'That's right,' Innes sneered, 'you think anybody who doesn't wear black and seal themselves up in a goddamn nunnery doesn't feel anything. That's just the kind of crack-brained reasoning I'd expect from you.'

'My way of thinking hasn't changed, and it's not going to change, and if you don't like it, you can just go away. And you can tell your precious Mr Fong that he can stop the barrage of flowers and cunning gifts. I'm tired of receiving tokens of affection from a man I don't even know.'

'What are you talking about? You won't see me, won't take my calls, and now I can't even send you flowers?'

'*You* haven't sent me anything. You never even enclose a note anymore, or anything to show that you've been thinking of me. I'm just a task that you delegate to your secretary. And I'm sick of it. Can't you understand, I'd rather have a daisy you picked with your own hand than an expensive tribute from Charlie Fong? Admit it, you haven't given me a thought from one day to the next, but now that my time of mourning is officially up, I'm supposed to leap blithely into your bed as though nothing had happened. But if you hadn't been in such a hurry to get me into bed, Gilbert would still be alive and so would Kit and everything would be all right.'

'Oh, so now it's my fault that your dope-crazed husband killed your slut of a sister. Sorry, Anne, but you're trying this maneuver out on the wrong guy. I don't burden myself with guilt when I haven't done anything wrong. I leave that kind of self-abuse to missionaries' daughters.'

Inside the house Albert murmured to Olga, 'I'd say your scheme was a screaming flop. We'll have to pull them apart in a second. And I don't mean from a lovers' clinch.'

'Shhh. It's not going so badly. You see how excited she is? Such a good sign. She'll be in his arms in a minute.'

'She'd better hurry. He's walking out.'

Innes bypassed the house and stormed out the front gate.

'Oh, dear,' said Olga. 'What should I do now?'

'Not a thing,' said Albert. 'You've done enough. It's my turn now. It's time somebody told her a few things.'

'No, Albert, she's not ready.'

419

'She's tough. I saw her in Paoting, after she killed two men. She can take it. Give her something to think about besides herself. That's what she needs.'

He carried a bottle of scotch and two glasses out to the garden. 'What, Jim's gone, has he?' he said innocently. 'Too bad. I brought a little liquid refreshment.'

'And included a glass for yourself, I see.' Anne hacked at the clods of earth under the rose bush with the claw-like cultivator. 'I thought you'd quit that stuff. So much for good intentions.'

'You wrong me, Anne,' Albert said. 'This other glass is for you. Well, no matter. Jim had things to do, I guess.'

'Oh, yes, workers to exploit, peasants to impoverish, opium to sell to babies. The usual. He'll be two million dollars richer by tomorrow.'

'Wish I had his talent,' Albert said enviously, mopping his forehead. The wicker armchair creaked under his weight. 'I don't know how he's going to keep things going, though, with Charlie Fong gone.'

'Charlie Fong hasn't gone anywhere. He sent me flowers this morning.'

'Well, if he did, he sent them from heaven, or more likely from hell. They found good old Charlie leaking like a sieve last month, in a whorehouse in Blood Alley. Jim was pretty shaken up by it, but not as shaken up as he was when an auditor went over his books and told him that good old Charlie had relieved him of a cool million over the past two years. Did a neat, efficient job of it, too. They never would have caught it – if Charlie hadn't caught it.'

Anne sat back and stared. 'I don't believe this, any of it. Why didn't he tell me?'

Albert shrugged. 'Embarrassed, I guess. Charlie made a fine fool of our Jim. Jim trusted him, you see. No man likes to put his faith in someone and then find out that he's been played for a sucker. Good idiom, that: played for a sucker.' He savored the words. 'Ah, I love the Americans. Good slang, good music, good bourbon.'

'If you're trying to imply that I, too, am guilty of playing Mr Innes for a sucker —'

'I'm not trying to imply anything,' Albert said. 'I'm just

filling you in on what happened between Jim and Charlie. I leave the meddling and the matchmaking to Olga, God bless her. I think it's a good thing that you and Jim have called it quits. He's in a pretty tricky position now, with Tu on the warpath. Anyone who was close to him could be caught in the crossfire.'

Anne stood up and brushed the dirt off her pantlegs. 'Wait a minute. Are you saying that Tu killed Charlie Fong?'

'That's the most logical explanation. Charlie stole a million, but nobody knows what happened to it. He didn't gamble, didn't smoke opium, didn't even chase women. He had no vices, and no bank account to mention. The only reasonable explanation is that Tu got to him, started to blackmail him.'

'How could he blackmail him, if Charlie had no vices?'

'That's easy when you're Tu: all you have to do is tell some poor sod that if he doesn't come up with a thousand dollars a week, you'll cut his balls off. Tu couldn't get to Jim, but Charlie must have been a pretty easy mark. Good joke, bleeding Jim through his secretary. Then the war between Tu and Jim heated up, and Tu realized that he could hurt Jim most by killing Charlie. Or maybe Charlie was being stubborn. We'll never know.'

Anne lowered herself into the other chair. She gripped the earthy cultivator. 'What war, Albert? What's been going on? Tell me.'

'More of the same,' Albert shrugged. 'Tu has decided that he wants control of the rivers. He's started to charge a tax to all boats – sampans, freighters, everyone. He calls it protection, but it's extortion, plain and simple. A lot of the boatmen have refused to pay. There have been bombs, bloodshed. A good many boats are lying at the bottom of the Whangpoo that weren't there last week.'

'And the freighters?'

'Their owners pay, too. Why not? It's better than seeing a ship full of cargo going to the bottom in flames.'

'But Jamie's not paying, is he?' she asked quietly.

'Of course not. He's leading the resistance. He's tripled the guard around his ships, and around himself, but it's just a matter of time. The Customs people are helpless.

Tu's bought too many of them, and the honest ones are looking after their own skins. Chiang can't do anything about it. The Japanese don't care. It's not their fight, and so far Tu hasn't demanded protection from their warships. It's the barge and tug owners and the ferry men and the shippers who are scared. Innes is trying to muster up some men to fight Tu's boys, but he isn't having much luck.'

Anne looked pale. Albert poured some scotch into a glass and pushed it over toward her.

'Everything he's worked for,' she said. 'It's not fair. Can't Sun do anything to help?'

'Sun has problems of his own. I heard this morning that his daughter tried to test the effectiveness of an entire bottle of Veronal. They pumped her out. She'll probably make it.'

'Why did she do that?' Anne asked, frowning.

Albert said, 'Who knows why young girls do the things they do? Star-crossed love, maybe? That's the most believable reason. But here's something interesting. Olga and I went for a drive several weeks ago, out to the temple of Kuan Ti.'

Anne nodded. She knew the place, a picturesque and somewhat remote spot honoring the god of war and peace. It was a favorite rendezvous for lovers.

'I saw a Chinese couple getting into a little blue sports car, just as we were pulling in. The car was Charlie's. And I'd swear the woman he was with was Eileen Sun.'

'You're saying that maybe Tu didn't kill Charlie at all. Maybe it was – does Jamie know about this?'

'I didn't mention it. Charlie was killed soon afterward. Jim thought he was being smart, keeping Sun in line, not letting him have too much responsibility, too much control. But it looks to me like Sun was the smart one. He had a pipeline to Jim's strongbox, and all he had to do was get his daughter to open the taps.' Albert heaved a sympathetic sigh. 'Poor Jim. I bet he's having trouble falling asleep nights, with all this on his mind. I don't know which is worse, the enemy within, or the enemy outside.'

'It's not having anyone to trust, or anyone to confide in,' Anne said. 'Is this all true, Albert?'

'Every word, except for the speculations about Sun.'

'You should have told me sooner.'

'I wanted to, but Jim made me swear not to mention it to you, and Olga backed him up. She thought you had enough on your mind. I disagreed. It's time you thought about someone other than yourself.'

Anne said, 'Would you please call a taxi for me, Albert?' She went into the house.

Albert picked up the untouched glass of scotch and gazed at it, then poured it onto the soil around the roots of the rose bush.

'You've been robbing me,' Innes said. 'You used Charlie as your dupe, and you've been robbing the company for the past two years. One million dollars, Sun. And you're going to pay me back, every cent.'

Sun said in a silky voice. 'That's an absurd allegation, my friend. And one that will be impossible to prove. Of course, the death of your friend and trusted confidant has placed you in a rather difficult position, and the revelations concerning him have been quite embarrassing. I can understand how you would like to vent your anger on a living person. But I assure you, I had nothing to do with Mr Fong. The missing money is entirely his doing. Or yours.'

'I wouldn't rob my own company,' Innes snapped.

'Nor would I. And this is my company, now. Forty-five percent mine.'

'Forty-five! You've never owned more than ten percent of the shares!'

'In the past few weeks, since the discovery of Mr Fong's thievery, the price of your stock has fallen very low. I had some spare cash to invest and I decided to take advantage of the opportunity. We are real partners now. And of course any losses the company has sustained will be forty-five percent mine.'

'The loss will be forty-five percent yours, when a hundred percent of it ended up in your pockets! You goddamned, sneaky, lying bastard. I ought to —'

'To what?' Sun demanded calmly. 'Break my neck? Cut my throat? It would solve nothing. My shares would simply go to my heirs.'

'You're out. You're not working for me anymore, understand? No more compradore, no more squeeze. Out!'

'You still need a go-between,' Sun said sensibly. 'Do you really think that you can find a Chinese who won't despise you, who won't squeeze you and rob you if he gets the opportunity? You are naive. You hate us, but that hatred pales compared to what we feel for you. Very well, I will not work for you anymore. But I will certainly demand my rights as a major stockholder in your company. I will call you to account for any discrepancies in your business practices.'

'Maybe I should ask Eileen about your relationship with Charlie?' Innes tried desperately to retain control of the situation, even as he felt the ground heaving under his feet. 'I'll bet she could tell me some very interesting things.'

Sun was unperturbed. 'Unfortunately my daughter is ill, dangerously close to death, in fact. If she and Mr Fong were acquainted, it was without my knowledge. She is a modern young woman; she doesn't need to ask my permission to socialize with any person she chooses.'

'She tried to kill herself, because you murdered her lover,' Innes said. 'Or maybe you fed her that Veronal yourself, to keep her from talking.'

Sun's cheeks paled slightly. 'That was an ill-considered remark. I shall overlook it.'

'Don't do me any favors. I'll buy your shares from you at current market value, which is more than you paid for them, and less the million you stole.'

'I will not sell,' Sun told him. 'You cannot force me out.'

Innes glared at him. 'I could kill you for this. I will, I swear it.'

'Ah, the American fondness for violent action,' Sun sighed. 'I am well aware that it is within your power to assassinate me, but that would not be to your advantage. Certainly, if you lost control of the company it would likewise not be to my advantage. I have no desire to work as hard as you do, or to be as visible as you must be. I perceive that we have arrived at a stalemate: neither of us will act against the other for fear of destroying ourselves. Not a bad way to maintain the status quo.'

'You're a thief.'

Sun stood up and adjusted his cuffs. He said, 'We can no longer even pretend to be friends, I see. No matter. You will continue to run the business, and I will collect my share of the profits, assuming that there are profits. That all depends on Tu's determination to destroy you and on your ability to outwit him. The odds-makers in the city favor Tu, but I am still inclined to give you the edge. Tu has everything to gain from his maneuvering, and nothing to lose. But you stand to lose everything you have worked so hard to achieve, and you will fight him with every ounce of cunning and courage you have. You will win. You may not destroy him, but you will surely drive him out of Shanghai for a little while.'

Innes gazed at him with hate-filled eyes.

Sun smiled pityingly. 'You have enjoyed the illusion of power, haven't you? You have reveled in it, delighted in it, wallowed in it. But you have failed to recognize that temporal power is simply that, an illusion. It is folly to think that you have captured the mountain if you haven't secured the surrounding foothills and all the passages to the summit. We Chinese recognize the insignificance of most human endeavors. Except creative achievement. Art. A piece of beautifully wrought gold or jade will last forever, but the mountain you have captured is no more significant than a pile of rubbish. The only grandeur it possesses is what you have given it in your imagination.' He glanced around with disdain, and left the office.

Innes slumped in his chair. He saw nothing, heard nothing. His new secretary, a young Englishman, buzzed him on the intercom, and getting no response came into the office to see what was the matter. Innes didn't look up when he spoke, and the secretary left the room.

'Looks like I won't have this job for long,' he told his friends later that evening. 'The company's practically insolvent, thanks to my talented predecessor, and Innes acts like a beaten man.'

Innes dismissed his car and his bodyguards and walked

out of the Innes Building alone, for the first time in years. He stood on the Bund, watching the traffic surge past. Passersby jostled him. Any one of them could have slid a knife between his ribs, or smashed his skull with a brick, but none would. Tu's assassins wouldn't be expecting him to expose himself.

He crossed the street and entered the park that overlooked the confluence of Soochow Creek and the Whangpoo. He leaned against the sea wall and watched the traffic on the river. A small freighter glided past, the red dragon of Innes & Company writhing on its smokestacks. It would be so easy to destroy a ship: an unseen swimmer could attach a mine to its hull. Overnight the fleet of Innes & Company could be at the bottom of the river.

His helplessness sickened him and he turned his back on the river. Looking down, he saw an anemic daisy growing out of a crack at the base of the wall. He plucked it and stared at it glumly, then he crushed it angrily and jammed his hands into his pockets. He left the park and headed toward the Cathay Hotel. He would shower and change, and then go out. He'd have himself a real spree, the kind he hadn't indulged in since he had started Innes & Company. He'd drink himself into oblivion, pick up a girl, maybe two girls, and if he ended up in Blood Alley with a knife in his back, so be it.

The private elevator glided up to the penthouse and he stepped out, his door key ready. He heard a whining noise, like a tracer bullet. He put his hand under his left arm and felt the hard coldness of his gun. The whining continued, stopped abruptly, then began again. He listened, amazed, as he heard the squeaking first line of 'Danny Boy.' He pushed the door open.

Anne was standing in front of the big window that overlooked the Bund and the Whangpoo. She was wearing the green and silver gown, and her hair hung loose down her back. Oblivious to everything else, she sawed away at her violin. Innes looked around. A mass of roses blazed in the jade bowl on the table in the middle of the room, and a fragrant armload of pink and white peonies filled the great antique fishbowl in the corner. A pair of sturdy shoes lay in his path, and an open suitcase spilled its contents over the floor near the bedroom door.

The first line of the song ended on a nerve-fraying screech.

'Damn,' Anne said under her breath. She flexed the wrist of her right hand, which held the bow.

'What are you doing here?' Innes demanded.

She whirled. The violin rested on her left shoulder. She wasn't wearing her glasses, and she stared at him with vague, unfocused eyes.

'What are you doing here?' he repeated.

She lowered her instrument slowly. 'That's a fair question. I'm certainly not making music. I guess I'm chasing demons.' She laughed. 'I ought to hire myself out for Chinese weddings, don't you think? A noise like that would scare any self-respecting demon into the next province.'

'How did you get in here?' She had had a key once, long ago, but he had changed the locks recently.

She shrugged. 'The assistant manager's secretary used to be a student of mine. I didn't even have to pay out squeeze. Just good will.'

He came farther into the room. 'Well, you can just pack up and get out again. I don't want to be saddled with some woman right now. Things are too complicated.'

She was unruffled by his coldness. 'Dear me, and they talk about women being fickle! This morning you loved me and wanted me, and now I'm just "some woman".' She set her violin and bow aside. 'You don't see my glasses anywhere, do you? I take them off when I play. I can concentrate better when I can't see the horrible grimaces on the faces of my listeners.' She felt around for them among the cushions on the couch. 'I may have left them in the bedroom, or the bathroom. I'm not very well organized. Sorry for the mess. I took a bath and washed my hair and when I was looking around for something to put on, I saw this dress and I just tried it on to see if it still fit. It's a little loose. I didn't realize I'd lost so much weight. Then I saw my violin. Olga shoved it at me through the window of the taxi and insisted I take it. It was so quiet in here, and I was tempted to see if I was really as terrible as I thought I was. Needless to say, I was not disappointed. It will take me years to get it back. Years. You'll probably go mad listening to me. I remember when I practiced, Kit always said, "Anne's killing cats again!"'

Innes watched her searching for her glasses, groping for them on the table under the roses, on the mantel, the shelves that held the artifacts that hadn't been shattered by the bomb blast.

'Stop it, Anne,' he said. 'It's no good. You were right, we don't belong together. It was all a game, a farce. An illusion.'

'Do you think so?' She cocked her head. 'I don't agree with you. So much is illusion, of course. It's a cockeyed, scrambled, senseless world, and the idea of being happy in such a world does sound like a dream. When I got here I turned on the radio and the madness just came spilling out: the Japanese in Amoy, fighting near Tientsin, rumors of war in Europe. You said long ago that a person just has to figure out what makes sense to him, and forget the rest. Well, the only thing that makes sense to me is loving you, and being with you. To hell with the rest of the world. I can't save it. I just have to do the best I can, in my own small corner.'

He said wearily. 'You don't understand what's been going on.'

'Yes, I do, Jamie. Albert is a good reporter: he doesn't add extraneous detail, and he doesn't leave out anything essential. I know all about Tu, and Charlie, and Sun. You should have told me.'

'I didn't want to worry you.'

'No, you didn't want me to come back to you because I felt sorry for you and because I wanted to cradle your head on my breasts. But what's wrong with that? I'm awfully good at it, and it makes me feel necessary, not superfluous baggage like "some woman",' she twitted him gently.

'They've got me,' he said, lifting his shoulders. 'I'm finished. It's stupid for you to stay around, just to watch the carnage. While I've been wallowing in my sense of power, as Sun so nicely put it this afternoon, he's been taking everything that wasn't nailed down. The company's nearly bankrupt.'

'You have your ships.'

'Which Tu will blow up if I don't pay him what he wants. I can't stop him.'

'What nonsense. You outwitted the whole Japanese army, just to save a bunch of goddamned candy-assed missionaries. You can certainly deal with an opium-soaked thug like Tu. Why don't you just ask Tiger Johnson to drop a bomb on his house?' she said with a sweet smile.

'I can't believe my ears,' he said. '*You*, suggesting something like *that*.'

'You must destroy him, before he destroys you.' Her voice was hard.

'Why should I bother?' he demanded bitterly. 'Why should I save my business, just so I can turn half of it over to Sun? I don't have to work like a son of a bitch, just to make Sun Yu-sing richer. With the money he stole from me, he bought up one third of the stock in the company, did Albert tell you that? He owns enough now so that he can pretty well tell me what to do. I'll be damned if I'll put up with that.'

'What difference does it make who else profits from your work, as long as you're doing what makes you happy? Whether it's Sun or a hundred other shareholders, it's all the same. Your pride has been hurt, because he and Charlie tricked you.'

'I was a fool,' Innes said angrily. 'A damned fool. I hated the bookkeeping aspect of the business, and I threw more and more of the boring stuff on Charlie. I trusted him. I should have known better.'

'Yes, it was a hard lesson,' Anne said. 'But you won't let it happen again. You'll never again invest so much responsibility on a single person – except me, of course. I hereby take responsibility for your happiness. I won't fail you, Jamie.'

He shook his head. 'No, you don't understand, Anne. I'm getting out. I'll let Sun have the business and I'll go someplace else and start over.'

She laughed softly. 'Come here,' she said, walking over to him and taking his hand. 'I want to show you something.' He held back. She said, 'Come on, I won't bite,' and led him over to the window. The evening sky over Pootung was deep blue, streaked with crimson. The lights of the city began to blink on. Shanghai sprawled at their feet. 'It's wonderful, isn't it? Enormous and filthy and crammed with the refuse of a hundred nations. And they keep coming. Not just Chinese, or even Russians anymore, but Jews from Germany and Austria. Every day someone knocks on Olga's door to ask if she'll buy their china or glassware or jewelry. They're dressed in heavy sweaters, woolens, the only clothes they have, and in this heat! They ask for work. They ask for food. I don't know why Shanghai just doesn't burst at the seams, or erupt into complete chaos. But somehow it manages to absorb them. It's not a good host. The weak ones die of heartbreak and starvation and a thousand other ills. But the strong make new lives for themselves. A man can come here with nothing – a refugee, or a sailor on the run from his enemies – and if he's smart enough and hungry enough, he can make a fortune, or five fortunes. Shanghai is a lot like you, Jamie. I love you both for the same reasons, because you're ugly-beautiful, aware of your strength, sure of yourself, alive. So alive. Innes and Shanghai: there's a match to be reckoned with. I hope that Jamie and Anne will be half so successful.'

'You're fooling yourself. You said yourself you couldn't live with my money, that you hated it.'

'How can I hate it, when it's part of you? It's part of Shanghai. Without it, Shanghai would be just one more Chinese city, picturesque and insignificant. I have some very grandiose plans for your money, you know: I'm going to establish a home for the children no one else wants, the children of mixed parentage, the half-breed bastards. Maybe I'll start my own school, or a maternity clinic. Oh, there's so much I can do! Your money will give me a start. I'm my father's daughter: I have a flair for preaching, and I'll bet I have a latent talent for squeezing money out of rich men. You and the other taipans in this town are going to be sick and tired of hearing from Anne Innes.'

He looked perplexed and exasperated. 'No, Anne, honestly, you don't know what you're getting into.'

She slid her arms around his neck. 'Pardon me, sir,' she whispered, 'but how would you like to donate to a worthy cause?' She kissed him lightly, and kissed him again and again until the tautness and the tiredness went out of his body.

'Somebody's always got his hand out in this town,' he grumbled. 'I don't believe in any charity except my own.'

'You shouldn't be so selfish. Let me tell you about the joy of giving.'

'Is it anything like the joy of receiving?' he said, tightening his arms around her waist.

'Better,' she promised.

'I'm a little strapped for cash right now.'

'That doesn't matter. The smallest token will be gratefully accepted.'

He reached into his jacket pocket. He opened his hand. A wilted daisy lay inside. 'How about this?'

'Perfect,' she said, taking the limp flower and holding it to her cheek. 'It's the most beautiful flower I've ever seen. Thank you.' She held him close. 'Thank you.'

'It should have been jade, or gold,' he murmured apologetically. 'It won't last.'

'Oh, you're wrong, Jamie,' she said. 'It will last, I promise you. It will last for a long, long time.'

RICH MAN, POOR MAN
by Irwin Shaw

Truly global in the scope of its humanity and passion, *Rich Man, Poor Man* is the story of a generation at war with the values of its past, the hypocrisy and tension of its present and the terrifying inevitability of a shipwrecked future.

Rudolph is the romantic, who learns to live with doubt and make a fortune at 30. His brother Tom is the brute whose acid-scarred American dream is coloured with boiling blood. Their sister Gretchen, seduced by the small town's leading citizen, is the beauty in urgent search of a man — the only man — who can save her from herself.

Irwin Shaw's book is a masterpiece in the truly modern manner: vision, myth, sex and violence unite in its pages to ignite the most explosive novel of the Seventies.

NEW ENGLISH LIBRARY

BEGGARMAN, THIEF
by Irwin Shaw

Here is the book that everyone has been awaiting
for seven years — the sequel to *Rich Man, Poor Man*.

Continuing in masterly style the saga of the Jordache
family, Irwin Shaw fills a huge canvas, moving with
consummate skill between Europe and America, as he
pursues the fortunes — the joys and sorrows, the
successes and failures — of each member of the family.

Beggarman, Thief will be enjoyed equally as sequel to
the internationally acclaimed *Rich Man, Poor Man,* and
as a brilliant novel in its own right.

NEW ENGLISH LIBRARY

THE STARS LOOK DOWN
by A. J. Cronin

This is a book about LIFE — ugly, beautiful, ironic,
heroic, and despairing . . . A book about PEOPLE, the
story of miners — their land, their lives, their loves, their
fights, and their scars. A book, deep in human sympathy,
to stir the conscience of a nation.

'His women are as brilliantly painted as his men. The
wretched Janny who pines for the genteel and comes
to so miserable an end, the Laura who gives Joe his first
big chance and permits herself to become his mistress,
her sister whom the war so subtly changes, and the
Sally whom a lesser novelist would have transformed
into a second Gracie Fields — all of them are wonderfully
good. It is a rich and rare panorama.' — *Sunday Times*

NEW ENGLISH LIBRARY

HATTER'S CASTLE
by A. J. Cronin

A soul-stirring novel of pride and greed, and its terrible retribution.

When her father forced her to leave school, and cut off all her contact with the past and future, Mary Brodie's whole life became the narrow compass of her family's cold, comfortless house in a small Scottish town. Her mean and ambitious father tyrannised his timid, obliging wife, his cowed, overworked younger daughter, and his spineless son. Four people were held in Brodie's merciless grip . . .

Until, like a breath of the outside world Brodie so much despised, came the young Irishman in whom Mary found a forbidden love and freedom, and who brought to her mother and sister the only release.

NEW ENGLISH LIBRARY

THE BEST PLACE TO BE
by Helen Van Slyke

Sheila Callahan had everything she wanted — comfort, security and a marriage that had lasted for twenty-seven years. Then, one summer afternoon in a Cleveland suburb, everything changed. Suddenly all she has left of her husband is the memory of his overpowering and free-spending ways — she is on her own. But can she face the problems of self-reliance, or will the pressures of her family drag her down? Is it too late to start again — and does she have it in her to do so?

NEW ENGLISH LIBRARY

THE MIXED BLESSING
by Helen Van Slyke

THE MIXED BLESSING continues the story of Elizabeth Quigly's remarkable family — and particularly that of her beautiful granddaughter, Antoinette Jenkins. For 'Toni' is the adored daughter of a mixed marriage that divided Elizabeth's heart and her family. Toni herself is torn — between loyalty to her mother and grandmother, who urge her to proudly acknowledge her heritage, and to her remorseful black father who begs her to deny it.

NEW ENGLISH LIBRARY

TIMES OF TRIUMPH
by Charlotte Vale Allen

Spanning more than three decades in the turbulent
history of our century, Charlotte Vale Allen's magnificent
saga traces the life and loves of a woman born to
struggle against every adversity with dauntless courage
and unflinching love.

Leonie came to New York with all the world against her
and built her tiny eating-house into a mighty business
empire.

Gray, the London journalist who followed her across the
ocean, was the father of her children and the love of her
lifetime.

Through the First World War, the hard and hungry years
that followed, through love and pain and bitter sadness,
through the growing years of their son and daughter
destined to retrace their mother's footsteps into a Europe
once again torn apart by war – Leonie's life was a time
of triumph.

POST A LITTLE HAPPINESS

Post·A·Book

A Royal Mail service in association with the Book Marketing Council & The Booksellers Association.
Post-A-Book is a Post Office trademark.

NEW ENGLISH LIBRARY

Book Tokens

Give them the pleasure of choosing

Book Tokens can be bought and exchanged at most bookshops in Great Britain and Ireland.

NEL BESTSELLERS

T51277	'THE NUMBER OF THE BEAST'	*Robert Heinlein*	£2.25
T50777	STRANGER IN A STRANGE LAND	*Robert Heinlein*	£1.75
T51382	FAIR WARNING	*Simpson & Burger*	£1.75
T52478	CAPTAIN BLOOD	*Michael Blodgett*	£1.75
T50246	THE TOP OF THE HILL	*Irwin Shaw*	£1.95
T49620	RICH MAN, POOR MAN	*Irwin Shaw*	£1.60
T51609	MAYDAY	*Thomas H. Block*	£1.75
T54071	MATCHING PAIR	*George G. Gilman*	£1.50
T45773	CLAIRE RAYNER'S LIFEGUIDE		£2.50
T53709	PUBLIC MURDERS	*Bill Granger*	£1.75
T53679	THE PREGNANT WOMAN'S BEAUTY BOOK	*Gloria Natale*	£1.25
T49817	MEMORIES OF ANOTHER DAY	*Harold Robbins*	£1.95
T50807	79 PARK AVENUE	*Harold Robbins*	£1.75
T50149	THE INHERITORS	*Harold Robbins*	£1.75
T53231	THE DARK	*James Herbert*	£1.50
T43245	THE FOG	*James Herbert*	£1.50
T53296	THE RATS	*James Herbert*	£1.50
T45528	THE STAND	*Stephen King*	£1.75
T50874	CARRIE	*Stephen King*	£1.50
T51722	DUNE	*Frank Herbert*	£1.75
T52575	THE MIXED BLESSING	*Helen Van Slyke*	£1.75
T38602	THE APOCALYPSE	*Jeffrey Konvitz*	95p

NEL P.O. BOX 11, FALMOUTH TR10 9EN, CORNWALL

Postage Charge:
U.K. Customers 45p for the first book plus 20p for the second book and 14p for each additional book ordered to a maximum charge of £1.63.

B.F.P.O. & EIRE Customers 45p for the first book plus 20p for the second book and 14p for the next 7 books; thereafter 8p per book.

Overseas Customers 75p for the first book and 21p per copy for each additional book.

Please send cheque or postal order (no currency).

Name ....

Address ....

....

Title ....

While every effort is made to keep prices steady, it is sometimes necessary to increase prices at short notice. New English Library reserve the right to show on covers and charge new retail prices which may differ from those advertised in the text or elsewhere.(7)